ATMOSPHERE

A NOVEL

Also by John Clarke

Middle Waters

Triangle

Praise for Atmosphere

Atmosphere is author John Clarke at his best – writing authoritatively about science in a compelling narrative that weaves what we know with that which we are on the verge of knowing. In this, the final installment of the Jason Parker trilogy, Clarke gives us the third act of an end-of-the-world saga in which the question is not just survival, but transcendence; at stake is the next step forward in human evolution.

The characters feel like old friends, especially Jason and his elusive love interest Laura Smith, and the imagined interplanetary and geopolitical background of the novel seems oddly familiar. Clarke builds on a story arc first established by *Middle Waters* that shatters our everyday view of the reality to reveal the surprising and sometimes terrifying truth that lurks beneath. What began as an adventure about frog-like aliens hiding in the deep oceans now becomes a desperate attempt to save humanity with the help of extraterrestrial technology.

In *Atmosphere,* Clarke has tackled one of the biggest challenges facing a writer of science fiction – what is there new and surprising to say about the end of the world? – and succeeds brilliantly.

— Max McCoy, award-winning author and journalist, writer of four licensed *Indiana Jones* adventures for Bantam.

Atmosphere by John Clarke – Top-notch hard science fiction well worth your time.

Atmosphere is the third book in the *Jason Parker Trilogy.* The author, Dr. John Clarke, is a diving expert, not just scuba, but diving in all its fascinating variations. In this series, Clarke explores saturation diving, not just to the relatively shallow depths that are the daily venue for oil-rig divers – 500 to 1,000 ft deep, but many times that using exotic gas mixtures predominating in hydrogen. I am an experienced saturation diver, and I can tell you that Clarke knows his stuff. Beyond that, he is an excellent writer. His characters are well developed and charismatic, even the non-human ones, and he places them within a fascinating plot.

Clarke's story backdrop is that humans have shared the planet with an alien species that has been here for a very long time. They know about us, but until Jason Parker, we really did not know about them. The first volume is about this discovery. The second is about the aliens leaving Earth for their own purposes. To get the most out of *Atmosphere,* you really need to read the first two books even though *Atmosphere* stands on its own.

Atmosphere is about Earth minus the aliens, but with some of their technology, and about what happens when Earth is hit with a near extinction level gamma-ray burst (GRB). The characters you come to know and care about, play significant roles throughout the series – especially Jason Parker and Laura Smith. Both are top-notch scientists, both are adept at "distance viewing," and their individual and intertwined lives form the connecting link for the entire *Trilogy.* Clarke's ingenious solution to continuing the human species despite the GRB will leave you astonished and breathless. He leaves the door open for further tales in this fascinating hard science fiction universe.

The *Jason Parker Trilogy* consisting of *Middle Waters, Triangle*, and *Atmosphere,* is top-notch hard science fiction well worth your time. — Robert G. Williscroft Author of *The Starchild Trilogy*

Atmosphere

A Novel

John Clarke

John Clarke

Wet Street Press
Panama City

Published in the United States of America by Wet Street Press, Panama City, FL.

This is a work of fiction. All characters, organizations, and events in this novel either are products of the author's imagination or are being used fictitiously.

ISBN-13: 978-0-9863749-4-4

ISBN-10: 0-9863749-4-6

Library of Congress Control Number: 2018915283

Cover Design by John Clarke

Cover Art by Susan Gerardi

"Far out at sea the water is as blue as the petals of the loveliest cornflower and as clear as the purest glass, but it is very deep .... Down there the sea-folk live." — Hans Christian Andersen

Other Books in the Jason Parker Trilogy Series

Middle Waters, Book 1 of the Jason Parker Trilogy

In the deep-sea canyons of the Earth lie aquatic aliens who soon must leave the planet. But they need the help of Jason Parker, a Navy dive scientist, and Laura Smith, a beguiling but eccentric graduate student in Oceanography.

The U.S. government is aware of this deep sea civilization and wants their weapons. This top-secret ambition puts the two unsuspecting divers in the middle of a volatile conflict between powerful military and intergalactic forces. Things could get messy for the divers, and for the entire planet.

Fortunately, Parker and Smith have some help from the strangest of places. The unlikely duo will have to survive incalculable odds if they are to single-handedly stop the Earth's first Alien War.

Triangle, Book 2 of the Jason Parker Trilogy

Two superpowers are in a race to recover and exploit alien technology. To compete with the rumored Russian retrieval of an alien spacecraft found deep in Siberia's Lake Baikal, the U.S. government orders two Navy saturation divers to risk everything to help salvage a spaceship that may not even exist. It is up to Jason Parker to make sure the divers return safely from the deepest man-dive ever.

To make matters worse, both the U.S. and Russia are targeting Parker and Smith for elimination if they don't get their way. As a result, Parker and Smith must struggle to survive at all costs while trying to somehow maintain world peace.

The balance of world power and the fate of the Earth itself may rest on a liaison between Parker, Smith and two mysterious men with most peculiar powers. One is a blind remote viewer, and the other is a Troll named Truman.

The world will never be the same.

Dedication

Atmosphere and The Jason Parker Trilogy is dedicated to Navy Divers like the fictional J.R. and Tom, who risk their lives at the "point of the spear" in the service of our country. Their brave deeds are legion, but due to the sensitivity of what they do, they will always remain unsung heroes.

Acknowledgments

The following have directly or indirectly inspired the creation of this volume: NASA for asking me the hard question about human adaptation to Mars; Astronaut/Diver Michael Gerhardt for suggesting I look at Phobos; NASA Engineer Donald Doer for questions about life support underwater and in space; the Office of Naval Research for asking about human gills; Terry Kennedy, Marine Recon diver of Osage heritage; cosmologist/dark matter researcher Aaron Manalaysay; fusion reactor engineer Larissa Cottrill; and of course the Navy deep Saturation Divers who inspired this work.

I am also inspired by the persistence and determination of women engineers such as Clarice Cote, Larissa Cottrill, Lori Zipes, and Holly Gardner, who flourish in a formerly male-dominated field.

I am deeply indebted to Navy Diving Medical Officers who inspired me to also ask the hard questions. A few of those, now passed, were Captains George Bond, Ed Thalmann, and Ed Flynn.

As always, I thank my test readers, my technical consultant CDR. Michael Runkle, Kris Farmen of Fireweed Editorial, journalist and novelist Max McCoy, and Navy diver and author George Williscroft. They have all helped me hone my craft.

FORWARD

Atmosphere is the third volume in the Jason Parker Trilogy.

The events in this trilogy begin in the near future and extend for roughly fifteen years.

In Volume 1, *Middle Waters,* Jason Parker was introduced as an action-addicted biomedical scientist and inventor working for the U.S. Navy. He held a Ph.D. in physiology and had a passion for flying and diving. He and his equally sensible wife, Sandy, lived in Panama City, Florida to be close to his place of employment, the Navy Diving Center.

As is appropriate for a government scientist, Parker was a practical man, well-grounded in reality, and subsequently curiously affected by a young graduate student in Oceanography who believed in UFOs and aliens. Most strangely of all, she actually thought she was an alien in a past life. Oddly, she was never quite sure if she was an extraterrestrial alien, or one long-ago trapped underneath the waters on the planet Earth. But that didn't matter to her. What mattered was that her supposed past life existence held more importance to her than her current life as a graduate student. As such, she was a challenge for her mentors, which included Jason Parker. As a rule, scientists do not entertain irrational beliefs, and yet Laura Smith, daughter of an Air Force Intelligence Officer, embraced an unprovable notion that to her was the essence of reality.

At their first meeting, Laura Smith felt an unexplainable affinity for the considerably older Jason Parker, which of course Parker found vexing. She was young and attractive, and he was married and committed to fidelity.

After flying his family to Mexico, Parker had an introductory meeting, of sorts, with aliens using their preferred mode of travel, spaceships. However, after that first meeting, the aliens had managed to insinuate themselves into his consciousness, a consciousness that refused to believe what it was seeing—and hearing.

The U.S. government was keenly interested in Parker and Laura Smith because of the attention they seemed to be gaining from a deep sea population of aliens called the Canyoneers. One person recruited by the dark side dealing with the aliens, took it upon himself to try to kill Parker and Laura. He would have succeeded were it not for the miraculous intervention of the aliens. Parker and Laura later returned the favor when they discovered the U.S was planning to nuke the aliens in their deep canyon homes.

With the help of Laura and Parker, the aliens demonstrated their mind-control powers, convincing the government that warring with them was not in anyone's best interest.

Eventually, the attention afforded Parker and Laura by the aliens paid off when they obtained a treaty so the aliens could leave Earth without being molested. They had been trapped on Earth for ten thousand years and needed to return to their ancient galactic home. In parting, the alien King, whom Parker dubbed a Frog, left Parker with a digital scroll of sorts with the complete history of man on Earth, but also with a "history" extending twenty years into the future. That history would take 100 years for humans to decipher, by the Frog's admission.

The only person troubled by the alien's departure was an investigative journalist who wondered if the alien departure was coincidental or an omen of things to come.

In Volume 2, *Triangle*, Russians discovered a triangular-shaped spacecraft deep underwater in a cave in Lake Baikal, Siberia. It was apparently left behind by the departing Frogs. Though promising to be a treasure trove of alien technology, gaining access to the craft was next to impossible, and once inside, the ship was empty. Jason Parker received hints that the Gulf of Mexico's DeSoto Canyon might also have a hidden alien craft. However, discovering it would require a heroic and pioneering deep hydrogen dive by two Navy divers.

In the meanwhile, a serendipitous discovery in the jungles of the Yucatan leads to a band of cave-dwelling bioengineered hybrids between humans and the alien aquatic species. They call themselves Trolls. The U.S. President wants them out of Mexico.

Through a partnership between the CIA and commercial DNA testing companies, an American citizen resident overseas was identified and recruited as a "remote viewer," using the most covert means of intelligence gathering. He was the best there was, even though he was blind.

Following the discovery of the *Frogs* in Volume One, the newly minted Ph.D. Oceanographer, Laura Smith, was put in charge of Alien Affairs for the Office of the Director of National Intelligence. After the revelation of the alien origins of the Trolls, Parker and Smith met up again while monitoring a secretive Navy hydrogen dive to 2,500 feet in the Gulf of Mexico. Shortly after the heroic discovery of another alien craft, Laura and Parker were kidnapped by Russian Intelligence.

The Russians wanted the American duo to help them activate their own salvaged alien craft, but things didn't go as the Russians planned. Laura and Parker escaped in the Russians' salvaged ship, thanks in part to the mental abilities of the newly immigrated Trolls.

Due to the experience gained from flying the Russian ship, Parker was finally able to activate and fly the triangular spacecraft recovered from the De Soto Canyon.

The Trolls sought and gained American citizenship, and the Intelligence Communities quickly learned how to exploit the Troll's uncanny skill sets, while ignoring their dark side.

CHAPTER 1. IMPACT

Four thousand and seventy years ago in a distant part of the Milky Way galaxy, a pair of gravitationally-linked stars began their death spiral, rumbling into a super energetic state that culminated in a gamma-ray burst beamed at light speed into a then-barren region of the Milky Way. In the 21st Century A.D., the Earth was racing at half a million miles per hour towards a cataclysmic collision with the brief but devastating burst of raw energy from that ancient star explosion.

In the city of Papeete, the capital of French Polynesia on the island of Tahiti, children from the local yacht club were on the water with a bevy of single sail dinghies, eight-foot-long training boats with seven-foot sails. Each dingy had room for just one child, so the tiny flotilla of snub-nosed boats was being shepherded by two sailing instructors in a motorboat, busily keeping the students corralled within their marked sailing practice area. There was a light breeze, ideal conditions for the Optimus training fleet, with enough force to propel the dinghies wherever the sailors commanded, but not strong enough to flip the boats over. The instructors' coaching could be clearly heard by the young sailors over the slapping of the waves gently jostling each boat.

It was 5:42 in the afternoon of November 23, but the sun was still high. The Milky Way galaxy lay unseen directly overhead the French Polynesian Windward Islands when a blast from a galactic neighbor, a binary star system in the constellation Sagittarius the Archer, descended like Sagittarius's arrow directly on top of the luckless Tahitians.

While the students were concentrating on wind and sail, the instructors in their bikini and boardshorts felt a burning sensation over all their exposed skin. Looking up, they saw a sky turning dark orange-brown, a sight never before recorded on Earth. The female guest instructor from California, with blond hair and blue eyes, felt her eyes stinging so severely she could not keep them open.

She shouted to her male counterpart, "I can't see!"

As he turned away from the darkening sky to look at her, he saw the skin on her face, arms, and thighs were suddenly bright red.

"What the hell happened to you?"

He was Tahitian, and his bronze skin and dark eyes were not as affected as hers, but even at that, he noticed his own arms and legs were burning at the same moment he became aware of the screams coming from the children. They jumped into the water in an attempt to cool their burns. Only one of them, a nine-year-old boy, remained on his boat, convulsed in a seizure.

Panicked, the female instructor shouted, "What's happening to the children? I can't see them. Help them, Ari!"

At the moment of the gamma-ray impact over Tahiti, a small meteor was tracking northward along an atmosphere-grazing trajectory when it suddenly changed course to the northeast. In a matter of seconds, it covered 4000 miles of the open ocean while still in space, then dipped into the atmosphere over Baja California. It was witnessed as a massive fireball passing directly over Isla Lobos, heading in the direction of the United States. Within seconds it had passed over the Southwest corner of Texas and disappeared just across the New Mexico border.

Minutes later, the U.S. Geological Service, Albuquerque Seismological Station, observed seismic activity. Civilian seismic reporting stations in El Paso and Lubbock, Texas, and the Mescalero Reservation near Alamogordo, New Mexico also reported in, allowing Albuquerque to triangulate a seismic event occurring near Carlsbad, New Mexico, with an apparent intensity of 3.0 on the Richter Scale.

The two government geologists on duty that night in Albuquerque were literally scratching their heads as their computers processed the incoming data. Even though the event equated to only a minor earthquake, the Carlsbad area was considered to be at low risk for seismic activity. The two scientists were not yet aware of that evening's devastating gamma-ray event over the South Pacific. The effect of the gamma-rays had covered the entire surface of the Earth facing the binary stars at the moment of impact.

Gamma-ray bursts are the most violent explosions in the Universe. The last time the Earth had been in the crosshairs of a GRB was on June 25, 2016, when a beam four times as wide as the moon and coming from a presumed black hole nine billion light-years away, found its way to the unsuspecting Earth. GRB 160625B emitted as much energy in forty seconds as our sun will in its entire lifetime. It came from the constellation Delphinus, the Dolphin, and lay in the northern sky not far from the now offending Sagittarius Constellation.

Ever since the discovery of GRBs, scientists had believed that such events only happen at cosmological distances, at distances too far away to harm anyone on Earth. However, the discovery that the *Apep* star system 8,000 light-years away in the constellation Norma was a potential GRB progenitor, taught astronomers that the Earth does not necessarily have the safety of vast distances. Any gamma-ray beam coming from nine billion light-years away will be too weak to harm anyone when it strikes the Earth. But star ranges of less than 10,000 light-years are a totally different matter, as the Earth had just discovered in Tahiti.

The short distance that gamma-rays had to traverse through the atmosphere directly over Tahiti meant that some ultra-high-energy gamma-rays made their way to the Earth's surface. Where radiation absorption did occur, ultraviolet radiation caused almost instantaneous burns to eyes and unprotected skin during the ten-second-long exposure.

Away from the Windward Islands, reaching towards Hawaii to the North and New Zealand to the south, the longer atmospheric path caused by the curvature of the Earth led to more atmospheric absorption of the gamma radiation. For those places, UV radiation was the primary cause of biological damage to people and crops.

Rampaging winds began spreading toxic nitrogen dioxide clouds around the planet, and within days, the earth was fully affected. As that dark cloud absorbed sunlight, the world experienced a cooling like that predicted from a nuclear winter, a cooling that could herald the advent of a mini-ice age.

An observatory near Sydney delivered the first report of the GRB. Then word came that more than half the satellites orbiting the planet had been lost. As a layer of apocalyptic nitrogen dioxide smog collected high in the atmosphere, Russia, China, and the United States began moving their elite and indispensable personnel into nuclear bunkers. Russian personnel started moving towards Mount Yamantau, a Washington D.C.-sized complex designed to protect hundreds of thousands of people for years at a time. They also started the transfer to the Mount Kosvinsky installation in the northern Ural Mountains, designed to harbor multitudes of military and government people for years, and perhaps decades.

John Clarke

China's ruling elite showed up at the Sanya Installation at Yulin Naval Base - Sanya, on Hainan Island, and other secretly fortified places not yet detected by American satellites.

Essential U.S. personnel were quickly shuttled to the Raven Rock Complex in Pennsylvania.

Chapter 2. Phobos

Two years before the gamma-ray burst struck Earth, Space Corp Tech Sergeant Clarice Williams could hear herself breathing inside her helmet as she stood alone on the surface of Phobos, mesmerized by the sight of Mars filling a third of her view. The red planet with its stark mountains, deep valleys, and sandy plains was visibly moving past as the former asteroid on which she rode sped along at almost 5000 miles per hour during its three times daily circuit of the planet. The Martian gravity had long ago captured the irregularly shaped rock that had been her home for the past year.

Mars had also captured the imagination of mankind. Yet, from Williams' vantage point, seemingly just a stone's throw from the dusty planet, she wondered if our vision had finally outstretched our wisdom.

As her eyes swept the planet looking for signs of life at the volcano Pavonis Mons, she understood how God might feel, looking mournfully upon the desiccated carcass of a planet colored red. She envisioned the redness coming from the dried blood of its people long ago destroyed by a planetary cataclysm.

She wished she could have seen Mars before it died. Seeing it now as a ghost of a planet brought no pleasure at all. She could never consider Mars her home, as much as the Space Corp wanted her there. She would be afraid that someday, somehow, her beloved Earth would suffer the same fate. And that, she could not bear to think about.

Williams' visit to the Mars side of Phobos was one of her monthly Bright Side rest and recreation visits. But this time, just as all the other times, she had eventually turned away from the planet, feeling overpowered by an inexplicable sense of loss. She returned to her Skimmer Scooter and headed towards her military post on the dark side.

The Phobos Skimmer Scooters were designed for one-person transport using a tracked mechanism but with a tail that swung down to bite into the asteroid surface whenever the scooter got light and tried to become airborne. This was a bit of a misnomer since there was no air on Phobos. With the very weak gravity of the tiny Martian moon, any vehicle "catching air" could find itself heading many meters away from the surface before landing again. Scooter landings were never graceful, so the grabbing-tail ensured the vehicle never got far from the moon's surface.

William's Space Corp monitoring outpost was on what Martian astronauts called the Dark Side of Phobos, but the Dark Side wasn't actually dark, at least, no more so than the Dark Side of Earth's moon. It merely faced away from Mars, just as the far side of Luna faces away from Earth.

Planetary scientists would say Phobos and the Earth's moons are tidally locked with their own planets, which means the far side of Phobos is a lousy place to view Mars, given that Phobos zips around the planet every eight hours. But it does make a great place to see the Cosmos.

The Cosmos is precisely what the U.S. Space Corp wanted to keep an eye on from its vantage spot on a distant moon, ever since learning there really were aliens out there. Even though Earth's ancient aquatic aliens were friendly, as revealed when they left Earth for good, the U.S. military could not afford to assume that other alien species would be as amicable.

So, on the dark side of Phobos, an observatory was built with top-secret sensor suites, staffed with uniformed military, all with top-secret clearances and an unassailable aptitude for keeping themselves busy and entertained while looking for mostly nothing at all for two years at a time.

Due to the interminable tedium of the Phobos deployments, the Dark Side military were given a once a month R&R opportunity to visit the near side to observe the Martian surface as Phobos swung around the red planet.

Due to the difference between the orbits of Earth and Mars, the two planets are only close every two years. Crew change-out missions were launched biannually to take advantage of that proximity, making each military deployment to Phobos a long haul.

With that in mind, each new crew first landed on the Mars side of the ex-asteroid, and once again upon departure, with monthly sojourns allowed. However, after a while, some crew members chose to give up their R&R time; there really wasn't much you could do on the Mars Side beside watch the red world go by above you. Once you had experienced a hundred or so overflights of the planet, you'd pretty much seen them all.

While Clarice was making her way back to the observation post, her crewmate and husband, Technical Sergeant Robert Williams, was waking up the pilot and only crewman of the incoming cargo ship.

"Good morning, Tobias. You got your morning wood on?"

"I can't believe you said that."

"Why not?"

"You should know it's never morning out here."

"According to universal time, it is 0600 hours, and we call that morning."

"You know, whoever let the Brits define universal time must be nuts. The universe is not a British colony."

"Good point, my friend. But I think 300 days in isolation has made you cranky."

"Not to worry. It's given me lots of time to think."

"What do you think about Tobias?"

"About how much I'm going to enjoy ripping you a new one when I get there."

"Like that'll ever happen. You forget, Clarice has my back."

"Am I supposed to be afraid of her?"

"You should be. I am."

"You crack me up, Bob."

"How'd you learn to talk like that? Ripping a new one?"

"From you, Bob."

Williams laughed. "Yeah, you probably did, Tobias. My mom always said I was a bad influence."

"I don't mind, Bob."

"Look, sorry to interrupt your wet dream, but I have to let you know we'll be launching our probe in a few minutes, to check you over before you land."

"Well, I'm nearing entry to Mars orbit, and all things look nominal from here. No sensor warnings, no spooky sounds. We're A-Okay."

"You know the rules, Tobias. We have to make sure no Clingon probes are hitching a ride. Don't want you to bring any parasites to our little moon."

"I'll try to give it a big smile. Which side do you think is my good side, Bob?"

"You handsome devil, you don't have a bad side."

After a brief pause in the conversation, Williams spoke up. "Hey, Tobias, are you smiling right now?"

"Yes, I am."

"I thought so."

A moment later Williams announced, "The probe just launched. You should have intercept in about thirty minutes. Try to hold still while it's checking you out."

"I'll try, but you do know I'm still traveling at twenty thousand kilometers per hour."

"Not to worry. The probe just locked onto you. You'll have company soon."

"Finally," Tobias said. "This is one hell of a long trip."

"Hate to have you make the trip this far from Earth, but we really need your supplies, especially that oxygen. Plus, Clarice said she's looking forward to having an intelligent conversationalist on board. I guess I'm not highbrow enough for her. I don't think she digs my sense of humor."

"You do take some getting used to Bob."

"I hear that a lot."

The relative closing speed of the probe and the cargo ship had been tremendous, so when the probe had closed about half the distance to the ship, it began decelerating, even when it passed the ship. Due to its feather-light weight, its ion drive allowed it to quickly accelerate in the opposite direction to come in behind the cargo ship.

As advertised, about thirty minutes after launch, the probe was circling the ship from all directions, looking intently for any signs of alien stowaway machines. The machines' original name, *seekers*, belied their sometimes-malevolent nature. Since that machine behavior had been detected five years before, the ever-reproducing *seekers* became known more appropriately as *Clingons*, reflecting how they liked to hitch a ride on the outer surface of spacecraft, supposedly searching for their long-gone alien masters, and as a not-so-vague reference to the Klingons of the old Star Trek franchise.

The outer airlock of the small Phobos Base activated, announcing Clarice's return.

"It's your lucky day, Tobias, you get to say hi to Clarice. She just got back from the Bright Side."

CHAPTER 3. CAPE EVANS

It was 8 PM on June 20, the date of maximum total darkness at McMurdo Station, Antarctica. The combination of Polar cold and total darkness made the U.S. Navy divers' work awkward and uncomfortable, but that was just another day for the most trusted dive team the Navy could assemble for this mission.

Jason Parker held an acoustical direction finder, homing in on a signal disguised by a background of marine noises: clicking shrimp, groaning seals, and distant whales. Buried within that natural cacophony were the navigation signals that Jason Parker's electronics could decipher, sending him straight to the bottom of the water-and-ice interface of Cape Evans, the glacial outfall from the volcano Mt. Erebus, not far from McMurdo.

Light discipline was severe at his diving site. Since it was the dead of winter at the bottom of the world, with a solid twenty-four hours of darkness, any stray light could betray to the ever-searching Russian satellites the fact that a top-secret military mission was underway, almost right under the noses of the oblivious overwintering U.S. Antarctic crew.

To no one's great surprise, overwintering was an extreme test for personal fortitude, relieved somewhat by the winter's supply of ten thousand condoms freely distributed by the meager medical staff on station. A pregnancy, or even worse, a medical complication from pregnancy, would put the pregnant party at high risk since medical evacuation flights during the darkest and most blustery part of winter, were rare, and dangerous for the flight crew. As they say, an ounce of prevention is worth a pound of cure.

One of the mechanics had been run over by a tracked vehicle, and his injury was severe enough that his transport out of McMurdo was a dire necessity, although a risky one.

That flight leaving Christchurch for "the Ice" had been Jason Parker's chance to catch a ride down to see what was going on 100 feet below the sea ice at Cape Evans.

Strapped into a rebreather modified for frigid water, and with a full-face mask, Parker slid down a line that led to the bottom of a

The inner lock door opened and Clarice walked up to the monitors after stowing her helmet. In Earth gravity, the helmet would be cumbersome, but on this tiny moon, it had almost no weight at all.

"Welcome back Clarice," Williams said. "Say hi to Tobias. He's coming up on insertion, and we're doing the final visual checkout."

"Boy, are we glad to see you, Tobias," Clarice said.

"Ah, you're sweet, but I know you just want my oxygen."

"Not true. I need someone cute to talk to."

Tobias laughed. "Yes, your husband said as much."

"We should be due for some repartee in fifteen minutes or so," Clarice said. "We're looking forward to it."

"Me too, Cla— *What the—!*" The last two words were shouted.

At that same instant, the probe camera showed the white paint and the American flag on the cargo craft charring from intense heat, and the craft veering off course. A split second later the video link with the probe was lost, and a second after that, all telemetry from both the cargo craft and probe was gone.

"What the fuck just happened?" Williams yelled. But his instructions were clear and his motion a reflex of training. He reached for the destruct button.

"No!" Clarice screamed.

She was too late.

From the station, the optics trained on the incoming ship, now exploded by Williams's destruct signal, showed a cloud of fragments approaching at up to twenty thousand feet per second, four times faster than the fastest bullet.

Clarice screamed, "Get suited up, now!"

His attention glued on the monitors, Bob shouted, "Incoming!"

In a thunderous crash, most of the laboratory was destroyed by the impact of a heat-exploded oxygen bottle and the charred titanium skull of the robot named Tobias.

cofferdam securely affixed to the vertical cliff where Barne Glacier, spilling down Mt. Erebus, met the Ross Sea. The Ross Sea was covered entirely in ice; had he been making a daylight dive, he would have seen the stark white wall dropping straight down from the glacier's edge to the rocky seabed, 100 feet below the surface. But in the dead of winter with no lights allowed, he could see nothing.

To ensure he would not get lost if the downline broke, Parker, like all the divers, wore a tactile stimulation suit that vibrated on his skin to point him to the acoustical beacon situated on the cofferdam on the way down. Going back up, it would lead them towards the nine-foot shaft cut through the ice to the surface. Of course, all of that navigation occurred in total darkness, with the only sense of downward motion being the need to equalize pressure in the diver's ears. It was so dark that the divers didn't know they were at the cofferdam until they felt it with their extended, gloved hand.

Unlike most cofferdams that have an open bottom, this one was more like a large box with a solid base. A rap on the bottom and one of the brawny divers inside would open an access port just long enough to yank the incoming diver out of the water and onto the box floor, lit only by a subdued red light. Within a matter of three seconds, the diver would be clear of the water, and the hatch would be sealed again. Due to the absorption of red light by water, and the thick covering of sea ice, even the most sensitive Russian satellite peering at that exact point during that three-second exposure, would detect nothing.

The diver who yanked Parker unceremoniously unto the cofferdam floor was an old friend, Tom Thomas, a former diver from NDC, and one of the two who had verified that a Frogship was hidden in a cave 2,500 feet deep, off the Gulf Coast of Florida.

"Doc, I don't think you'll be flying this spaceship anytime soon."

"You don't think duct tape and Bondo will help?"

"Highly unlikely, my friend. How the hell are you?"

Thomas helped get Parker to his feet and started assisting him with removing his diving rig.

"Shit, it's cold in here."

"Better keep your electric suit turned on."

Another diver, J.R. Jackson, shorter and usually more animated, entered through a closed door separating the entry space from the rest of the project space. When J.R. got quiet, his fellow divers began to worry. He was a trickster extraordinaire.

"What Tom meant to say," J.R. offered, "is you'll freeze your ass off. And where we're taking you is even colder. And in there you'll have to turn your heating off. We're told that area must remain deep-frozen."

"That's what I hear. What do you think it is?"

"Frozen guacamole. That's just what it looks like, but smashed flat as a flitter."

"Flitter?" Parker repeated.

"You know, a cow pie."

"No, I don't know. Any bones?"

"Not that we can tell. The firmest structure seems to be more like cartilage like sharks have," Tom said.

"But it's mostly squished muscles and soft insides," J.R. added. "Like maybe guts."

"Wonder if this was a food bank for the frogs. Like maybe they collected this stuff to eat."

"Could be anything," Thomas added. "Follow me single file, but don't get stuck. I don't want you blocking my exit."

"And I'll be following close behind you Doc," J.R. said. "So do me a favor and don't cut the cheese."

Parker smiled. Sketchy as this was, it felt good to be working with his diver friends again. As two of the most experienced and highly cleared divers in the Navy, they were a hoot. But they could be deadly serious and deadly efficient when the occasion demanded.

Tom and J.R. got on their hands and knees and started crawling through a crevice in the side of the alien flying saucer. That crevice had been pried open by hydraulic jacks. With a hundred feet of glacial ice on top of them the jacks, still in place, were not able to open up any more of a crawl space.

Eyeing a couple of the jacks as they slide-crawled past them, Parker couldn't help commenting. "Do these jacks ever fail?"

"They could," J.R. answered. "Then we'd all be flat as flitters."

"But not guacamole flitters," Tom added. "More like ground beef flitters."

Parker decided to ask no more questions and instead concentrated on crawling and slithering as cautiously as he could, making sure not to bump into the jacks.

Another five minutes of scooching between icy cold bent metal and ancient ice had Parker wishing he'd lost five pounds before coming to McMurdo. He was concentrating so hard he almost bumped into Tom, who had stopped and was peering ahead.

Parker inched up beside him. J.R. did likewise.

"This is what you came all this way to see," Tom said.

"It's not much to look at," J.R. added.

He was right about that. There was no way to gain any height on the stuff before them, to see what it was, but Parker's first impression was that of an inflatable Christmas Santa Claus that had lain deflated and frozen for thousands of years. Except the color was wrong. There was no red in it—all green, gray, and dingy white. And in spite of its firmly frozen condition, it seemed to exude a somewhat astringent odor. Fortunately, it was not the sickly odor of death and decay.

"How big is this?"

"Not very," J.R. answered. Maybe five by five."

"Feet?"

"Yeah."

"So, I guess there's no way to slide it onto a blue tarp and extract it out of here?" Parker asked.

"Not a chance, Doc. It would be torn to pieces," Tom said. "And if we start warming things up above the craft and melting the ice so we can open up a larger space, this stuff will probably decay very quickly."

"Turn into green pea soup," J.R. opined.

"Not good," Parker said.

After another three hours of inspection, decompression and return to the surface, the three cold and tired divers arrived back in McMurdo Station as the day shift was coming in the mess hall for breakfast. You could only tell it was morning by looking at the clock because the absolute darkness never changed during the depth of winter.

The men picked up their trays and moved through the serving line. It didn't take long since the over-wintering crew was small compared to the rush of scientists and technicians who poured in when the weather improved in October, and the sun was up for most of the day.

Parker, Tom, and J.R. sat by themselves, their trays loaded with piles of high-calorie food. They were considered outsiders by the rest of the crew since they had not been on-station in the past, and they never talked about their work. The only one of them who received attention this morning was J.R., from a cute blond with a cold-reddened face and a body that showed a few pounds packed on for the winter. Parker watched her wink at J.R. and J.R. smile in return. She glanced at Parker, perhaps wondering where the new guy came from, but J.R. did not speak. She nodded her head, seeming to realize there had only been one flight in, and the new guy must have been on it.

"She seems to like you, J.R."

"We have fun," he said. "But I'm too damn tired now to think about chicks."

Tom looked at him with a look of surprise, which Parker noticed.

"I see you Navy guys pretty well keep to yourselves," Parker said.

"Yeah, it's safer that way. Loose lips sink ships, you know."

"So Doc," Tom said, changing the subject, "Have you been a ship without a rudder since you left NDC in Panama City?"

"Actually, no. I'm more of a free agent now, still on Navy salary but serving whoever needs me."

"Whoever needs him to fly a fucking alien spaceship," J.R. whispered. "Nice gig if you can get it."

"Haven't done that in a while. But I'm here to see how you guys are doing? Getting all the support you need?"

"No complaints," Tom said.

"How do the others get along with you guys when you have to mingle?" Parker asked.

"Oh, come on, man," J.R. said. "You know we're party animals when it's appropriate."

Tom smirked at Parker. "The only social concerns are that the other guys are pissed that J.R. seems to be claiming more than his fair share of the rubbers." Then, looking back at J.R., "After all, they do have to last all winter."

Parker looked at J.R., with amazement. "More than your fair share of ten thousand?"

"What do you say we change the subject, Doc," said J.R. around a mouthful of French fries. "What are we going to do with our guacamole?"

Parker assumed that no one within earshot would have any idea what the real subject was. "I have no clue. I think I need to sleep on it, which I plan to be doing about ten minutes from now. But I do have another question. What's the most dangerous part of this job?"

Tom didn't hesitate but kept his voice low. "It's not the diving. It's the glacier. One of the Underwater Construction Team guys disappeared down a crevasse in the glacier just above our dive site. He couldn't be retrieved because of the collapse of the crevasse walls."

"Really?"

"One day a couple of hundred years from now his squished body will get kicked out by the glacier as it heads underwater. Some future diver may find him."

"I would think the crevasses are being constantly mapped," Parker said.

"We did too. But there's some interesting scuttlebutt. Some said he was bedding a young lady here, and in the course of the evening started talking too much. Turns out, the chick was supposedly a Company gal. She ratted him out. And then he disappeared into that crevasse. Very convenient."

"Are you guys shitting me?"

"No, he definitely fell into the crevasse."

"But I think if she were really CIA," Parker said, "you guys would never know."

"Maybe. But some think the guy was too smart to fall. He must have been pushed."

Parker was becoming more skeptical by the minute. He'd been in enough remote work camps to know how rumors and aspersions fly every which way in such an isolated environment.

"Where's the CIA gal?" Parker asked.

"She left on the flight that brought you in. You just missed her."

How convenient, he thought. "So, you think her bosses called her in from the cold?" Parker chuckled as he said it.

"Could be. I doubt she was supposed to get that close to the folks she was watching."

"Who was she watching?"

"Us," J.R. said.

"We're the only ones with secrets down here," Tom added.

Parker looked at J.R. with a smile. "Did you…?"

"I'll never tell," J.R. said with a deadpan expression on his face.

They sat quietly for the rest of their breakfast, enjoying the warm food and camaraderie in a barren place a universe away from home. Then Parker got up to refill his orange juice, marveling at the thought of the availability of orange juice in the winter, thousands of miles from the nearest oranges. The Polar Program Office of the National Science Foundation takes good care of their over-wintering staff.

And then he had another thought. Returning to the table, he said, "J.R., you just said something that gave me an idea. This poor guy down in the crevasse. The glacier is moving, right?"

"Yeah, slowly, but the crevasses open and close quite often. He's squished down there somewhere. Probably killed in the fall, then buried by an ice cave-in from above. They tried to reach him, but it got too dangerous. Not worth risking another life to bring up a frozen corpse."

"Yeah, I completely agree. And I think I know what we can do with our guacamole."

Chapter 4. Guacamole

Parker was topside at the infrared-camouflaged dive site canopy. A spy satellite, no matter how sensitive its sensors, would detect nothing but an undisturbed glacial expanse slowly tumbling into the frozen, snow-covered Ross Sea.

Parker was on the satellite phone with a Navy Lieutenant friend at NRL, the Naval Research Laboratory in Washington D.C.

"Don't ask me why," Parker explained, "I just need to know if you have any of those crawler scanners you were telling me about. Or is it just vaporware, nonexistent?"

"No, Jason. They're real. The sponsor lost interest in the scanners, so they're sitting on a shelf. We have ten or twelve of them."

"Good, I need all of them. They have to ship out tomorrow, along with at least three of the computers to run them."

"Tomorrow's Saturday, Jason."

"Just make it happen."

"And they're going where?"

"McMurdo Station."

"Holy crap Jason. That'll be seriously difficult."

"But not impossible."

He sighed. "No, not impossible."

"Good."

Parker hung up and scrolled through the contacts on his laptop until he found the number for his next call. It was ETH Zurich, the Swiss Federal Institute of Technology. The university had produced an astounding number of Nobel Laureates and thus attracted the brightest students and professors in Europe. Recently, one of the professors in the natural sciences department, a Dr. Helmut Reuter, had been in the news for his use of a new computer algorithm to reconstruct a three-dimensional, lifelike image of an ancient man removed from a melting glacier.

The man called Otzi had apparently fallen into a crevasse high in the Swiss Alps, and when the glacier melted, his crushed and mangled body had been recovered. It was then digitized and reconstructed by the computers in the professor's laboratory.

Parker and Reuter had met years before when Reuter was taking a sabbatical at Emory University. Being a good bit older than Parker, Reuter had taken a fatherly interest in Parker, and Parker grew to respect him for both his kindness and expertise.

"I can't give you our trade secrets," Dr. Reuter said in a thick Swiss-German accent, "but I will tell you that we make certain assumptions about symmetry. And it doesn't have to be a person—it works for animals too. Natural bodies are symmetrical, and if we crush a digital model of a body with an almost unlimited set of conditions, we can compare the crushed body to the original. That gives us our reconstructive algorithms. So, when an already crushed body comes in, once it's meticulously scanned, we run our algorithm in reverse and reconstruct what it must have been like."

"Does it work on flattened road kill?" Parker asked.

"Most certainly. That was one of the first calibration tests we ran on it. We knew it was a rabbit, scanned the remains, and sure enough, were able to tell what it looked like in real life. In fact, that was how we got funding to enhance our computers and improve our algorithms. And we were just in time for the Grindelwald Couple. The result was rather stunning. National Geographic is coming by next month to do an in-depth article on us."

"Nat Geo? That's impressive. Congrats!"

"So how many bones are we dealing with?" Reuter asked.

"I think none."

"None?"

The Swiss Professor sounded shocked. "Look, we can't do amoebas. We have to have some anatomical structure to work with."

"It might have cartilage. Can you do a shark or ray?"

"I don't know," Reuter admitted. "We haven't tried."

"While we're generating the data, maybe one of your students could experiment with that."

"It would be a challenge, but I like the idea."

"How much data do you need to work with?" Parker asked.

"Our modeling needs at least twelve terabytes of data. But that's assuming we have something we know, like a bony structure. With cartilage, I'm not sure. Like I said, that will be new for us."

"Twelve terabytes, we should be able to do that."

"So, what is your mystery object? You've piqued my interest."

"We really don't know. That's why it's a mystery."

"Honestly, I don't know. I guess it's anyone who sends me a message to report."

The next morning Parker rode the Terrabus to the Ross Sea landing strip. From the bus's headlights and the surface lights outlining the embarkation point, he could see the shape of the waiting C18, but it was too dark to discern details of the craft. His watch said it was 11:30 in the morning but the surreal phenomenon of *diamond dust* ice crystals suspended in the air, rendered a magical spell on Parker's closing moments at McMurdo Station. The ice crystals reflected whatever artificial light was available, looking like fairy dust just barely visible in the dim light. He had never seen it before, and likely never would again.

Once on board the behemoth jet, he took up one of the many empty seats arranged in wide rows in the forward third of the aircraft. Parker was almost embarrassed to be surrounded by empty seats in such a behemoth plane, but orders were orders and not to be questioned. Transportation back to New Zealand would take four hours in the C18. If he'd had to take a C17, it would have taken five.

All Parker had been told was that on arrival back in Christchurch, he would barely have time to turn in his red Antarctic parka and other polar clothing before he caught a night flight to Los Angeles. Beyond L.A., he had not been told his final destination. He would be briefed once he arrived in the States.

As the plane soared over the shore of the Antarctic continent and finally passed the edge of the sea ice, he began to see a brightening in the northern sky. The farther north they traveled, the more sunlight they would see. That was the most sunlight he'd seen in weeks, and despite the circumstances of the trip, it made his heart soar.

By the time the rugged Southern Alps of New Zealand's South Island came into view on the western side of the jet, Parker had begun to let go of his emotional ties of responsibility for the Navy divers still working in the dark, now 2,500 miles away. They were well trained, highly experienced, and most of all knew how to keep their mouths shut about the work they were doing on the Ice, or more precisely, under it.

After arrival in Christchurch and a hop to Auckland on the North Island, Parker was headed home on a twelve-hour flight across the

Pacific. He wasn't sure why he was recalled from the mission, but he did enjoy a mystery.

Chapter 5. Air New Zealand

Jason Parker didn't know if all pilots preferred window seats, but he certainly did.

He was relieved the middle seat to his left was empty. When the lady sitting in the aisle seat unbelted and headed to the back of the plane, Parker looked over at the man sitting on the far side of the aisle, a hipster-looking type with a spade beard and a western-cut snap shirt, watching a movie on a display device of some kind.

Parker remembered another time when he was headed across the Pacific towards Guam and saw the ephemeral image of a smiling Frog sitting on a businessman's lap. Apparently, the man had not been aware of the ghostly presence sharing his seat.

Parker couldn't remember exactly why the Frog had been smiling, but the fleeting image was both puzzling and unsettling because, as he discovered later, the actual Frog was thousands of miles away and thousands of feet underwater.

Ever since that flight to Guam, from his window-seat vantage point on all other flights, he would look across the aisle to see if by any chance that ephemeral image would reappear. But it never did.

It was in Guam that he and Laura Smith had drawn close, a forced intimacy due to confinement at the hands of a former friend turned rogue NSA agent. It was during their escape from that confinement, triggered by a warning from the same ephemeral Frog that Parker realized three things. One, the U.S. government seemed insanely jealous of his natural discourse with the alien aquatic species. Secondly, those creatures who called themselves *humans* but whom Parker called Frogs, to avoid confusion, apparently had an invested interest in the survival of both Parker and the Starchild oceanography graduate student, Laura Smith.

Thirdly, a former friend attempted to murder him. The physicist, whose brilliant mind had been twisted by an exaggerated sense of self-importance would have succeeded in killing him had it not been for the miraculous rescue and medical intervention of Frogs.

Usually, Parker would have selected the local wine offered on this Air New Zealand flight. On this day, however, with his under-stimulated mind wandering between Frogs and the women in his life, such as Laura and his apparently disgruntled wife, he stopped the drink cart as it rattled close by and asked for a miniature bottle of Stolen Dark rum to add to his coke.

Sandy had always said she was not bothered by Parker's friendship with the much younger Laura, and he never had a reason to doubt her, until now.

Separation after twenty years? What was she thinking?

With the day-night terminator racing west at supersonic speed, and the jet flying east at near sonic speed, twilight lasted little longer than a hiccup, quickly plunging the plane into the utter blackness of the Pacific night. At that point, the value of a window seat was lost, and Parker turned to his portable aviation navigator to entertain himself.

The tablet-sized navigator Parker carried with him on such flights gave him a simulated view of the outside world and the cockpit instruments being used by the pilots. Some of that information was available to all passengers, but Parker preferred the better visuals provided by his device. It made him feel like he was in the cockpit, which was the one place where every pilot is the most comfortable.

It also allowed him to test the boundaries of the mind control that served him well on Frogships. Watching the extremely sensitive heading indicator and artificial horizon displayed in front of him, he felt empowered by the rum to see if his mental concentration could jiggle the needles, altering ever so slightly the jet's heading or pitch.

In spite of his mental gymnastics, the flight bore on through the night as if on rails. But as he doubled his efforts, there was a short series of bumps, followed by the seat-belt light coming on.

The copilot came on the intercom in her decidedly Kiwi accent announcing she had turned on the seat-belt light for passenger comfort. Alarmed, Parker aborted his mental effort, followed by a hint of a smile of satisfaction. However, in spite of his stopping his ill-advised concentration, the mild turbulence continued for several minutes. Clearly, it wasn't his doing.

Okay, Parker thought, *we'll chalk that up to coincidence.*

Apparently, he couldn't mentally control this Boeing ship, even if he wanted to. And in all honesty, he didn't want to. He was just—curious.

It was a good thing the ship's autopilot didn't give a damn who was sitting in the passenger cabin, but for Parker, it was a far different story with the Frogship.

Parker had heard whispers that hotshot American pilots had attempted to replicate his flight in the DeSoto Canyon Frog ship, without success.

Hell, he thought in a self-satisfied way, *supposedly they couldn't even get the damned door open.*

As a result, every time he was in a military pilot's presence, they seemed to react toward him with a mixture of awe and disdain.

He hated that reaction since he really wasn't a member of their club. He'd served an ROTC hitch in the Army right out of college, during peacetime, but never claimed to be a military pilot like his brother had been. He'd never fired a shot in anger, or dodged an incoming missile, or ejected from a crippled airplane.

However, to his credit, he had survived a couple of light aircraft crashes, and for some reason, he had an uncanny ability to fly the hottest aircraft in the world.

At least he had that one time.

But that one time had been enough to earn him the enmity of those Russians who knew he'd escaped Lake Baikal in the one Frogship they had salvaged.

Except he really hadn't. It was true that he and Laura had been able to activate the Baikal ship, a feat no Russian had been able to do. But once launched, the craft actually flew itself to Nevada following a flight plan uploaded mentally by a recent Mexican emigre that called himself a Troll with an unpronounceable name.

Through a bit of State Department collusion with the Mexican Trolls, before the U.S. finally returned what the Russians considered stolen property, that same craft had been used to extract every last Russian Troll from their captivity in Siberia. Conveniently, those Trolls might have the innate capability to upload Frogship flight plans just like their Mexican brethren. Without them, the Russian's salvaged ship had no means of control. It was an empty shell, and therefore of no tactical or intelligence value to the Russians.

Even though the Russians had caused an international incident by kidnapping both Laura Smith and Parker, the Russkies were hopping mad they weren't able to keep them. They were also peeved that their collection of Troll slaves had disappeared about the same time, although the Russians never seemed to make the connection between the two events.

Shortly after the American's own ship had been salvaged from the De Soto Canyon in the Gulf of Mexico, Parker had been given a chance to make a short flight, under his own mental direction without the help of Trolls. That was where his remote viewing skills came into play.

He and a blind remote viewing assistant, Joshua Nilsson, had flown at low altitude and then submerged to the depth of the canyon, returning once again to the location where the craft had been found. But like a horse comfortable in its stable, it had been reluctant to leave its home at 2,500 feet. But, at last, with worried urging from Parker, it abandoned its deep ocean cave and returned to the Navy shipyard at Pascagoula where it had been taken after being salvaged.

After that, Parker lost track of the ship, which seemed to be part of the government's security plan. Parker and Laura had been kidnapped once by the Russians after being a little too careless, so who was to say it wouldn't happen again. It was best for everyone if Parker was kept in the dark about the ship's whereabouts.

Looking out his window to the south, Parker saw towering cumulonimbus clouds illuminated internally by lightning. Those storms reached up to the jet's altitude, and beyond. From this safe distance, the raw power of nature was a thing of beauty. But once upon a time, as a young man, he flew off-shore at night only a mile above the waters of the Gulf of Mexico. It was a beautiful flight until he encountered a series of rapacious storms venting their fury uncomfortably close to his aircraft's wings. As the storms raged, his knees uncontrollably tapped out a message in something like Morse code. They seemed to be saying, *What the hell are you doing here, Parker?*

From that experience, he could appreciate the value of flying jets in the stratosphere, above the majority of the weather. Better yet would be operating in space where there is no weather at all.

But even space travel can be dangerous, which makes a compelling argument for seeing what you want to see remotely. As a species, the Frogs had evolved the remote viewing method of moving their consciousness around without their bodies, without ever leaving the safety of the high pressure, low oxygen environment their physiology demanded. There are no thunderstorms in the deep sea.

While the Frogs took their remote viewing capabilities for granted, Parker had struggled to acquire a limited skill in remote viewing. But clearly, the Master of all remote viewers was the blind man named Joshua Nilsson, one of the CIA's most carefully guarded secrets.

As Parker called for another Stolen, neat, he concluded what he had always known. The ET Frogs were weird in many ways, but they had saved the lives of both Laura and himself, so he was reluctant to think ill of them in any way. In fact, after the mass departure of thousands of their ships rocketing out of the deep sea canyons of Earth during The Great Leaving, he had to admit he missed them.

He wondered where in space they were.

CHAPTER 6. ALIEN EMERGENCY

Emery Reed, M.D., Navy Captain, was a six-foot-tall man with dark hair that sat like a tightly tailored cap over his piercing eyes, eyes that were almost always offset by a teeth-revealing smile. He had the kind of good looks and hard body that would qualify him for a spot in a Kalvin Klein ad, but he chose to serve his country. He'd served as the chief medical officer on highly secretive submarine missions and was trained in emergency medicine and psychiatry, which qualified him for the high prestige of being a sitting President's personal doctor. He was also the Navy's only physician qualified simultaneously as a diving medical officer, submarine medical officer, and flight surgeon.

Dr. Reed, now the Senior Medical Officer at the Naval Diving Center, NDC, was staring at the young patient in front of him. She was a thin child, nine years old, and with a heavy cough. She reminded Reed of the way his own daughter looked at that age, with big brown eyes and a high forehead. She had already lost all of her baby teeth, well ahead of her peers.

Although her gross appearance was overall human, genetically she and the rest of her kind were self-described Trolls, hybrids between the aquatic aliens and humans. The aliens colloquially called Frogs created the hybrids to serve as slaves for mining minerals in caves, hence the Troll moniker. The Trolls could tolerate Earth's oxygen levels, but that same oxygen was highly toxic to the Frogs.

The men beside her were a strange-looking bunch. Her father was a gaunt man wearing clothes that hung poorly on him as if hurriedly borrowed from a Goodwill bin. He was cleanly shaven in the extreme, with no sign of stubble. It was as if he had no facial hair at all, only a dark head of hair that hung down his back.

The other man was angular looking, dressed far blacker than seemed appropriate for a Floridian.

Reed was a man known to be discreet and who could be trusted to keep secrets. In this case, the secret was the girl and her father. The enigma was the other man who was scrutinizing the Captain's every move.

Reed motioned to the man who identified himself as an agent with Homeland Security. They stepped out into the hall for a moment's privacy. It was a Saturday night, and the usual bustle of divers and Navy corpsmen was absent. They were alone and could speak freely in muted tones.

"The cough could be viral, bacterial, or fungal in origin. Considering the dampish cave she's been living in, the Marianna caverns, my best guess would be fungal, and that's especially concerning."

"But it can be treated, right?"

"Yes, but we have a problem."

"What kind?"

"You said she's not entirely human; there are DNA differences."

"That's correct."

"Even among humans, the susceptibility to fungal infections, and in fact, many diseases, are influenced by race. But if she's not entirely human, we know nothing about her prognosis if we don't treat her."

"Doc, why would you not treat her?"

"We don't know what effect our antifungal medications would have on her. It might kill her."

"What?"

"Let me give you an example. You've heard you should not feed chocolate to cats and dogs, right?"

"Yeah, because it could kill them."

"Exactly. Chocolate has theobromine which is poisonous to our pets. Humans can process it just fine, but our pets can't do that. So theobromine accumulates to toxic levels, and they can die."

"I got that, but she's not a pet."

"The point is," Dr. Reed said, "we don't know exactly what she is. She and her kin, the so-called Trolls, were bioengineered by the Frogs to be like humans. There can be a big difference between being *like humans* and actually *being human*."

"So, what are you saying?"

"Her phenotype is human, so chances are her genotype is human too, but there are exceptions. And those exceptions could kill her."

"In plain English please, Doc."

"The cure could be worse than the illness."

"She sure looks human to me."

Reed said, "But I heard somewhere that they are UV emitters."

"Yeah, but I can't see it."

"Of course, you can't see UV," the doctor said. "But let's do a little demonstration just to confirm."

The two men reentered the physician's office and donned white cotton smocks. Addressing the girl, Reed said, "I'm going to turn the lights out for a moment to check your eyes."

Holding his ophthalmoscope with one hand, he approached her eyes.

Speaking to the agent, "Jim, would you turn off the lights for a moment? I'll tell you when I want them back on."

As soon as the room went dark, Reed's coat began to glow in a bluish-white color. He shined a soft infrared light into the girl's eyes, which showed on an infrared detector that the girl's pupils were slightly dilated, but not as much as he would have expected for a typical patient.

"Light back on, please."

When they came on, the Doctor saw the pupils constrict, as he would have expected.

Reed looked the girl in the face, warmly smiling. "Your skin lights came on."

"Yes, they always do that when it's dark. Don't yours?"

The Doctor looked at the girl's father and addressing both of them, he said, "No, I don't have that talent."

"Why not?"

"Because you have superpowers I don't have. That's awesome."

Reed reached up to give her a high-five, an act she knew about but had not much practice doing. She managed it with enough confidence that she passed Reed's impromptu neurological exam.

"Can I touch your forehead?"

"Sure, if you want."

It was warmer than it had been.

"Does your skin always get warm when your skin lights come on?"

"I don't know. I guess."

The agent was motioning with his head that he wanted to talk in the hall again, but Reed ignored him.

"Did you notice how my jacket was glowing so brightly?"

"Sure. That's what our homes do as well," she said.

"It was fluorescing, from your skin lights. I couldn't see your skin lights, but the cotton in my jacket was responding to it."

The girl reached out and touched his coat. "It doesn't feel warm."

"No. When something reacts to your light, it doesn't get warm like your skin does."

"Oh."

Both the agent and Reed noted that the girl had stopped coughing during the examination.

Dr. Reed crossed his arms and looked at her. "I think the best thing to do for now is nothing. If I gave you some medication, I might be making things worse.

"Why not admit her to the hospital?" the Homeland Security agent asked.

"They won't watch carefully enough. And they'd likely give her something inappropriate before they released her. I don't want her going home until this resolves."

"Whatever you say, Doctor."

Reed pulled the dark-suited man out into the hall again and spoke quietly. "If need be, we can take her to Bay Medical ER. But we'll cross that bridge when we get there."

"What can you tell them?"

"I'll tell them she's immunosuppressed and we have to be very careful. They'll be able to get the X-Rays we need, culture her sputum, run the usual blood and urine tests."

"Is she immunosuppressed?"

"I have no idea. I know nothing about these Trolls' immune system, or their metabolism, or anything, really."

"They survived just fine for thousands of years in the Yucatan without Doctors."

"But now we've placed them in a different environment, North Florida."

"North Florida, the Yucatan. Six of one, half dozen the other."

"I don't know how the microclimate compares. Different microclimates, different pathogens. If we lose this girl, we may have to move them somewhere else."

"You think we could lose her?"

"It could happen. We don't know how to treat them. In fact, we don't know much about them except they only have one lung instead of two. If something bad happens to that one lung, they're dead."

"So maybe we should have left them alone."

"That's true. But they wanted to leave Mexico, and POTUS was all too happy to oblige. In the meanwhile, I want her kept here in sickbay overnight."

Turning to her father, Reed asked, "Are you alright spending the night with her here? We have food in the fridge, and these beds are mighty comfortable."

The father, his face wrinkled with worry, unconsciously swept his dark hair off his forehead.

"We can stay here until morning, but then we want to go home."

"We'll discuss that in the morning," Reed said. "If you don't mind, I'd like to swab inside her mouth so we can check for strep. It's not pleasant, but it's not too uncomfortable, either."

"Do what you must."

After swabbing the girl's mouth, Reed placed two swabs inside a vial, sealed it tightly, and placed the vial in a container with a cold pack.

"We should have an answer in a few hours. In the meanwhile, if she gets more uncomfortable, call me immediately. I'll be sleeping in my office, but I can be here in two minutes."

What Reed didn't say was that one swab was for the strep test, and the other was for DNA analysis. He needed to know more about the genetic makeup of these Trolls to establish a baseline for medical treatments. The DNA sample would be sent to Emory University who worked with the Max Planck Institute for Evolutionary Anthropology in Leipzig, Germany, the world's foremost genetic comparison lab.

Unbeknownst to him, part of the biological samples from Jason Parker's crushed Cape Evans craft was also being sent to the Max Planck Institute, in addition to the samples going to ETH Zurich.

There was an awful lot of people interested in anything relating to the genomes of Frogs and Trolls. The genetics community had not been this excited since the days of Watson and Crick.

CHAPTER 7. NEVADA DEEP

The arrival at LAX was a smooth blessing. As much as he loved to fly, he looked forward to staying on the ground for a while. It had been a very long flight from Antarctica, and as a result, his ears were ringing, his back was aching, and his sunny disposition had expired about halfway across the Pacific when the old John Wayne movie he had started watching crapped out due to "an equipment problem."

Not flying for a while sounded like a great idea.

As Parker stood to get his belongings from his overhead bin, the hipster sitting across the aisle moved closer to him and showed him a Sky Marshal badge.

Parker looked at him, quizzically. "What's this?"

"I'll be escorting you to people who will take you from here."

"People, what kind of people?"

"Navy people."

"You don't look like a lawman."

The hipster raised an eyebrow. "That's the whole point."

Parker had been hunted by the Russians, maybe the Chinese, and a host of other not so friendly nations. He and his Starchild cohort, Laura, had already been kidnapped once by the Russians, right under the U.S. government's nose in Pascagoula, Mississippi. And before that, a rogue NSA agent had tried to kill them. Still, being escorted by an Air Marshal seemed a bit overkill. But he was in no shape to argue that point, not with all the dull and fatigued faces staring at him, silently urging him to move down the aisle.

From the baggage claim area of LAX, two humorless men in civilian attire and closely cropped hair waved off the Air Marshall and attached themselves to Parker. They didn't talk except to say, "Follow us. We have another plane waiting for you."

"Where am I going?" Parker asked.

They didn't answer.

Great. More flying.

After a forty-five-minute run in a futuristic-looking twin-jet Embraer, they passed close over the small desert town of Indian Springs and approached Creech Air Force Base from the east, landing on the nine-thousand-foot-long east-west runway.

Creech was best known as a base for the Reaper remotely controlled aircraft. For that reason, and the fact that it was only about forty miles south of Area 51 where the Alien Triangle had last been parked, and having a very low density of people living nearby, made it an ideal location for covert work on the recovered triangular alien ship.

The fact that Creech was in open desert ringed by distant mountains meant base security had no problem detecting the presence of unwelcome visitors. A small hill on the base just north of the runways made an ideal observation platform and housed an impressive array of sensors. Even a stray mouse could not enter the base perimeter without being detected, and if need be, exterminated.

Parker knew none of this when he landed and was ushered off the aircraft, then down the ramp fifty yards or so into another waiting aircraft, a high wing Cessna 182. Compared to the plane he had just arrived in, the Cessna was guaranteed to arouse no curiosity at all in airplane watchers.

As much as he wanted to sit in the copilot's seat, he was directed into the back two seats.

"Where are we headed now?"

"You'll find out soon enough. It's a short trip."

Indeed, it was. Fifteen minutes later, they landed, passing a sign as they touched down that read, *Yucca Airstrip*.

If possible, the area around Yucca Airstrip looked even more desolate than Indian Springs.

When the plane taxied to a stop, the pilot kept the engine running but warned Parker not to walk forward of the strut supporting the wings. Parker had no desire to get his face chopped off by the plane's spinning propeller.

What the hell is this place? Parker thought. *I see nothing of interest here.*

As two men in Air Force khaki uniforms approached, Parker realized this still was not the end of the road. The two men opened the luggage compartment and pulled out Parker's belongings and carried them to a waiting Humvee. Through the noise of the plane's engine, they beckoned Parker to follow them and to take a seat in the middle bench of the sand-battered car.

By the time he had fastened his seatbelt, the Cessna had taken off again, headed back in the direction whence it had come. Curiously, everyone seemed to be in a hurry, considering this appeared to be a place where time itself was as fossilized as the dinosaur bones in the surrounding hills.

After leaving the airfield access road, the driver turned left and headed up a road leading towards a low range of hills.

"I'm guessing you won't tell me where we're headed."

Parker silently mouthed the words as the man next to the driver looked back at him and said, "You'll find out soon enough."

After a ride up to the base of the closest range of hills, they pulled up to what appeared to be a hefty garage door. The door raised as they came to a stop, and a man in some sort of military uniform waved them into what appeared to be a small garage with a grated floor. They stopped, and the uniformed man asked the driver, "So this is him?"

A mechanical device of some sort moved back and forth below the grated floor. It may have been scanning the underneath side of the vehicle to make sure that nothing looked suspicious.

When Parker looked up from the scanning apparatus, the uniformed man held out a retinal scanner. Parker placed his face close to the handheld device, and after a second or two, a green light lit up the screen, accompanied by a cheerful beep.

"Yep, this is him."

The man waved to another man in uniform, and the back wall of the "garage" began to rise with a hydraulic whine.

"Nice to meet you, Dr. Parker," the guard said. "I hope you enjoy your stay."

Parker nodded his head at the guard, and just had time to say "Thanks," before their vehicle moved forward into a steel-lined tunnel that quickly became a rock-lined tunnel. It was long and sloped downward as they drove past intermittent rows of what seemed to be sensors in the ceiling, with an occasional armed guard.

"What is this place, Fort Knox?"

"You'll find out soon enough."

At least they were consistent.

He estimated they had only traveled about a mile before the vehicle came to a stop once again, in front of yet another door. Once again, a uniformed man stepped up to the open window and scanned Parker's eyes. After the beep, the soldier simply said to the driver, "Proceed."

The door opened onto a tunnel which turned abruptly to the right. Rounding the turn, they passed through another array of sensors, then entered a cavernous room. There in the middle of the floor, bathed in megawatts of light, was the Triangle craft he had somehow piloted into the depths of the DeSoto Canyon.

But somehow, it looked different. It seemed to have a sheen he'd never noticed before.

A man in civilian clothes approached, and as he opened the truck door, Parker recognized him as his one-time nemesis, and now a friend with one eye askew, Hans Richter. Richter had always claimed to be from the NSA, but Parker had never been able to confirm that. Nevertheless, he was the only person who would be likely to explain where he was and why.

"Howdy, Jason. How do you think she looks?"

"Different."

Parker shook Richter's hand as the spook smiled back at him, seemingly much enjoying the little surprise they had waiting for their civilian Navy scientist.

"I'm surprised you noticed, but yes, we have made some changes, mostly sealing the craft so it should now hold pressure."

"And inside?"

"Nope, it's still as empty as ever."

"How did you seal it?"

"Monofilm on the inside. We've done nothing to the outside. We were afraid to touch it, other than to lightly clean it."

"Hans, where in hell are we?"

"Where do you think you are?"

"Somewhere in Nevada, I'd guess."

Richter laughed. "Somewhere, yes. Remember when we said we had to move the ship to a more secure area, more secure than Area 51?"

"Yes."

"Well, this is it. But we're only twenty-three miles away from the Area 51 runway."

"This certainly seems secure. I thought we might be in Cheyenne Mountain, but the geography isn't right."

"That's a good thought. Security is about the same as Cheyenne Mountain."

"Why am I here?"

"You haven't figured it out yet? We need you to fly it again."

"Well, it's about time. Who's my copilot? Laura Smith?"

Before answering, Richter looked at him and smiled.

"You don't need a crutch, Jason. We think you can do it all by your lonesome."

As much as Parker looked forward to the chance of flying the hottest aircraft in the world, he had severe misgivings about making a solo attempt. After a year of continual probing and prodding of the spaceship, government scientists still had no idea how it flew. No one could fathom what the propulsion system was.

Ironically, Laura Smith had become far too important of an asset for the intelligence community to risk her life on an experimental flight, or so Richter explained.

"So, I'm expendable?" Parker asked Richter.

"That's not it, Jason. You're a highly competent pilot, but they aren't. So why risk them when they provide no added value?"

"But you guys said you think Laura is like me on steroids."

"That was true, at one time. But we think you can enhance your skills with a little practice."

"Sweet Christ, that's what we did in Russia. I don't like the sound of this."

"We think you can do it. Follow me, and we'll brief you on what we've learned in the past year."

"Okay, I can practice, but let me tell you this, I'm not leaving the ground again before I talk to some folks about propulsion systems."

"As you wish. We can make that happen."

Richter led Parker to a door guarded by a Marine.

"Good grief," Parker exclaimed. "This room's more secure than the rest of this fortress?"

"You'll see why shortly."

"But he doesn't have a gun."

"Doesn't need one. He's a lethal force with just his hands. Besides, we don't want any stray rounds ricocheting around here. Wouldn't want to hit our craft."

"You still calling it the USS Canyoneer?"
"We're actually calling it TFAS for short."
"TFAS?" Parker repeated. "Meaning what?"
"The Fucking Alien Ship," Richter said, smiling.

Parker was not sure what he was expecting to see once they entered the guarded room, but there was absolutely nothing of interest. There were tables, chairs, and the ubiquitous screen and projector.

"Let me guess, death by PowerPoint?"

"We only use holograms here."

At that moment, a door in the back of the room opened and a shiny-faced man of thirty-something years strode across the room and shook Parker's hand. A little too aggressively actually.

"Dr. Parker, so good to meet you. I've heard so much about you."

"And you are…?"

"Weiss. Jacob Weiss. I'm the senior electrical engineer."

Richter leaned in close to Parker, "Don't be fooled by his boyish appearance. He's a mega-genius."

"I heard that Hans," Weiss said.

Turning to Parker, Richter said, ""But it's true. All our scientists and engineers are geniuses here, but Jacob is the best."

Ignoring Richter's flattery, Jacob motioned Parker to have a seat as he walked over to the nearby hologram projector.

"We've had great luck getting information out of that Antarctic craft. Let me show you what I mean. For this briefing, I'm going to concentrate on the metal samples we took from what we think is the pilot and crew area."

"You mean where we're scanning the squished green stuff?"

"Yes. Now here's a microscopic view of this material, and you can see it's a metallic nanofoam. Does it remind you of anything?"

"Actually, it looks a lot like gray matter in the brain."

"Exactly our thoughts. So, we started looking at this nanofoam as a model of the human brain. Now, the human brain has 100 billion neurons and a quadrillion synapses. Based on what we believe is the full extent of this foam over the crew cabin, we're estimating several quadrillion metallic neurons. And I can't even think of how many synapses we're talking about."

"Metallic neurons. I've never heard that before. But for what purpose?"

"Best guess is it's an antenna, picking up pilot brain waves, and a CPU which interprets the pilot's intentions, and converting those into control and guidance information."

Parker's eyes got really wide.

"I see you're skeptical, but you know we can control a car with our mind. Sure, it takes a skull cap now to pick up the brainwaves and send them to a steering control computer, but given ten thousand or a million years of science and engineering advancement we'll have sensitive enough sensors that physical contact will not be necessary."

"Okay, I'll say it," Parker said. "That's quite a reach."

"We think not, thanks to you. Remember that up North a little while ago, you wanted the craft to move, and it sensed that and controlled the lights which somehow modulated whatever propulsive forces were acting on it. The result? You wanted to move one way or the other, and it responded. That's a fact, not a stretch of the imagination."

Parker was quiet, mulling over what the so-called genius had just said. The guy did have a point.

"Okay, I'll give you that. But what about the propulsion system? Do you have any speculation about that?"

Weiss shrugged and looked over to Richter. Richter knew just how frustrating that search had been.

"We're not there yet. You said it might somehow be tied into dark energy, but we still don't know what that is. And you did say a Frog told you that their return to their home star only seemed to be faster than light speed because of their use of the space-time warping effect of dark matter."

"That is true, but I don't understand it."

"We don't either. But taking them at their word, they're using a propulsion system we don't understand, but which works."

"I'll tell you what I told Hans. I'm not flying this thing again until I talk to some folks first. And one of them happens to be nearby."

Chapter 8. The Odor of Blue

There is never an end to a thing once it is started, according to astrophysicist Peter Green. One can call it an end, but that doesn't make it so.

A person can be born, grow old, and die, but his or her energy goes on, somehow. It may not be recognizable, but physics says it must be that way.

Even a universe is born, grows for a seeming eternity, yet eventually, it too must die. Some say in its end, there is a new beginning.

Dr. Peter Green knew those facts better than most. As an astrophysicist working with colossal machines of physics research at CERN, Switzerland, machines that have the power to peer into the beginning of the universe, he'd often thought about not just the beginning, but the ending, the ending that precedes what comes next.

His specialty was dark matter, and something perhaps related, dark energy. Neither can be seen, but physics says they must exist for the universe to be what it is.

Either that, or physics is wrong, and neither Green nor his scientist colleagues had ever found physics to be in error.

But he did wonder, if a universe dies does it leave behind a ghost, unseen but somehow there, with a mass that exists at grand scales, but nonexistent at human scales?

And if so, must not the nature of our universe, the shape of our galaxies, depend on an ever-growing graveyard of dead stars, galaxies—and people?

Where does it end? Well, it doesn't, not really.

At least that's how Dr. Peter Green saw it.

In spite of the attention Peter garnered from his devoted parents, he was a bit—odd. As a child, he was clearly intelligent, but he saw things differently from most kids. For instance, he had always known his last name smelled like a baby's scalp with a pinch of gardenias. As for red, it was his favorite color, but not his favorite smell, somewhat like fractured granite with a hint of garlic, from the arsenic he supposed.

As a synesthete whose brain moved like fluid throughout all of his senses, his world was wildly stimulating, but at the same time lonely. As a young child curious about the differences between boys and girls and the blue and pink colors so often associated with them, he once asked his parents why boys smelled like old shoes and girls smelled like the earth before a rain.

That was the first time his parents were at a loss for words, but not the last. As he later realized, those smells didn't actually belong to boys and girls, per se, but to the colors he had been taught to associate with them, blue and pink.

In preschool, teachers excused his irrational odor association with colors as caused by his immature language skills. For instance, he frequently confused the colors yellow and blue. And why not? They smelled almost identical to the dank odor of slightly moldy leather. Yellow was just a tad mustier.

His parents and teachers assumed that by the time he reached first grade, he would know all of his primary colors, just like the other children. But during first grade, he came to understand that he was not like the other children. They did not think blue smelled like old shoes and thought he was rather peculiar for thinking it did.

Several years after the Great Leaving, when the world's deep ocean frog-like aliens left Earth, and after two alien ships had been salvaged and flown, the now fully-grown Peter Green was concentrating on finding secure hand and footholds as he scaled a cliff in the Red Rocks Canyon on the western outskirts of Las Vegas. His face was pressed close to the red sandstone that smelled like a hot iron scorching cotton shirts.

But then the scent changed. The color didn't change, but something was new. It smelled pungent, and as he inched higher towards a ledge, his intended rest stop, the odor became increasingly unpleasant. His nostrils stung, and his mind recalled the ammonia solution his mother used when cleaning windows.

Desperately needing to rest his now aching arms, he dug his fingers into the rock face even harder and willed his legs and arm muscles to pull his sinewy body up onto that ledge.

As he was tensing to launch his body onto the relatively flat surface, he spied the tawny coat of a cougar at the same instant that the disturbed animal's paw found Peter's head. With his view twisted downward from the impact, Peter saw only one thing: He was falling.

Peter Green did not know how long he had been unconscious, but he knew he was tightly wedged by his hips into an ever-tightening, ever-narrowing crevice approximately twenty feet below the top of the crack into which he'd been knocked by the cougar. As he attempted to push against the side of the crevice with the legs he could no longer see, he realized that his legs were numb from the constant pressure, and each wiggle caused him to slip a little deeper into the crevice.

From the look of the narrowing fissure, he realized he must be no more than ten feet or so above the bottom of the crevice, but he could hear movement, and snake sounds below him; rattling sounds. Rattlesnakes apparently were able to access the thin crack from the desert floor, and seek shelter from the unrelenting heat. If Dr. Green had fallen to the bottom, snake venom likely would have finished him off before he could be recovered.

But as it was, his chances for recovery were not looking good. As he took stock of his situation, he was at least thankful that his arms were free. But with his hips solidly wedged in, his effort to claw his way higher were foiled as his gloved hands slipped off the fragile sandstone which held him.

His brilliant mind, able to compute the rate of expansion of galaxies, had quickly calculated that on his own devices, his condition was intractable.

But still, large problems get solved one little step at a time, so he continued clawing at the wall, trying to dig small impressions into which he could insert his strong, sinewy fingers, anything to give him leverage for a push upwards.

After an hour, struggling through a headache and possible concussion caused by the panther's impact and the ricochet impacts as his helmeted head contacted the crevice walls during his fall, he had managed to rise maybe a centimeter. That was just enough to release a little pressure on his left hip, but not enough to free him or to give him hope.

He must have passed out again because it was now noticeably darker in the bottom of the crevice, and the air was beginning to cool around him as the desert prepared itself for the night. Then small grains of sand started raining down upon him, disturbed by something above. His instinctive concern was that the cougar had returned.

He looked up, cupping his hands over his eyes to protect them from the falling sand. And there stood a man, bent over at the waist peering down at Peter Green.

"Well, I'll be damned. Are you prospecting down there?"

After a dazed second, Green asked, "Am I imagining you?"

"Nope, I'm real."

Green's next question was, "Do you have a rope with you?"

"I do. Let's see if I can help you out."

"I'm wedged in by my hips, but if you can make a loop, I should be able to slip it under my arms. I'm afraid you may have to do a lot of pulling."

"Not to worry, we'll have you out of there before you know it."

The man quickly threw an expert bowline to make a loop and then dropped the loop down on Green. Green slipped the loop over his shoulders and secured it with the carabiner on his climbing harness, taking some of the tension off his armpits.

"Are you ready to get out of there?"

"Hell yeah. Let's do this."

The man began pulling at the same time that Green began trying to pull with his hands and wiggle his lower extremity. But there was no real response.

"Damn, you're really stuck, dude."

"My hips feel a little looser. Let's try it again."

"We don't have much choice, do we? Let me put my back into it this time."

Both men grimaced and grunted with the exertion, and after a few seconds, Green's hips broke free, and he lurched up high enough that he could get his feet up against the crevice walls. Now freed, the sides of his feet began pushing against the wall, gaining more and more traction with each step.

A few seconds later, Green pulled himself onto the top of the crevice, lay on his belly, taking deep breaths of air while the stranger lay down on his own back, panting.

A few moments later, the stranger said, "Good thing you had a helmet. It took a hell of a beating."

"It did?"

"Yeah, those look like big claw marks. What did you get into?"

Green began unbuckling his helmet, removed it, and looked at it.

"A mountain lion. Felt like it tried to rip my head off."

"If those claws had dug into your skull, he might have succeeded."

"I'd say I got my money's worth out of that helmet."

Then looking at his rescuer, he asked, "By the way, who are you? And how'd you find me?"

The rescuer smiled at him. "You don't remember me? I'm Jason Parker. Your family and mine used to hang out together in Virginia when you were a kid. I haven't seen you since you grew up, but your Dad's been keeping me abreast of your career."

"Well, not to look a gift horse in the mouth, Dude, but why are you all the way out here? Were you looking for me?"

"I was. Your Dad said if I needed to see you right away, my best chance would be to find you here."

Green stared at Parker for a moment, then whisked his hand across his face to wipe off some of the rock dust.

"I never knew you were a rock climber," Green said.

"In my college days," Parker explained. "If you know the Atlanta area, I trained on weekends until I could handle Tallulah Gorge pretty well."

"I don't know the area," Green said. "I cut my teeth in Virginia and Pennsylvania. But as you see, this area is no challenge for solo free climbing. No rope required. In fact, I'm surprised you have a rope."

"I used to be a Boy Scout. I just had a feeling."

"Good. I like those kinds of feelings," Green said, grimacing while stretching his limbs.

Parker continued. "I tried calling you, but your Dad explained how you cut off the world when you come out here."

"That's true, I do, but I may have to rethink my ways after this. I'm damn lucky you found me."

"Let's get off this rock before it gets dark," Parker said. "There's still a mountain lion out there somewhere."

There's something primal about sitting around a campfire. Perhaps a little pride is involved, the successful harnessing of a potentially deadly force, combustion, and turning it into warmth and light. But it's more than that, really. The flames and sparks draw one's thoughts inward. It's a time and a place for introspection.

Between the flames and the chilly, starry night sky, Parker and Peter had been quiet for several minutes, communing with their private thoughts. Parker stirred the fire with a long branch, sending sparks bounding upward, sparkling like stars then dying out as they rose higher within the column of heated air. As the sparks rose to be absorbed by the field of stars above, Parker wondered what forms of life those stars were supporting. Gazing upward, it was impossible not to believe that someone was looking back.

"Peter," he asked after a while, "how did you come to astronomy and cosmology as a career?"

Peter Green kept watching the fire with his knees pulled up and his arms resting on top of them. "Oh shit, man, that happened so long ago. But I guess, I can really trace it back to when I was a third-grader lying on my back in a grassy field up on the Skyline Drive in Virginia. My older brother and I were using my Dad's binoculars to explore the sky above us."

Green swiveled his head around, covering the entire starfield above them.

"There was an unobstructed view of the dark sky, just like there is now. It was the first time I can remember seeing the Andromeda galaxy. I found that amazing, to see another galaxy, one a lot like ours, and yet so far away."

"Can we see Andromeda tonight?" Parker asked.

"Actually, we can. Lay on your back and look straight up. Let your eyes adjust to the darkness, and in a minute, you should see it as a fuzzy light."

The desert pavement of pebbles, sand, and clay felt pleasantly cool on Parker's back, but the air was chilling rapidly.

"I see the Milky Way," Parker said, pointing above and drawing a line from high above him down to the western horizon.

"Andromeda is just west of the Milky Way. Actually, right now it's directly above us. Do you see it?"

"Not yet."

"Don't look directly at it. Shift your gaze just a hair."

"Oh, now I see a smudgy spot."

"In about 4 billion years the Milky Way will be colliding with Andromeda. It should be quite a show in the night sky."

"People don't stargaze much anymore," Parker said.

"Nope. Too busy watching TV. But that's why I come out here to the dark skies. It's a yearly pilgrimage."

Green rolled over to his stomach to face Parker, who was still staring straight up.

"It's not the same looking through a telescope or a computer monitor," Green said. "What you see here is the raw image, unprocessed, as close to our roots as we can get."

Parker didn't speak. He just listened.

"Did you know I'm a synesthete?" Green blurted out.

Parker raised his head to look at Green. "Did you say a synesthete?"

"Yes. I'm surprised Dad never told you about that. My teachers thought I was a strange kid."

Well, that was random.

Parker rolled over and sat up to face Green. "Were you?"

Green also pushed up into a sitting position, groaning.

"Are you alright?" Parker asked.

"Just sore, I don't think anything's broken. But to answer your question, hell yeah, Dude. I was a weird one. But look, I turned out okay."

Parker laughed. "If you say so, Peter."

After a few more minutes listening to the desert sounds, Parker realized he was shivering.

"I may not be as tough as you, Peter. I need to get back around the fire."

They both moved back to the fire, trying to soak up as much heat as they could, considering they were surrounded by cold desert air on a clear night.

After half a minute of silence interrupted by the howling of coyotes, Green turned his head to Parker.

"What brings you out here, Jason?"

Stretching his interlocked hands in front of him, Parker started slowly.

"Well, I have a problem. Have you heard about the Frogships?"

"Of course. Everyone has."

"Well, here's the thing. We have no understanding of what propels them."

"Rocket engines, maybe?" Green asked.

"Speaking generically, I'm going to say no. I've wondered if they could be antigravity machines," Parker said.

"The only problem I see with antigravity machines," Green suggested, "is they could work great if you have gravity, like from a planet, or a star, black hole, or a galaxy. But in interstellar space, you might be a long way from a gravity source."

"I guess the ship would just coast," Parker added.

"But still, have you seen the way our space program uses gravity to assist in accelerating our craft out of the solar system?"

Parker thought about that for a moment before answering.

"You mean like they go looping around various planets? Certainly isn't a straight line."

"Exactly. And I can't believe that a really advanced civilization, like your Frogs, for instance, wouldn't find a way to accelerate in a straight line, especially if they're trying to reach some fraction of light speed."

Parker felt satisfied with the way he was directing this conversation.

"So you're saying that would rule out antigravity devices?"

"For initial acceleration, antigravity might be great, but once you get out of the gravity field of Earth, then no more acceleration."

"What about dark matter?" Parker asked. That was what he was really getting to.

"Aha, that's my field. Well maybe, if we're talking science fiction. But the diffuse gravity of dark matter seems to hold galaxies together. I don't know how it could have enough gravity to affect something tiny, like a spaceship."

"Okay, but I'll hazard a guess we really don't know enough about it."

"That's true. Not yet, anyway. Maybe someday."

"Like maybe a million years from now, we can do it?" Parker asked.

Green laughed. "Okay, I see where you're going with this. Yeah, if we conduct scientific research for another million years, we might end up as smart as the Frogs, and know how to take advantage of dark matter. But right now, we don't even know what dark matter is."

Parker smiled, knowing that Peter indeed knew exactly what he was aiming for.

"But until then," Green warned, "I wouldn't step foot in a ship with an unknown propulsion system. You might end up trying to bore a hole right through the sun."

"But what if you have to?"

"If you had to?" Green rubbed his chin.

"Well, I could be glib and wish you luck, or philosophical and say birds don't understand aerodynamics but they fly just fine. Sometimes you just have to trust the creator of the design. If it works, it works. You can let the next generation figure out how it works."

"What about dark energy?"

"What about it?"

"Could it be used for propulsion?" Parker asked.

"That's an even harder question. Dark energy, if it exists at all, is based on quantum fluctuations around a ground state. We know of no way to generate unidirectional force from random fluctuations."

"This problem is beyond me," Parker said, "but according to the word on the street, you're one of the brightest people in the field. I was really hoping you had a grasp on it."

"I hate to disappoint you, Jason, but I'm clueless. But I'll think about it and let you know if I have any thoughts after I get back to the university."

"When do you get back?"

"Two weeks."

"Rats," said Parker. "That won't do me any good."

"Why not?"

"It just won't."

The rest of the night was spent with the two men in their respective sleeping bags arrayed around the dying embers. Sleep did not come easily for Parker, but when it finally did, he dreamed of the cold of interstellar space.

Apparently, he needed to invest in a warmer sleeping bag.

Parker awakened to the smell of coffee coming from Green's camp stove. There was light in the sky, but the sun had not yet broken over the jagged horizon to the East.

"Did the coyotes keep you awake?" Green asked as he was pouring a packet of oatmeal into a cup of hot water.

"Something did," Parker said as he unzipped the sleeping bag, stood up and starting stuffing it into a neat roll.

"You heading out already?"

"I am. I'm on a tight schedule today."

"I hate that for you. It's a gorgeous morning. Where are you headed?"

"I've got some business up north."

"Well, I can't say it enough, thanks for saving my ass."

"And thanks for giving me some inspiration," Parker said as he walked over to Green and shook his hand. "Tell your Dad you did good."

"Shoot, I didn't give you much," Green said.

"To the contrary. I'm going to think like a bird and trust the designer."

"Alright, good luck with that."

As Parker was driving away, he called Hans Richter.

"Hans, I'm coming back. I should be there in a couple of hours."

"Learn anything useful?"

"Not really. But it was good to see the kid. He's all grown up. And I did save his life, sort of."

"What?"

"I'll tell you about that later," Parker said.

"Well hurry back. An old friend is here to see you."

"Who might that be?" Parker asked.

"Dr. Harry Kincaide."

"You kidding me? Last time I saw him, he wanted to flog me."

"Why?" Richter asked, sounding surprised.

"Because I proved to him that his most precious alien artifact was nothing more than a toy, a training aid for Frog kids. I thought you might remember that."

"I must have missed that part."

Chapter 9. A Ship is Alive

Sixty-one miles off the East coast of Taiwan, due east of Xiulin and its coal-fired power plant, bobbed a brightly colored fishing boat with a red-trimmed prow arcing from the main deck in a smooth curve up to a height even with the top of the boat's bridge. Elsewhere on the superstructure were outlines of yellow and blue surrounding red shuttered windows on the lower deck. For a working boat, it appeared almost gaudy, but in the eye of the skipper and crew, non-nautical colors were a welcome diversion from the endless gray of the Philippine and East China seas.

The waters beneath the *Shy Chan No. 5* were ten thousand feet deep. The bottom was a transitional zone between the 7000-foot-deep Okinawa Trough just to the north and the 21,000-foot Ryukyu Trench to the south.

The easy to reach shallow water had been fished out, and the crew of the *Shy Chan,* like the whole Taiwanese fishing fleet, had been forced to move further from shore, into more treacherous waters in the hopes of grabbing their share of the growing market for deep sea fish such as sea bass and orange roughy. Ecologically, the shift to deep water fish was a fast-growing disaster for the offshore fisheries since deepwater fish had extremely slow reproduction and growth rates. The skipper and crew of the *Shy Chan* knew that deep-sea fish were becoming increasingly difficult to find.

For that reason, the boat's owner had, after many queries, agreed to take on board a secret weapon, a Buddhist monk from Thailand. For sure, this would be the only Taiwanese fishing vessel with such a spiritual being on board.

Whether the saffron-robed monk would help them find fish was yet to be determined, but at least Phra Theratapati showed restraint in his eating and upkeep so he would not be putting a significant dent in the boat's operating budget.

The sun had been up only an hour as the *Shy Chan* ran slowly north, paralleling the coast of Taiwan, and remaining over deep water. The trawling nets had not yet been deployed overboard since the skipper was waiting on a word from the Monk who was meditating. It was a gamble, betting on a meditating monk to find large schools of fish, but Phra Theratapati had been very convincing, and after all, the Skipper had nothing to lose except a little time. If the monk's claims were valid, the ship could earn a fortune on this next transit.

The monk's visage on the right side of the bow seemed out of place, and indeed it was. Men with plucked eyebrows, shorn heads, and right shoulders bared belonged in Monasteries throughout Southeast Asia. It was not unusual to see them by themselves waiting on flights from Taipei to Bangkok, and vice versa. But on a commercial fishing boat? Never.

But here he was, sitting in a half-lotus position for stability against the gentle swells, seeking out the mental clues that he was convinced would indicate a large school of much-prized fish. By a pre-arranged signal, the Monk would raise his hand then drop it suddenly as an indication that the ship was approaching the school that only he could see in his meditative mind. With that signal, the trawl would be dropped behind the vessel and guided down to whatever depth was indicated on the fish finder sonar.

The helmsman maintained the correct course previously arranged with the monk, and all waited for the anticipated signal from the robed figure. Then sure enough, just as the forward-looking sonar began picking up a scattered signal, the Monk gave his sign, and the Captain radioed for the trawl to be released. Both the current and the ship's slow forward motion caused the trawl to back up on the fish school, giving the net time to dive down to the depth of the school.

Curiously, as the Captain had his eyes glued to the fish finder, the jagged reflections from the school seemed to be rising towards the surface, complicating the Captain's planned intersection of the school and the net.

In Chinese, the Captain shouted, "The school's rising quickly. We may not catch it."

Then he gave a precise order, "Reel in the net closer to the boat!"

As the sonar reflections from the approaching school continued to rise, the size of the school continued to expand.

"There must be millions of fish. We may need a bigger boat," he said, laughing.

By this time the Monk had left his position at the bow and walked back to the stern where he was hoping to see the school of fish snared in the trawl net.

All eyes were now on the surface of the water behind them, and excitement grew as the water began to mound up over one of the largest schools any of the crew had ever seen. Then as it broke the surface, the brilliant flashes expected for a large school of silver-sided fish appeared but then consolidated into something continuous, and solid appearing.

It was not fish at all, but a giant metallic structure, far larger than any possible school of fish, and it kept rising, slowly now, out of the water under its own power and draped in the *Shy Chan's* trawl net. Within seconds the craft began pulling upwards on the net so that the stern of the ship was lifted, pulling the rudder and twin screws out of the water, so that the boat bobbed perilously on its bow.

Phra Theratapati was in shock. This was a far cry from what his visualization during meditation had him expecting. Then the saucer-shaped craft splashed back into the water. It floated for a second behind the trawler, then began sinking, still securely netted in the ship's trawl. The Captain was quick to realize the large craft would pull the boat under unless the crew was able to separate the net, not an easy task in any situation, but especially in an emergency. Ordering in Chinese again, the Skipper yelled, "Cut away the net."

The crew hands on the stern realized as quickly as did the Skipper the peril they were in and took to the twin securing lines with broad axes. As they chopped the thick lines, designed to prevent accidental severing, the stern of the ship was pulled further downward, closer to the waterline. If the lines couldn't be severed in time, the *Shy Chan* with its entire crew would be scuttled by the stern to wherever the metallic craft was headed, approximately ten thousand feet below.

The final cut was made as water began pouring over the transom. The severed line snapped like a bullwhip then disappeared over the side. The ship recoiled with so much force that a deckhand was launched overboard, flying thirty feet in the air and splashing down a few yards from the boat.

The only person with the wherewithal to notice the deckhand's disappearance was the monk. Due to his awareness, the crewman was safely recovered with nothing more than a compressed vertebra. Only the fact that Phra Theratapati had saved one of their own kept the sullen crew from throwing him into the sea.

The startling words, "A ship is alive," echoed quietly through the darkest depths of the Defense Intelligence Agency within minutes after being uttered on a secure phone by the leader of the Mexican Trolls. The news from Argxtre was spread by whispers from the DIA to the Pentagon Priesthood.

The person receiving the call was Kelly Brightman. Brightman had been a former electrical engineer and analyst for the NSA, and his experience with the defense department working on diving programs for the Navy Diving Center, NDC, put him near the top of the list of qualified applicants for the new position, DIA Director of Alien Affairs. But what clinched it for him was that he was only one of two people who had first encountered Argxtre in the bowels of a cave in Mexico's Quintana Roo province, a tourist area riddled with cenotes and mostly flooded caves. The other person was Jason Parker.

Unlike Brightman who quickly rose to an unusually secretive, and usually ignored side branch of the DIA, Jason Parker had remained somewhat aloof of any particular intelligence or scientific agency stovepipe. DARPA, the Defense Advanced Research Agency, wasn't sure what to do with him once the apparent reality of extraterrestrial aliens, or at least of their combination underwater and interstellar spacecraft had been revealed. The aliens were gone, and two abandoned craft had been recovered. Of course, everyone was hoping the U.S. might find another, but that job of searching and recovery was assigned to the DIA. Actual recovery efforts, if any, would be planned and conducted by the combination of the DIA and CIA, with close oversight by the Office of the Director of National Intelligence, ODNI.

Parker's friend, Laura Smith, was another person snatched up for a new Alien Affairs job at the ODNI. She had a little more prominent exposure than Brightman, but only because the ODNI had oversight of the lower intelligence agencies like the CIA, DIA, and NSA. But in a way, Brightman's role was seen of more immediate importance than either Parker's or Smith's. He was connected by secure phone to the only Mexican Troll known to fly a Frogship, as Parker called them. And since the Trolls were now U.S. citizens, he had the means to monitor every detail of the Troll citizens' lives. Brightman's former ties to the NSA guaranteed that he had access.

The prevailing wisdom was that should the U.S. Government recover another alien craft, the two people who would initially be kept far from the fray were Drs. Smith and Parker. Some said they were too valuable to risk with too much knowledge too soon. Nobody wanted them getting kidnapped again, by any competing government, let alone the Russians.

Others would say that the two friends, Parker and Smith, were too unpredictable. That might apply to Parker since he was a free agent. The Navy paid him, but he answered to any government entity which needed him for a mission.

Some said behind closed doors, and at some professional risk that Laura Smith was a cute but annoying pain in the ass. Young women like her who rose to a vaunted position because of a rare event, such as the discovery of the Frogs and their ships, were not well-liked by those who rose up the hard way, clawing their way to the middle altitudes.

But as Parker always told Smith, the cream rises to the top. "Don't worry about those left behind. You only live once, Laura," he would say when she confided in him, which of late was not often.

Then again, Laura didn't believe you only live once. To her, reincarnation was a real thing, though she kept that secret bottled up best she could. She knew the ODNI didn't want any fruitcakes on their payroll.

Parker had grown fond of Laura, especially since they had on several occasions shared life-threatening experiences, and against all the odds had survived. Strangely, Laura felt even a stronger connection to Parker, based on her belief in former lives. But that was also something she had learned to keep bottled up.

As for Kelly Brightman, he was as far from strange as you could get. Standing tall and straight behind a Department of Defense podium, taking questions from the press, he looked like a large Nordic god with military-short blond hair and confident speech. He looked every part the Washington professional.

Parker was proud of Brightman, who he had mentored. Brightman had kept his cool when confronted with an alien hominid in the depths of a cave with no assured safe exit, and now he had done well in D.C. His ascension to such a trusted and valuable position was a relatively rare feat.

"Is it the Russian ship?" Brightman asked Argxtre.

"No," the Troll said. "It's another ship."

"Where is it?"

"Near Taiwan."

"Coordinates?"

"24°15'21.07" N, 122°00'59.04 E. But it was a brief exposure."

"What do you mean?"

"It wasn't alive long. I'm guessing it came on and then shut down again."

"That's bizarre."

"That's all I know."

"Okay, thanks, Truman. We'll check it out."

"That's not my name."

"Yeah, I know. Thanks for the head's up."

"The what?"

"The warning."

It was true that Argxtre's name was impossible to pronounce, so Parker had come up at the spur of the moment with the alias, Truman Baltazar. Argxtre well understood the Americans' difficulty with his random name, but he never missed the chance to remind his American friends of their linguistic inadequacies.

Joshua Nilsson was eating his lunch in a common eating area, wishing he was anywhere except CIA Headquarters on such a gorgeous day. Even though his cortical blindness prevented him from seeing how beautiful it was, he could smell the flowers which optimistically expose their pollen on just such spring days. He could smell the beauty.

Nilsson was relatively short for an American male, five foot seven, with black hair and bushy eyebrows. Although he had once been slender and active before his tumble down a flight of narrow stone stairs in Stockholm, his blindness had slowed him down considerably. Combined with his taste for shredded pork and imported beer, which he liked a little too much, he had recently acquired a growing beer belly.

There was nothing distinguishing about him except his habit of randomly looking off into some direction other than towards the person he was speaking to. Of course, he was not actually looking but listening to random sounds that unconsciously grabbed his attention. He had not yet learned that distracting habit was socially discomforting to those speaking to him, mainly because no one had mentioned it to him.

Nilsson had planned to stay in Sweden, the home of his ancestors, but once the CIA learned of his Remote Viewing capabilities, they made him an offer he could not refuse. Instead of being perceived as handicapped, he was returned to Washington and Langley Virginia as one of the CIA's most important intelligence assets. As far as remote viewers were concerned, his gift was in a class all by itself.

Nilsson stopped chewing his ham sandwich when he heard footsteps approaching.

"I have something for you, Joshua."

"Oh, it's you, Fowler. You do see I'm eating, right?"

"I'll buy your lunch tomorrow. This can't wait."

"Of course not. It never can. But, well, lunch does sound good. Barbeque?"

"Sure, whatever you want."

Bill Fowler walked ahead of Nilsson on the concrete path leading to Nilsson's viewing room. Nilsson refused to be guided by touch and was quite adept at following the sound of Fowler's footsteps on the concrete path.

Nilsson could do his work anywhere he liked, but the Agency was willing to oblige Nilsson with anything he wanted. And what Nilsson wanted to know was just how far they would go to please him.

For his efforts, he was provided the most relaxing room at Langley. In fact, it was probably the only relaxing room at Langley. As he walked into his space, soft ambient music began playing and by a spoken word, he could change the mood of the music from forest sounds, to soft music, to basically anything he wanted.

Before he settled on some throw pillows, he announced "Eastern mystic music." And just such music began playing.

Speaking aloud for the recording equipment, he said, "I want to set the mood since this is in the Far East if I know my longitudes well."

The Agency's rule was that no one would respond. Nilsson was to be left entirely on his own.

That requirement irritated the hell out of Fowler, a rather conceited agent who despised analysts and anyone else who he felt was lacking. In Fowler's mind, Nilsson was little more than a pampered and highly overrated oddity who should not be gracing the halls of his Langley.

Although Nilsson did not need coordinates to track a human, whatever this was, was probably not human. The first time he viewed a new thing, he did need coordinates.

Nilsson held the Braille-encoded piece of paper in his right hand, subconsciously rubbing the fingers of his left hand over the bumps.

"Well, I'm not surprised to find I'm over some water. And since nothing is within sight, I guess I'll have to get wet."

Nilsson was speaking figuratively. He could not get wet of course, but that was his description for the process of willing his conscious mind, and fully sighted mind, down into the water.

"I don't suppose you're going to tell me how deep I need to go."

No one spoke.

"Of course not, that would be too easy," he said sarcastically.

No one knew. They frankly didn't know if anything was at that location, or if it was, at what depth it would be found.

"Shit, this water is really deep. You sure there's anything here?"

By the protocol, nothing was returned but silence.

"Freaky. That is one weird-ass looking fish." Nilsson turned his head to the right slightly, as if he was actually looking at something.

"Okay, this is now getting boring as hell."

A minute later, "Ignore my last. I'm looking at a pile of garbage, no, cloth. Damn, it's a mound of fishing nets, and they're covering up something massive, and metallic. It's, it's"—His voice trailed off—"Oh shit, it's a spaceship. It looks like a flying saucer covered in fishnet. But it's not a triangle. It's disc-shaped, like the one in Antarctica."

Those listening were now excitedly but silently gesturing to each other.

"I wonder if this netting is an attempt at some sort of camouflage. If so, it's amateurish, if you ask me."

"Okay, I'm on the bottom, and nothing else seems to be around here. So I'm guessing this is what you're looking for. I'm coming off the target now."

Nilsson was exactly right. That was the good news the DIA was hoping for. Uncle Sam just might be able to snag another alien ship.

Chapter 10. The Plan

Within a matter of hours, a U.S. spy ship was diverted from the west coast of Taiwan to the eastern side by way of Taipei and the north end of the island. They were tasked with getting robotic eyes on the target to see how much of Nilsson's viewing was correct.

If it was, the U.S. had a problem. The assumed alien craft was presently way too close to Communist China. Already word was being received of a wild story about a fishing vessel, a Buddhist monk, and a flying saucer that tried to sink a fishing boat. Fortunately, the story was being told and retold in bars by drunken sailors, so the crew's veracity was seriously in doubt. But those bars were known hangouts of Chinese spies, so it was only a matter of time before Beijing would become interested.

And China certainly didn't need another reason to invade Taiwan.

President Harmon Whitney had only been in office for a few weeks when it was time for him to be briefed by the Advisor on Alien Affairs, Office of the Director of National Intelligence. He had heard rumors about Dr. Laura Smith, but this was his first meeting with her.

In spite of the Director of National Intelligence's effort to protect Laura by keeping her out of the know, POTUS insisted she personally brief him on the events in Taiwan. Her education came quickly.

Just a few intense hours after being read-in, Laura was dressed in a no-nonsense dark grey pants suit, accentuated with a minimum of jewelry. Everything about her appearance was conservative, a carefully crafted understatement. There was only one flamboyant person in the Oval Office, and it wasn't going to be her.

"Dr. Smith, I have five minutes on my schedule, so let's get to the point."

The President was sitting scarcely five feet away so he could see the card she was holding with the graphical action plan and timelines printed on it.

"Mr. President, these are the thing's we'll be doing to exploit this alien craft if that's really what it is."

"You seem to be our alien expert. What do you think it is?"

"An alien craft, perhaps like the one we're working on in Antarctica."

"Then let me hear the plan," Whitney said. He seemed impatient.

"First, we want to verify the stories. We'll locate and quarantine the fishing vessel's crew, including any reputed Monks involved if they can be found. Then we'll identify and impound the fishing vessel and examine it for damage to nets and superstructure. While that's happening, we'll get robotic eyes on the alien ship. If we get confirmation, we'll initiate plans to covertly remove the craft from the deep waters where it was found and transport it to the closest Japanese waters. Then we'll continue transport to the U.S. Navy base in Sasebo, Japan, 900 miles away."

"What's the risk?" POTUS asked.

"The first step would be a challenge, considering U.S. assets would be operating in a foreign country, but that's where the CIA's methods and operators really shine. They are already in place and working their human intelligence."

"Nice," Whitney said.

"The second task will involve a lie, but an excellent one, in our opinion. The DIA would put forth a compelling case that a Taiwanese flagged fishing vessel damaged U.S.-owned deep ocean intelligence-gathering equipment used to monitor potential threats to Taiwan coming from the East. After all, the potential enemy, China, in this case, is perfectly capable of flanking Taiwan and attacking simultaneously from the east and west. With that cover story, no Taiwanese court would refuse a request for the U.S. to impound and inspect a single fishing vessel."

"The lowest risk operation will involve NAVOCEANO, the Navy Oceanographic Office, which already has a deep diving glider operating in the area, controlled remotely by its operators in the John C. Stennis Space Center in Mississippi. It's a slow process. Gliders are not speedy, but they are cheap and available, and ideal for an initial fly-by. As for what they will survey, the unclassified story is they will be collecting typical oceanographic data, water temperature, salinity, currents, the type of routine data only an oceanographer like me could get excited about."

"Why do oceanographers get excited about that?" Whitney asked.

"That data is used in computer models of submarine operations, informing submarine Captains about how best to hide from adversaries, if the need arose."

"Well, let's hope we don't need to hide on my watch. What else can those gliders do?"

"They can see. They have miniature deep-sea cameras."

"So we should be able to get a first look with the gliders?"

"That's right, Mr. President. We really need to get confirmation of what Mr. Nilsson saw."

"I was briefed that he did it by remote viewing. Is that right?"

"Yes, Mr. President. It is."

"That's some bizarre stuff there, Dr. Smith. Can you do remote viewing?"

"Not at all, Sir, but I know someone who can."

"And who would that be?"

"Dr. Jason Parker."

"Oh yes, I heard about him too."

Whitney's head began oscillating back and forth.

Laura asked. "Is anything the matter, Mr. President?"

"I had no idea what was going on. None whatsoever."

"Not many people do, Mr. President."

"Can I ask you a personal question?"

"I suppose so, Sir. What is it?"

"When you and this Parker fellow were being held captive in Siberia, did they treat you with respect?"

Smith laughed. "Well, except for the kidnapping, the drugs, the cold stone jail cell, the cold shower with a creepy male guard watching the whole time, I guess it was tolerable. But I'm not giving them a positive review on Yelp."

Whitney smiled. "You're tough, Dr. Smith. We're lucky to have people like you in government service."

"Thank you, Sir. Now, can I ask you a question?"

"Sure."

"Normally this material would have been briefed by someone higher up, like maybe my boss, the Director of National Intelligence. I'm curious why I'm here."

POTUS nodded his head, smiling.

"I bet you are. The simple fact is, I've known Mr. Schlenker for decades, and in spite of his impressive credentials he's never stolen an alien spaceship from under the Russian's noses. I wanted to meet the person who did that."

Two days later, the Navy received their first visual indication from the gliders that something unusual was sitting on the bottom, enveloped in what in all likelihood was a tangle of fishing nets. That was all it took for Washington to put enough credence in Joshua Nilsson's remote viewing observation to order a NAVOCEANO 330-foot oceanographic survey vessel, the USNS Johnston, to take up station over the location marked by the glider. Once on station, the Johnston deployed its autonomous vehicles to survey the site, feeding information back to Washington where a combination NAVSEA and DIA team was planning a recovery operation.

What was astonishing to Laura was that for the second time in five years, the U.S. Navy was planning the recovery of what may have been an alien spaceship. Unfortunately, the depth at which this target lay was far too deep to use the assistance of Navy deep-sea divers. Everything would have to be done remotely.

Once the craft was recovered, the transport plan called for the first phase of relocation from the bottom site sixty-one miles east of Taiwan, to the closest and most western Japanese island, Yonaguni-Shima, then up to Okinawa, followed by the long water transit to Sasebo. But at least once it was in Japanese waters, the craft would not be threatened by China, unless they were willing to start an unwinnable war.

CHAPTER 11. EXECUTION

His name was not important. It was only a false persona since he was doing the Agency's bidding, and loving every second of it. He was Chinese-American, dressed, and groomed to look more Chinese than American, and was one of the first agents to fly into Taiwan from Los Angeles on this new mission.

He was very good at blending into the Chinese-Taiwanese population since there was nothing about his appearance that looked out of place among other Asian males in their thirties. Because of the need to blend in, he had been exempted from flying into Taiwan on an American carrier, the usual requirement for Federal workers. The Boeing 777 carrying him to a one-of-a-kind encounter belonged to Eva Air, a Taiwanese airline jammed with Asian passengers. Most Americans had never heard of it.

From his trained attention to the actions and speech of those closest around him, either friend or potential threat, he heard the voices of Vietnamese, Thais, Taiwanese, and Chinese. Apparently, the passenger manifest was multinational but almost entirely Asian. In fact, the only American he spied on board was an older, maybe late sixties, grossly obese American traveling alone to Thailand. The Agent guessed the man was traveling for sex tourism, but he could be wrong.

The agent's task was to beguile Taiwanese boat owners without revealing the slightest connection to the U.S. government. His fake persona on this mission was that of an American boat engine manufacturer looking for investments in the Asian markets. His calling, if you believed his false cover story, was in helping modernize the aging Taiwanese fishing fleet. And there where many thousands of working boats in need of modern marine engines. That meant there were thousands of Taiwanese boat owners who could be misled into revealing useful information in the hopes of receiving new engines at a well-discounted price.

Through wholly believable deception, he was assured of sooner or later finding a boat owner who had a recent run-in with an alien craft. All he needed to find the owner was time and an inexhaustible supply of bullshit.

As the 777 was making its western approach into Taipei Taoyuan International Airport, skirting at ever lower altitudes across northern Taiwan, the Agency man, sitting in his preferred window seat, saw a slender, silvery rod racing across the ground at a speed which seemed to exactly match that of the descending aircraft. The agent knew the plane would be locked into a speed of 250 knots considering their proximity to a large city, so the object had to be going at least 170 knots. Because of how well matched their speeds were, and how lockstep their heading was towards downtown Taipei, the agent realized he was watching the Japanese-styled bullet train that ran from Zuoying district of Kaohsiung City in the south, proceeding north along the western side of Taiwan towards the capital.

That sighting was ironic, he thought because he knew that on that very same bullet train, another operation was planned for a personnel intercept before their target had a chance to disappear into the mass of faces at the Taipei train station. That target was one of the crewmen of the "USO boat," as the agency had nick-named the Unidentified Submerged Object.

Out of habit, the CIA agent had the video display on the seat back just in front of him showing the flight map. It was part of his rational desire for situational awareness. As the big jet was being vectored to the west for an extended left-base approach to runway 05-R at the Taoyuan International Airport, he noticed that the islands and the mainland of China appeared alarmingly close on the video screen. In fact, the Strait of Taiwan was only about eighty-one miles wide at that point, and in a matter of minutes, his jet could be over Chinese soil.

Since any hijacking of a Taiwanese jet would prove problematic for an American CIA officer, he monitored the map display carefully for the first hint of a return to a northeasterly course.

When that turn began, he sighed out loud, causing the Vietnamese seatmate to his left to look at him with a puzzled look.

"Are you airsick?" the man asked in a concerned tone and with only slightly accented English.

"I'm better now."

The air at the lower altitude over the western side of Taiwan had been bumpy as usual, so the question was not an unreasonable one, but perhaps the American's answer had not been convincing. The Vietnamese man pointed to the window seat airsickness bag, just to make sure the quiet American could reach it in a hurry.

"Thank you, but I'm fine now."

The Vietnamese man scooted a little further to the left in his seat, just in case.

Zuoying District of Kaohsiung City was the home port of the Republic of China Navy, and also a likely port for damaged fishing vessels needing repair. The local bars served both Taiwanese sailors and fishing boat crews, and bragging sessions were frequent. But one fisherman's bragging was of particular interest to CIA agents visiting the bar for drinks after their shifts.

The American agents were especially interested when two suspected Chinese spies approached the fisherman just as he was leaving the bar late at night, and handed him tickets for the high-speed rail to Taipei.

After a call back to Langley, the American agents were ordered to monitor the crewman best they could. When and if he headed to the Zuoying terminus of the rail, the two agents were told to join him and discourage him from getting off at the Taipei Station. The means to that end would be a roll of hundred-dollar bills, and a ticket to Nangang, only eight minutes east of the main Taipei Station.

As the big jet's wheels were touching down on runway 05-R, the agents on the bullet train were making their move. The boat crewman's seatmate headed back to the toilet, and one of the agents moved up to take his seat, while the second stayed behind to distract the fellow returning from the bathroom.

"I have ten thousand American dollars for you if you take this ticket, bypass Taipei, and get off with me at Nangang."

The man's Taiwanese Hokkien dialect was spoken too quickly for the linguistics-trained operator to grasp everything, but the man seemed to say he was meeting someone, and they were paying to talk to him.

In the universal language, the agent pulled out the roll of U.S. Treasury notes. Apparently, the crewman wasn't being paid that well by whoever he was meeting because he unabashedly reached for the ticket in exchange for the roll.

By the time the two seatmates reached Nangang, the man was a U.S. asset.

High on the list of questions awaiting this man, once he was settled into the safe house arranged by the Agency, was the credibility of the stories he had been broadcasting while intoxicated, about a Buddhist monk raising a craft from the sea. Was it true?

The opinion among oddsmakers in the American staff was that it was the alcohol talking.

"He called himself Phra Theratapati, but he wasn't from Taiwan. He had been at a monastery near Bangkok before joining our crew."

"Who invited him?"

"The boat owner. The monk said he had some sort of power over schools of fish, and our owner was interested in giving him a try. The Monk wanted a cut of the profits, but wasn't taking as much as the rest of us."

"Seriously? Some special power?"

The interrogator immediately thought of another Holy Man, thousands of years ago who did, in fact, have that sort of power over fish. But if this monk actually believed he had that same power, then he might be afflicted with a messianic complex. That would sure muddy the intelligence waters.

"That's what he claimed. It seemed strange to many of us because Monks generally disavow any interest in money. But maybe he just wanted enough to get a flight back home, so I didn't think the arrangement was too surprising."

"Do you know where the monk is now?"

"No. None of us got paid by the Captain, and I suspect he's in hiding."

"Where do poor monks hide?"

"Only one place. Monasteries. There are lots of them in Taiwan. Maybe he's hoping someone with generous alms will give him a ticket back to Bangkok."

"Why would someone believe that a Buddhist monk could draw fish to a fishing boat?"

"Simple. We are running out of fish, and Monks are highly revered in our society. We thought he could do no harm."

He looked around the groups of agents who had befriended him and made a sinking sign with his hand. "But we almost died."

"Can you describe this monk?"

"He was skinny and tall, and orange."

Well, that's pretty generic for any monk, the interrogator thought.

"And facial features?"

"They all look alike. They shave all their hair, even eyebrows."

"You wouldn't happen to have a photo of him, would you?"

"No, but the boat Captain would. He always photographs his crew members."

"That's nice."

"Not really. If we get washed overboard, he just wants the family to have the last photo. But I guess it's better than nothing."

"Who's the boat Captain, and where is he?"

"We just call him Boss, but it seems like it could be something like Xian Youqian or Xian Youquan, kind of a weird name. He's in Kaohsiung City at the boatyard overseeing boat repairs."

Chapter 12. Team Mates

Mark Fuller, a CIA Analyst, was also traveling to Taiwan at the behest of the Agency. Fuller, a tall, muscular, bald black man with glasses, had not ended up on the career path he had imagined. Then again, perhaps few CIA personnel do.

He had planned on an academic career in Comparative Religion, but during a summer break, he traveled to a Buddhist monastery in the Sagaing Hills of Myanmar, nestled unobtrusively along the Irrawaddy River. He had planned to immerse himself in a three-week silent meditation retreat.

During the beginning of that retreat, he and a handful of other foreign visitors had the opportunity to ordain as Buddhist monks. In Myanmar, becoming a monk does not require a life-long commitment. Temporary ordination allows a novice Buddhist to become a monk for as short as a few weeks with none of the western guilt associated with "back-sliding" if they revert back to hedonism at the end of the training.

By the time the retreat ended, he and his fellow students had to choose to return to lay life or proceed down the education and training path to being a fully ordained monk. The latter path led about as far away from modern American life as you can get. But since Fuller had committed to the full twenty-one days, he focused on the one task given to him, meditation.

That was when, amid forced inactivity and contemplation, he realized that what he truly wanted was a life of adventure. Oddly enough, within the influence of the Sagaing Hills of Myanmar, he began to fancy himself working not with students for the rest of his life, but with the CIA.

Fuller's plane landed at 5:55 PM local time, and after clearing customs, he was nestled into the Novotel Taipei airport hotel by 6:30, and asleep by 7:00 PM, Taipei time.

Seven hours later at 2 AM, 2 PM Washington time, he was awakened by the sound of a subtle movement in his room. He had kept the fan on the room air conditioner running on continuous to provide some ambient background noise, to help him sleep. He lay on his back for a moment, wondering if perhaps the perceived movement was part of a dream, a byproduct of nerves jangled by a long northern Pacific flight, and the stress of knowing his assignment was going to be the most critical and challenging of his life.

He may have imagined the sound. It may have been nothing, but just in case, he reached for the Sig-Sauer P320 pistol tucked neatly away in a mattress holster close to where his right hand rested. The cloth fabric of the holster was supple, just barely covering the cold steel and plastic of the handgrip.

But there was nothing. No sound, no movement, no shadows.

As he started to relax his right hand, he found his face covered by a pillow. A tenth of a second later his hand found the gun again and withdrew it from the holster.

Someone turned on the lights. "Wake up, douchebag!"

As Fuller pushed the pillow off his face, someone whose features Fuller could not see clearly without his glasses said, "You should be at peak now. It's 2 PM your body's time."

Fumbling for his glasses, Fuller shouted, "Jesus fucking Christ, I almost killed you assholes!"

The overhead lights reflected off Fuller's bald and sweat-glistened head. He was standing beside his bed in his boxer shorts, still holding the pistol in his right hand.

"Put that away before you hurt someone," one of the interlopers ordered. His voice was decidedly nonplussed.

"Why didn't you knock on the door like normal people?" Fowler asked.

"This is what we do."

Fuller, being an analyst, had always assumed that what his fellow analysts said about CIA agents was right, that they were aggressive, filled with self-importance, and reckless. But now he had verifiable evidence of that, at least in the case of these two clowns.

"You could have been dead right now," Fuller reminded the unknown duo.

"Yeah, about that. You have no military grade door locks or proximity alarms in this room. You could be the one dead right now."

The second, gruffer agent snidely said, "Apparently, we have our work cut out for us."

The first agent, the one apparently in charge ordered, "Get dressed Fuller, moonlight's wasting. We're taking you to our stash house. We need you to talk Monk-talk to a boat crew member who's cooperating with us."

The second agent said, "You're not at all what I figured a monk would look like."

The agent in charge looked at Fuller quizzically. "Would you really have shot me?"

"You were a second away from eternity."

The agent smiled. "I don't think so."

"Why do you say that?"

"You still had the safety on."

The sun was over the horizon by the time the scrappy agents arrived in Nangang with Fuller and ushered him into his room. The fisherman was stirring in the kitchen. He seemed to find it more to his liking than either his home kitchen or the mess area on the many fishing boats he had been aboard for the last twenty years. Indeed, he seemed content getting used to western standards of living, and with a fat bankroll in his possession.

When Fuller walked into the kitchen to pour his morning coffee, Fuller and the boat crewman met eyes for the first time. The crewman spoke something quickly, and one of the housekeepers translated.

"You're new. Are you the monk they've been talking about?"

Fuller nodded, and the translator spoke something back. It was best to skip the details.

Then the crewman followed up with an additional comment which the translator repeated as "I've never seen a monk like you."

"In what way?"

"You are dark."

"Well, you have now."

"Where are your robes?"

"In my luggage."

The lead agent said, "Don't get too comfortable in your room, Fuller. We hope to have a photo of the monk this evening so you can go hunting tomorrow. I suggest you use your time wisely to debrief sailor boy here. You'll need all the info you can get."

That was an entirely accurate statement. Fuller wanted to discover as many details as he could that might help him find and then connect with this strange monk. Did the man chant anything memorable? Did he talk about any particular monasteries? Did he share in any conversations with the crew? Did he keep to himself? Did he eat smaller portions than the crew members? Did he meditate? Where did he sleep? Did he ever explain why he thought he could bring fish to the boat?

The two of them chatted most of the day, gradually filling in a picture of the mysterious Phra Theratapati and the bizarre events on the boat.

"As I understand it, as the boat was getting closer to the position where all the weirdness began, he was just standing by himself at the furthest point on the bow, and the crew was standing amidships ready to deploy the nets on the Captain's command."

"Actually, he was sitting, meditating."

"The monk didn't signal the deployment of the nets."

"I don't know. Boss was watching the sonar looking for a fish school. About the time the monk left the bow and started walking amidship, the Captain saw a large school rising from the bottom. Or so he thought."

"And the monk did not detect anything unusual."

"If he did, he didn't say anything."

"And you said it got fouled in the net and started pulling the stern up."

"Yes."

"Why do you think it dropped back down?"

"I don't know."

"Did the monk seem surprised?"

"Very. We all did."

The first agent interrupted, "Yeah, yeah, we all know about that. But what I want to know, Fuller, is where you're going to find the Monk?"

"There are lots of monasteries in Taiwan, but if he needs money for a ticket home, he's probably hanging around the big metropolitan monasteries. More likely to get a nice handout from a sympathizer, especially a Thai expat."

"So that would narrow it down to, what, fifty or so monasteries?"

"At least twenty. Maybe more. But I have to start somewhere."

"Well, let me remind you, there's a whole lot of people wanting to talk to this monk before he disappears even deeper into the woodwork."

Fuller nodded his head repeatedly. "I know."

The midnight oil was burning at the headquarters of the Naval Sea Systems Command in the Washington Navy Yard on the banks of the Anacostia River. The Office of the Director of Ocean Engineering, Supervisor of Salvage and Diving, otherwise known as SUPSALV, would not be sending anything more than a detachment of divers to Taiwan to assist with the recovery of the alien craft, but every piece of hardware in its salvage inventory would be employed.

As the plans became more detailed and more expensive, a few officers in the know could be heard quietly cracking jokes about the difficulty they would have lifting the ship.

"Let's just get the monk to do it," they often said.

In truth, if the Monk could be found, he probably would be asked to do the heavy lifting, as incredible as that seemed.

The Agency already had one unique asset in its employ, Joshua Nilsson, but they were also keen to latch onto this supposed holy man. But so far, all anyone had been able to do was send a single CIA analyst with untested skills to identify the monk and bring him in. The Taiwan operation had the monk's photo now, but little else. All the Agency could do was make sure their field agents protected Fuller. As an analyst, what he didn't know about spycraft could get them all killed.

CHAPTER 13. REUNION

Joshua Nilsson was lounging in his robe, listening to the Sunday morning news programs. Those programs based in Washington D.C. were broadcast not far from his apartment in McClean, Virginia, which in turn was an easy commute for his driver to CIA Headquarters at Langley.

A two-toned ding-dong alerted Nilsson that a visitor was at the door to his apartment building. His TV muted automatically so he could hear who was at the door. Before he could move from his seat, speakers in the ceiling of each room of his apartment gave a description of the visitor.

"Sally Simpkin, 29 years old, Stanford University, government contractor, social media friend, no known security risk. She is alone. Provide access? Yes or no."

"Yes," Nilsson said with enthusiasm.

The CIA was taking no chances with their only blind asset. They had installed a Government User Identification and Detection System or GUIDS facial recognition alerting system to let him know who was requesting access.

A few moments later, there was a knock at his apartment door.

Once the GUIDS system confirmed the person at the door was the person initially requesting access, and hearing "Come In" spoken in Nilsson's natural voice, his apartment door unlocked.

Simpkin hesitated.

"Hello, Joshua, this is Pipi Longstocking. Can I come in?"

"Yes, by all means, come in, Sally."

Once she entered, she stood just inside the door, looking around.

"Hi, Joshua. This is kind of spooky. How did you know it was me?"

"Easy. Listen to this," he said. "GUIDE, repeat the last alert."

"Sally Simpkin, 29 years old, Stanford University, government contractor, social media friend..."

"GUIDE, enough."

"Wow, GUIDE's pretty smart."

"It's tied into the NSA database. It knows all about everyone except the unborn. And they're working on that."

"What do you mean?"

"You know those 3D ultrasounds of fetuses that are so popular now? Where do you think those images end up?"

"You're kidding me, right?"

Nilsson smiled.

"Joshua, you're letting this Agency job go to your head."

Nilsson shrugged.

"And speaking of that head, I have something for it."

She grasped his head in both her hands and kissed him squarely on the lips, with passion.

"Am I invading your personal space?" she asked after the kiss.

"You can invade it any time you want, Sally," he said grinning and feeling a little tension below the waist.

When Sally Simpkin gave herself the moniker Pipi Longstocking, she revealed a side of her persona that Nilsson found exciting. She was youthful, but not childish, and with a lilting voice that for him embraced the very concept of femininity. From his illicit remote viewing experience, he knew she had a body that any virile young man would desire. What little physical contact he had with her in the past had confirmed his mental image.

On the other hand, Nilsson's own physique, firm, and athletic in college, was deteriorating from a lack of exercise and attention. The only thing that seemed to be growing was his paunch. What muscles he had once had, were fading from disuse. For those and a multitude of other reasons, Simpkin's kiss was the first passionate kiss he had experienced in quite some time.

She must want something, Nilsson thought cynically.

"I should have let you know I was coming," she admitted, "but it's sort of a last-minute thing. I was in town meeting with Dr. Kincaide, and he asked me a question I couldn't answer."

Dr. Harry Kincaide was the chief physicist at Stanford Research Institute in Menlo Park, California. He had organized and run the remote viewing program for the CIA and DIA and had been profoundly flummoxed when he tested Jason Parker and Laura Smith after the Great Leaving. He was convinced that he had in his possession a powerful alien artifact, a parting gift from the Frogs, which was a multicolored glass sphere of some unknown purpose. Alas, Parker and Laura Smith had proven to Kincaide that the globe was nothing more than a training aid for Frog-children, designed to teach them the ways of psychokinesis.

"What makes you think I can answer it?" Nilsson asked.

"Because you're the best-damned answer finder there is."

"You want something remote viewed, I suppose."

"Yep, the DeSoto Canyon."

"I've already done that," Nilsson reminded her.

"But not recently. We're picking up some biological activity."

"What does that mean?"

"That's exactly what Kincaide asked me. I have no clue, but I know someone who might?"

"So why isn't the Company tasking me? Why are you involved?"

"Because it's not the Agency's business—yet."

"I'm not sure I should be working off the payroll. My bosses have pretty strict rules."

"Hey, we're all on the same team. You're too valuable of an asset to not share."

"So, all you want is for me to check out the canyon?"

"Yes, and if you find something interesting, take careful mental notes."

Nilsson lowered his blind eyes toward the floor, thinking of the potential repercussions.

After a few moments' hesitation, Nilsson said, "I guess there's no harm in that. There shouldn't be anything there, anyway."

"There you go. So, now would be good."

"Like, right now?" he asked, surprised.

"Sure. Is that a problem?"

He thought about that for a moment, then said, "I suppose not. I'll give it a go."

When Nilsson held one of his remote viewing sessions at Langley, it was a staged production. It invariably included meditation music or geographically relevant sounds, accompanied by subdued lighting. It also required the comfort of a form-fitting chair with adjustable positions. The Agency had spared no expense to get Nilsson "in the mood."

That was all part of Nilsson's slightly devious plan. The ability to remote view was the only skill he had that other CIA analysts did not possess. He reasoned, why not take advantage of it?

However, as he was about to show Simpkin, he could also plop down pretty much anywhere, furrow his brow for effect and "be there."

As Nilsson began his viewing, he described what he was experiencing.

"I'm in the water, and it's dark, but even at this depth, there is a little bit of ambient light. Very little, but perceptible. Now I can see a faint greenish glow in front of me.

Nilsson turned his head back and forth as if looking around.

"It's all pretty featureless except for the green glow. Oh, now something is blocking part of it. I can see something approaching. It's silhouetted by the glow so I can't make out any details. It's taller than wide, though."

For several moments Nilsson said nothing.

"It's getting closer. Seems to have a vaguely human shape. I'm sensing that it's aware of my energy presence."

He took in a deep breath. "It's here. Still can't tell what it is, but I don't get a sense that it wishes me harm."

Nilsson had had that ironic feeling before. His virtual presence, his *energy* as he described it, could not be harmed when it was out of his body, but nevertheless, he was always able to sense the intent of any contacts, just as if he was physically onsite.

"The thing is reaching towards me."

Nilsson jerked his head back. "Oh, what a rush!"

Then remembering the need to describe what was happening, he said, "It touched me. I got a blast of information. Way too much for me to understand. But now an image of…incubators. Lots of baby incubators…all empty."

Nilsson was overcome by a pang of profound and unfathomable sadness. Simpkin could see tears welling in his eyes.

"What is it?" she asked.

"I have no idea, but the situation is desperate. I…I can't go on."

After Nilsson regained his composure, he said, "I could use a stiff drink right about now."

Simpkin asked, "Has that happened to you before?"

"Never. If it had, I wouldn't be doing this."

"You were feeling its emotion?" she asked, haltingly.

"I guess," Nilsson said, shaking his head in disbelief.

"That blast of information you got, will you be able to process it?"

"I don't know. Maybe eventually."

"If you do, please contact me and nobody else."

"Why you, Sally?"

"My boss, Kincaide, is still the point of contact for all Frog stuff."

"Frog stuff?" he asked with a quizzical look on his face.

"I'll let myself out, Joshua. Thanks for your help."

"Sure," he said absentmindedly. But what he was thinking was, *Really, Frog stuff?*

Chapter 14. Target Practice

Harry Kincaide, it's been a long time," Parker said, extending his hand. "Are you still mad at me about the Frog toy?"

"Not at all, Jason. In fact, that's one of the reasons I'm here to talk to you."

"So, you've moved on from that day at Andrew's Air Force Base."

"Yes, and so have you," Kincaide said. "Did you learn anything from your cosmologist friend?"

"About possible propulsion systems? No. He doesn't think we're smart enough to understand it."

"That may be true, but we have figured some things out about navigation. At least we think we have it figured out. You'll be the one to tell us if we're right or not."

"How so?"

"Remember how the Frog toy was a telepathy training aid for young Frogs?"

"Yes," Parker said, smiling. "And I remember you were none too happy when I told you that."

"Yes, that was the last thing I was expecting to hear. So, beyond telepathy, what is the most important distinguishing characteristic of the Frogs?"

"Uh, I guess that would be remote viewing?"

"Absolutely," Kincaide said.

"And you're probably the world's expert on the subject," Parker noted. "At least the CIA seems to think so since you built their entire program for them."

"I understand you have skills in that area too," Kincaide replied.

"Maybe, some. But I hear we have a common friend, Joshua Nilsson, who's the best there is, in my opinion."

"You're right, he is incredibly capable. There's only one problem with Nilsson, he's not a pilot."

"Uh, what does that have to do with anything?" Parker asked with a puzzled scowl on his face.

"Navigation. As a pilot, you know all about aerial navigation."

"Of course, I have to."

"Jason, we think the craft is the best flying platform ever built. We think it's equipped to automatically handle every flight regime and problem it might ever face anywhere in the universe."

Wow, that's quite a presumptuous hyperbole, Parker thought.

"But only the pilot knows where it should fly to," Kincaide added.

Parker was still confused. He had no idea where this conversation was headed.

"I understand Jacob Weiss told you we think the pilot's cockpit is a probable brainwave receiver, simply based on its seeming neural net infrastructure. It's likely either an entire quantum computer or part of a quantum computer. Hell, the whole ship could be one for all we know."

"He did share that with me," Parker admitted.

"Now imagine this. By remote viewing a target, you and the Frogs are receiving an image of a target without breaking the conventional rules of space and time."

"I don't know about that."

"Well, you can't deny it happens," Kincaid noted.

"Somehow."

"Yes, somehow. So, if you can see the target, and the ship can read your mind, then that means the ship can see it as well."

"And following your logic," Parker said, "if the ship can see it, you think the ship can navigate to it?"

"Now you get it. As long as it knows where you want it to go, it figures out the fastest and safest way to get there."

"Why are you so sure?"

"Past experience. Look at how our aviation technology has advanced in a hundred years or so. Multiply that a thousandfold, and where do you think we'll be? We've advanced from lights and bonfires, to pinpoint accuracy making a landing on a fog-bound runway. And that's only in a hundred years, and using human brains and primitive computers which are severely handicapped compared to what the Frogs have to work with."

"Okay, I enjoy the academic discussion," Parker said. "But why did you come all this way?"

"We want to test our theory."

Jason Parker was isolated in a room with windows that had been covered with heavy draperies. His isolation was to ensure no clues could be provided by smiles, frowns, or throat clearing. Sensitive microphones were recording every breath Parker took, but no sound came into the room. It was so quiet that he could hear only tinnitus, a mild ringing in his ears brought on by years of aviating in noisy piston engines, and of diving with its continual assault on his eardrums.

Parker had been handed a piece of paper with the following coordinates:

37°29'16.09" N, 116°13'41.65" W

His task was to remote view the location of those coordinates, just as he had learned from the *Coordinate Remote Viewing Manual* written by none other than Kincaide and a handful of other *psychic spies*, as they were often called.

Unbeknownst to him, the target he was trying to visualize was located forty miles to the northwest of the present location of the ship. He had never been there and was working only from the latitude-longitude coordinates he had been given. He knew from the coordinates that it was not far away. Thus he had a good idea of what the terrain would be like; not much different from the terrain right outside the heavy steel security doors protecting the underground complex.

"I'm standing in the middle of circles, a series of concentric circles. The area looks like a dry lake bed. It's featureless except for the circles. The rings are not entirely complete, some have broken places like they are old and weathered.

There seems to be sandy roads, straight lines running through the lake bed, with three intersecting in the middle of the smallest inner circle. They make a Y-shape within the rings."

He paused, frowning.

"I'm guessing on the size of the circles, but I think they're over a football field away from each other. They may be closer to 500 feet than 300 feet apart. I feel there are five of them.

"I'm looking further away now. To the east are mountains and to the west. Also, some to the south. They're not very high. There may be mountains further away, to the north. But the north seems to be mostly open, and flat."

In the room where Hans Richter, Harry Kincaide, and a few Air Force officers were gathered, there were, in fact, a lot of smiles. Richter and Kincaide exchanged high fives.

"As long as he has coordinates to go by, he's almost as good as Nilsson."

Richter shook his head. "He's remarkable. I think we're ready to test your little theory. When can we do it?"

The senior Air Force officer, General VanDyke, answered. "Tomorrow. We'll go at dawn. There are too many mountains out there to risk flying completely blind. I don't want to take any chances."

Richter laughed. "You think he can do anything about it?"

"Yes, we reviewed the video and radar tracks from his flight from Pascagoula to the DeSoto Canyon, and he was pretty much in control. For close-in work, he's very much in control, mentally."

"Okay, then, who's breaking the news to Parker?"

"I will," Kincaide said. "I'm the one with this crazy idea. I trust he'll tell me to fuck off if he thinks I'm full of shit, or if he thinks he's not ready."

"And if he does tell you that?"

"I can be pretty persuasive, but ultimately it's his life on the line. He'll have to make that decision."

The officer said with all seriousness, "That's why I wish we had a military man who could do this. They can be voluntold."

Everyone except Hans Richter was surprised when Parker jumped at the chance to fly the craft again. He had no reservations, trusting in both the alien technology and his own skills; foolishly some thought. But that was Jason Parker.

He had no doubt that in the millions of years the Frogs had been navigating interstellar space and deep oceans, their craft would be fully intelligent, with quicker reasoning powers and reflexes than any pilot, human or otherwise.

As the sky began to brighten and the surrounding mountains began to cast long purple shadows, the thick metallic roof of the underground facility slid back into its recessed storage location, giving Parker a view straight up into a cloudless sky ringed with pink-tinged mountains as he willed the alien craft's entry door open, just like before. He was relieved that the ship seemed to welcome him by promptly opening the otherwise hidden entry.

Parker assumed the craft had the sense to fly over the mountains rather than through them, but just in case, he was heavily restrained and surrounded by shock-deployed airbags. He was also wearing a NASA spacesuit in case the pressure boundary sealing operation failed. Being a short flight, the craft should not gain much altitude, but if it lost its mind and rocketed into space, he wanted to be prepared for anything, even loss of cabin pressure.

He ran a comms check while sitting in a seat that overlaid the original seat, molded to better fit a human body than the Frog body.

He had comms. The cabin entry door was shut and sealed.

Now, there was little else to do. There were no switches to throw, no dials to read, no screens, no levers.

All he had to do was prepare the ship for flight using nothing more than his mind.

Easy day.

With all quiet in the hangar, he once again focused on the imagery of his target. That feat, awkward at first, was becoming easier with each attempt.

All the ship had to do was gather the imagery from Parker's mind, convert that into the three-dimensional flight plan that not only allowed it to reach the target but to do so considering optimal altitude and speed at every point in the route.

That's all.

The goal was to hit the bullseye of a target that looked amazingly like a huge archery target with its concentric circles while avoiding the mountains lying along the ship's potential flight path.

Of course, no flight is complete without a smooth landing. In this case, it was to be performed with no human control input of any kind whatsoever.

A little scary, to say the least.

Now the critical step for Parker was convincing the ship to fly while keeping the acceleration forces to a reasonable level. He had managed that in Pascagoula and the Gulf of Mexico once, so supposedly it should work this time too. Somehow.

Parker said over the comms, "Alright folks, it's Showtime."

He visualized the area in front of the craft becoming transparent, and the ship obeyed. He could now see the hangar in front of him, and an assortment of gawkers, cameras, and sensors.

Now he visualized the craft slowly climbing vertically. He had to rise past 200 feet or so of bedrock before it would clear the hill overlying the base.

And as he imagined that, the craft rose obediently, majestically, and silently.

After clearing the hill, the craft accelerated at two Gs towards the northwest, rising three thousand feet to avoid the hills near the target. It just as quickly started decelerating at negative two Gs and within a couple of minutes extended its legs and gently set down in the middle of the targeted ring of circles.

Through the still transparent front of the triangular craft, he could see Jeeps heading his way, leaving trails of dust behind them.

Over his comms he could hear "Jason, your top speed was 1300 miles per hour. That's Mach 1.7. You're riding a speed demon, Parker."

"Am I in the right place?"

"You hit the bullseye. Literally."

"What is this place?"

"You're in an old bombing range."

"Is it radioactive?"

"Heck, no. We wouldn't want our baby to get contaminated."

"Or me, thank you."

"Nor you."

"I didn't have much time for sightseeing, but I thought I saw a bunch of deep pits and such. Are those nuclear craters?"

"Sure are. You crossed over a nuclear testing area. Some of that area just might be radioactive."

"What do you call this place?"

"The Kawich Valley, restricted area R-4807A."

"My escorts are here so I'll sign off from inside the ship and do a meet and greet. They're taking photos already, and I need to go smile for them."

With that, the transparent window became opaque. As Parker approached the exit door, it obligingly opened for him.

Chapter 15. Blake Plateau

The NOAA Research Vessel *Gordon Gunter* rolled lazily in gentle swells 240 miles east of St. Augustine, Florida. The Milky Way galaxy swung back and forth across the night sky as the ship rolled, floating gently over a fixed point on the seafloor 3000 feet below on one of the deeper portions of the Blake Plateau. The plateau was a remarkably broad, deep, and flat plain separating the continental shelf off Georgia and Florida from the much deeper Abyssal Plain in the Atlantic Ocean.

About 200 miles to the south lay the Bahama Islands, and over 300 miles to the north lay Beaufort, North Carolina. The only thing interesting near the ship was an instrumented deep-water codfish equipped with a low light camera for observing luminescent light from small deep-water fish which were potential prey for the large cod.

The National Marine Fisheries Service was funded to research the interaction between food fish species and deep-water fish which used fluorescence as a way of attracting either mates or prey in the under-populated deep waters off America's east coast.

The predatory cod, typically found in waters as shallow as two thousand feet, had recently been observed at the three-thousand-foot level. Scientists had begun to wonder if the deep-diving fish were taking advantage of the bioluminescent flashlights of deep water, potential prey species.

There was a growing belief among marine fishery scientists that just as human fishermen were searching ever deeper for fish, so were predatory fish like cod because of the increasing sparsity of their usual prey found at more moderate depths.

The fish's instrumentation included a miniature high data rate acoustic modem which relayed low light images to the ship. Like tracers from a machine gun, occasionally a low-intensity strobe would fire, providing to the scientists on the *Gunter* a visual image of the codfish's surroundings.

Oceanographic technicians had woken the project leader Andrew Syski because the cod had just targeted and devoured some small fish, the first successful interaction of the night so far. He'd told them that if the cod finally began eating, he wanted to witness the action.

Syski entered the wet laboratory at the ship's stern. Instead of the usual aquaria that would generally line the hull for specimen storage, there was a bank of large flat-screen monitors revealing the action down below.

"Andy, he's focused on another bit of luminescence, but he's unusually wary this time."

"Maybe he's full," a female intern remarked.

"A codfish is never full," Syski answered from his many years of experience. "Has the strobe flashed yet?"

"No."

Unlike tracers on a machine gun, the strobe was set to go off randomly so the cod wouldn't learn to wait for the strobe before striking. Cod are smart, as fish go, but not smart enough to understand the concept of random patterns. They were also too impatient, and hungry, to just wait for the flash before striking.

The screen flashed white, and as the computer began processing the image, the closest technician to the screen said, "There you go. Can't tell…"

Syski interrupted him, "It's all teeth. He's too damn close to an angler fish!"

"I thought they were pretty small?"

"Do you see those teeth?"

The front of the Angler fish's head was taken up entirely by inward-curving teeth, or so it seemed.

"That thing can swallow a fish several times its size. Any more signals?"

The technician paused before answering with what they desperately did not want to hear.

"No."

"Still nothing?" Syski asked again.

"As you can see, nada."

Then a flash filled the screen again.

"The black frames are coming in now, as clear as ever."

"Great. He must have been hiding," Syski said. "I would too if I were him."

After several more minutes of black screens and no movement, another flash occurred and simply showed the flat muddy bottom seeming to be just a few inches away from the camera.

"Okay, that's it for me, troopers. I'm headed back to my bunk, so let me know if anything else interesting happens."

"Roger that. Sweet dreams."

Syski smiled and paused before opening the heavy watertight door to the laboratory.

"I imagine our pet cod will be having nightmares for the rest of its little life."

His technicians laughed.

The intern said, "At least he's a survivor."

With all of the technicians looking at Syski, none of them saw what Syski saw on the screen at that moment.

"What's that?" Syski asked, pointing to the screen.

All eyes switched back to the screen as the processor seemed to have a tight lock on what appeared to be a searchlight.

"What the hell? That's not biological."

The bright light seemed to be growing larger, and brighter, finally bathing the camera and fish in a light that seemed stronger than sunlight. And there it froze, just as did the cod.

Instinct would have had the cod quickly leave the area, but his previous trauma, and now this light, seemed to be overloading its neural circuitry. Perhaps it thought that if it didn't move, it wouldn't be noticed. After all, the cod's colors blended in well with the muddy clay of the Blake Plateau.

"Our fish may be injured," said another technician.

The fact that the cod's body had betrayed him became apparent when the next strobe flash revealed the image of a helmeted human with an outstretched arm.

"Jesus, look at that!"

They all peered closer to the monitor as Syski reached over and pressed a red button to freeze the image.

Sure enough, a helmeted human diver could clearly be seen.

The intern looked expectantly at Syski.

"Can humans dive to three-thousand feet?"

"Not that I know."

Syski had been a saturation diver in the Navy, many years before getting his degrees in marine biology and taking the NOAA job. He had personally never dived deeper than one-thousand feet, but he knew the Navy Diving Center in Panama City had pressed experimental divers to 1800 feet in their large pressure chamber. He also knew the pressure effects had been problematic for the divers, so he didn't think a three-thousand-foot dive was humanly possible.

Yet here it was, a vivid image of the impossible.

"You think the Navy knows about this?"

"I don't know, but if they don't, I bet they'll be very interested."

After a moment's thought, Syski announced, "I need to call some people. Are we getting any more images?"

"No. But we'll keep recording just in case."

Unfortunately, the image of the human diver reaching out for the NOAA cod was the last image recorded.

After Syski called his friends at the Diving Center, they contacted their bosses in Washington, and soon the Pentagon had handed the Master of the RV *Gunter* a new task. Even though NOAA did not have an overt DoD mission, they were assigned a covert mission until Navy assets could be assembled and deployed. The *Gunter* was to stay on station and try to discretely identify the object the diver came from.

For a research vessel filled with civilians, the discreet part was a tall order.

CHAPTER 16. PENTAGON

Five days after the *Gordon Gunter* discovery, the four-star Admiral, Chief of Naval Operations, threw his hands up in the air as he was absorbing the implication of the message he had just been handed.

"Jesus Christ, you mean to tell me we have a Chinese lockout submarine parked on the Blake Plateau, with Chinese divers walking around on the bottom. And they don't seem to care we're scanning them on side scan and photographing them with our ROV?"

"Afraid so, Sir."

The man answering was a dark and brooding GS-15 civilian from the Defense Intelligence Agency. He wore his concern on his face, at least when reporting to the senior operational Admiral in the U.S. Navy. There was no upside to his visit to the Pentagon this morning.

"At least they don't seem to be a missile sub, so that's about the only good thing I can see. On the downside, they're downrange of our NASA and Space Corp rocket launches from Cape Canaveral. If we splash one in the area, they'll be on target first to salvage the goodies with their divers. But that's pretty unlikely, Sir, don't you think?"

The CNO was thinking out loud and didn't bother to answer. "But my real concern is if they can operate at 3000 feet, then they're free to sit on the bottom anywhere on the Blake Plateau, which means they can follow our subs coming out of Kings Bay."

"Maybe they're disabled."

"If so, they're sure being quiet about it on diplomatic channels. No comms from Beijing at all. And besides, if they were in trouble, they wouldn't be splashing divers to check out a damn codfish. Even one that takes photos."

"I suppose not, Sir."

"Speaking of that, can our boys do that? Walk around at 3000 feet?"

"No, Sir. We've been to 2500 on the hydrogen dive salvaging that alien ship, but we have no interest in 3000 feet. It's too risky."

"For whom?"

"The divers, Sir. And for us, if one of them dies without a good reason."

"It's that risky?"

"Yes Sir."

"Well, I think the Chinese just gave us our good reason. Tell whoever was running that DeSoto Canyon dive I want to see them in my office tomorrow morning."

"That was quite a few people, Sir, including our Intel folks."

"Then get them all in my office, 0630 tomorrow. I've got to brief SecDef tomorrow, and I need some new ideas."

"What are you going to tell them?"

"I'll tell them my hunch is the Chinese are just trying to rattle us. And I want to know a way we can safely rattle them back, other than increasing our presence in the South China Sea."

"Maybe this is a tit for tat."

"Maybe," the CNO replied. "But I sure don't like being bested by them this close to home."

The halls of the Pentagon are vast and continually echo with the footsteps of men and women in both military and civilian attire.

Dr. Laura Smith had been called into a high-level Pentagon meeting to monitor a dispute among the Joint Chiefs of Staff. The Chairman of the JCS, Army General Anthony Lillo, was President Whitney's principal military adviser, but the Chairman was duty-bound to fairly report the opinions and concerns of the other JCS members. As it stood, there was far too much rancor to report to anyone. The Joint Chiefs had been stressed more than usual deciding on mission priorities.

"For God's sake, please stop shouting!"

The person attempting to disrupt the mayhem was none other than Laura Smith. She had been quiet during the meeting so far, so her interruption came as a shock. She, like a child, was expected to listen, not speak.

The Chairman glowered at her.

"I don't give a flippin' damn if POTUS wanted you here. You raise your hand to be recognized if you wish to speak in my meeting."

"With all due respect, General, my hand has been raised for five minutes."

"Oh, for God's sakes. What's so damned important, Dr. Smith?"

"Whitney expects me to report back to him in an hour with my recommendation, so I need to summarize what I think I'm hearing."

"Bloody hell," the General said, "That's my job. Not an intelligence weenie's job. Why do you have access?"

"So directed," she responded curtly.

"Then let's get this over with. Just remember, you do not speak for the Joint Chiefs. Only I do that."

"I understand the protocol. This will just take a moment."

The General nodded his head for her to begin.

"This is what I've heard so far. The Chinese submarine camped out on the United States' doorstep is an ever-present threat." Turning to face the Admiral on the staff, "Admiral, you're pushing for the removal of that threat to be the priority for the first target assignment for Jason Parker and his unarmed alien ship. Perhaps that could be done without starting World War III."

The Admiral nodded his head.

Turning to the Space Corp Admiral, she said, "The Space Corp has a compelling reason for wanting the alien craft to first rescue the remaining crewman on the Phobos outpost. For one thing, if Parker flew the craft into the Chinese sub, or crashed it into the water, it would be out of commission, and the rescue of the American on Phobos would be impossible. Did I get that correct?"

"Yes, that's accurate."

Turning back toward Admiral Lillo, "He's not here, but the Secretary of Defense is inclined to do nothing. Let Clarice Williams die. She will probably be killed one way or another before the Triangle could even get there if it can get there at all. Any way you look at it, the odds are heavily weighted against Williams. To SecDef, it seems much better to let the Chinese have their fun in international waters rather than risk both the alien ship and, so far, the only person who can fly it, Jason Parker."

All in the room were silent. The Chairman, initially expressionless, slowly began to smile.

"Well, Ms. Smith, that's a pretty damned good summary, for an intel weenie. And with that, I think you can leave, right?"

"Yes, sir."

"And just so you know, if we end up with a different conclusion, I'll be the one to brief it to POTUS."

"I understand Sir."

Standing up, she exited the room as quietly as she could.

As Laura retraced her path through the rabbit warren of hallways out of the Pentagon, she thought to herself, *You did good, girl!*

After later listening to Laura's concise summary, President Whitney thought that the U.S. might have another alien ship anyway, the one in Taiwanese waters. If the Triangle came to a bad end, it wasn't necessarily the end of the world.

Of course, to Laura, that meant either she would lose Jason or her own life. Either way, it could be the end of her world.

The Pentagon always reminded Jason Parker of a beehive, with the queen bee, or bees, hidden safely inside locked places to which very few in the government had access.

Parker had no idea why he had been called there, but none other than a Space Corp Lieutenant Colonel had met him at the main entrance and escorted him to a waiting room adjacent to a SCIF, an extremely secure facility reserved for discussing the nation's top secrets. And then he was left alone. To pass the time, he picked up a copy of *Aviation and Space* magazine to browse while waiting for whatever was going to happen.

Curious, he thought, *it's like a doctor's waiting room, but with no other patients.*

He started speeding through an article on the peacetime uses of military drones, but it just made him relive the frightening experience of the supersonic alien drones released from a Russian submarine in the Gulf of Mexico.

He was startled by a familiar voice.

"Like a bad penny, you keep showing up."

Parker looked up into the fetching eyes of Laura Smith, who had approached silently within a few feet. He stood up and hugged her, whispering into her ears. "There's a bit of luster left on this penny, my dear."

Laura was a former graduate student of his, and a rumored paramour, but they had been through more than one dangerous situation together. They'd been the target of rogue assassination attempts, rescued by aquatic aliens, as well as the now-famous kidnapping by the Russians. Their emotional ties ran deep.

But what impressed Parker more than anything at this moment was that she had not been escorted. Apparently, she belonged here, somewhere deep within this beehive.

When he last spent time with her, they had both had to hide her association with the Director of National Intelligence.

"Are you part of this meeting?" Parker asked.

"I am."

Laura had a sly smile. Although technically still married, Parker could never entirely hide his affection for this strange young woman with almost unlimited talent and unequaled imagination.

Ironically, it was her imaginative association with the past-life alien species that had landed her a job with ONI, as a specialist in alien species.

But even more bizarre was her heartfelt conviction that she and Parker had once shared life together as alien beings either on a distant planet or on Earth. That was one little detail she had never been clear about. But that uncertainty had not terribly concerned her, certainly not in comparison to her absolute certainty that they had a shared life at one time in the distant past.

Parker being the pragmatic Navy scientist, had never shared that sentiment with her. But he did have to admit that the bond of mutual survival had forever tied them together in this life.

The nearest door swung partly open, and a man dressed in navy blue pants and a light blue shirt came out, pointing to a box by the door. "Drop your phones in here before entering."

He then left the area down one of the halls leading away from the conference room, or whatever it was.

Parker looked at Laura and said, "I guess that's our cue."

Obediently, Parker dropped off his phone. Laura came prepared, having left her phone somewhere else in the vast complex.

Parker motioned towards the door, "Ladies first."

She pulled the door open to take a peek, and then motioned to Parker, adding, "They're waiting for us."

The room was smaller than Parker had expected, and not a single person was in uniform. The five men and one woman had no name tags, which Parker found disorienting. He had nothing to judge who these people were.

"Drs. Smith and Parker, please have a seat at the table." The woman speaking pointed to two chairs side by side, with their name tags.

Parker took an instant liking to this lady. Her figure and voice reminded him of his English teacher during his senior year of high school. She looked matronly, relatively tall, and spoke in a stern authoritarian voice. But then as now, he perceived a softer side.

"And who might you folks be?" Parker asked as they sat down.

"It's not important for you to know," she said. "As far as you are concerned, we have no names."

Parker had a bemused look on his face as he half laughed. "Okay, then. This is a bit strange, but I guess you know that."

"Dr. Parker, what you are about to hear cannot be repeated outside of this room. It is far above top secret."

She seemed to be the only person who spoke. The others sat quietly across the table from him and Laura.

She then handed the two of them nondisclosure agreements. After quickly glancing over it, Parker saw nothing that would help him understand what this meeting was about. Nevertheless, he signed and dated it, just as he knew he must, and handed his signed form back to the lady without a name. After Laura had done likewise, the woman spoke again.

Appearing to single out Parker, she asked, "What do you know about Phobos?"

Parker was not yet ready to begin the inquisition, and stalling might buy him some time to think about that question before blurting out an answer.

"I don't mean to speak for Dr. Smith here, but can you do me a favor before we begin?"

The oldest appearing male, maybe in his fifties, nodded towards Parker, silently giving him permission to continue.

"I have a sense that you folks have more advanced degrees than I, and maybe more than the both of us together, so can we dispense with the formality of titles? I'm Jason, and this is Laura."

He quickly turned to Laura and asked, "Is that okay with you?"

Laura nodded her head.

The woman seemed to speak for the group. "As you wish Jason. Now, what do you know about Phobos?"

The short delay had given Parker just the time he needed to search his memory for a reasonable answer. "I assume we're not here to discuss Greek mythology, so I'm guessing you mean the closest moon to Mars. I do know that NASA has been trying to gain support for crewed landings on Phobos before attempting landings on Mars."

The older gentleman smiled. "This may not take as long as I thought," he said. His voice sounded strained as if he was recovering from a cold.

The woman continued. "Yes, that is true, NASA has said that publicly. But actually, that has been a diversion."

"How so?" Parker asked.

"Just so you understand, if word of what we are about to tell you gets out, and is traced back to you..." she tapped her pen against the tabletop. "Well, you will be declared *persona non grata*, at the very least. You are an imaginative man, so I will let you fill in the blanks."

Parker recognized the threat for what it was, but he also understood the rules. He was not about to blab anything he might learn. He was simply curious why he had been selected to hear it.

"I understand."

She sounded more like his English teacher all the time. It was making it hard to take her seriously. She looked at the rest of them, focusing primarily on the older gentleman, and when he nodded, she continued.

"We speak for the President of the United States and the Secretary of Defense."

She paused to let that sink in.

Okay, not so much like my English teacher, Parker thought.

"We have been on Phobos for twelve years," she said. "And on Mars for ten."

Now Parker was impressed, but also disbelieving. Laura, on the other hand, did not react.

"You are kidding me, right?" Parker said slowly.

"If you don't believe us, ask Laura. She knows."

Parker looked at Laura, silently asking, *Is it true*?

She nodded.

The nameless woman continued, "We set up an over-watch on Phobos to get a sense of the safety of an eventual semi-permanent presence on Mars. One side of Phobos is always facing Mars, and one side faces away. Twelve years ago, we set up sensors on the Mars-side as we call it, and ran the cables over to the space-side of Phobos. That's where our Phobos station is located. It faces away from Mars, so we can detect and identify any potential unwanted visitors that might do harm to our Mars base."

"Unwanted visitors?"

One of the younger gray-suited men spoke next. "Your so-called Frogs are not the only visitors we have. Conveniently they all seem to come from the outer regions of the solar ecliptic, so Phobos is conveniently located to spot them, and if needed, to give an early warning to the existing Mars base."

Parker shook his head. "You can't be serious. How did you hide a launch large enough to establish a Mars base without someone noticing?"

"Secret military missions to Phobos was the real reason Space Corp was established. From Phobos, the hop down to Mars was relatively easy. It took us a couple of years to stockpile the materials we needed on Phobos for the Mars base. By taking our time, we were able to disguise the shipments."

Looking at Laura, he asked, "And you've known about this all along?"

"Yes," she said, keeping her poker face.

Laura never ceases to amaze me, Parker thought.

"Well, yeah, that's really interesting," Parker said. "But why am I here?"

"And Laura too," the woman said.

Parker was getting impatient and wanted to cut to the chase. "So why are *we* here?"

"We need someone to fly the Frog-ship to Phobos on a rescue mission."

"There you go with the comedy routine again," Parker said, knowing that he was risking insubordination. But frankly, he didn't care. What that lady just said was bordering on insanity.

"Mars is on the opposite side of the sun," the lady said. "We have no other way to rescue our assets there because we'll have to wait another year to do a normal Earth-launch. But the astronauts don't have that much time."

"How many are on Phobos?"

"Two."

"Wait a minute, wait a minute," Parker said emphatically. "I don't want to overthink this, but exactly how do you plan to get us back? Reentry can be hell, and we have no way to control it. Maybe we can dock with the space station?"

"No way. That's an international asset, and this remains a top-secret mission. And besides, NASA wants us nowhere near the ISS."

"That should tell you something," Parker said sarcastically. "How long do you think it should take to get there?"

"Based on our tracking data when the Frogs left, they quickly accelerated to somewhere between 0.1 to 1 percent of light speed. Frankly, we're not sure we can measure those high speeds accurately, but since Mars is about 249 million miles away from Earth at the greatest separation, it should take anywhere from one and a half days to fifteen days to cover a straight-line distance."

Parker wasn't an astronomer, but he knew a bit about the planets and the stars from studying celestial navigation as part of his Ph.D. work. "Wouldn't that put us right through the sun?"

"It would, so you need to follow a curving path around the sun, roughly at the distance of Earth from the sun. Considering the increased distance that requires, I'm guessing total travel time would take anywhere from a week to a month."

"How long does it normally take to get to Mars?"

"At its closest approach, it takes about 300 days. At its furthest, over 400 days. But our astronauts only have a couple of months of oxygen left."

"Oh," Parker sighed.

"So, you see there's some urgency here," the woman said.

"But this is crazy. Once we're at speed, we don't know how to slow the ship down."

"Let me remind you, the Russian craft brought you all the way home from Russia, with you being unconscious for the first half of the trip. And you landed safely."

Parker was skeptical in the extreme.

"I'd like to bet my life on something with a bit more evidence," Parker said, "and a lot less speculation."

"Let me put it this way. We need the outpost on Phobos. Our fledgling Mars station needs the overwatch. We cannot abandon that facility and leave our astronauts there to die."

"Why?" Parker questioned.

"Why?" The responding man seemed puzzled for a moment. He locked eyes in turn with both older gentleman and the nameless woman before saying, "You don't have a need to know."

Parker didn't like that at all.

"Since I don't know who I'm talking to," Parker said brazenly, "I won't call bullshit on that, but I should."

Everyone at the table smiled at that, except the older gentleman who seemed a little too full of himself. He now broke his silence. "Before you head to Mars, Jason, we're sending you on a strictly Navy mission which will give you confidence in both the craft and your ability to fly it."

"What kind of mission?"

"I understand Harry Kincaide briefed you on Remote Viewing, and the ship's ability to navigate based on that view."

"We did more than brief it. I actually did it."

"And what was your thought about it?"

"It worked. I was extremely surprised, but it got me back to Area 51 in no time at all."

"Right. Well, we have something a little more challenging for you. It involves a Chinese submarine and a contingent of deep-sea divers who seem to be staking out a claim to the Blake Plateau."

"Wait, what?"

Outer space and undersea? You've got to be kidding me.

"The Blake Plateau, off the East coast about—"

Getting snippy now, Parker interrupted the man.

"I know all about the Blake Plateau. I've been there, done that. But where on the plateau?"

"We know very well where it is, but you have to find it for us, by remote viewing it. If you can't *see* it as you remote viewers like to say, then you'll never be able to navigate to it."

"So it's a test."

"Indeed."

"Has Joshua Nilsson found it?"

"Right away."

"Can I take him with me?" Parker asked.

"No. We have Mr. Nilsson doing higher priority work for us. Plus, we've got him under protection. He's one of our best assets."

That gave Parker a hint that the man who finally spoke was likely CIA. "So, I've got to do something that could cause an international incident, and I have to do it all by myself. That's great."

Parker's sarcastic tone was unmistakable, and in most circumstances would earn him a reprimand. But the assembled persons had already been briefed on Parker's likely response—by Laura.

"No, no, I'd say you GET to do something no one else has ever done."

To the group's credit, they knew exactly how to work Parker.

Laura looked at Parker and smiled. "Jason, the ship knows what to do. All you have to do is visualize the target and what you want to do after reaching it."

"Just so I understand," Parker said addressing the group, "Laura's not coming on the first mission, but she's on the one to Phobos. Right?"

"Yes. We need her on Phobos."

After the initial shock, Parker began to like the prospect of such a mission.

His wife would hate it, but she wouldn't know. And as she'd already made perfectly clear, she didn't want to know.

"Regarding the Chinese sub," Parker said, "can I scare the bejesus out of them?"

They all nodded their heads in unison, smiling. "That's what we want you to do," the woman said.

"What about the Troll, Truman Baltazar? What's he doing these days?"

"Relocating his fellow Trolls to a dryer climate," one of them said. "But we don't use Trolls for classified missions."

It was beginning to dawn on Parker that he might be an easy write-off if things went seriously awry. But then again, Parker had a habit of accomplishing the impossible.

So far.

Chapter 17. Juno Caliber

Straight after his briefing at the Pentagon, Jason Parker was once again deep underground near Yucca Flats, Nevada. He was about to undergo a flight physical exam with Captain Emery Reed, the former Senior Medical Officer at the Navy Diving Center, and an old friend he hadn't seen in years.

Of course, being a former President's personal physician bought Reed a lot of credibility among Special Projects people. This project was as special as they come.

Parker walked into Reed's medical office for the first time and extended his hand. When Reed shook it, he pulled Parker in for a manly hug and a pat on the back.

"Look what the cat drug in," Reed said. "You sure get around."

"I'd same the same for you. Last I heard you were at NDC."

"I had no idea I'd end up here," Reed admitted, "but I'm delighted to be working with you again, Jason."

"I certainly didn't expect this either," Parker admitted.

"You know the routine," Reed announced. "Pee in the cup behind the curtain, and when you get back, I'll have my gloved hands warmed up for you."

"You get right to it, don't you?"

"Daylight's burning, and I know you want to fly."

"Hell yeah, let's do this."

An intense hour later, Parker was removing the dozen ECG leads from his chest and extremities when Dr. Reed looked up from his tablet where he'd been making notes.

"Jason, if I didn't know better, I'd say you're getting younger, not older. Based on the last angiogram, you've got the heart of a twenty-five-year-old. A physically fit, non-smoking twenty-five-year-old. Pretty impressive for someone in their fifties."

"Hey, as long as I'm fit to fly, I'm happy."

"That you are. And you may need all of that fitness and muscle tone if you're to tolerate the high G loads your bird is capable of."

As Parker put his shirt back on and started buttoning it, he said, "I'm glad you mentioned that. I'd like to talk to you about Gs. You've been briefed on my G exposures?"

"I wouldn't be much good as your physician if I hadn't been."

"I hear you're a G-monster."

Reed paused, looking up as if remembering past flights and then said, "Yeah, I miss that. Nothing like doing a low altitude run through the mountain passes at 500 knots to get your juices flowing."

With boyish enthusiasm, he flattened his hand, thumb, and pinky extended to simulate a jet banking into high-G turns.

"How many Gs have you pulled?" Parker asked him.

"Nine. Maybe a brief peak at ten."

"What are your thoughts about twenty Gs?"

"Oh yeah, your departure from Siberia. Well, it's no wonder you and Laura were unconscious. But as you see, no harm came to you, except for that little tilt of your head that didn't use to be there."

"What?" Parker said squinting.

Reed broke into his toothy grin. "Kidding."

"This is what I'm wondering about," Parker said. "We all seem to think this craft thinks for itself, with some super-quantum bejesus computer embedded in its skin."

"So I've heard."

"And it seems to accurately calculate the lowest energy trajectory for a flight of any given distance. If the distance is far enough, it goes suborbital if left to its own devices."

"Seems it does, but you can control it, as you've seen."

"Unless I'm unconscious," Parker said.

"So don't be."

"If it decides to pull 20 Gs again, there won't be anything I can do about that. And since we're planning a 2300-mile flight, it just might decide that's the way to go. And that worries me."

"Just go along for the ride," said Dr. Reed.

"Except I'm planning to buzz a Chinese submarine. I may need to override the quantum brain if it gets too close to the sub. And I can't very well do that if I'm unconscious."

"I see your point. But here's another interpretation. I've actually lost some sleep thinking about this very same problem. So, when you and Laura escaped from Siberia, did you want to do it as fast as possible, or at a leisurely 3-G acceleration?"

"A slow departure would have gotten us shot out of the sky."

"Yep. I'm sure you were worried about that. Now if your brain waves are being picked up by a flight computer, it would have understood what you needed—a survivable exit strategy. And it delivered, better than we could have imagined."

Parker looked at his friend with a puzzled look on his face.

"You think this thing knows what I want and then delivers?"

"If you have enough computer power, and sensing power, the machine can be every bit as smart as that."

Parker paused a minute, thinking this was strange talk coming from a physician.

"Did they teach you this stuff in med school?"

"Oh, Heavens no. It was on-the-job-training as a NASA flight surgeon."

"Good grief, Emery. Is there anything you haven't done?"

"I've never been to McMurdo."

The next day Parker was sitting in the Frogship, a craft that was almost becoming familiar to him. But not quite.

Remote viewing the Chinese submarine sitting at 3000 feet on the bottom of the Blake Plateau had been surprisingly easy. His skills seemed to be improving with practice.

The flight across 2300 miles of the country would be a challenge for him, at least in part because he would have to remain out of the water off the coast of Georgia until 100 miles offshore. The edge of the continental shelf east of Sapelo Island, Georgia was too wide and shallow to risk a high-speed supercavitating entry. In a matter of seconds, the craft could plow straight into the bottom.

The only problem was, he really didn't know how to do that. But if Dr. Reed's idea was correct, maybe the ship could figure that out on its own. And if Reed was wrong, Parker's end would at least come swiftly, probably too fast for him to feel anything.

Sandy probably expected as much. But all things considered, the ride would have been worth it.

This would be Parker's fifth attempt to fly the alien beast. He felt like he was getting the hang of it, but this time he realized he might end up at a suborbital altitude in a ship that might or might not be pressure-tight. Granted he had survived such a flight before, but this time he would be combining a high-altitude flight with a presumably high-speed water entry followed by a deep ocean penetration inside a supercavitation bubble. That was something no human had ever done before.

The time had come, determined by a few brief minutes when there were no satellite transits to observe the opening of the deep hangar roof. As the roof began to open, Parker willed the ship to life, which cleared the ship's hull in front of him, and which started the gentle levitation off the hangar floor.

Once the roof was fully open, Parker and his craft were committed.

"Ship, let's do this thing."

The Frogship launched vertically in a blur, just like Siberia. Once again, Parker, overcome by G-forces, blacked out.

When he slowly regained his senses, his first awareness was of a voice coming through the earpiece in his helmet. The detached voice sounded distressed.

"Phantom One, how do you read? Phantom One, do you copy?"

Parker struggled to remember, then he realized, that was him. It was his call sign. He was supposed to answer his F-22 escort, Angel Four.

"Angel Four, Phantom One reads you loud and clear. What's my altitude, speed, and heading?"

"Sorry dude, but this is Angel Eight. You passed Four like he was standing still. I'm at my ceiling, and you're tracking fifty angels above me and still accelerating eastward. You'll be out of my radio range in a few miles. Right now, you're headed on course for the New Mexico border, and if this speed continues, you'll be in Texas in two minutes."

"Holy cow, how fast am I going?"

"Radar says roughly five thousand knots."

Parker only had one more thing to say before he was out of radio range of his tracking jet.

"Damn."

Houston was tracking Phantom One, but for some reason, it was having difficulty communicating. At over Mach 6, there may have been some ionization around the craft, but compared to spacecraft reentering the atmosphere, Phantom One was relatively slow. Radar had it projected as quickly passing over the barren expanse of the Texas Panhandle, followed by Oklahoma, then far above the Ouachita Mountains in Arkansas, just south of Little Rock, followed by the

Mississippi River which was so far below the craft it might not even have been visible to Parker.

As the craft crossed the Georgia border near Columbus and Fort Benning, it started descending at a rapid rate, about 25,000 feet per minute.

Inside the ship, Parker felt weightless as the ship was in free fall, but along an eastward trajectory that carried him ever closer to his constantly remote viewed target 260 miles offshore. In spite of his initial period of unconsciousness, Parker's mind now seemed to have a lock on the foreign sub's reported coordinates, and apparently, that lock was guiding his hypersonic craft.

Navy P3s had dropped sensors over the mid-region of the Blake Plateau as soon as the Chinese submarine had been detected. From the ship's location near the Blake Spur, an area fifty miles north and south of the sub's location was saturated with sensors. If the sub moved more than a few meters in any direction, it would be detected, and its location positively identified.

It wasn't clear to anyone on scene what they were to do if the sub did move. The rules of engagement were to not engage since the sub rested in international waters and was not in a particularly sensitive location. The only potential concern was that ballistic missile subs coming into and out of the sub base at Kings Bay, Georgia would be transiting through that area. But that was nothing new. American nuke submarines had been tracked by Russian subs for decades. If the Chinese now wanted a piece of that action, there wasn't much to be done about it, short of declaring war. Of course, first they had to be able to detect the American subs, and that was no easy task for any foreign Navy.

Some in Washington merely thought the Chinese were playing a chess game. The U.S. was routinely sending ships through the South China Sea to reaffirm our freedom of navigation in international waters. The Chinese sorely resented American presence in what they claimed as their ocean, but by international law, the South China Sea was not China's territorial waters. So in a tit for the United States' tat, it was supposed by some politicians that the Chinese were simply proving they could play that game as well. But in this case, their game was to plant their flag on a piece of the muddy bottom 250 miles from the U.S. coast.

Signals from the sensors were being analyzed at AUTEC, Andros Island, Bahamas, and also by a Navy ship that had replaced NOAA's *Gordon Gunter* on station over the sub.

At a change of the mid-watch one night, a Navy Chief noticed something different on the screens.

"How long has the sub been off the bottom?"

"It is? I didn't notice," the Sonar Operator, Petty Officer Briggs, said sheepishly. It had been his job to notice.

On a second computer screen, the Chief brought up the X and Y coordinates where the sub had been just two hours earlier. It had been parked at that position for the last week.

"And look here," the Chief said, alarmed. "It's now one-kilometer further west. And still moving west, at one knot."

"Oh shit," Petty Officer Briggs said.

"How the hell did you miss that?" the Chief yelled at the Petty Officer.

"I guess the alarms aren't working."

"The alarm in your head should be working," the Chief yelled, knowing that he would ultimately be blamed, not the Petty Officer.

"Now that you're awake, Briggs, how far off the bottom is it?"

"Fifty feet and the bottom is slightly rising."

"Do you believe that?"

"Yes, Chief I do. We checked the calibration this morning."

"Well, that's just great."

Parker and his ship were now approaching high clouds that zoomed past the cockpit window at an incredibly fast rate. There was not the slightest hint of turbulence, unlike a standard airplane. Once below the highest clouds he could see the Georgia coast fast approaching as the ship continued its descent.

When he realized they'd soon be crossing the shoreline, he had a troubling thought. Before the descent had begun, he'd been able to get a clear focus on the remotely viewed submarine, but now he couldn't. In fact, he seemed to be looking at empty space. The coordinates were clear in his mind, but the image was altered. It was still an underwater space, but only a muddy bottom remained where there used to be a submarine. That troubled him, but he couldn't figure out exactly why. Perhaps it was nothing more than fatigue—he'd been focusing mentally from before takeoff until now. Except for when he was unconscious.

A minute later, the ship was over Georgia's barrier islands. To those looking up at that moment, it could be seen as a silver streak in the sky over Sapelo Island. Somehow, perhaps because Parker willed it, the ship leveled off its descent, keeping a safe distance from the perilously shallow waters between the coastline and the Florida Hatteras Slope. But once beyond the slope, the bottom quickly sank to the level of the Blake Plateau, and the ship finally entered the water, riding effortlessly in a supercavitation bubble of air.

Startled fish too close to the ship's path were pummeled by intense pressure waves riding ahead of the almost supersonic craft, and then turned to mush by the impact of the collapsing cavitation bubble. The energy imparted to the water as the spacecraft passed was returned to the water through a mechanism much like the thunderclap of air collapsing around the void created by lightning. Water, being much denser than air, transmitted a great deal more energy, enough to violently shake anything close to the collapsing bubble.

Once past the Hatteras slope, the water began to clear as the ship entered the Gulf Stream. As the ship continued its descent, the water darkened enough for Parker to see the glow from the craft's large colored lights reflecting off blurs of unidentifiable things in the water. What Parker could see through the forward portion of the hull was being distorted by the shimmering bubble of air created by the force of the craft rocketing through the water, shattering the water into its gaseous components.

At a depth he guessed was about a thousand feet, total darkness prevailed. By Parker's estimation, he was a third of the way to the bottom where the submarine lay. He couldn't resist smiling at the surprise awaiting the Chinese.

Although Parker had no instruments to show him his depth, he did have a pressure gauge displaying the pressure inside the craft. As long as the needle remained pegged at one atmosphere, he was safe. If it began rising, then he knew the ship was no longer pressure-proof. It would have started the process of flooding, a process that would accelerate until he was crushed and drowned.

Unlike human-built submarines, he knew the craft would not implode. It had been built to withstand the water pressures at the depths of the Mariana Trench or deeper. It had also easily withstood the pressure where the craft had been recovered, at 2,500 feet in the DeSoto Canyon, so Parker had not been particularly concerned about this dive to three-thousand feet. He was much more concerned with what would happen when it encountered the interloping submarine. After all, he could see nothing in the blackness.

Without warning, Parker was slammed hard into the bottom of his seat as the craft briefly pulled Gs in an upward correction. It was a violent maneuver that only became clear as he saw the brief flash of what might have been a submarine hull zipping just below him, perilously close.

Onboard the Chinese submarine the sonar operator was screaming as he heard the supersonic, unidentifiable target on a direct heading towards the submarine. He and the skipper of the sub could only assume it was a new American weapon hunting them down. At the incredible rate of closure, they had no time to adjust course to thwart the attack.

At the moment of predicted impact, there was a deafening explosion that seemed to envelop the submarine from all directions, jarring the sensibilities of all onboard. However, the sound did not break any piping or damage any control surfaces. It seemed to pass without any permanent effect, except to terrify the entire crew.

As the sub's Skipper called for a damage assessment, and all stations reported normal operations, with no fires or flooding, the Captain called for full right rudder, bearing 090°. They would be leaving the area at flank speed, heading back to sea. They also decreased their depth to a safer level of 600 feet. They had been attacked at 2,500 feet, and at that depth, superstructure damage could destroy the submarine. The Commanding Officer did not know if the impulsive noise had weakened the hull, but he felt no reason to take chances.

The Chinese Captain had done what he had been ordered to do. The Americans had been shown that China could assume sea bottom autonomy at will, wherever they wanted, whenever they wanted, and there wasn't a damned thing the U.S. could do about it. Starting a war over a submarine squatter hundreds of miles from the U.S mainland was something the Americans would never do. They were far too practical and predictable.

And now it was the Skipper's duty to survive to report back that they had been attacked by a new American, supersonic weapon.

It was eerily silent as Parker and his ship sat on the bottom of the Blake Plateau, very close to where the Chinese sub should have been.

How did this go so wrong? he thought as his heart rate began to drop from stratospheric levels. He was shaking, worse than when he had been in a small plane skirting the edge of thunderstorms at night, over the ocean.

This could have ended very badly.

What a fool I am. I was saved only by the smarts of this machine. What if it hadn't been quick enough to respond?

My family would have been told that I had been lost at sea. They would never know what really happened.

Sandy's fears would have been realized.

I can't do this to her. I just can't.

Parker discovered on his first real mission with the alien craft that he could not track a target if it changed location. Now all he had to do was get off the bottom three-thousand feet down, and fly back to Nevada to report what he had realized. Like it or not, it seemed like a blind remote viewer would have to join the flight missions if they were to intercept mobile targets.

CHAPTER 18. JANUS SILVER

"Not only no, but hell no!"

The Director of National Intelligence pounded on his desk as two intelligence officials, one CIA and the other from the Defense Intelligence Agency had just explained why they had been arguing.

"I've already said I want Laura Smith on the Phobos mission. If the Space Corp wants Jason Parker as the pilot, then that's fine too, as long as he and Smith are still getting along. But I agree with the Agency that Joshua Nilsson is not going on the flight—I don't care if Parker wants him. He stays put. We're not risking our best asset."

Just like that, it was decided who would be flying the Triangle to Mars to rescue the surviving Space Corp astronaut on Phobos.

Technical Sergeant Clarice Williams had been both smart and lucky so far, often switching into survival mode, and carefully stretching her oxygen supply by sleeping and allowing her core temperature to drop to just above sustainable levels. To relieve the tedium of staring at the stars and black sky while waiting to die, she had made a trip over to the Mars side.

Watching the beautiful Martian landscape, trying unsuccessfully to spot the small and secret military colony there, she considered just sitting down and waiting for the oxygen supply in her suit to run out. By design, the oxygen would go before her carbon dioxide scrubber would fail, but if it didn't, and the helmet carbon dioxide got too high, she'd just vent some of the pressure in her suit, venting the CO_2 while simultaneously lowering the atmospheric pressure, accelerating the hypoxia which would eventually put her to sleep one last time. That had to be better than dying the way Robert had, from traumatic injuries and instantaneous decompression.

She thought it the ultimate irony that other Americans were so close on Mars, and yet they had no way to reach out to each other. As far as they knew, she was dead. Even though the Phobos station status reports had been relayed to the Mars side of Phobos, and then sent by telemetry to the Mars base, that relay had been destroyed by the crash of the resupply ship. The Mars station was blinded from the Phobos station telemetry.

There was still enough of the Phobos station left functioning to relay signals back to Earth whenever she was on the dark side. She sent a daily message back to Earth to give the status of her food, water, oxygen, and other essential supplies needed by a woman in her thirties. But if she ended things on the Mars side, then no one would know what happened, until her frozen and desiccated body was eventually found. If it ever was found.

Houston had been lying to her, saying help was on its way. She was no fool. Mars was at its greatest distance from Earth, on the far side of the solar system, so it would take many months for a rescue mission to arrive. And with the crash destroying half the base's food and oxygen supplies, she didn't have months.

Sadly, it occurred to her that if Robert had survived, they would have had to share the remaining oxygen, which would have given each of them even less time.

Why was Space Corp giving her false hope? There was no salvation coming.

She had not intended to watch the indication on her oxygen supply, but she had mentally calculated how much oxygen she would need to get back to the wrecked base, just in case she changed her mind. Oddly enough, when the numbers reached that critical level, she did exactly what she thought she wouldn't do. She got up, turned around, and started the transit back to Phobos base, to be with Robert's remains, and to live again to face another day, and another three circuits around the planet she would no longer be able to see.

The instinct to live was stronger than she'd thought.

After she got back and plugged in for an oxygen refill, she reported to Houston, and once again after a forty-minute delay Houston responded with the same inane message, "Help is on its way."

"Bullshit," she muttered to herself.

Dr. Emery Reed had sequestered Parker in his small office adjoining the examining room at the underground hangar complex near Yucca Flats, Nevada. While Parker was tucking his shirt back into his pants and zipping up, Reed flipped through the chart and summarized his findings.

"Well, your blood pressure is still perfect, you have no signs of illness or anything else that could impact your flight. So, I declare you cleared for flight."

"I could have told you that."

"Watch it, smartass. If I listened to you, I wouldn't be doing my job. And remember, I do know that pilots will do anything to keep from being grounded, so I never take their word for it when they say they're good to go."

"Why, Emery, I'm shocked."

"Now here's something that will shock you. I'm going with you to Mars."

"What?" Parker stared at him, then began to smile. "Ha-ha. I get it. Fat chance."

"No, I'm not kidding. The astronaut you're picking up may need medical assistance and attention."

"Oh."

Then after a pause, Parker followed with, "Okay, I see that, but wouldn't you want to send the more junior docs? There is a risk, you know. We've never tried this."

"I understand, but it's the right thing to do."

"What you're really saying, you sly dog, is you'd die to fly in a spaceship. Right?"

"Well, yeah, I guess so."

"So, we're going to be loading up the bird with medical gear? We'll have to find a way to secure it because the takeoff Gs are something else. If that stuff breaks loose, we could be killed."

"Not a problem. I used to select my gear and pack it whenever we traveled overseas with the POTUS and Veep."

"How much are we talking about?"

"Only a few Pelican cases. I'll have a portable X-ray machine, a miniature pharmacy, some trauma surgical equipment, blood stasis devices, stuff like that."

"All that fits in a few cases?"

"As long as money is no object."

Parker looked down at his watch. "Shit, I've got a meeting to go to. You coming?"

"I can't. Laura's my next exam."

"She's here already?"

"She arrived this morning. I imagine you'll see her at lunch."

The astronavigation session for the Janus Silver mission had already started as Parker quietly entered the back door of a large classroom with video screens covering the entire wall at the front of the room. The room was packed with maybe fifty personnel, some in uniform but most in civilian clothes. The number present surprised Parker since he didn't think many people knew about the upcoming flight.

You could tell the Washington civilians; they looked considerably overdressed for a desert environment.

And of course, it was easy to tell the NASA astrophysicists. Somehow the ones with badges looked stereotypical of engineers at NASA Houston. Some of them wore short-sleeved dress shirts, narrow ties, and thick black-rimmed glasses. They could have stepped right out of the seventies. The only thing missing was pocket protectors.

Curious, he thought.

At the front, a lady with a NASA badge, visible only when she turned to face her audience, was pointing to the path of a space probe to Mercury. Its course around the ecliptic plane of the solar system was laid out on the screen, and animated to show the probe's looping path.

"We used a gravity assist from Earth for our first acceleration, then headed for Venus for another gravity assist, looping around the solar system before finally getting into position for several high-speed passes by Mercury."

"That's not what we're doing," said a tall man in a grey Space Corp uniform who rudely interrupted. "We're going to Venus and Mercury, past the sun, and then straight on to Mars."

She sighed. "I know that General. I'm just showing how we got that close to the Sun, once upon a time. Gravity assists were essential."

Someone else from across the room now interrupted.

"But that's not an alien ship, and you're not thinking like an alien."

Parker turned his head to look. It sounded like Peter Green, but from where he sat, Parker couldn't see him.

"And what exactly does that mean, Dr. Green?" the lady in charge asked.

"You're constraining yourselves to deal with a craft with deficient thrust, needing incredibly inefficient means to gain velocity."

"Of course."

"And by so doing, you're constraining yourself to maneuver within the confines of the ecliptic."

Holding his own laser pointer in his hand, he pointed to the vast volume of empty space above and below the planetary ecliptic. "If I was piloting an alien ship, this is where I'd go if I were planning to go really fast. Nothing in my way until I reached Mars on the other side of the Sun."

"You don't need to lecture us. NASA is intimately aware of the properties of our solar system. Everything outside of the ecliptic is mostly empty space," she reminded him.

Good for her, Parker thought. *Peter's sounding a bit arrogant.*

"Nothing's empty. Space is filled with dark matter, dark energy. All of that might be used for propulsion."

Hey, Parker thought, *that was my idea.*

The lady tapped one of her feet in exasperation. "I'm well aware you're a dark matter and dark energy researcher, and I'm educated enough to know that so-called empty space is filled with it, but the fact remains, we don't know what IT is. And we certainly don't know how it could be used to propel the ships. Unless you do. Do you?"

"No, but I'm damned sure the aliens know."

She shook her head. "If they do, they're not talking. Unless they're talking to you. Are they, Peter?"

Parker could hear a few faint chuckles in the room.

"No, they don't."

Now Parker had no choice except to speak up. "I get what Peter is saying.

"Oh, Dr. Parker," the NASA lady said, "I'm glad you could make it."

Her voice had just a tinge of sarcasm in it. Of course, that might be the way she always talked.

Parker continued. "Dr. Green and I had this same conversation not long ago. But let me tell you this. It doesn't matter what all this theoretical machination determines, the craft has a mind of its own, and I personally don't think any of our minds can match it."

"What's your intuition about the path you'll take?" she asked.

Parker laughed. "Intuition? Considering this august assemblage of minds, that's funny. But if I were a gambling man, I'd say there is a lot more empty space in the solar system than that along the planetary orbits. So, I'd say the planetary path is improbable."

"You don't think planetary gravity is important?"

"Not to our craft. And besides, if you'll humor Peter just a bit, if there were anything at all to his musings about dark matter in the solar system, it likely would have been cleared over the eons by the passage of the planets. There shouldn't be much of it left in the ecliptic."

"NASA and the Space Corp went to a lot of trouble to get us here for this meeting," the lady reminded Parker, "and you're saying we're wasting our time?"

"Our musings are very entertaining to think about, but I bet you this craft will surprise us all. It surprises me every time I fly it."

The lady in charge said, "Then I guess we'll just have to wait and see. For now, folks, we need to clear the room. We have another group coming in."

With that, those assembled began to noisily excuse themselves, with many giving Parker sideways glances as they left. Except for Peter Green. He approached Parker.

Peter laughed. "I'm glad I set you up with our conversation the other evening."

Peter shook Parker's hand, vigorously.

Parker said, "As for what you all were saying, I think the ship knows which way to go."

"We'll soon find out," Green said. "The ship has a tracker on it now, and these eggheads will be poring over the data during your entire flight out and back."

Parker gave Green a strange look.

"Uh, we've never flown it with a tracker attached," Parker said, sounding alarmed.

Green looked surprised. "Really? I heard you flew it with a Limpet mine attached, until it fell off."

"That's true, in Russia. But the Limpet wasn't transmitting high powered signals. Since the lights on this thing are somehow moderating its power source, and lights are electromagnetic radiation, a high-frequency tracker transmitter might interfere."

"You think so?"

"Who do I need to see to get the damned thing removed?" Parker asked.

"Don't ask me. I have no idea."

Parker's reaction was stern. "We're not flying until the thing gets gone."

CHAPTER 19. DEPARTURE

The morning before departure, the three crew members were introduced to their robot assistant.

"Jason, meet Tobias II," Laura said. She was beaming.

Tobias II was an anthropomorphic robot that looked nothing like a classical mechanical robot. It looked very much like an American male of medium height, five foot nine inches tall with realistic-looking hair and soft, textured skin. He was dressed in a Space Corp grey jumpsuit with the winged Space Corp emblem on it.

Parker was not in the least bit pleased that his request to have Joshua Nilsson on board had been denied. He didn't need a robot. He needed the best damned remote viewer there was.

"What can this thing do for us?" Parker asked, obviously irritated.

"For one thing, it can remain conscious regardless of the number of G's we experience."

"I don't care. What's its history?"

"It's an updated version of the robot used for unmanned shipments to Phobos and Mars. The first Tobias had an amazing success rate as a navigator and pilot, and this version is even better. Tobias never screwed up a delivery, and best of all, it never complained about the boring trip."

"But what can it do for us?"

"I don't know, but it's better than nothing," Laura said. "And he's a pretty good conversationalist."

"Long as I can tell it to shut up. I don't want a yakking mouth at a critical phase of flight."

"It does have a quiet mode," she said. "And in that mode, it's a high definition recorder. Our lead technician will give you and Emery a rundown on its operation after lunch."

"How'd you get to be so knowledgeable about this robot?"

"I've spent time with it. He's kind of cute, for a robot."

Parker and Reed raised their eyebrows.

"I saw that," she said smiling. "I was asked to take it home and document the naturalness of his verbal skills in a natural setting. He's a lot more interesting to talk to than most men I've dated."

"I'm not sure how that will help us, but we'll see. Frankly, I'm more concerned about that tracking transponder. Did it get removed?"

"I was told it had been," Laura said, nodding her head.

"Good."

The day for departure dawned with its usual desert coolness and pink clouds in the eastern sky. Parker, Smith and Dr. Reed were in place and awaiting launch clearance from NASA who had been monitoring the global circulation of space junk. The International Space Station was safely on the other side of the Earth just in case the launch of a spacecraft with a mind of its own took an unexpected course.

Compared to the position of the ISS, the clearance of satellites and other space junk was a more delicate and imprecise matter. NASA needed to have some idea what path the ship would take, and rather than accept Parker and Green's notion that the ship would not follow the solar ecliptic, they were betting that it would. So the path followed by the sun and moon in the daylight sky was the path they were hoping to find an empty spot through which the ship could safely fly. If the ship departed on any other course, survival would simply be a matter of luck.

That clear launch window was just moments away as the three spacesuited astronauts were seated, ready to go.

"This doesn't look like any aircraft I've seen before," Reed said, twisting his head left then right. "I won't know what it's doing."

"No worries," Parker said. "You'll have plenty of situational awareness. We have ship environmental control system instruments for you to monitor. The most critical are the internal pressure and temperature monitors, G-meter, and inertial navigation system. Other than that, there isn't much else we can monitor from inside the craft. And frankly, no one knows if the inertial navigation system will work on this flight."

"But it doesn't guide the ship, does it?"

"No. It just tells us where we've been, and where we might be headed next if nothing changes. I'm afraid you'll have to trust my brain to tell the ship where to go."

"Should I be worried?" Reed asked.

Laura was the one who answered. "You don't want to live forever, do you, Reed?"

"Very reassuring, Laura," Reed said sarcastically, shaking his head.

Laura assumed an uncharacteristically pensive look about her.

"Actually, Emery, I feel very much at home in this bird, and I must admit I have no idea why."

"And Jason, what am I supposed to do with this thing?"

Reed was looking back at Tobias, the anthropomorphic robot that had been fitted into the ship overnight.

"Nothing. It's just along for the ride."

Reed was tasked with keeping an eye on the instruments, such as they were, while Parker focused on their target, the Martian moon of Phobos. Laura was there to provide her strangely gotten insight on the alien mind, especially if her perception had anything to do with increasing the odds of surviving this inaugural space flight in an alien craft.

Parker and Laura Smith had already briefed Dr. Reed that launch might render them unconscious, and no one could guess where they would be when they regained consciousness. NASA had done what they could to provide tightly fitted water-filled suits for launch, with the hope that the suits would help the crew regain consciousness sooner than if they only wore the usual G-suits for fighter aircraft.

Centrifuge tests had shown the water suits were somewhat useful, but the centrifuges could not exceed 12 G acceleration. And on two occasions now, the alien craft had. So, once again, the three crew members were little more than well-educated guinea pigs, a point not missed by the National Academy of Sciences who as a body could not understand why intelligent people would expose themselves to that level of risk without some guarantee of survival. But for the crew on board, some risks were worth taking, both personally and for the greater good of the nation.

At the launch minus three-minute mark, Parker visualized energizing the craft, turning on its lights and clearing the viewing window just as he had in Russia. The lights came on as expected, and at the two-minute mark, he attempted the delicate process of levitating the craft about five feet off the ground.

On the last flight, he could feel himself developing a finer control of the ship, and he hoped he could repeat it this time. But the most important thing this bird had taught him was humility. Sometimes things went as planned, and sometimes not. Perhaps that's an unavoidable consequence of working with a quantum computer embedded within the shell of the craft. In the quantum world, nothing is definite.

But to Parker's relief, it worked this time. He had it hovering just off the hangar floor.

At the one-minute mark, the massive roof of the heavily disguised complex slid back, exposing the craft to the sky, and above that, the now invisible stars hidden by the sun which would soon break above the horizon.

Due to the tight time constraints, Parker had agreed to let Laura launch the craft using her James Patterson-inspired invocation. It had worked once, so perhaps it would work again. They had no time to spare.

As the final seconds ticked down, Parker looked back at Reed who nodded, then over to Laura. She was doing her best to concentrate and take mental control of the craft.

At the T minus four-second mark, Laura began speaking, one forceful word per second.

"Up ...up... and... away."

Nothing happened.

Laura looked at Parker with a distressed look on her face as their planned departure time slipped by.

"Don't pause between words," Parker said. "Just blurt it out, like you did in Siberia."

She gritted her teeth. "Goddammit, up up and away!"

And they were gone.

"Wake up, darlings." The sound was from a male with a pronounced Southern accent.

"I have a surprise for you."

Reed, the crew member with the highest G-tolerance, was the first one to begin processing what Tobias had said.

"You have a surprise?" Reed said, not fully comprehending what had been said.

"For sure. We're headed right for the moon."

At that, Reed's mind and body sprang into action. He leaned forward and shook both Parker and Laura.

They shook off the inevitable mental confusion caused by the sudden loss of consciousness, and looked forward.

Sure enough, ahead of them lay the moon, already three times larger than usual, and growing rapidly.

"Holy hell, we're in the ecliptic," Parker said. "How long have you been awake?"

"About two seconds before I woke you. Didn't you hear Tobias's warning?"

Laura looked at Parker in disbelief. "We're headed straight for it. Quit daydreaming Jason. Focus on Mars."

"What do you think I'm doing? Maybe this craft's not so smart after all," Parker said.

Reed calmly reported back, "But we're making great speed. At this rate, we should impact in less than five minutes."

"Yes, I agree with your estimation," Tobias said. "Actually, it will be four minutes and 37 seconds."

"Four minutes? What the hell can I do in four minutes?" Parker asked rhetorically.

"Pray," Tobias suggested.

"Feels like we're still accelerating," Parker said.

"We are. But were accelerating at a slower rate than takeoff. It's looking like a steady five-G pull."

Laura looked at Parker, clearly distressed. "Slow it down. Give us more time."

"You see any brakes on this thing?"

Reed turned toward Laura, "Parker can't do it alone. You launched us, so you slow us down."

"I'll see what I can do."

"Wish I could help," Tobias said, "but I can't talk to this ship."

In Houston, Mission Control was chaotic. Of all the things they had anticipated, losing the U.S.'s only alien craft on her first space voyage by flying it into the moon, had not been considered. The senior executive Director in the control room had not voiced her fear, but she was thinking it, to the exclusion of almost anything else. Parker had refused to fly with a tracker, but at this Director's insistence, they had covertly hidden one in an inconspicuous place, deep inside the recently donated robot, Tobias II. And now, it looked like something, perhaps the tracker, was causing the craft to lose control at an incredible speed.

"What do we do?" a technician asked.

The Director didn't answer. She knew there was absolutely nothing that could be done. The fate of the mission lay only in the craft and its luckless crew.

She also knew the crash investigation would undoubtedly pin the blame for the ship's loss on the stubbornness of the executive in charge, namely her, in total opposition to the demands of the only man in the U.S. who was able to fly it.

Her career was over.

With the lunar landscape growing larger in the view out front, Laura silently prayed. Parker looked over at her and said. "It's not working."

Reed said, "Still accelerating, 5 Gs."

Parker felt a sinking pain in his stomach unrelated to the acceleration. "What the hell is it doing?" he shouted. "What the hell!"

Reed called back, "It slowed to 4.2 Gs."

"Not enough."

Just then the view out front shifted an almost imperceptible amount toward one edge of the moon.

"Did I imagine that?" Parker said.

"No, the INS picked it up. Our velocity vector is still going to impact, but it may not be straight in."

"Well, that's great consolation." It took a great deal of effort for Parker to keep from reaching for the stick that wasn't there to steer with.

"We're still shifting to the right," Laura called out. Her voice sounded almost jubilant.

"What *is* it doing?" Parker said.

Laura said, "I feel sideways acceleration."

"Let me check," Reed responded. A moment later, he had news. "We are accelerating laterally. We may just miss it."

Parker said, "Laura, you can pray for me any day you like."

"It's going to be close," came Reed's voice, "but I think this is intentional. It may be a slingshot past the moon. Using a gravity assist, maybe."

"Well that's a damn paltry assist," Parker said.

"Better than nothing," Reed answered.

Parker said, "I hope the cameras are recording. This should be spectacular, a high-speed fly-by of the moon. If we miss."

"Big *if*," Laura retorted.

The mountains of the moon had grown to Mt Everest size, and the radial acceleration was increasing to the point of being uncomfortable.

"We're turning," Parker said.

"Skimming the ranges," Reed said, beginning to grit his teeth, bearing down against the new G-forces. "Or so it looks like here. And we're still accelerating."

Inside the cockpit, things grew silent as Parker and his crewmates simultaneously bore down against the Gs from the turn. Parker also uttered his own silent prayer. It couldn't hurt.

"Jeee-*zus*, Jason," Laura said under her breath, "you can't drive this thing better than this?"

"It's on autopilot."

"You mean autocrash?"

Lunar mountain tops streaked by in a blur, and then the view out front went black.

For a moment, the cockpit remained silent.

Then Laura said, "I think I just peed myself."

Parker, still trying to visualize Mars, asked: "Emery, where are we headed?"

Reed smiled, staring at the INS but did not answer immediately.

"Dr. Reed," Parker repeated, "where are we going?"

"It tells us where we've been, and not where we're going, but it looks to me like we're now headed at a right angle to the ecliptic."

Laura looked over at Reed with a quizzical look on her face. "Meaning what?"

"We're headed to about as deep space as we're likely to find on this trip," Parker said.

"Why couldn't it have done that in the first place?" Laura asked rhetorically.

"Good job, Ms. Laura," Tobias said.

"What? Why did you say that?"

"I suggested you pray, and you did."

"Hate to burst your bubble, Tobias," Laura snapped, "but that had nothing to do with you."

The Red Phone rang in mission control, and after a couple of seconds while the person picking up the phone listened intently, he handed the phone to the Director. With some hesitation, she took it.

"No, Mr. President, we have no idea why it did that. But it seems to be on course now."

She listened again for another moment.

"Yes, sir, the spacesuits do accommodate bodily waste, but we're hoping they haven't needed it, yet."

The Director looked around the room, checking the monitors.

"Yes, Sir, we're all waiting, and they are still accelerating, so we don't have an estimated arrival time."

"Yes, Mr. President, it was my idea to put the tracker on the craft. Actually, we placed it in the robot. Parker would never think to look there."

For the first time in several minutes, she was smiling.

"I'll pass your appreciation on to the rest of the team."

As she hung up the phone, the room erupted in cheers. Disaster had been averted, and President Whitney was pleased.

As the noise quieted down, she spoke so all could hear, "We still have a long way to go folks. And we still don't know how this thing works, so steel yourself for any eventuality."

CHAPTER 20. CRUISE

There was a profound silence in the cockpit, silence like that before conception when what is, was not. There was no engine noise, no vibration, and nothing outside to suggest movement. The crew members were suspended in time except for the gentle push at their back, reminding them of low but steady acceleration.

The 20-G launch that rendered them unconscious had accelerated them within seconds to the escape velocity of 25,000 miles per hour and sent them to the moon within minutes. The craft's acceleration had now decreased to the point where it was only barely perceptible, but nevertheless, within half an hour, their velocity had increased well beyond that of any other man-made spacecraft.

Physically, the three crewmembers could move around, but none left their seats. If they were like Parker, the reality of what had just happened to them was finally sinking into their still somewhat woozy brain.

During the excitement of preparation, he'd had no time to really think about this mission, other than in grandiose, overly-simplistic ways. After a total of four flights, Parker thought he knew what to expect, but he had been entirely wrong. The craft had been spit out of the Earth's atmosphere as if it was a toxic substance being vomited from the planet's innards.

None of the brightest bulbs on the pre-navigation team had anticipated that the craft would come within meters of colliding with the tallest of the lunar mountains. And to what effect? For a ship seemingly immune to the effects of gravity, it seemed to be using lunar gravity to affect a change in course from the solar system ecliptic, to turn perpendicular to it.

And now it was headed in the general direction of the sun. Mars, hidden by the solar glare, was on the far side of its orbit around the sun, relative to the Earth. Would the craft choose to graze the sun as well? If so, the spacecraft and the astronauts contained inside would be consumed by the heat of thermonuclear fires.

But Parker thought the craft was smarter than that. It had a mind of its own, which was likely far superior to that of humans, or human machines. Arguably, any advanced brain operates on a precept of survival. It would not intentionally destroy itself.

Parker shifted his attention to Laura. Did she have the same level of trust in this craft as he did? If so, then why?

And more importantly, why would the nation's top intelligence officers so willingly risk their only extraterrestrial alien expert? It seemed to him that they not only allowed her to go on this dangerous trip but in fact, they seemed to be directing her to go.

Why would that be?

"Well, that was a trip."

The voice came from Reed, a short way behind Parker.

"I'm going to go check on the medical supplies. Want to make sure they're still secured after all those Gs."

Reed unstrapped and stood, a little wobbly due to the acceleration along the axis of flight.

"Before you leave," Parker asked, "how fast are we going now?"

"We're hauling ass. There are now so many decimals places I can't even keep count."

"That not very useful," Laura said.

"I'll give you a better answer when I get back. I really need to assure myself we still have good medical cargo. Otherwise, there's no point to my being here."

As Reed moved around an interior wall separating the cockpit from the passenger and cargo section of the craft, the silence returned.

What's with Reed? He was the previous President's physician, and he's been ordered to ride along in a craft we don't understand? This could be a suicide mission.

It almost was, and they were just getting started.

So what's so damned important about one Space Corp enlisted woman who's been stuck on a wrecked observation post? Is she worth three lives, and the only alien craft the U.S. has?

Parker looked over at Laura, engrossed in adjusting her harness. Something didn't add up.

It didn't take long for Reed to return.

"All's well with the gear. Won't be a wasted trip, after all."

"Good. Now buckle back in," Parker said.

As Reed strapped in, he asked, "We expecting rough air, Captain?"

"You gotta watch out for those vacuum pockets."

"By the way," Reed said nonchalantly, "we're now going roughly 840 thousand miles an hour and climbing."

"Damn," Parker said. "Too bad it doesn't feel like it."

Laura remained silent, looking dead ahead into the black emptiness. The sun was in the corner of their view, which provided a comforting indication that they were not headed straight for it. *The Frog Ship must realize the wisdom of remaining a safe distance away from stars,* Parker thought.

"I've been thinking," Reed continued. "Assuming we survive this expedition, this ship needs a real name. An epic name, something suitable for future legends about it and its fearless crew."

"Fearless, huh? Is that what we are?" Laura asked.

"Of course," Reed answered.

"Well, you did hear me say I peed myself back there."

"You probably weren't the only one. Guys don't talk about such things."

"Offends your masculinity. I get it," she said. "So, what name are you thinking of?"

"Actually, I do have something in mind. But I'll share that with you later. I want to try and figure out what this thing is doing, and how."

"Ha. When you figure that out," Parker said, "a whole lot of folks will want to know how you did it."

Laura looked back at Dr. Reed. "He's a Brainiac, Jason. Don't you know you have to be, to be the President's physician?"

Parker looked back at Reed, smiling. "Well if he's so damned smart, why is he riding all the way across the solar system in a ship we don't understand, and which may not bring us back?"

"I could ask you the same thing, Jason."

Parker laughed. "And I'm not sure I have a good answer. My wife thinks I'm a flipping fool to fly this thing."

Without looking back, Laura said, "I assume she doesn't know about this mission. Right?"

"Of course not."

And she doesn't want to know about it, either, Jason thought.

"Good. Just checking."

"What about you, Laura?" Parker asked. "ONI only has one person like you. Why in hell would they risk you on such a crazy adventure?"

"The person we're rescuing is vital to us."

"Rumor has it she's just some enlisted chick who got the worst duty in the solar system."

"She's doesn't see it that way."

"How do you know?"

"She knows stuff—important stuff."

"What kind of stuff?"

"Stuff you don't need to know."

"Oh, so we're risking our lives for something we don't need to know. That's just great."

"Don't give me that bullshit, Jason. You're risking your life because you get to fly the hottest ship known to man. That's all."

"Well, now that you put it that way, yeah. That's basically right."

Laura smiled at him. "I know you, Jason. Don't ever forget that."

The group remained silent until Reed couldn't stand the suspense anymore.

"About that. You two have known each other for a long time?"

Parker laughed. "You haven't heard?"

"Heard what?"

Parker looked at Laura and said, "Are you going to tell him, or should I?"

"Knock yourself out," she said.

"Well, there's a chance we won't survive this, so you might as well hear the story. It will amuse you."

Laura cut a stern glance over at Parker.

"Laura believes in reincarnation, and she believes with all her heart that we were paired romantically in a past life."

"Soulmates. I get it," Reed said. "A lot of people think that when they find a natural affinity for each other."

"Except this is different. She believes we were Frogmates."

Reed's eyes got big, but he said nothing.

"Not the kind of frogs we have at home, amphibians, but extraterrestrial alien Frogs. Like the ones who built this spaceship."

Reed smiled. "You're shitting me, right?"

"No, that's why we're the only two people on Earth, other than the odd Troll or two, who can fly this bird."

Laura wasted no time in snapping at Parker. "Since you brought it up smart-aleck, why do you think we can fly it?"

"Well, to be honest, it's a mystery to me."

"So don't dismiss it out of hand," she warned him sharply.

"Is what he said, true?" Reed asked Laura.

She sighed. "Well, I didn't expect Jason to add so many personal details, but I did give him permission to speak. I won't make that mistake again."

"I'm just a little surprised ODNI hired you, Laura. That sounds a bit schizophrenic, from a physician standpoint. Do they know?"

"Actually, yes," Laura replied. "That's why I got the job."

"So what is your job, Laura?" Reed asked. "Advisor on alien affairs? What does that mean?"

"It's complicated."

Apparently wanting to deflect any more personal questions, Laura asked Reed, "What's our speed?"

"Still climbing. I think the light speed needle is coming off the baseline. No human being has ever been this fast. And it keeps getting faster."

"Awesome," Laura said excitedly. "So, if we near the speed of light, will Jason no longer be a dick?"

There was utter silence in the ship as it continued to accelerate.

As planned, the crew took turns sleeping, with one person awake at all times, keeping track of their progress towards Mars and its two moons. While Parker slept, Laura took over the visualization job, which she seemed to do well enough to keep the ship on course. While Reed slept, either Laura or Parker also had the watch. In other words, neither Laura nor Parker trusted Reed to have the watch alone. He was not, as he admitted—frog-minded—whatever that meant.

During one of Laura's sleep periods, Parker had found his mind wandering quite a bit, and still the position of the ever-enlarging Mars out in front of them had not shifted. Perhaps the navigational lock was more robust than they had imagined. Maybe it was true that the human or Frog mind was not as essential as they had believed.

Not long after the Sun slid out of view behind the Frogship, the three astronauts began to sense the gradually increasing G-forces of deceleration. When they first sensed deceleration Mars was nothing more than a red dot in the distance, but at the incredible velocity they were still traveling, it soon reached the size of a pencil eraser viewed from the end, at arm's length. At that point, their deceleration forces had reached two Gs. Due to the growing deceleration, movement about the cabin was difficult if not impossible, and all three of them settled into their seats and securely buckled their harnesses.

"Jesus, Reed," Laura said, "how long is this going to keep up?"

"The computer says several more hours unless the deceleration forces get worse. And I have a sneaking suspicion they will get worse because at this rate, we'll overshoot Mars entirely."

"Well, that would suck," Laura said, crinkling her nose. "Jason, can't you visualize a little better?"

"The visualization gets us there, but the ship determines exactly how we get there."

"Yeah, and I think the ship was made by Frogs," Laura continued. "We have no idea how many Gs they can tolerate."

"Thanks for reminding me," Parker said.

Parker had remained relatively quiet once the Gs starting coming on. He had in fact been absorbed in doing precisely what Laura asked for, trying to communicate to the ship's quantum computer the fact that their G tolerance was limited. Of course, he couldn't know if the ship's brain cared. It had been given a mission, and it was programmed to complete that mission without destroying the ship. If the ship's occupants took a beating, well, that was not its primary concern.

The three of them remained mostly silent while trying to adjust physically and mentally to the new deceleration forces. Then Reed spoke.

"I know the name."

"Name for what?" Parker asked.

"The ship. It should be called Dioscuri."

"Dios what?"

"Curi. Dioscuri. You say it like *Dye-ohs-cure-ee.*"

"What the heck is that?" Laura asked.

Apparently, Tobias could not resist showing his erudition.

"The Dioscuri were twin Greek demigods who helped sailors with safe naval voyages. Their individual names were Castor and Pollux."

"You're a robot of many talents," Laura said. "I didn't know you were a student of Greek mythology."

"I like to read."

"In all honesty," Parker said, "I figure once we get tired of calling this thing XFS, some politician's kid will insist on calling it the *Enterprise*."

Reed said, "Maybe, but if we survive this trip, I think it deserves something more original and dignified than Enterprise."

"Makes sense to me, but I've never heard of the Dioscuri."

"Then maybe you should read some more," Tobias said.

Laura's head whipped around to look at Tobias, who seemed to ignore her glance.

"Don't be rude," Laura said.

Ignoring her, Tobias continued. "Castor and Pollux are stars in the constellation Gemini, 51 and 33 light-years away respectively. The American Gemini space program was named after that constellation."

Parker looked at Laura and said, "You said that thing has a quiet mode?"

"Don't be rude," Tobias admonished Parker.

"You're getting this close, Tobias," Parker said holding up his right hand with thumb and forefinger spread about two inches apart.

"Close to what, Jason?"

"The kill switch."

"Oh."

Things were quiet in the ship for the next few minutes.

Eventually, Laura's curiosity was too much to abide total silence.

"Emery, why name the ship after twins?"

"Because it's both a submarine and a spaceship."

"Oh, that makes sense, I suppose."

"So, what does XFS stand for?" Reed asked.

Parker and Laura gave each other a knowing look, smiling best they could through the forces of deceleration.

"You tell him," Parker suggested.

"It was actually my boss's idea," Laura said. "The more I talked about Jason's and my experience on the Frog ship, he started jokingly calling it the Ex-Frog Ship. Some Admiral heard that, and next thing you know, the official title was changed from Canyoneer to XFS."

"Ah, I see," Reed said, "so D.C. likely won't change it, but I do think Dioscuri is more fitting."

"Dioscuri is harder to say," Parker noted, "but it has class. And considering all the calculations and energy transformations this ship is going through, I'd say it deserves a classy name."

"So true," Laura agreed.

After several more hours of constant deceleration, Mars had grown large in their view, and both moons could be seen. Diminutive Phobos, closest to the planet, was orbiting at breakneck speed, much faster than they had anticipated. It's one thing to know the moon's exact velocity down to meters per second, but something altogether to see it in action.

"Are you two thinking what I'm thinking?" Parker asked.

"Don't know about you," Reed said, "but I'm wondering how we're going to land on that little thing."

"This is where it gets interesting," Parker replied. "The manned and robotic ships managed to do it, so I'm hoping this bird is at least as smart."

"That's why you need a highly intelligent pilot like me," Tobias said.

"Except you're not piloting anything, Tobias."

"That's true. But I should be."

"Maybe someday, Tobi," Laura said.

"Oh, I like that," Parker said. "From henceforth you're Tobi, not Tobias."

Tobias seemed to sigh, which is an unnatural thing for a robot. But somehow it managed it just before it said, "Whatever floats your boat."

As Tobias spoke, the deceleration dropped to about one G according to Reed's inertial computer.

"Wow, that feels better," Laura said. "I was getting a bigtime wedgie, and there wasn't a damn thing I could do about it."

"Gs are still dropping," Reed updated them. "We should be getting light in our seats pretty soon."

"Awesome. I'm kind of missing the weightlessness," Laura said.

"According to this," Reed noted, "we should be getting there any second."

Parker spoke up. "Looks like we're orbiting Mars folks."

Parker looked back at Reed. "I don't think we thought this through. Emery, hop up here and take my place next to Laura. I want to keep an eye on that readout."

"Okay, but I don't think I can hop. Float, I can do."

The two men passed each other, and Laura looked over at Reed. She was smiling again, something a lot easier to do at zero Gs than 2 Gs.

"Welcome to the best seats in the house," she said.

"I'm just hoping Parker doesn't lose his concentration."

"As I thought, we're closing in on the same orbit as Phobos, and it's behind us where we can't see it."

"Oh, great," Laura groaned. "Can it run into us?"

"Potentially, yeah. This is where I hope your trust in this machine is justified."

"Your Inertial Navigation System doesn't show us Phobos?"

"No. It knows where we are, but not where Phobos is. We don't have radar."

"Maybe it's a terrible time to ask," Laura said, "but why not?"

"This hull is impervious to solar radiation and cosmic rays," Parker answered, "which keeps our radiation exposure down to nil, but it also makes it impenetrable to radar. And we don't dare mount anything on the outside of the hull since we're not sure how the hull works."

"I better get a raise out of this," Laura remarked out of both fear and annoyance.

"Look," Reed shouted.

From the front, a rounded rocky surface slowly rose into view.

"We're landing," Parker said.

"Whoa Nelly," came the Southern voice from the back.

After another five seconds with the rocky terrain rising slightly higher, they felt a bump. A metallic thud reverberated throughout the hull.

"We've landed!" Laura said. "Good job, Jason."

"I didn't do shit. The ship did it all."

Chapter 21. Twenty Feet

The three space-suited astronauts entered the airlock together. When the outer lock opened in the hull of the ship, Parker and Reed stood at the precipice with Laura beside them.

"Holy Mother of God," Reed said, "we're actually on a moon of Mars."

"What a kick-ass view of the stars," Parker said gleefully.

"It's a long way down, boys," she said, "and I don't see a ladder."

"Not to worry," Parker said. "This moon has a minuscule gravity. We'll float down."

"You first then, Mr. Confidence."

"Hold my beer."

Parker stepped off the edge and slowly floated to the smooth rock surface.

"See, the laws of physics still apply."

Seeing that nothing terrible had happened to Parker, the others quickly joined him.

Parker first inspected the ship which seemed none the worse for wear.

Reed was scanning the horizon for his patient. "After the longest house call in history, I sure hope my patient shows up. How far away from the base are we?"

"Can't be far," Parker answered. "This whole rock is only fourteen miles in diameter. We landed on the side away from Mars, which is the side the base is on."

"You couldn't have gotten us closer, Jason?" said Laura ribbing him.

"Considering how fast this moon is traveling, I did well to get us within walking distance. Besides, I don't want to risk landing on the wreckage."

"Or Sergeant Williams," Reed offered.

"So true," Parker said.

"She should be homing in on my beacon," Laura said. "But I suggest we meet her halfway."

Having looked at the comms status panel in her helmet's heads up display, Laura added, "Her beacon is still operational, so that's a good sign." Pointing her arm at an approximately ten o'clock angle from the direction they were facing, she said, "And my sensor says we should walk that way."

"Why walk when we can bounce?" Parker asked, making a jump in the right direction, a jump that pushed him ten feet into the air. "I think the trick is to bounce forward, not straight up. But don't push off too hard—no telling where you'll end up."

"Yeah, you don't want to get to Mars the hard way," Laura muttered.

They bounded off in the direction Laura had pointed, trying their newfound bouncing skill. It took some getting used to, but was fun, and took their mind off the seriousness of their task, at least for a few minutes.

Perhaps it was because she was the youngest, most athletic and coordinated of the three, but Laura got out ahead of the rest by a good fifty yards. She froze at the edge of a shallow depression, the remains of a small crater.

"It's here," she said.

"Any sign of Williams?" Parker asked.

"Not yet."

When Parker and Reed caught up with Laura, they saw the partially shattered remains of what had been the Phobos station. From one side the station appeared perfectly intact, but the side closest to them was destroyed. And sitting in a chair as if awaiting their arrival, was the naked body of a human.

The body's sex could not be immediately determined due to physical damage to the body, in the chest, midriff, and pelvic area.

"It must be her husband," Parker said.

"I hope it's not her," Laura answered.

"Clarice, if you can hear us, we're here to take you home."

Very gingerly, the three voyagers began to inspect the wreckage, looking for the best way to approach the intact portion of the facility without tearing their suits on jagged debris scattered by what was clearly an impact of a large object at high speed, based on the wide dispersion of the metallic remains.

It seemed miraculous that as much of the structure remained intact as it did. Apparently, there was enough structural integrity left to support Clarice Williams during her time alone on the moon. But where she was now, was a mystery.

Parker examined a collection of large oxygen cylinders stacked outside the complex. A quick glance at the color-indicating pressure gauges show that many of them were empty, meant to be refilled by the supply craft that crashed. But not all were empty. It looked like there was enough left to supply Williams for another few weeks.

Out of the corner of his eye, Parker caught movement. Turning to his right, he saw a spacesuit. "I'm here."

It was Williams.

Strangely, she did not move closer, but Laura almost sprinted with her hops till she was next to the immobile Clarice Williams.

"I can't believe you're really here," Williams said. "I thought I was hallucinating. Earth is so far."

"This ship of ours can really move," Laura said, wanting to hug her. But spacesuits don't accommodate hugs very well. "We'll have you home within a couple of days."

"What are you doing out here?" Reed asked. "Isn't it dangerous without radiation protection? You're so exposed."

"Not really. The crash dug out a little hollow over there," she said, pointing behind her, "with an overhang that protects me from radiation whenever I go outside. Plus, I can hide if I want to."

"Hide from what?" Parker asked.

"Plus, I was using up my oxygen operating the outer lock to gain entry."

Parker repeated his question. "Hide from what?"

Williams looked toward Laura, who shook her head in her helmet.

Williams changed the subject. "Poor Robert is freeze-dried now, so we'll have to be careful when we move him. Parts of him tend to break off."

"You sure you don't want us to cast him off into space for an astronaut's burial?" Reed asked.

"You can't. He'll come back eventually, and probably break up even more. And if you push hard enough, he would be caught by the Martian gravity and become a shooting star."

"Cremation by reentry," said Reed. "I wouldn't mind being a shooting star if I was in Robert's condition."

"I want him home. And I'm sure his family does too."

Parker looked at Reed. "Doc, should we be worried about contamination?"

"I think not. He's freeze-dried and irradiated. That's enough to kill any bugs. And besides, the body bag I brought is impervious to gas and fluids if there were any left, which I doubt there would be after this exposure."

Turning to Williams, Reed said, "We should be able to get him home okay. I'm optimistic."

"Okay, just be careful moving him. Like I said, things break off."

Laura said, "Yeah, I noticed he's missing a few parts."

"I'll fill you in on that later, Dr. Smith."

"No formalities please. We're all risking our lives out here."

"You're right about that," Parker said. "Let's pack up your husband and get in the ship. Dr. Reed needs to examine you to make sure you're okay for the trip."

"Okay or not, you're getting me off this damn rock."

"Don't you want us to load up your husband's body?"

"Never mind that—I've changed my mind," Williams announced. "There's no way we can put him in a bag and carry him to the ship without breaking him all to pieces. I think he'd rather be left here, keeping watch over Mars for eternity, so that's a happy thought. As long as—"

"Long as what?" Parker asked.

"Nothing. Nothing at all. Before we go though, I need to send one last message home, to let them know you're here and I'm okay. And then I'll pick up our recording decks and set the destruct sequence."

"I hope this won't take long." Parker was growing impatient.

"What's the rush? Besides, I'll get one last Navy shower. I can't stand myself anymore."

"Ah, negative on the shower. Secure your records, Sergeant, but we're getting the fuck off this rock, pronto."

"Yeah, whatever."

"But what if something comes to visit while we're out here," Laura asked.

"They hardly ever come by, but if they do, let them sniff your fingers."

"Like a dog, eh?"

"Not exactly. They'll probably take a finger or two, but with luck, they'll leave the rest of you alone."

"You're shitting me," Laura laughed. "You'd die soon as you take the glove off."

"Oh no, we're talking inside the shelter. They're interdimensional, come and go as they please. So you're better off out here."

Williams opened the remaining pressure lock one last time, stirring the dust that had accumulated during her absence. Before she stepped inside the lock, she turned towards the three of them.

"And yeah, they do bite."

After she disappeared inside the remains of the complex, leaving the rescue crew outside, Parker asked Reed, "Is she okay?"

"I have my doubts, but I don't exactly know what's normal for this situation."

While the astronauts waited for Clarice's return, the three astronauts looked around a little more nervously than they had on arrival. Williams had given them something to think about.

"I don't buy that interdimensional crap," Laura said.

Reed, attempting to be the most analytical one, said, "Giving her the benefit of the doubt, she's been scared and lonely for so long she's invented scenarios more exciting than the one she's stuck in."

Even imaginary monsters can be a relief when you're all alone, Reed thought but didn't say.

With another stirring of rock dust a few minutes later, Williams showed up, properly suited and carrying a stack of gold disks, invaluable records for later scrutiny by Space Corp and the DIA.

"I'm good to go," she said. "Let me tell Robert goodbye, and then we're out of here."

She hopped over to stand in front of the partially disfigured but still lifelike corpse of her husband, mouthed something silently to him, then saluted. After waiting for a moment, perhaps imagining a returned salute, she faced her newfound companions and hopped back to them.

"Okay then," Parker said. "Let's get this show on the road. Are you up to hopping a good ways Clarice? If not, I can carry you. You must weigh all of two pounds in this gravity."

"I'm up to it. I'm a Spacewoman, you know."

"You are indeed," Reed said. "First one I've ever met."

It only took five minutes of hopping to get to the ship. Once there, Parker paused, not sure how to plan their jumps up to the open airlock. He pointed up at the ship, saying, "Clarice, how should we plan this jump? I don't want to overdo it and launch into orbit."

"No, no. Don't do that. We'll never get you back. Remember when you were a kid riding an elevator, and you'd jump up a little when the elevator was stopping at the top or the bottom?"

"Yeah, actually, I do," Parker said.

"Nothing more vigorous than that. Just a little hop."

"Okay, I think I got it."

"No wait, I'll go first," Clarice insisted. "That way if you shoot too high, I can grab you and hopefully stop you."

And with that, Clarice hopped up the twenty feet, landed on the platform, and turned back to face the three astronauts still on the Phobos surface.

"See, it's easy," she said.

"You first," Parker said to Laura.

"If you insist, but don't laugh. I don't feel very graceful in this getup."

And she jumped, arms and legs flailing, but close enough for Clarice to grab her and pull in her into the outer lock.

"That was fun, boys," Laura said. "Who's next?"

"After you Emery," Parker said, pointing up to the open space.

"Okay, I'm going to think like a kid and not get too athletic."

"We don't have all day," Parker reminded him.

"Hey, don't rush me. You'd feel pretty shitty if I go into orbit. Just let me channel my inner child-in-an-elevator-with-my-dad for a moment."

Parker sighed. "Okay."

A second later, Reed launched, yelling "Wheee!" all the way up. Unfortunately, he was going too fast to land on the platform, and Laura jumped out to grab him and keep him from going too high. Her weight arrested his rise, but her momentum pushed the two of them out about thirty feet away from the ship, in the direction from which they'd come, where the partially shattered moon base and its lone, desiccated sentinel remained.

"Be careful landing, guys," Parker shouted.

Fortunately, their descent was slow enough that both of them had time to get their feet firmly beneath them, preventing a fall.

"Nice save there, Laura," Williams said.

From a distance, it was hard to see Laura's scowl. "Too much testosterone there, Reed," Laura said. "Gentle next time, like a kid. That's what she said."

"I'll go back up first, but don't make me have to catch you again."

Just as quickly as she did the first time, Laura effortlessly jumped up onto the platform. As she turned around, she said, "Okay Cowboy, a little less 'yee-haw' this time around."

"Okay, like a kid, here I go," Reed said. "The elevator is coming to a stop, and I jump..."

This time he got it exactly right. No rescue was needed.

Reed turned to peer down at Parker. "I have been redeemed, Jason. Now show us how it's done."

"No promises," Parker said. He was, in fact, a bit nervous.

"Alright, it's happening now," he warned as he gently bent his knees and pushed off.

He rose surely, but slowly. Wary of jumping too high, he actually jumped too low. However, he was able to grab the bottom of the platform and hoist himself upon it.

Laura laughed at him. "Well, you certainly didn't overdo that."

"Oh hell," Reed exclaimed, "If I didn't have my head screwed on ... I meant to take a picture. I'm going back down. This is too historic. It'll just take a second."

"Oh, for crying out loud, Emery," Parker moaned. "Make it snappy. We can't enter the ship until we're all together."

"I'm sorry. I'm just a little wackadoodle about us being where we are. I have to document it. I'll be right back. And give me your biggest smiles."

Reed pulled his space-approved camera from a storage pocket, and dropped to the moon's surface, landing gently.

He started hopping away from the craft.

"Where you going, Reed?" Parker asked.

"Gotta get far enough away to get the whole ship in the shot. This is an incredible view."

"Hurry it up, we got things to do."

"No worries." Reed turned towards them, raised his camera, and froze.

"Geesh, Reed, take the freakin' picture already. I can't hold this smile forever."

Reed did not respond.

"Good God, Reed, my wife can take a photo faster than you."

Laura looked at Parker, worried, then back out into the darkness.

"Emery, what's wrong?"

"Something's not right," he responded weakly.

"Get back here, Emery. Now!" Parker barked.

Energized by the command, Reed hopped the distance back to the ship in a matter of seconds and then bounded up to the platform and the waiting astronauts. But his landing was awkward, throwing him to the floor and knocking Williams down in the process.

"Welcome back, Grace," Parker chided him.

"I couldn't see where I was landing."

"What?"

"After I jumped, everything went white."

"Can you see now?"

"Yeah. It's weird like someone flashed a blinding light in my eyes."

"But you're okay?"

"Seem to be."

"Why'd you say something wasn't right?"

"I got a weird taste in my mouth. And... I don't know, I felt time-shifted or something. Can't explain it."

"Time-shifted? What does that mean?"

"Don't know why I said that."

"But you're okay?"

"I said yes. Let's get going."

Chapter 22. Pavonis Mons

When they had shed their spacesuits and changed into jumpsuits, Reed, apparently recovered, showed Sergeant Williams around the ship. As they left, Laura pulled Parker close, smiling.

"What's this?" he asked, pleasantly surprised. Laura had been standoffish on the trip so far, making no effort to be her usual playful self.

"This is me telling you you're a fuckin' jackass," she said as her mock smile quickly faded. "I don't know what's wrong with you, but this is not the Jason Parker I've come to know. If you tell anyone else our personal history, especially my private thoughts, I'll make sure your oxygen bottle has nothing but nitrogen in it."

"You could have stopped me, you know."

"I wasn't going to embarrass you in front of Reed. But I will kill you if you do it again."

Parker looked straight in her eyes, expecting her to crack a smile. But she didn't.

"This is where you say you're sorry," she said in a reprimanding tone of voice.

Parker remembered the times Sandy had asked him to apologize for the times he had been in *harm's way* with Laura. But he never could, because he was not really in control of his destiny. But this, yeah, this he could do.

"I'm sorry, Laura. I wanted Emery to know, but I should have let you tell the story. It's your story, not mine."

"You're damn straight," she said, finally cracking her smile.

Getting the feeling he'd been forgiven, and being anxious to move on, Parker asked, "Speaking of straight, do you think we're getting the straight scoop from Williams?"

"I don't know," she said, shaking her head. "That's why I came, to find out for myself."

"So, you've known this?"

"Yes. But we don't know of any such species. If they're real, we really need to know if they've been interfering with the Mars colony."

"And if they're not real?"

"That's the main reason Dr. Reed is here. He's had quite a bit of experience dealing with schizophrenic paranoia and hallucinations."

"Wow, so you definitely have your doubts," Parker said.

"We never heard about these creatures and their black ships until her communications right after her husband died."

"Could be a coincidence," Parker admitted.

"Could be. That's why we're reserving judgment until we get her home. But tell me, what do you think about the naked husband and her hiding outside of what remains of the base?"

"That was weird. Who strips their dead husband and parks him outside?" Parker asked. "Plus, I think being outside, exposed to radiation, would be a horrible choice for her health."

"I agree," Laura said. "But if you take her at her word, she seemed to think she could hide outside, but not inside."

"It almost sounds like dementia if she doesn't feel safe in her home," Parker said.

"Yeah," said Laura, "it sounds like paranoia doesn't it? And don't forget, she didn't believe she could possibly be rescued. So mentally, I think she was prepared to die."

Parker studied her eyes. He knew Laura was hired because she could keep secrets. "On the other hand, I imagined virtual Frogs, and they turned out to be real, in the flesh." He swept an arm around them.

"And we're flying in one of their ships."

She smiled. "That's true."

"So let's go easy on Sergeant Williams. She might be completely correct."

Laura shifted her eyes away from Parker and looked down.

"I hope not."

Laura seemed worried, and Parker knew that when Laura was worried, he had better worry also.

"But, thanks to your getting us here safely, I have a surprise for you."

"Am I going to like it?" Parker asked.

Laura's smile faded into a serious look.

"You're not smiling," Parker noted. "I prefer surprises where the girl is smiling."

"You might like this, and you might not."

"Let me guess. We have another mission before going home?"

"Very perceptive of you. You think you can get us to Mars?"

"Why do you ask?"

"Cause the plan was that if we made it this far, we would move on to the second phase."

"I hope the third phase includes us going home before we get eaten."

"It does."

"I suppose you have secret squirrel stuff to do on Mars."

"Maybe."

"Do you have lat long coordinates for where we're going?"

"In Martian coordinates, yes I do. Do you think you can remote view those coordinates?"

"We'll find out. Where's zero degrees latitude?"

"It's a crater called 'Airy-0', near the equator."

"And our target location?"

"Pavonis Mons, in the Tharsis Mountains. I'll send the coordinates to your communicator."

Parker felt a vibration as the device on his wrist lit up, signaling a new message. It said, 0°28'36.94" N, 112°56'52.20 W.

"It's on the equator. Will we be warm there?"

"Warm for Mars. It might actually get above freezing while we're there."

"This is a mountain?"

"A volcano. Our base uses the volcano's old lava tubes for protection from solar and cosmic radiation."

"Let me see if I can find this place," Parker said, signaling the need for silence. He sat in his chair and furrowed his brow, concentrating on the coordinates.

"Sure wish we had Joshua Nilsson here," he said.

"Well, you don't. The Agency's never going to let him get far from Langley. Now hush up and concentrate."

Just then Williamson and Reed returned. Spotting Parker in his seat, she asked, "Where do I sit."

"Nowhere just yet, Clarice. Dr. Parker's trying to get a navigational fix."

"You don't know where the Earth is?"

"I'll explain later. Let's be quiet so he can concentrate."

Parker was growing irritated. "Yes, no interruptions, please."

It was difficult for the two women to remain perfectly quiet. Williams was understandably anxious to get back home, and Laura was growing antsy about revealing the truth of where they were headed next. Williams would not be happy.

The silence was broken only when Parker said, "I got it. It really is a volcano."

Williams looked at Laura, startled. "Volcano?"

"Mons Veneris," Parker said.

Reed glanced at Parker with a lifted eyebrow.

"No, I mean…what did you say, Laura?"

"Pavonis Mons."

"Yeah, whatever you said," Parker said a little sheepishly, realizing the extent of his verbal blunder.

"On Earth?" Williams sounded incredulous.

"No, Mars. Now that I found it, that's where we're headed."

"You have got to be shitting me. You're not taking me home?"

"It's the very next stop after Mars," Parker said. "Agency orders."

I've had worse orders before, Parker thought. *This could actually be fun.*

"Well, that seriously sucks," Williams said, scrunching up her mouth.

"Hey, you can't get to Heaven without stopping in Atlanta. This is sort of like that. We'll be headed home before you know it."

"Do you see the caves?" Laura asked.

"Yep."

"Good, then you've got the right place."

"Wait, what's with this 'see the caves shit'?" Clarice asked.

"He's remote viewing. That's how we control the Frog ship," Laura said.

"So that's what this is. How'd you get it?"

"They left it," Parker answered. "And apparently, I can fly it."

"Well yeah, but God almighty, do we seriously have to stop by Mars Base?"

"You know the base?" Parker asked.

"Oh, hell yeah. We had to check-in at least once a day with them. We were their overwatch. And ever since the accident, they tried to cheer me up. Both they and Houston told me you guys would get here soon, but I didn't believe them. We're on the opposite side of the sun from Earth now. It shouldn't be possible."

"And yet here we are," Parker said.

"I'm not a rocket jockey," Williams admitted, "but how does this thing handle atmospheric reentry? That's pretty critical from what I recall."

"You're absolutely right," Parker answered. "And we have no idea how it does it."

Williams scratched the back of her head. "Let me get this straight, you're planning to enter the Martian atmosphere, but you have no idea how to do that?"

"Correct. Now before you think we're nuts, let me brief you on what we think this ship is. We think the hull is filled with billions of sensors, all tied into some quantum computer embedded within the hull. The hull reacts to the environment, perhaps even sensing the environment before it reaches it, and sends control signals to the network of lights arranged around the edge of this thing. And then the lights modulate the interaction of the hull with some yet to be understood energy field. Maybe dark energy, or dark matter. Who knows? It doesn't matter."

Williams cleared her throat. "It matters to me."

Parker continued. "We think the interaction is controlled by both the light energy or frequency and the position of the lights. When the interactions are balanced, the ship levitates. When the ship is energized, but the lights are not controlling horizontal motion, you get a full power vertical ascent. When the lights are not balanced, then you get direction in one vector or another. There's an infinite number of possible speeds and directions which can result."

"Oh my God. We are doomed," Williams said.

"Not so fast," Parker said. "We've made several high-altitude flights so far, and one transitioning into a supercavitating water entry. The ship is highly maneuverable."

"And it does all that on its own?"

"Yep. All I do is tell it where I want to go."

"Tell it?"

"Well, think it, actually."

"Remote view it is the correct term," Laura added.

Williams shook her head. "I knew it, we're gonna die."

"I bet not," Parker said.

Tobias, who had been uncharacteristically quiet, piped up. "I don't know. The odds against us are mounting."

Laura was apparently tired of William's doubts. "Let me remind you, Sergeant Williams, and Tobi, we flew across the inner part of the solar system, flew past the sun on a route never taken before by human-engineered craft, all to rescue you. And here we are. We traveled at, oh I don't know, five million miles an hour or so, and made what looked to us like a blind landing on this moon which was threatening to run over us. And best of all, we have no fucking controls. No joystick, nothing. This baby has the best autopilot ever, so we're just along for the ride. If you want to get home, you better become a believer, fast."

With that dressing down, Williams slowly chose one of the two empty seats behind Parker and Laura's seats. She and Tobias looked at each other, both cocking their heads in disbelief.

"Let's get going," Williams said weakly.

"We will as soon as the ship is ready. It has to sense my intentions, and then we'll be off. And tighten your harness because this baby can pull Gs."

Tobias said, "If you all are wondering, I'm good to go."

"That's good, Tobi," Laura said, "I'm glad you're happy."

"I'm A-Okay!" he chirped.

For the first time in Parker and Laura's experience, they did not blackout on takeoff. With very little gravity on Phobos, there was next to nothing holding them on the surface. And with the surface of Mars only 3700 miles away, the ship's initial maneuvering seemed to be in preparation for atmospheric penetration with a final landing somewhere in a mountainous equatorial region. Considering the rapid speed which Phobos was whizzing around Mars, neither Parker nor Laura had any idea just how far they would have to travel to reach Pavonis Mons. But both of them trusted that the ship knew how far it was, as well as the safest route to the landing zone.

"You know Laura," Parker said, "Reed is right. This ship does need a proper name. And if we reach our target without crashing, I for one am going to adopt Reed's name for this ship. *XFS Dioscuri.* It's got a nice ring to it."

"Uh folks, I can hear you," Reed said. "But I agree, she deserves a proper name."

"Sounds mysterious," Williams added.

The first indication that *Dioscuri* had encountered the thin Martian atmosphere was when arcs of plasma began shooting past the forward-facing viewing port of the craft. Compared to similar reentry plasmas on Earth, this one had a yellower tinge to it, perhaps reflecting the almost complete absence of oxygen in the Martian atmosphere and an overabundance of carbon dioxide.

Parker had expected some buffeting, but the ride was smooth and fast. Before the ship inclined itself above the Martian horizon, they could see the Martian terrain slipping past at a dizzying speed. Even on reentry, *Dioscuri* was a speed demon.

Approximately two minutes after reentry had begun, the plasma arcs dissipated and the nose of the craft dipped low enough for them to see a range of mountains on the distant horizon. Within another minute, those mountains were no longer so distant, and Parker began to get the feeling those mountains were precisely where they were headed. When their forward progress slowed, and the mountain ridges began to grow closer, Parker was confident their landing spot was not far below them.

Within seconds, they could see the tops of the Tharsis Mountains rising in front of them which meant they were descending steeply now.

"Tighten your seat belts, ladies. We're about to touch down."

And then there was no more movement.

"Welcome to Mars folks. Let's get suited up. It's time to disembark and let Laura do whatever spooks do on Mars."

After a fraction of a second delay, while Tobias was apparently looking up the most probable meaning of "spook" in this instance, he laughed, inappropriately.

Laura did not seem amused.

A few minutes later the three of them stood in the outer lock as the exterior door swung open to reveal a reddish desert view with men in spacesuits running towards the alien-looking craft. To the arriving crew's dismay, three of the men were pointing laser rifles in their direction.

Parker looked at Laura with alarm. "Shouldn't they be coming up on our comms?"

She nodded and tapped her wrist communicator to sweep all potential UHF frequencies they could be using. Since she was standing close by Parker's side, he could see the wrist-mounted communicator cycling endlessly. There were no comm frequencies alive.

"They're not broadcasting," she said, alarmed.

"Well they sure as hell want to know who we are," Parker said emphatically.

"Show them our American flags on our suits," Williams said.

It was as good an idea as any. They all three simultaneously turned to their right to expose the stars and stripes patch on their left shoulder.

As they did, the three armed men dropped their weapons and waved to them.

"You're a genius, Williams."

"I've been in this goddam suit way longer than you, Parker. I know it inside and out."

Laura was now thinking about the next step. "How do we get down now? There's gravity here, and I'm not jumping and breaking a leg this far from home."

"Oh, shit. Let me check my checklist for landings in a gravity field."

"You're kidding me, right?" Laura asked.

"No. We rehearsed a nil gravity landing. No one said we'd be landing on Mars. This is what you get for springing a destination change on me at the last minute. And ... ah, here it is. An aluminum ladder is stored in bin A36. I'll be right back."

"You ever used it?"

"We'll figure it out. It's not rocket science."

The outer airlock door had to close before Parker could regain entrance to the ship.

Closing the outer door is probably going to confuse the hell out of the Mars crew. But it can't be helped.

Thanks to someone's advanced planning for any eventuality, Parker was led straight to the proper storage bin and returned to his shipmates in a matter of minutes. Once the inner door sealed, Parker was able to open the outer door.

This time, the number of Mars crew gathered below them had doubled, and they had raised their weapons again. Apparently, the unexpected closure of the door had alarmed them. But when Parker fitted the ladder into its attachment points, the armed men relaxed. They seemed to intuitively understand what had happened.

Once the ship's crew and passenger were on Martian soil, the armed men peered carefully into the helmets of the newcomers and recognized Sergeant Williams. All of them smiled and patted her shoulders. Parker could see them mouthing something to her, but no one heard anything. It was as if the Martian comms were not working.

"All I got out of the lip-reading," Williams said, "was 'Glad to see you.' I think."

Then they saw two space-suited men carrying another man who appeared to be unconscious, or worse, towards a cave entrance. Based on the labeling, it seemed to be the main entrance to the underground base.

The armed men motioned for them to follow as they trudged toward the door.

Williams and the *Dioscuri* crew were a little unsteady in the Martian gravity. It had been a while since any of them had experienced anything other than a negligible weight. They moved slowly, testing their steps, making sure they didn't fall.

It didn't help that between steps the newcomers to Mars were also looking every which way, trying to take in their new surroundings.

This is amazing, Parker thought. *I'm on freaking Mars.*

Before they reached the cave entrance, the men carrying an astronaut laid their load down just outside the heavy steel doors and turned to head back out into the desert. As Parker looked in their direction, he was startled to see a larger than usual astronaut carrying another over his shoulder. He also saw two more men further away carrying another astronaut.

"What the hell's going on here?" Parker asked his colleagues.

"I don't know," Laura said, "but it looks bad."

Reed said, "They're not particularly gentle when they lay them down. Makes me wonder if they're dead."

As they got closer to the door entrance, Laura said, "Well, then it appears we have four bodies here and more being brought in."

"My God," Williams sighed loudly. "These are the guys we were trying to protect."

"From what?" Parker asked.

Williams did not answer.

Chapter 23. Mars Base

When the armed men and the Phobos four were behind the inner lock, tightly closed against the poisonous Martian atmosphere, they could all remove their helmets.

One of the three Martian crew who escorted the Dioscuri crew into the base turned towards Williams and asked, "Is this the rescue team sent to bring you home?"

"It sure is. I thought I'd never see them."

"Then this must be the Frogship I've heard about."

"It is," Williams answered. "I'd still be up there if it weren't for these folks."

"What in God's name is going on here?" Parker said, cutting to the chase.

"And you would be?"

"I'm Jason Parker. This young lady over here is my copilot, Laura Smith, and our physician is Captain Emery Reed."

"Well, what happened is, we were attacked. Half of our team was just killed. Everyone who was outside."

"Is that why you were holding guns on us?"

"Damn straight. We didn't know who you were. Thought you might have been the ones who did it."

"Did it? With what?"

"Who knows? Some sort of death ray. They all died at the same time."

Parker frowned. "Death ray?"

"That's what I said."

"How many are left?"

"Ten. We always keep half the team in the cave when the other half are out tending the plants and the rats."

"Rats?"

"Nutria, basically a big rat. They're all dead too. But come on, we need to take you to Lieutenant Commander Meyers, our Officer in Charge."

Chris Meyers, a tall blond-haired officer, had the honor of being in charge of the most secret laboratory being run by the U.S. military, and the only manned laboratory on Mars. Much to Parker's surprise, he was told it had been operating for ten years, and over those ten years, it had steadily grown in size with the accretion of materials, resources, and funding as its secret mission met with ever greater success.

Until now.

Meyers was visibly stressed. He was one year out from rotation back to Earth and was looking forward to one of the highest honors the Space Corp black op community could bestow. But now, disaster had struck, and he had no idea how his team had been so fatally attacked. As far as U.S. intelligence knew, there were no enemies who even knew about the Mars Base. Rumors and suspicions, perhaps, but no hard evidence.

"Dr. Smith, I was informed a week ago that I was to brief you on our situation, but all that is overcome by events now. As far as I'm concerned, you're a well-timed rescue mission for us survivors. I guess I'm going to have to commandeer your ship."

Parker quickly added, "Commander, you don't have to commandeer anything. We're happy to take you back. I trust you have some ice to bring these bodies back with us."

"How long will it take in that thing?" Meyers asked.

"Roughly sixty hours."

He whistled. "Damn, that's fast. But it doesn't matter because they're not going. The protocol is that anyone sick or dead stays. We can't take the risk of contaminating Earth with whatever killed these guys."

"Oh geesh," Laura said. "Don't we need the evidence to know what killed them?"

"I'm pretty sure we'll know." He held up a badge with a radiation symbol on it. The symbol was black. "One of our radiation health guys had rotated outside and was wearing this when he was hit. Its black color means the radiation level was off-scale, enough to cause instant death."

"What kind of radiation?" Reed asked. From his years as a medical officer on nuclear submarines, he was an expert on radiation and radiation sickness.

"Don't know. The badge measures all ionizing radiation. So we'll need to take this back with us so rad health folks can probe its internals and figure out the type."

"This happened when?" Reed asked.

Meyers checked his watch. "Roughly three hours ago."

"That's about when I got whacked," Reed said while looking at Parker.

"What do you mean, whacked?" Meyers asked.

"When we were loading up to leave Phobos, I experienced this wave of weakness and nausea. And I tell you what, I'm not feeling so good right now."

"And you are?" Meyers asked.

"Dr. Emery Reed, medical support for Sergeant Williams. Lucky for her, she's in better shape than we expected."

"Yeah, I'm one tough chick."

Meyers' voice softened the tiniest bit. "I'm glad to hear it, Williams. But what happened to you, Doctor?" He seemed to be struggling to remember Reed's name.

"Reed. I was outside the ship taking a photo at the request of the DoD and could tell something wasn't right. But a few seconds later, when I was jumping back to the ship, I felt like I received an electrical shock, and all I saw was white. I landed on the ship blind, but I could see a few seconds later."

"That sounds familiar. You need to talk to our Doc when he's free. He's trying to reach the Chief Space Corp Flight surgeon, but not having much luck."

"What time delay do you have this far from home?" Reed asked.

"Thirty minutes. It takes an hour to get a question answered. You just hope you don't have an emergency. Except now we do."

Addressing Parker, Meyers asked, "While we're waiting for our Doctor to show up, let's talk logistics. Can you take ten passengers onboard?"

"We have lots of room. Might not be comfortable, you'll have to rack out on the floor, but this thing has carried over two hundred folks before."

"Well, that should do."

"There's only one catch. It pulls 2-Gs or more for hours. You guys will not be comfortable."

"We're used to roughing it. Mars is not exactly paradise, and it'll be worth it if it means we get home sooner."

"So, what can we do to help?"

"Nothing. We've got it covered."

"Do you need help carrying the bodies inside?"

"They stay outside. Our engineer is scramming the fusion reactor, in case we get back here someday, and then we seal the base. We don't want whatever killed these men to get into the base and potentially contaminate it."

Commander Meyers motioned over a passing astronaut.

"Sergeant, grab Schultz and Browning and start loading ice, water, and food on board this ship. We're going home."

"How much Sir?"

"Take all we can. Our fallen won't be needing it, and we might."

"Roger that, Sir. We'll get on it."

Just then, an older looking man rounded a corner and gawked at the strangers.

Meyers, sensing the man's confusion, said, "These are the Americans who rescued Sergeant Williams from Phobos. They picked her up in our alien ship, the Frogship.

The man did not seem impressed. "Did you happen to see who was shooting at us?"

"No, why would you ask?"

"Cos Phobos was passing overhead when we got hit."

"We couldn't have seen because we were on the stellar side, facing away from Mars."

"Then that means this particle beam came from someplace beyond Phobos."

"Why do you call it a particle beam?" Parker asked.

"That's the weapon of choice for ... uh....". He looked at Meyers, "Are they cleared?"

"The two women are. Don't know about this guy."

Parker was getting annoyed. "Look, I'm risking my life out here just like you guys, and I'm the one flying you home, so maybe you better cut the security shit and read me in."

Laura shrugged. Addressing the Commander, she said, "He's got a point. I can vouch for him. He was with me when we made contact with the Frogs. He's a true Frogship flyer."

"Okay. Then know there are hostiles out there. An alien species that doesn't like what we're doing, so they take potshots at our gear from time to time. They haven't hurt anything except a few rats, until now."

"Wait a minute," Parker said. "A hostile species?"

"Don't worry, they're not your Frogs. They're big fuckin' insects."

CHAPTER 24 MARTIAN RATS

Everyone engaged in pulling bodies into the base kept a wary eye on the sky. Whoever attacked them could come back at any moment.

Parker noticed a gun emplacement high over the cave entrance, seemingly scanning the sky for something that needed killing.

"You sure noticed that quickly," Meyers said. "It's not manned, it's autonomous. It almost blew you guys right out of the sky, but we secured it just in time. Bad timing on your part."

"We didn't know." Turning to point back to the ship, Parker said, "This baby has no radios."

"Well, you got lucky this time. After losing half our manning in an instant and never seeing the attacker, we got a bit trigger happy."

"That's understandable," Parker admitted.

"What do the enemy craft look like?"

"The only person who's seen one is Sergeant Williams. She said it was black on black with black trim. Which is to say that with it approaching from the blackness of space, you couldn't see it, not even on radar."

The under-the-mountain facility was a comfortable and steady sixty-eight degrees Fahrenheit. In the summertime, the temperature outside was actually a balmy seventy degrees outside during the day, dropping well below freezing every night. But the warming power of the fusion reactor not only kept the facility warm but provided much-needed heat to the areas outside.

The remaining personnel attended to the evacuation protocol in something close to a frenzy. Critical equipment and records were carried to the ship; everything else was being pulverized into dust.

Parker was walking with Lieutenant Commander Meyers as Meyers was checking on the shutdown procedures. "Why aren't you using burn bags, Commander. Am I missing something?"

"There were no burn bags on Mars. There's not enough oxygen for flames, and even if the material was carbonized from the heat of the reactor, there was still a chance carbon dioxide would escape. There's too much of that on Mars already."

"Well, I feel stupid. I should have thought of that."

"It takes getting used to. It also takes getting used to living where we do. Most of this facility is in old lava tubes. We couldn't be better insulated, and these tubes have been around for millions and maybe billions of years. We get no tectonic activity at all here, which makes it an ideal location for the fusion reactor."

The first door they came to was glass-paneled so they could see inside. The door was heavily secured.

"That looks like a nursery for plants."

"It is, but we can't go in. That's Martian air in there. Lots of warm carbon dioxide. The plants love it."

"For your salads?"

"Some, but mostly for the Nutria. The Nutria eat the veggies, and we eat the Nutria."

"Really?"

"Good source of animal protein to supplement our diet. And it's low energy expenditure to grow them. The Nutria get along just fine on the plants and garbage. All we have to do is keep them warm and fed."

"But why are they outside?"

"Because these are Martian rats."

"You're kidding me."

"No. Come see. We have a little walk, and I'll explain on the way."

They were passing by a multitude of windows looking into more nursery areas.

"If we are ever to colonize Mars, we have two choices. Either we geo-engineer the toxic Martian atmosphere to make it more like ours, or we bioengineer humans to tolerate the atmosphere we are given."

Parker laughed. "Surely, you jest."

"Actually, not. The latter was chosen as the most likely means of success. Until today."

"So, you bioengineer humans here?"

"Oh, absolutely not. This started back on Earth in a university laboratory working on mice, and then once established here, we moved up to Nutria. We wanted zero chance of these creatures getting loose back home. They've never known Earth, and in fact, they can't survive in Earth's atmosphere. Ironically, there's too much oxygen for them on Earth."

"But surely there is not enough oxygen in the Martian atmosphere," Parker asked with a skeptical look on his face.

"That's true. We have to supplement it, but they are way more hypoxia-tolerant than Nutria on Earth."

"If they escape from the cages, they die, right?"

"Exactly. That's why they are kept outside. It's part of our biological isolation protocol."

"How'd you do the genetic modification?" Parker asked.

"We used the old CRISPR-Cas9 technique to edit out the genes for oxidative metabolism in mice egg cells, and insert the genes for, well basically, fermentation."

"Where did those genes come from?"

"We started with bacteria, but had more success with Remipedes."

"Remipedes?"

"Blind cave-dwelling crustaceans."

"I know Remipedes well," Parker said.

"I know you do. We thought about them as substitutes for bacteria after reading about them in the Fortean Times article. I think Samuel Putnam said the Frogs raised giant Remipedes for food."

"They do. I saw the buggers with my own eyes. They were huge, and dangerous."

"Well, these little critters are too small to hurt us but lethal for the Daphnia we feed them. And then we use the Remipede genes to insert into the rodent genome. We knew how to do it for the mice on Earth, and the Martian Nutria weren't much different."

"So now the Nutria live outside?"

"They did. Now they're all dead, remember? As are half of my men."

Satisfied that all the outer reaches of the cave system had been secured, Meyers turned and retraced his steps.

"For flight security reasons," Parker said, "I need to know what you know about your attackers."

"We call them bugs because that's what Sergeant Williams told us. They scared the hell out of her up on Phobos, and she doesn't scare easily. After her husband died, they were snooping around, so she stripped his body of all clothing and put him outside. That way, they would hopefully associate his naked body with humans and maybe not notice her in her spacesuit, as long as she stayed hidden either inside or outside."

"Did it work?"

"Must have. They didn't eat her."

"What about her husband?"

"They pawed at him a little bit. Ripped his dong right off. That was shocking for her to watch."

"She was outside at the time?" Parker asked.

"Sure was. She saw it all. Really pissed her off."

"Well, here's our tactical problem," Parker said. "We had to rescue Williams because of the incident with the supply ship. It was attacked by something unknown. Do you think the bugs have directed energy weapons?"

"As many casualties as we suffered, I'd say they have to."

"Then they may pick off the rest of us on the way out," Parker cautioned him. "We have no defenses."

"Who's ever heard of a Space Corp ship with no defenses?"

"It's a Frog ship, and I think their defense was speed and maneuverability."

"I hope you're right," Meyers said, looking at Parker sideways.

"Commander, it's entirely up to you as to whether you brief your surviving crew, or not."

"No need to tell them they might still die. We all know that."

An alarm went off, and lights started flashing in the base corridors.

"Five minutes to evacuate. Five minutes to evacuate."

"I guess we have to leave?" Parker asked Meyers.

"That might be smart, but nothing will happen until I count heads, and you confirm the ship is ready for boarding. Once it is, I'll initiate the scram of the reactor, and seal the main doors."

"So, you'll be the last one off."

"I hate to leave ten dead men behind, but those are the rules. We all know that when we come here."

"Well, at least in the cold, and with no bacteria, they'll still be just as they are whenever you come back."

Meyers gave Parker a hard look, then nodded, seemingly in partial agreement.

"If we come back."

Parker, Laura, Dr. Reed, and Sergeant Williams stood in the open door of the outer lock looking out upon a Mars they would soon leave behind. Below them, the surviving members of the Martian Space Corp detachment stood at attention in four rows just below the entrance to the Frogship. While one of them kept a skyward watch, the

Command Master Chief began a roll call, just as he had so many times over the past year. For each name called but without a response, there was a pause, followed by a smart salute.

Ten times that was repeated.

The four original crew members returned to their places as the remaining Martian crew began climbing the narrow ladder up to the ship. Williams collected them all and led them to the back of the ship where they would stow their spacesuits, change into the fresh Ecosuits they had brought for the trip, and prepared their seating areas as comfortably as they could, in preparation for the next three days or so.

After Parker sealed the hatch, Dr. Reed briefed the survivors on what to expect for the trip home. It would not be pleasant during the prolonged G phases, but it sure was better than waiting to get picked off by the bugs while the Earth slowly began to catch up with Mars.

As Reed left, Laura asked Williams how she was doing.

"I really want to get out of here," Williams admitted.

"Keep in mind," Parker reminded her. "This is not like an Earth launch. We'll be accelerating at Gs for hours. So, if you think you have to pee, this is the time."

"I already did, just now."

"Oh," Parker said.

"Aren't these suits amazing?" Laura added after a respectful pause.

"Good thing they're disposable," Williams added.

Parker chuckled. He knew they didn't have any spare Ecosuits for handling body waste. It could be a long trip home once the porta-potty filled up.

When Reed returned to the cockpit area, Parker had completed visualizing both Earth and their intended landing spot at Area 51. He had time to look over at the Doctor as he settled back into his seat and shifted around to get as comfortable as he could.

"How are you feeling, Emery?"

"Don't ask me no questions, and I won't tell you no lies."

Turning to Laura, Parker said, "I've got this. With the weaker Martian gravity and new passengers not securely braced, I want us all to maintain consciousness. Agreed?"

"You're the Captain," she said, smiling. "I'll keep my mouth shut."

Parker looked at Laura, then Williams, saying, "You ladies ready?"

Both nodded.

Parker renewed his visualization effort, imaging the desired target, Earth, on the opposite side of the sun. After feeling that his mental lock was secure, he vocalized, as he always did. "*Dioscuri*, let's go."

The viewscreen began to clear, and the ship seemed to levitate a few feet off the ground.

But nothing more happened.

Laura looked over at him, "Want me to help?"

"Silence, please, we agreed."

"Suit yourself."

Remembering his first incantation with the ship, the one he used on departure from Siberia, he said, "Superman wants to fly."

The ship rose a few more feet, wobbling back and forth.

"Okay, I give up," Parker admitted.

"You're asking for my help?" Laura was smiling, glancing back at Williams.

"Yes, please."

"Ship, listen to me carefully," Laura said sternly. "Up up and away!"

The moment the last word faded, all the ship's occupants were forced downward in their seats with the force of eight Gs.

Tobias was unfazed by the G-forces as he shouted out, "Girl power!"

The view out front showed the Tharsis Mountains shrinking in size, and soon through the Martian haze, they could see the curvature of the red planet. After a shift in spacecraft orientation, they saw only stars and a distant sun. Beyond that, they knew would be an even more distant Earth.

Chapter 25. Easy Time

Parker had goosebumps as he reflected on what they had just done, and were yet to do. Traveling at relativistic speeds across the solar system was more than a dream. It was a miracle.

Sure, Star Wars and other cinematic space adventures envisioned faster than light speed drives to transit the universe, but the Frog Ships did not appear to have that capability. But remembering what the Frogs had told him, a trip can seem to occur at superluminal speed because of the warping of space-time. How that worked, he had no idea. In fact, a greater mystery was how an alien spaceship with no moving parts was propelling them at all.

The Easy Time, as Reed had come to call it, was that time when acceleration had dropped ever so slowly down to the point where they were at maximum velocity. It became apparent as a lightening of their bodies, no longer pinned down by overwhelming G-forces. Shortly after that, they could float weightlessly.

During that time, the crew was able to snack, and Reed would bring them forward to see the view out the front. The sun was slowly changing position relative to their direction of travel, sliding ever so slowly off to the side of their view. Reed would also report on the readings from their inertial navigation system, which was reporting their velocity as an astonishing 1,009,800 miles per hour, a detectable fraction of light speed.

Williams greatly enjoyed being weightless again, which reminded her of her near-weightlessness on Phobos. Addressing both Laura and Parker, she said, "You think I'll be safe going back to the back with all that pent-up testosterone?"

Parker said, "They're probably too nauseous from the zero-G to even think about bothering you."

"Unless you want to be bothered," Laura added, winking at Williams.

"Never crossed my mind, and won't for a long time." She emphasized the "long."

"Just in case," Reed said as he returned to the cockpit, "I'll escort you."

Laura said, "You're a true gentleman, Dr. Reed."

Parker, more concerned with Reed than Williams, asked, "How are you doing Emery?"

"A bit nauseous."

"Space sickness, maybe?"

"Maybe."

Every two hours or so, Parker would get up and stretch his legs. Either because of, or in spite of Laura being a very capable copilot, the ship did not change course during his time away from the pilot's seat.

During one such stretch, Parker pulled Lieutenant Commander Meyers aside.

"We lucked out Chris. Nothing attacked us."

"So far, so good," he said. "I suppose if the ship had to evade other ships, we would have noticed, right?"

"Oh yeah. Unlike in the movies, G-forces would be slamming us around. We would probably suffer some injuries since we're not tightly strapped in."

"That thought did occur to me," Meyers said.

"You had a huge responsibility running Mars Base," Parker said.

"How long did it take you to get it running at full speed?"

"Five years to transport enough material to build the facility and another five to get the biology working right."

"That's actually surprisingly quick."

Meyers smiled, apparently proud of his team's accomplishment.

"It is, considering we only launch every two years when the Earth and Mars are closest."

That smile lasted only a few seconds. It quickly faded into a desperate scowl.

Throwing his hands in the air, Meyers raised his voice and shook his head.

"But now, it's all for naught. I lost half my team."

"You can't be blamed. You did all you could."

"Nice sentiment, but you don't know that. That's for the Space Corp to decide, and fatality investigations rarely end well for the mission leadership."

"I'm so sorry. You had such a small team, I know you all had to be very close."

"We were family. And to think some fucking beetles could have destroyed it."

"And why do you think it was beetles?"

"Sergeant Williams saw them and said they kind of looked like big beetles."

"But you haven't actually seen them. And we don't know yet what actually happened on Mars."

"I don't know of any other bad guys out there, and I'm guessing you don't either."

Once Parker and Laura were alone again, she told him, "I asked Emery to give Williams a subtle psychiatric exam at the first opportunity. I'm hoping this is it."

"She's made some interesting claims," Parker said.

"All of which are potentially believable since we don't know what is out there," Laura reminded him.

"Extraordinary claims require extraordinary evidence," Parker reminded her. "And no one on Mars has seen anything yet."

"So how long was it before we had evidence of the Frogs?"

"Physical evidence? Not until I got shot and had the surgical scars to prove it."

"Surgery that we can't do," she reminded him. "I rest my case."

A while later, Reed showed up alone.

"Williams decided to hang out with the guys for a while," Reed said.

"They've grown very close since the death of her husband."

"That's good on several levels," Laura said. "It also gives us a chance to talk. And if you don't mind, I'd like to bring Parker into this discussion."

"Okay."

"So," she continued, "Emery, what do you think about Williams and her monster story?"

"First, I don't think she sees it as a monster, but it is concerning for her. Tampering with her dead husband was not appreciated."

"So, you don't think she's lying?" Laura asked.

"Not at all. But that doesn't mean she's not delusional or hallucinating. Under the hugely traumatic circumstances, I wouldn't be surprised if that's what it is."

"We can't know if it's true or not?" Parker asked.

"Not by simple questioning," Reed said. "She seems absolutely convinced of what she saw."

"Well, that's a big deal for me and the Intelligence community," Laura said. "We've never heard of these guys. They're a new species, and if they've attacked our Mars Base, then that's an act of war."

"But if they're a new species," Reed said, "you don't know how to fight them."

"I've got Orkin on speed dial," Parker joked.

Reed frowned. "I'm just reporting on our bereaved astronaut the best I can under the circumstances. As things stand now, I can't tell if she's a remarkable individual who's witnessed scary things or a mental health patient. Unless something changes that is clearly abnormal, we'll have to be satisfied with the ambiguity."

Laura was looking irritated. "I do have to report to my boss when we get back."

"Just report on what I've observed. In the meanwhile, we need to continue treating her just as we have. If she says anything more about it, listen but don't pry. And don't play amateur psychologist."

"Understand. Patient confidentiality."

"She's not a patient," Reed said. "At least not yet."

CHAPTER 26. AREA 51

Dioscuri's arrival back in Nevada was understated. The first interplanetary rescue mission for the craft had been heroic, but as is typical for black projects, few people would ever know about it.

There was no fanfare outside the craft, but plenty of noise inside the craft when the survivors of the Janus Silver mission realized they had landed back on Earth.

As they were making the final approach for landing, Parker could see ambulances and other emergency vehicles standing off at least a half-mile away. They must have wanted to give the landing craft plenty of room to set down. But once the ship was solidly settled on the hard-packed sand, Parker saw those same vehicles racing toward them as the clear frontal viewing area slowly became opaque once again. The craft had done its job perfectly all the way across the inner solar system.

As expected, the craft had been airborne for roughly seventy-two hours. Before they left the sun behind at the half-way point, everyone on board had come forward to view their star from an angle no one had ever before seen, from outside of the planetary ecliptic, the plane around which the major planets orbit the sun.

When Parker opened the outer door, a throng of emergency vehicles was parked close to the craft. But none were needed. The only person feeling ill was Dr. Reed. Having once been on nuclear submarines, he had been well trained to recognize the signs of radiation poisoning. When he admitted that self-diagnosis to one of the physicians waiting below, they slipped him onto a stretcher, ignoring his protests that such silliness was unnecessary.

"Let them take care of you, Emery," Parker shouted after him.

As he was carried away, he raised his hand to acknowledge what Parker had said.

Everything the ship's crew and passengers had been wearing was stripped off and incinerated, and their bodies were doused in disinfectant to make sure they were not carrying any Martian bugs. Then everyone, covered in no more than disposable plastic coveralls, was subjected to intense medical screening. It was during those examinations that the Chief physician came in to check on Parker.

"How are you feeling, Dr. Parker?"

"I'm feeling grateful to be back."

"We need to make absolutely sure because the Mars Base radiometer results have been analyzed. It showed an off-the-scale reading for gamma radiation."

"Holy shit."

"And it appears that Dr. Reed has a case of radiation poisoning like he suspected. A mild one to be sure, but there was an awful lot of gamma radiation out there. Assuming your checkup remains negative, be attentive to anything unusual. Sometimes it takes a while for symptoms to develop."

"How's the Martian crew checking out. And Laura?"

"Dr. Smith is fine, and the Martian crew seem to have been lucky."

"Sergeant Williams?"

"She's been through a lot, so it will take a while to recover. But physically, she's fine."

"*Dioscuri* did a good job then," Parker said.

"*Dioscuri*?"

"The name of our ship. It got us there and back safely all on its own, so it deserves a proper name."

Following his medical clearance, Parker was ushered into a small conference room, where he found both Laura Smith and Hans Richter waiting on him.

"Well, there he is. The best pilot in the Solar System."

That accolade from Richter was hard-won.

"Hello, Hans. I'm sure Laura let you know that the ship pretty much flew itself."

"Yes, and she said she actually got you off Mars." Richter was actually smiling.

"She sure did," Parker said, nodding his head in appreciation.

"I'm not sure why," he continued, "but sometimes I need a little help getting the ship's attention. It seems to listen to her."

"That's what I hear," Richter said.

"What do you make of our dual rescue?" Parker continued.

"Could not have worked out better," Richter said. "That is one amazing machine."

"It is. And I'm kind of glad you didn't tell me ahead of time that Janus Silver was a two-part mission."

"Considering the uncertainties, we didn't want to burden your mind too early in the mission."

"That was wise, especially since we almost crashed into the moon on the way out."

"Yeah, that was a scary time in Houston," Richter said.

"Well it was a little bit more than that for us," Parker said winking at Laura.

"Now, let's talk about gamma-rays," Richter said. "We're flying Dr. Peter Green in this evening to talk about the fact that we presume high dose gamma-rays killed half the Mars crew. Based on Dr. Reed's account, we think he got a glancing dose of gamma-rays too."

"I was afraid of that."

"He has clear signs of radiation poisoning, with his exposure occurring at essentially the same instant the Mars crew was killed. That timing is far too close to assume it's a coincidence. If we were attacked, President Whitney has some big decisions to make."

"Commander Meyers thinks it was a particle beam weapon that killed his people."

"Particle beams don't shoot high-intensity gamma-rays. They shoot particles."

"As far as we know." Parker had a compulsive habit of playing the devil's advocate. He didn't like jumping to conclusions.

"What we also know, is that no craft of any type, alien or otherwise, was observed within a five-thousand-mile radius of Phobos and Mars."

"What about stealth spacecraft?" Parker asked.

"According to my engineers at the NSA, there is no craft stealthy enough to avoid detection by our sensors. But I wouldn't bet on it."

"So, what are you thinking?"

"We'll wait until Peter Green gets here. Don't go wandering off. We'll start the discussion at 1700 hours this afternoon."

"Can't it wait until tomorrow? I'm bushed," Parker said.

"No, it can't."

In Coordinated Universal Time, there is no lunchtime per se, but to Parker, Laura, and the Mars crew, regardless of the time, it was time for chow. After being warned by their keepers to say nothing to anyone, they were allowed to eat the usual Wednesday lunch of three meat meatloaf, mash potatoes, buttered corn, milk or tea, and yeast rolls. Nothing fancy, but compared to cold MRE's it was a feast.

After Parker cleaned up and took a nap, he and Laura were escorted to one of the most secure rooms in what is arguably the most secure facility in the world. Once there, he once again saw Hans Richter and another familiar face, Harry Kincaide. Emery Reed was not present since he had been flown out to Naval Medical Center San Diego to start treatment for his radiation sickness.

As promised, at 5 PM Pacific Time, the briefing began.

"Folks, for those who don't know me, I'm General Morrison, and I'm responsible for briefing SecDef in a few hours. It's up to us to prepare our section of the President's Daily Briefing in the morning. It's already 2000 hours there, so we don't have much time. Consider it an all-nighter if need be. It sucks, but it can't be helped. We're waiting for one more person to get cleared through security, so we have maybe fifteen minutes before we start. Get yourself some coffee. We have donuts if you get hungry because we're likely to be here a while."

Parker turned towards Laura. "You work for ODNI so you must have a good idea what the President needs to hear about our trip. What do you think is the priority?"

"To me, it's obvious. Are we or are we not in a space war with ETs? If so, will we be fighting on Earth in the near future?"

"I don't think we know," Parker opined.

"I agree, but we have lots to talk about from a lot of different viewpoints. So hopefully our 'group think' will come up with something better than a shrug."

"For what it's worth, if we're venturing into a space war, I think it will be no contest. We'll get our asses kicked."

Laura looked at Parker with a look he had only seen once before, during their internment in Russia. Her big eyes were welling up.

"It could get ugly," she admitted, nodding her head.

A few minutes later, the General returned to the head of the long conference table and announced, "Please finish getting your coffee and return to your seats."

Peter Green was escorted into the room and paraded to the front of the table. Green and Morrison spoke softly to each other before the leader turned and said, "This young man encountered a little difficulty getting through security because he kept insisting Area 51 did not exist. He wanted to know where he really was."

There were chuckles throughout the room.

Parker rose and greeted Peter. "I had no idea I'd be meeting you again so soon. Did they use a team of horses to drag you out of the desert?"

"Just some gentle persuasion."

As they stepped away and Parker pointed to an empty seat, Parker said softly, "I'm not sure exactly who General Morrison is, but he smells like trouble to me."

"No, he smells like purple."

They both laughed and went to refill their coffee cups.

"Okay folks, we have our last member here, so let's get going."

Parker told Peter he was sitting with Laura Smith, and he'd introduce him to her at the next break. Green smiled at Laura as he saw Laura was looking at him.

"I better get back to my seat," Parker said softly.

The General continued. "The way this is going to work, when you address the group, facial recognition software will identify you and place both your photo and credentials on the screens in front of you, so you'll know who's speaking. It will also display it on the large screen in case you're taking a stretch break."

"Thank goodness," Parker whispered to Laura.

"We don't have much time to get a consensus. Our last member is Dr. Peter Green, a cosmologist who's done work on dark matter at CERN, and theoretical work on dark energy at UCLA. Jason Parker met him recently to talk about alien propulsion systems, but now that he's here I think we can take advantage of his great intellect to help us sort out what happened to our Mars crew. As you may have heard, Dr. Emery Reed could not be here because he got a dose of gamma-rays on Phobos and he's undergoing treatment for radiation poisoning at UC San Diego. That fact will figure into our estimations of what happened."

"We got clobbered," interjected Commander Meyers.

The General pointed to Meyers. "Lieutenant Commander Meyers here was the OIC on Mars Base, and I asked him to give his impression of what happened. Commander?"

Behind General Morrison, a large screen lit up with the moment to moment positions of Mars and its moons Phobos and Deimos. Phobos was much closer to Mars than Deimos, and traveled much faster, about 5000 miles per hour, racing around its planet in eight hours compared to the thirty hours Deimos required.

Meyers remained seated, as much from accumulated fatigue from the attack and from the stress of the trip from Mars. Trying to sleep during prolonged periods of G-forces was next to impossible.

"Phobos was passing directly overhead," Meyers said, "when we got hit. Every Vitals monitor we had on the men outside, all ten of them, alarmed at the same time. Within a minute, all showed flat lines. I wasn't far from the cave entrance when they alarmed, and when I ran out, I instinctively looked up. I didn't see any ships, just Phobos. I figured some bastard was on the moon firing a particle beam at us. But when I learned that they'd also winged Dr. Reed, I realized they had to be somewhere we couldn't see them."

Several people in the group were pointing to the screen and whispering to each other.

The Commander continued. "The energy in that beam had to be incredible to kill them all within a minute. They didn't cry out. They just dropped where they were, scattered over an area of at least one square mile."

"Any radiation detectors?" Green asked.

"Yes, one of our fusion techs was out there and was still wearing his badge. It came back reading off-scale for gamma radiation."

The General said, "ADAM is plotting the real-time positions of Phobos and Deimos relative to Mars. Our view is from an arbitrary point in space six thousand miles away from the Martian surface."

While the General gave the audience a few moments to get oriented, Parker leaned over to Laura and asked, "What's ADAM?"

"The fastest supercomputer in the world. Artificial Intelligence at its best."

"What does it stand for?"

"Something Biblical, I think. But the word around here is it stands for A Damned Arrogant Machine."

"ADAM, go to the time of the event and hold. Show Mars Base."

The view shifted to the perspective of Mars Base. Just as the Commander had said, Phobos was directly overhead, and Deimos was nowhere to be seen.

"ADAM, out."

The view returned to a point in space where both the base and Phobos could be seen. Deimos was peeking around the backside of Mars, not visible yet on Mars Base.

"Those views explain why the Commander thought he was being shot at from Phobos. And that could happen. Sergeant Williams was not at her post when the shot occurred, and the Phobos Base sensors had been severely degraded by their own accident months before."

"ADAM, show Reed, ship, base."

The view shifted to reveal the outward-facing side of Phobos, the Phobos Base and the supposed position of Reed when the hit occurred. The XFS showed as well.

"So now this is where our medical opinion provides some insight. Based on Dr. Reed's symptoms, we believe he received only a glancing blow, at a low angle of inclination. Furthermore, the others standing in the open door on the ship received no irradiation. They would be Dr. Laura Smith, Dr. Jason Parker, and Sergeant Williams."

"ADAM, triangulate shot and show source."

Three lines from Reed, the ship's door and Mars Base converged on a point in front of the image being shown.

"ADAM, go to the source. Show distances."

The view shifted to a point where the lines converged, with the view facing both Mars and Phobos. Deimos was again hidden somewhere behind Mars. The distance to all targets was shown, 3600 miles to Mars Base, 2000 miles to Phobos Base, and an approximate forty-five-degree inclination to Mars Base. The shot had apparently not come from directly overhead.

"So, this is our best guess where it came from." The General said.

"The only problem is, our sensors detected no targets. Nothing was flying."

Dr. Green raised his hand.

"Yes, Dr. Green?"

"Will ADAM recognize my voice?"

The screen seemed to speak. "I know you, Peter Green."

Addressing the General, Peter asked, "May I ask it to recompute?"

Before the General could answer, the screen said, "Yes."

The General shrugged. "What it said."

Laura leaned into Parker, "You see what I mean about arrogant? Sometimes ADAM gives orders, not the General."

"ADAM, assume the gamma-rays came from directly above Dr. Reed. Compute all potential sources."

Turning to the group in the room, "I'm assuming the rays were perpendicular to the surface of Phobos, so Reed would be hit dead on."

"Dead on is right. What are you doing?" Kincaide asked, sounding exasperated. "Dr. Reed would be dead."

"No. Dose is as much a function of time as intensity. Reed was jumping and may have had a very brief exposure."

"Done," ADAM said.

"ADAM, show potential sources on solid objects one at a time ranked by distance, closest to furthest."

On the screen, a long list appeared. At the top was the Earth.

The muttering in the room got louder.

"ADAM, identify geographical region on Earth."

"China," it said out loud. ADAM didn't sound alarmed, but many in the room were.

"ADAM, higher resolution."

The screen zoomed in to an unmarked position on the Tibetan Plateau.

"What the hell!" the General exclaimed. "There's nothing there."

"Are you sure?" Peter asked.

"Who's got the National Reconnaissance Office on speed-dial?" the General barked. "We need to know the window for our next pass over this area."

A hand raised. "Got it, Sir." The lady who responded excused herself from the room, presumably to place a call.

"ADAM, next on the list."

Titan, the largest of the Saturn moons, popped up.

"ADAM, show distance."

ADAM spoke, "744 million miles."

"ADAM, compute solution within our Milky Way galaxy."

Thousands of lines appeared on the overall view of Mars and Phobos.

"ADAM, select the closest in our galaxy and show distance."

One line showed, originating just below the constellation Scorpio, with a distance of 8,000 light-years.

"ADAM, details."

ADAM spoke this time.

"It is a potential gamma-ray burst source originating in the Apep star system.

"ADAM, how strong would a GRB from Apep be?"

"In plain English, it would release more energy in ten seconds than the Sun in ten billion years. A GRB from the Apep star system aimed at Earth would be a civilization-ending event."

"ADAM, is Apep likely to be a GRB repeater?"

"There is a fifty-fifty chance of that happening."

"ADAM, what is the meaning of the word Apep?"

"Apep, the Egyptian serpent-god of chaos."

Addressing the General, Peter asked, "Can I give my opinion?"

"Please do. I can hardly wait." The sarcastic tone in Morrison's voice was readily apparent.

Standing to address the group, Green said, "One reason the base got walloped, is that the Martian atmosphere is fragile and has a miniscule amount of ozone compared to Earth, mostly because of the paucity of oxygen in the mostly carbon dioxide atmosphere. And there is virtually no ozone in the equatorial regions where the base is located. So there was next to nothing attenuating the gamma-rays when they hit."

"Is that true?" someone Parker didn't know asked.

"I wouldn't say it if it weren't. Now let's focus on the math. According to Dr. Reed's medical condition, ADAM has shown us that the gamma-rays could have been centered on the observation post, and not hitting it from an oblique angle like Commander Meyers thinks."

"Then why wasn't Captain Reed fried?"

"Like I said, a short period of exposure. From what I've been told, Reed was mid-jump when the rays hit, and a split second later he was pulled into the shielded ship. Jason, if you, Laura, and Williams had not gotten on board the ship when you did, I think all of you would probably have been killed."

Parker whispered to Laura, "Well, that's a sobering thought."

She did not take her eyes off Green.

Someone asked, "Is there such a thing as a gamma-ray laser?"

"Yes, there is," said Kincaide. "Theoretically possible, but not practical."

"Not for us at least," said the General.

"If aliens wanted to destroy us, there are much more efficient ways than to fly around a big-assed nuclear gamma-ray laser," Kincaide said. "A visible-light laser would do just fine."

All in the room knew that Kincaide was arguably the foremost laser expert in the world. His opinion on this topic would not be questioned.

"What if they don't want to destroy us?" Green asked. "What if it just happened, an accident? What if it wasn't an ET alien at all, but the one thing all civilizations fear?"

"Like what?" asked the General.

"A collapsing neutron star or a black hole called a Blazer, creating a gamma-ray burst."

"Why wouldn't our gamma-ray satellites have seen it? That's what they're up there for."

"A GRB is like a laser in that it produces a thin beam. But it would have to be pointed right at Earth for us to see it. Fortunately, it hit 250 million miles away from us. If we'd seen it that would mean it was pointed towards us, and we humans would be going extinct right about now."

"Why don't we hear more about that threat?" Morrison asked.

"The Fermi II telescope spots GRBs all the time in some far off galaxy or other. But, statistically, our galaxy seems to be quieter. But it could, and probably did happen just now, to a near neighbor. Admittedly, once a neutron star collapses, the GRB is over. It won't happen again to that collapsed star. But a Blazer is a black hole that burps a relativistic jet of gamma-rays whenever it eats a star. And that can repeatedly happen with the same black hole."

"Damn!" said someone wearing a NASA short-sleeved dress shirt.

"You may have noticed that even ADAM doesn't know where the radiation source is located, perhaps outside of our galaxy or perhaps in it. The Apep star system is the closest potential source for a GRB, according to ADAM. But as our galaxy and our solar system are constantly moving through space, we could be lining up right now for the next burp. We'd never see it coming until it was too late."

"Jeeesus Christ," Kincaide muttered.

With a face contorted by uncharacteristic anxiety, the General moved closer to Green, "Why do you say this would be an extinction event?"

Someone else said, "Millions of people would die outright."

"True," Green said, "But that's not it. Our protective ozone layer would be damaged, and quite possibly a large part of our atmosphere could be blown away. Our oxygen levels in the remaining atmosphere could plummet precipitously. Solar radiation would slowly cook us. Our food supply would be killed off, even the fish and the plankton at the bottom of our food chain."

"We wouldn't get a warning?"

"I think we just did. But the next volley could come at any moment. And since we don't know where this star or black hole is located, we have no way of knowing if we're moving into or out of range for the next blast."

"Well God damn it," the General blurted out, "we have to do something."

To the General's obvious displeasure, no one said anything. Generals give orders knowing their words have power. Those subservient to them take their orders as direction and scurry off to do their bidding. But doing "something" was not an order that could be acted upon. It was a plea, a plea that everyone in that room was feeling, all at the same time.

Just then the lady who went to check on satellite schedules came back into the room.

The General looked up at her. "Bridgett, what's the word?"

"1400 Eastern time tomorrow. That's the soonest."

"Well that's useless," the General snorted.

Out of habit, Green raised his hand. "Sir, may I add something?"

"Yeah, why not. I'd love it if you would un-confuse me."

"Let me tell you all something I've learned about stars. They give life, and they taketh away. They are born, and they die. But when they die, they take a hell of a lot of living things with them. Our space-faring ETs know that, and maybe based on what our friend Jason Parker has told us, they have been trying to warn us all along."

"Well they don't have to be so damned cryptic about it," Morrison complained.

Parker thought, *Maybe that's why the Frogs were in such a hurry to leave us. Maybe that's what Samuel Putnam was afraid of.*

Parker called out, "Has anyone been monitoring the oxygen levels on Mars since the attack?"

One of the General's aides spoke up, "Yes, it's been cut in half."

"We assumed the sensors had been damaged by gamma-rays," Kincaide said.

Green said, "I think we'll discover the atmosphere of Mars has been damaged by gamma-rays."

Hans Richter, his left eye askew as ever, had little to say throughout the commotion. Like Parker, he was a practical man and introspective. An idea that had been welling up in him ever since the discovery of the Frogs came bursting forth during a brief moment of quiet in the room.

"Diaspora."

"What?" the General asked, exasperated.

"Diaspora," Richter repeated. "If humanity is to survive, we must scatter. As long as we remain only on Earth, we're sitting ducks."

Morrison was visibly growing impatient. "Folks, we're running out of time. I have only one question. What do we tell POTUS? Since we had no sensor readings of any craft, alien or otherwise within thousands of miles of Mars at the time of the incident, I'm inclined to tell him we're not under alien attack. If you agree, raise your hand."

Parker raised his hand immediately, but Laura turned to Parker and whispered, "What about what Williams is saying?"

"We have no evidence, only hearsay. Peter Green makes more sense." Parker replied quietly.

Laura then slowly raised her hand, which became part of the majority opinion.

"For those who did not raise your hands, I'll give each of you thirty seconds to tell me why you disagree."

The first, identified as Carl Weathersby, Ph.D., Cal Tech department of Physics, said, "The GRB idea is a huge gamble, without a single bit of evidence. It's inference only, and I hate to bet the survival of the human race on inference."

"That's fair," the General answered. "All I would offer is we've detected no alien craft anywhere near Mars or Earth. So there's no evidence for an incipient frontal assault either. Now, is there anyone else?"

Next, a woman in Navy dress blue uniform stood and was identified as Commander Patricia "Pat" Werner, M.D., Ph.D., MPH, Science Adviser to the President.

"Ninety percent of the drivel I've heard just now is junk science. It's one thing to think out of the box, but you do have to know where the box is."

"Do you know this person?" Laura whispered.

"Oh shit," said Parker. "I used to know her back in graduate school. I haven't seen her in at least twenty years. She was full of herself back then, and it looks like she still is."

"The spotlight's on you now, Dr. Werner," the General said. "So, please explain."

Laura leaned over to Parker again. "Did you know she works for President Whitney?"

"No, I didn't," Parker whispered back.

Werner rose high so the camera would pick up her rows of ribbons, lending her the appearance of importance.

"It's like Weathersby observed," Werner said, projecting her voice across the audience so no one would miss a word. "This is all inference. You're making up stuff."

Peeved by the appearance of his old nemesis, Parker spoke up, "We didn't make up the dead astronauts, Pat."

"Jason Parker. Bless your heart. We'll talk later."

"I'm waiting for specifics, Dr. Werner," the General said brusquely.

"First of all, you're listening to Peter Green. Did you know he's a freak? He smells colors. And conveniently, he works in a field where they study things we can't see and defy the laws of physics. For all we know, he and his buddies could be making up incomprehensible mathematics to study fairies. It's a nice gig if you can get it, but do you really want to make life-changing decisions based on his input?"

"Oh my God," Laura whispered. "She's rotten to the core."

Morrison put his hands on his waist, showing his impatience.

"Either give me specifics to consider, Dr. Werner, or we're done here."

"I'll rest. This is all a joke."

"I doubt she'll be invited back," Laura said softly to Parker.

Looking over all the hundred-pound heads gathered at the table, General Morrison's eyes were exploring for more comments, helpful comments, and not finding any.

"Going once, going twice, forever hold your peace."

After one more sweep of the faces, Morrison said, "Okay, the word to POTUS in the morning is that Mars experienced a catastrophic gamma-ray burst from some unknown star or galaxy. It was a cosmic accident, not an act of war."

And then, as if lacking in confidence, he said, "In case we're wrong, I want eyes on Tibet, STAT."

With that, the meeting was concluded. As Parker stood up and stretched, he said to Laura, "Thank goodness that didn't take as long as I thought it would."

Parker had his back towards Pat Werner, so he didn't see her approaching, though Laura did.

"Shit, Jason, she's coming towards us."

"Ignore her," he said. However, he couldn't ignore her when she touched his back to get his attention. That touch sent chills down his spine.

"The last time we met, Jason, you were about twenty pounds lighter. Been eating too much Southern food?"

"No, Pat, it's called growing up," he said.

"Up and out maybe," she said. "I see you're still stuck with the same employer."

Trying his best to avoid a confrontation, he said, "If you enjoy what you're doing, that's all that matters."

"You always were a lightweight, Parker."

Werner and Parker had dated for a while in college. Her self-confidence and sexual appetite appealed to him compared to the previous girl he had dated. She had been Parker's polar opposite. It didn't take long, however, for him to realize Werner fancied herself a dominatrix. Parker's revulsion ended the relationship abruptly and, he believed, mutually. Somehow, they had managed to avoid contact until today.

Laura snapped back at Werner, who was deliberately getting in Parker's face. "I don't care who you are. Fuck off."

Shifting her sneer over to Laura, Werner asked, "And who is this Parker, your girlfriend? Does your wife know about her?"

Laura kept her cool. Looking the Commander up and down, she simply said, "The President deserves better. I'll let him know."

"Ha, like he'll listen to a cunt like you."

Laura simply smiled, knowing that POTUS would indeed listen intently to the Director of the Office of National Intelligence's science advisor for alien affairs. DNI had funded Werner's participation in this secret forum.

"You're a disgrace to the uniform, Werner," is all Parker was willing to say.

Fortunately, Werner kept moving toward the exit, but Parker and Laura hung back, putting some distance between themselves and the Commander. As they waited there, General Morrison approached Laura.

"Dr. Smith, I understand your boss invited that officer. Tell him that if he ever does that to me again, I'll kick his ass."

"Roger that, Sir. I'm definitely taking that for action. She's a disgrace."

"Despicable is more like it," the General said. "Now, I have to apologize to Dr. Green. The President needs to know what a crazy bitch she is in public."

Parker cracked a smile.

The ghost from Parker's past had incredibly complicated matters for General Morrison, and he may not have realized it yet.

The consensus of the Panel had been that Peter Green's assertion of a natural source for the gamma-rays on Mars was more plausible than the alternative explanation of an alien attack from an unknown and undetected alien craft. That was what the General had to report immediately to the Chiefs of Staff and then the POTUS.

The complication was that now the President's personal Scientific Adviser lambasted the credibility of Dr. Green. She offered no alternative to Green's assertion, but she, of all the people in attendance, had the personal ear of the President. So, would the President pay heed to the scientific panel or to the rantings of a Dominatrix?

Ironically, it could be that the survival of the world depended on whether or not the President was into BDSM.

CHAPTER 27. BALBOA

The nurses at the Naval Medical Center San Diego, commonly called Balboa Hospital, were all atwitter over the tall, dark and handsome Navy Captain and physician Emery Reed who was admitted with radiation poisoning. No one at the hospital had seen such a case before, so for a military teaching hospital, it was a rare find. It was also lucky for both them and the patient that the relatively light dose of gamma radiation required little more than supportive care, something on the order of a flu patient.

The primary medical concern was keeping up with his fluid loss from vomiting and bloody diarrhea. The staff's management concern was keeping interns and residents out of his room when his wife, a well-known model and musician, showed up to be with her husband.

Of course, if anyone in the medical community had known how he was irradiated, it would have been an even bigger headache, with journalists clamoring at the door. But since this was a military hospital, all anyone had to say was that the details were classified, which of course they were. People could imagine all they wanted, but no one would ever be able to guess what actually happened to him.

Despite the hullabaloo that came with his famous wife, Reed did not feel at all like a celebrity. He was too nauseated to feel anything except the overwhelming desire to get better. But having worked hand-in-glove with radiation safety officers on submarines, he knew the only cure was tincture of time. That was the treatment plan, the standard of care, and the only things that could derail that course of treatment were infection and dehydration. That was the fight Balboa's doctors were waging, and so far, it was working.

When Jason Parker paid his friend a visit, he wore a surgical mask, booties, and coveralls to protect Reed from any stray bugs.

When Reed saw Parker, he greeted him with a smile.

"Well, my friend," Parker said, "you're looking better than the last time I saw you. When you left, you looked like you were about to toss your cookies."

"I've tossed quite a few since then. Thank God it took a few days for the bad effects to set in."

"We have a lot to be thankful for, but mostly I'm glad you're looking better. While riding the elevator, I heard some nurses talking about you. It seems you've become their favorite patient."

"Patient—ugh. I'm not a very patient patient. I keep telling the staff how to treat me, and they keep ignoring me."

"And well they should. Being a doctor is not your role right now. Aside from the stomach issues, how are you doing?"

"Mentally, I'm a wreck. I keep thinking about—well, you know. Dead astronauts."

"I know. I have the same problem. It takes away the thrill of being on Mars. I've been taking Ambien to get me past it. You getting meds to help you sleep?"

"Whatever it is they give me, knocks me out," Reed said. "But I still wake up with nightmares."

"Maybe what you need is something to think about besides how lousy you feel. You up to helping me with a project?"

"Maybe. What's on your mind?"

"While you were beginning your treatment here, we had a meeting of some brilliant people to decide what to tell the President. At the time, we didn't know if we were under attack or not."

Reed smiled. "I know the story. They updated me."

"You know it was most likely a gamma-ray burst."

"I do."

"Here's something you may not know. According to astronomers at the University of Texas at Austin, a GRB is suspected of causing a major extinction event on Earth 443 million years ago. Based on the geological evidence, a GRB sufficiently powerful to cause whole scale extinctions would not only wipe out life on land but also in the shallow seas. However, life in the deep sea would survive. Water is a great absorber of gamma-rays."

"But wouldn't the atmosphere be destroyed or damaged?" Reed asked.

"Absolutely. If you were deep underwater during the blast, you wouldn't want to surface anytime soon. With Earth's ozone wiped out, ordinary solar radiation would make life untenable, and the joining of oxygen and nitrogen caused by the gamma-rays would make a killer nitrogen dioxide smog that blocked out sunlight and killed all the plants."

"That could happen?"

"Statistically, it could. And it did. If it did it to Mars, it could do it to Earth. Since Mars' atmosphere is a hundred times thinner than ours, and with less oxygen, it's more susceptible to damage on the surface. But if we've already had one extinction event, and maybe more, we could certainly have another."

"That would certainly suck," Reed said, smiling.

"You think it's funny?"

"No, I don't," Reed said.

"We only have two choices as I see it. No matter what you do, a large percentage of humanity will die. Plain and simple, no getting around it. But if we create enough underwater refuges, deep sea refuges, some people at least should survive long enough for the Earth to recover. We'd have a nucleus of people left to start over."

Reed was positively grinning at this point.

"What in the hell is so funny?"

"Give me that notepad over there, will you?"

Parker did as instructed, and Reed wrote something down and handed it back to Parker. It read, "D. Baxter@NASA.gov, Kennedy Space Center."

"What's this?"

"Contact this guy. I hear you know him."

"Yeah, I do. We used to work together on a Spec Op project."

"Then, not much has changed."

Jason Parker knew the think tank assembled by General Morrison was not enough, and he wanted badly to put serious thought into more and better guidance for the Chiefs of Staff and POTUS. He was not really interested in returning to Kennedy Space Center to rehash old ideas with a friend, ideas that he knew were not related to the problem at hand. Reed didn't quite recognize the seriousness of what had just happened. And neither did Washington apparently, or they'd be moving quicker than they were. They did not seem to appreciate just how badly lack of attention to the Mars problem could playout for the United States, or for that matter, the entire human race.

Parker knew it was literally a far-fetched idea, and one that might take a hundred years or more to implement, but someone had to start thinking about it sometime. After the close call for Earth by way of the Mars hit, this was as good a time as ever. After all, NASA had been tasked with protecting the Earth from a killer asteroid, but no one had been thinking about protecting humanity from a gamma-ray burst.

And ultimately, there was no practical way to protect the Earth. What was needed, just as he had initially suggested, were a variety of ways for ensuring the survival of the human race should a cosmic catastrophe strike. After all, that was the whole idea behind Diaspora.

As had just been shown, colonizing a single planet in space was no sure solution. Mars had long been considered the best off-planet candidate for colonization, and look what happened to it. In fact, there had been speculation that Mars might have had flourishing life at one point in the distant past, but something catastrophic had happened to strip away much of the atmosphere and the oxygen contained within it.

And now that threat was staring humankind in the face. It could happen to Earth, at any moment, without warning. It would be a crime against humanity if we were not prepared.

But how?

The Frogs had left mankind with a gift of their technology and identified two people, and a race of Frog-designed Trolls who had the innate ability to fly the craft, the craft Dr. Reed dubbed *Dioscuri*.

So one priority had to be learning how to use it, and build more.

But since *Dioscuri* was the master of space and oceans, which would provide the safest haven for survivors should a cosmic explosion devastate Earth's atmosphere?

Space or the oceans? That was the hugely expensive question.

Chapter 28. Diaspora

Once again Parker found himself waiting outside a closed Pentagon door. He had thought about visiting Don Baxter at NASA Kennedy Space Center, as Dr. Reed had suggested, but he had been on the road or in space nonstop since leaving McMurdo. He was tired and had no time or energy for any more courtesy visits.

As much as I hate to admit it, this is precisely why Sandy left me.

He had been briefed that there would be in attendance Admirals, Generals, and high-level civilians. A couple of months ago he would have been intimidated by the combined ranks of these people, but since then he had flown an alien craft at speeds never before achieved, through virgin space to a destination that could have killed him and his passengers. That earned him street cred if nothing else.

Truth be told, Laura deserves as much credit as me. She shared the same risks, took over the mental contact with the ship when I needed a break, and was every bit as brave. Tell a Navy SEAL he's got to carry a ten-pound alien life form inside of him for nine months and then push it out his butt and we'll see who's brave.

The tension relaxed when a Navy Commander opened the door and ushered Parker into a nondescript room containing two or three personnel from what seemed to be every branch of the military. Before he closed the door, the Commander leaned in close to Parker and said, "Make it concise."

Parker did not have time to respond before the door was shut.

A four-star Admiral stood at the end of the room and spoke. "We as a nation, are indebted to you, Dr. Parker. Thank you for your heroism, and that of Drs. Smith and Reed. And thank you for returning our prize back to us unharmed. I hear you have a name for it besides XFS.

"Yes, sir, we do. Dr. Reed named it *Dioscuri*."

"Then, from henceforth, it will be called that, informally. Its official name remains the same, however."

"I understand," Parker said.

"So, what is it you want to tell us?"

Turning to face the assembled group, Parker started his monologue.

"We have nuclear submarines constantly cruising the depths to ensure we will always have a nuclear strike capability no matter the circumstances. We may not be the first to shoot, but we'll be the last. Now that we know a first strike could come not from an enemy, but from space like it did on Mars, we need a similar approach in place. That approach would not be offensive but would guarantee the survival of the human race. The Earth could be a far different place after a gamma-ray burst. The ozone layer will be gone, a toxic smog will envelop the whole planet. Humans, plants, and animals will die on a scale not witnessed since the death of the dinosaurs.

"There is a chance that part of the atmosphere will be ripped away, carrying away what oxygen did not combine with smog. It may take decades before the Earth's atmosphere returns to normal, and even longer before the biosphere that we are so dependent upon recovers. If it recovers. There is a possibility that after an especially energetic GRB, when the smog finally dissipates, our planet could be left looking like Mars."

There was an audible gasp from the hardened Flag Officers and Senior Executives.

"What we need is a fully autonomous refuge, fixed, not dependent upon a propulsion system and steering controls, fixed to the bottom on land we call our own. For really long-term survival, it cannot be manned by submariners. It would need a much larger population, a breeding colony, and farmers of sorts, biologists and medical care personnel. It would be large, it would be expensive, but it might house the last vestiges of the human race."

Parker paused for a minute before asking the obligatory question.

"Any questions?"

The Admiral spoke. "We don't know that the attack was not a hostile action, or that it was a cosmic blast. The full evidence is not yet in, so we must reserve final judgment."

How the hell are you going to determine that? Parker thought. But he was wise enough to not let his skepticism show.

"But as for what you want us to consider, we will consider it. In the meanwhile, my adjutant will give you the name of someone we want you to contact. Again, thank you for your flawless rescue mission, and for teaching us we can trust the alien technology in our possession. That is a priceless contribution. And please convey our best wishes to Dr. Reed, we wish him a speedy recovery. Thank you again, and you are excused."

And with that, it was over. Parker was led back to the door, and once outside he was handed a card with the following name: Donald Baxter, NASA, Kennedy Space Center.

I guess I'll be making a visit to Don after all.

Donald Baxter was an uncelebrated hero in Parker's eyes. He had been an officer in Naval Intelligence and retired as a Captain in the Naval Reserves doing what he had done best, working Intelligence issues. But for his day job, Baxter was the Senior Engineer for astronaut life support for the Space Shuttle Program. It was through that endeavor that he and Jason Parker had once worked together for the benefit of the Navy Special Operations community. They both were designing diving equipment for unique Navy and NASA missions, and at some point, collaboration just made sense, especially when Baxter transitioned into a NASA diving mission to rescue NASA astronauts. Now, a decade later, who could have imagined that Parker would be the one rescuing astronauts, on Mars, with an alien spaceship.

Then again, life is full of surprises.

The flight down the east coast from Washington D.C. to Space Coast Regional Airport, followed by the drive across the causeway to the Kennedy Space Center held no surprises for Parker, which was much appreciated. Lately, it seemed everywhere he turned he encountered something mind-altering.

Once on the secured portion of the NASA facility, Parker felt lost. The building where Baxter was located was so nondescript as to be impossible to find. He had been there years before, but his vague recognition was not enough to navigate to the proper location. Out of desperation, Parker called Baxter and got turn by turn directions until he pulled up in a parking lot behind the two-story building.

As Parker walked around to the front of the building, Baxter was there to open the door and escort him to the sign-in desk. From there, he left his phone in a lockbox, and followed Baxter down winding halls until they ended up at a door that had a title plate that read, *Senior Engineer, Life Support.*

As Baxter punched in his code in the cipher lock, he turned to Parker and said, "I have a surprise for you."

"I'm getting weary of surprises to tell you the truth."

The door swung open, and Parker saw the silhouette of Laura Smith outlined by the light through the thick windows facing the parking lot.

"I should have known you'd be in on this," Parker said.

"The bad penny turns up yet again."

She stood up and walked over to him, trading a handshake for a hug which was more of an embrace than Parker had expected.

Parker turned back to Baxter. "When Captain Reed sent me to look you up, I had no idea you two were in cahoots."

"Well, I try to know personally all the Intelligence assets that might prove useful to me."

Laura Smith was wearing a tighter fitting dress than the last time Parker saw her, which made it difficult to take his eyes off her. But he was here for business, and this NASA business seemed to be reflected in a diversity of wood and plastic models in Baxter's office. Most were of easily identifiable space-related craft, and interspersed among them was a full-scale model of a cryogenic supercritical air backpack and breathing apparatus. Parker knew that one well.

But another one puzzled him. It didn't look like any spacecraft he knew. In fact, it didn't look suitable for space at all.

"So when Doc Reed called me," Laura said, "and told me he was sending you here, I told him I just got rid of you. And now we're together again."

"Maybe you have too many fingers in too many pies."

"Yeah, that's what my boss tells me. But I think you'll be glad I'm in this one. I told them we needed you."

"You told NASA?"

"Them and others."

"So, what's going on, Don? I'm all ears."

Baxter smiled, looking at Laura like the cat who swallowed the canary.

"Our respective work has crossed paths many times," Baxter said. "without you knowing it. I helped design the life support system for the Bond and Barry Cannon habitats. I know you've been there."

Baxter then pointed to the brown model that Parker couldn't identify. "And then there is that."

Parker walked over to examine it, looking for some label or other identification, but there was nothing to reveal its identity.

"Can I get a clue?"

"Don't look at it from the outside," Laura said. "View it as if you were inside."

"But it's solid, there is no inside."

"It's just a model Jason," Laura said. "In reality it's hollow, and you've been in it."

"You're kidding. Seriously?"

"Yep."

Parker shook his head back and forth, trying to make sense of the object and what he was being told.

"I have…," Parker started to say *no idea,* but then it hit him. "Oh, no, you're kidding me. This is Mars Base?"

"It is," Baxter said. I designed the life support system, just like I did for the habitats. And it worked beautifully for ten years."

"So, you must have gone there, Mars, at some point."

"Sure did. I was on one of the first secret assembly launches. It helps when you work for both Navy Intelligence and NASA."

"So that would explain why I haven't heard from you in ages."

"I have been busy. Plus, I couldn't talk about this. The only reason I can now, is that you've been there. You know our secrets."

"So," Parker said, "why am I here?"

"Let me shield the windows." Baxter stepped over to his desk and pressed a button on a remote control, and all the windows began vibrating randomly, projecting noise out into the outside environment, blocking any laser or acoustical listening devices from hearing the conversation inside. Inside the room, the projected noise was only barely audible, a multi-frequency hiss, white noise.

"When the windows are stimulated, this entire office becomes a SCIF, with no electronic or acoustical signals leaving the room. Pretty neat, eh?"

"I'd say," Parker admitted. "I guess working for NASA has its benefits."

"Actually, Laura's bosses had a lot to do with it," Baxter said. "And now that we can talk freely, you better take a seat."

Parker saw that as a sign this was going to be good. They sat.

Laura spoke next. "You're not the only one who's been thinking about a deep undersea base."

"How deep is deep?"

"The Blake Plateau."

Parker whistled. "Two thousand feet deep?"

"Or deeper."

"I think you know why I thought of it," Parker said, "but why did you guys think of it?"

"Blame it on China," Baxter said. "They've been building territory and trying to occupy the South China Sea for years. But when they became squatters on the Blake Plateau, we'd had enough. So first, you chased them off with the Frogship."

"*Dioscuri* is what we call it now," Laura corrected him.

"You named it? Cool. I like that," Baxter said.

"Dr. Reed named it," Laura said. "And since it saved Reed's life by getting us back so fast, the name is staying."

"Anyway, as I was saying," Baxter continued, "if we want to claim territory for national security reasons, we have to occupy it. Thus, the deep sea habitat idea was born. And since I'd designed the life support system for three autonomous habitats, including two undersea habitats and Mars Base, and I'm still a Captain in Naval Intelligence, I was tapped for life support design."

"That is absolutely rad," Parker said, so genuinely impressed that he reverted to the slang of his youth. After a moment's reflection, he added, "But why am I here?"

"We'll get to that in a minute," Laura said. "Occupying deep-sea territory was the first reason to design a new habitat. But what you probably don't know is that before you scared the Chinese away, I had identified a snippet of unencrypted Frog writing on two frames of a video taken by Tom and J.R. on their DeSoto Canyon hydrogen dive. Feeding that into our best supercomputer, we were able to decrypt a tiny bit of the Frog code they gave you."

"And."

"Well, it appears the Frogs left because something bad is going to happen."

"Like what?" Parker asked.

"We don't know. That's the problem."

"Well, that's also what Samuel Putnam thinks."

"We know, and now the Chinese are speculating," Laura admitted.

"I thought you guys were the best at keeping secrets."

"They are trying hard to find out what we know."

"As always," Parker said. "Do you think we have a leak?"

"Not that we know of," Laura said. "Not yet anyway."

"So now we've had the Mars Base attack. Either there's a potential alien invasion or Peter Green is right, and Mars got hit by a gamma-ray burst."

Baxter added, "Both seem unlikely, but we have the evidence that something like a GRB happened to Mars. If it happened there, it could happen here, any day, without warning. That seems to be the growing consensus at NASA."

Laura continued, "So, a deep sea base provides protection from a GRB since water absorbs gamma radiation, or it would hide a breeding group of humans from alien attack."

"Whoa, you're making my head hurt."

"So, we now have three pressing reasons, pardon the pun, for making this habitat work. And we still think the Blake Plateau is an ideal site for it."

"Except," Parker added, "you want to make a human-friendly, autonomous base at two thousand feet for I guess long-term habitation?"

"Here, let me show you."

Baxter pulled up the 3D holographic depiction of the proposed station. The hologram, projected from the ceiling, floated between Don and Parker.

"Don, you think you can design such a thing?"

"There's a complication, and that's where you come in. For long-term structural integrity, we want to have zero pressure differential across the design's hull."

"You're not talking about a one-atmosphere environment inside?"

"Nope, two thousand feet equivalent pressure. And you're one of the best, if not *the* best scientist to understand how divers can breathe that atmosphere for months at a time."

At that moment, Parker noticed something just outside of the structure. It looked like a holographic diver.

"Are you two kidding me? Is this a joke?"

"No, the structural engineers say it's the only way to ensure long-term survivability of the structure."

"No, I get that. I mean this diver here. Is he on scuba?"

"Of course not. He's using artificial gills. The people can't stay inside forever. He would be doing stuff like EVA repair missions."

"Don, gills don't work on people. We need much more oxygen extracted from the water than seawater contains, especially at two thousand feet."

"Okay, so we need to design people who require less oxygen like we were trying to do on Mars."

Shaking his head, Parker said, “Okay Don, I get it. You guys need my help.”

Laura stared at Parker and said, “I love it when your eyes sparkle.”

Baxter led Parker down a hallway to a door that had numerous warning signs on it, too many for Parker to read as they quickly passed through the door. Inside was something that looked like an engineering school research laboratory. They paused in front of a diagram on the wall. It seemed extremely complicated, a fact which Baxter tried to remedy by, as he said, “dumbing it down.”

“We’ll start at the left side of the diagram with the one element that can make this whole plan work for an autonomous undersea base. It’s modeled on the Mars Base concept which clearly worked well for ten years. This block is the power source, our small fusion reactor. It provides power, but it also produces helium which we need for our breathing medium. As craft come and go to the base, we’ll inevitably lose a little helium, and so we need a way of restoring those losses without dependence on anything topside or shore-based. Secondly, using your approach to deep diving in the DeSoto Canyon, we’ll need a hydrogen source. Then, from our desalination process for obtaining freshwater, we’ll be able to electrolyze the freshwater. From that, we get oxygen and hydrogen.”

Baxter paused in front of what was obviously a pressure chamber based on the ruggedness of its construction.

Parker said, “Hydrogen, eh. You know there’s one downside of hydrogen diving.”

“Explosions?”

“No. Not enough oxygen for that below 600 feet. I’m talking about hydrogen psychosis.”

“We may have a solution for that.”

You mean Zanax? Parker thought.

“We have a theory that a prolonged compression will allow for adaptation. Let me show you. This chamber is rated to 100 pounds per square inch, a pressure equivalent to 225 feet of seawater. But we think the secret to avoiding hydrogen psychosis is by allowing the addition of helium from the fusion reactor, and hydrogen from electrolysis to be controlled by the rate of water electrolysis.”

Baxter directed Parker’s attention to computer screens with the visual representation of standard round gauges. For some reason, Parker found that display familiar and satisfying.

"See these gauges for hydrogen and helium flow? A computer is controlling the electrolysis process, making sure that the contained oxygen never reaches an explosive mixture as we're taking the chamber to depth. And since this is considered a refuge, we can take a month or more getting down to maximum depth. We're in no hurry. That slow rate of descent should give the divers' bodies time to adjust to the hydrogen."

"Well, 225 feet is not very deep."

Baxter laughed. "Oh, no. This is just a test chamber to prove our ability to control the electrolysis and depth change. I know you left NDC last year so you may not know we're on their schedule in six months to go all the way down to 1000 psi, or 2250 feet of seawater, more than we'll need for a Blake Plateau habitat."

"Good for you. But I'm surprised NDC will let hydrogen in the chamber."

"We've had to do some convincing, but, after all, this is a national imperative."

Parker looked over at Laura, then back at Baxter. "Some might argue this should be a world imperative."

"Baby steps Jason," Laura answered. "Baby steps."

"Okay, so the overall plan doesn't suck too bad," Parker said, "but the devil's in the details."

CHAPTER 29. SOUTH CHINA SEA

The Spratley Islands had been receiving more than the usual attention from U.S. Naval and Intelligence sources ever since China made their outrageous and illegal claim to the South China Sea. In spite of dissenting international opinion, China had built new land by dredging the shallow waters of the Spratley Islands, and occupying that new land located over 650 miles from the closest Chinese island, Hainan, and much closer to the Philippine Island of Palawan.

Squatters' rights are built upon tenuous international laws, but in China's case, they were willing to reinforce the claim on land they created by a military presence. Perhaps inspired by the old Russian empire, China was aggressively extending its reach and claims to both the Arctic and the South China Sea. Geographically, those claims were preposterous, but China wanted to make a point: they considered themselves to be a global power, not just a regional power.

A young Chinese Naval Officer of rank *Shang Wei,* equivalent to Lieutenant in other Navies, watched nervously as the crane on his barge slowly lowered a thirty-meter-diameter acrylic dome into the azure waters just offshore of Fiery Cross Reef, a man-made and fortified island, one of many in the appropriated Spratley Islands.

In spite of its size, the dome was relatively light because it was not designed to protect the inhabitants from the pressure at 200 meters. Instead, it was intended to protect the inhabitants from animal predators. The fact that it was flooded with ambient seawater would ensure no pressure gradients could weaken its thin surface.

Lieutenant Zhang's jet-black bushy eyebrows belied the fact that the hair underneath his officer's cap was almost non-existent. He knew a lot was riding on the correct deployment of this habitat. The intent was to place the dome on the slope of the Spratley Islands chain so it would be deep enough to protect it from surface events like tsunamis and other atmospheric or celestial events yet shallow enough to make sure a plentiful fish population was available. It also had to be shallow enough that it wouldn't be a physiological burden on the *Shui er* or *water children* who would soon be occupying the domed hemisphere.

Under the Lieutenant's watchful eye, the clear dome entered the water, concave side up. It bobbed in the waves for a few moments before its weight pulled the edge of the upside-down dome just beneath the surface, allowing seawater to entirely fill the structure. Once it had been lowered forty meters beneath the surface, cables cradling one point on the curved surface would be tightened while the ones on the opposite side were loosened, allowing the structure to flip over, assuming the appearance of an umbrella floating to the sandy bottom far below.

Ever since a Chinese-born biochemist in the United States had worked out how to do gene editing on mammalian DNA using the CRISPR-Cas9 method, Chinese biochemists and geneticists on the Chinese mainland had been working overtime to develop *a super-soldier* and a *super diver* using methods forbidden by ethicists in the U.S. and most Western countries.

In Lieutenant Zhang's point of view, his Motherland had every right to defend itself using whatever means available. So what if many genetically altered human embryos were lost in the process of experimentation? Surely their destruction would be less traumatic than the millions of more completely developed fetuses deliberately destroyed every year by Western nations. It seemed to him and his fellow officers the very height of hypocrisy to condemn human genome editing for scientific research while at the same time supporting the killing of unborn children for convenience.

He often told his military friends that if the mistaken sense of morality of the naïve and self-righteous Americans allowed China to overpass it on the battlefield, then it must be a consequence of the superiority of Eastern logic.

Walking back into the ship's bridge, he watched the monitors showing images from the two autonomous vehicles following the dome as it descended. If it looked like the dome was going to settle in an inauspicious spot, the ships' dynamic positioning thrusters would gently move the dome whichever direction would assure a smooth landing on a sandy bottom with a minimum of slope.

A remotely operated vehicle or ROV had already discovered an ideal location, which was no easy feat since by the time the bottom contours reached 200 meters they were already beginning their plunge down to truly deep waters, three-thousand meters.

Zhang didn't know much about the scientific details of the *Shui er*, except to know that the test tube children were either chimeras or something entirely new with genes spliced from humans and something else. That something else was a contribution of the genetic material of an unknown source from a Russian Genetics Institute, under the requirement that absolutely no inquiries into the source of the material would be permitted, under pain of death.

As the dome was passing 120 meters a panicked school of fish, being chased by a tiger shark, sought refuge in the dome as it continued its steady descent. The fish's strategy seemed to work as the shark kept bumping its head against the dome, trying to get to the fish circling at the upper-most portion of the transparent dome. To those on the bridge of the ship, the scene captured by the ROV cameras was comical. However, the fish themselves were still panicked. They could no more work out why they were being protected from the shark's jaws than the shark could.

Zhang turned to the senior enlisted sailor close to him and said, "Looks like we'll have some fish to deal with when we get this thing on the bottom."

As the dome and its captive fish school continued heading into dimmer light, the shark was following it down, with his body arrayed vertically like the fluttering tail on a kite.

The sonar on the vessel called out the depth of the dome as it neared its sandy destination.

"150 meters, 160 meters, 170 meters."

At that point the winch operator shifted into low gear, slowing the dome's descent for a soft landing. As the dome reached 180 meters, the shark must have finally realized what he had to do. With a quick flick of his powerful tail, he raced down the curved side of the dome and slipped under its edge just as the dome contacted the bottom.

What happened next was a scene of utter chaos. The once safe fish now had nowhere to run or hide, and the Tiger shark earned its reputation as a killing machine, slashing ruthlessly through the ball of fish, then tracking each of the survivors down and swallowing them whole. Within less than a minute, all of the fish were consumed, and the blood of those ripped in half by the cavernous jaws colored the seawater in the dome.

"Well Lieutenant, the Chief Petty Officer said, "I'd much rather deal with a school of fish than a single Tiger Shark. What do we do now? Pull the dome back up a bit and hope the shark leaves?"

"We can't *xiǎo Wáng*. Remember, on contact with the bottom, penetrating bolts all around the dome fired, anchoring the dome to the coral base. It can't be moved, even by a typhoon. We'll just have to let the *Shui er* deal with it."

"Surely not, they're children."

"You don't know these children. They'll probably skin it alive and eat it for dinner."

The CPO looked at the Lieutenant with a half grimace and a half-smile on his face. "You're kidding, right?"

Lieutenant Zhang just smiled. "And they are our secret weapon against the Americans."

"Won't the SEALs just kill the children?"

"Never intentionally. That is one of their greatest moral taboos. And one of their weaknesses which we will exploit."

Lieutenant Zhang smiled again, this time with a smile that was more of a sneer.

"Their weakness is our strength," the CPO recited from one of the People's Liberation Army training manuals.

Zhang patted his subordinate on the back in a paternalistic way. "You have learned well."

Chapter 30. The Oval Office

The Director of National Intelligence walked into the Oval Office without knocking.

"Samuel, a knock is customary, you know."

"Mr. President, we received a Red Flag communication from Laura Smith a little while ago. And now we have a confirmation."

The President paused, still holding a half-full cup of coffee. His hands and right arm began twitching, and to stop the palsy, he threw the cup across the room, staining some of the most precious carpet in the world.

Dr. Emery Reed had been waiting in the West Wing for admission to the Oval Office. He really thought he would never see the inside of that office again. Having spent eight years serving two Presidents, by all rights he should be left with nothing but memories, both good and bad. But for some inexplicable reason, he had been requested to return and was now waiting to meet the current POTUS, Harmon Whitney.

Reed still felt sore, and perhaps would always be burdened with that discomfort. Once damaged, nerves take a long time to heal, but maybe with time, the pain would improve. No one knew for sure. There just wasn't a patient population upon which to make inferences since gamma-ray bursts are fortunately rare. But it did make for an unusual medical case study, which had been classified before it was even written.

As Reed bided his time, he could hear agitated voices coming through the door. He recognized one as the President's. Though muffled, it was not the sonorous, composed voice usually heard by the public. It was a full pitch higher. Reed could sometimes make out an occasional *damn* and *hellfire*.

And then silence, followed by the opening of the door closest to Reed. Through that door marched an intense appearing dark-haired man who in passing gave Reed a glance with his very dark eyes that silently asked, *Who the hell are you?*

Reed was wondering the same thing but had the well-practiced sense to not betray his thoughts.

"You may see the President now," said the middle-aged, a bit thick in the middle, and matronly woman controlling Presidential access. He could not see her shoes, but considering her station in life, he presumed them to be sensible-yet-stylish. She had that air about her.

Reed paused. He was not a man quickly troubled or intimidated, but this visit seemed to be ill-timed. And he didn't know why.

"The President is waiting," the lady said more emphatically this time.

Indeed, he was. When Reed entered the great office once again, he had a strong feeling of *Déjà-vu,* except the face and body rising from the President's desk was different. For a moment, he felt disoriented, but he knew better than to let that be known. But one thing he could not help notice was what appeared to be a large coffee stain on the oval rug in front of the President's desk.

Perhaps the President strode quickly over to Reed out of consideration for Reed's pain, or maybe he was merely more energetic and youthful acting than Reed had realized. He grasped Reed's hand firmly and shook it, carefully at first and then more forcefully.

"Well, you are every bit of what I'd been told."

"Yes, sir." For Reed, this begged the question, *what had he been told?*

"But you look like you're in pain so let's find you a seat. I assume you're not taking pain meds today?"

Under standard etiquette rules, such a question would be out of bounds, but Reed understood that POTUS had a right to know the mental state of those he was addressing. After all, POTUS's conversations were rarely casual.

"No, Mr. President, I wanted to be unencumbered when meeting with you."

"Good. I don't think we met during your stint with the previous Presidents. But I've heard a lot about you. And now you're the only man in the world who's survived a blow from a cosmic gamma-ray burst. That makes you pretty special, Dr. Reed."

"I'll take luck anytime I can get it."

"So do you prefer to be called Dr. Reed or Captain Reed?"

"Actually, I prefer Emery."

"Okay, Emery it is then. Can I offer you water before we start our chat?"

"No, thank you, Mr. President. I had some outside. I'm good."

"Okay, but look, let's dispense with protocol here. It can get really awkward if you keep calling me Mr. President, so for the time being, and this one time only, just stick with Sir."

"Whatever you say, Mister, I mean, Sir."

"Good, we don't have all day. Now I assume you have no idea why you are here. Is that correct?"

"Correct, sir. I have no clue."

"Well, it's about that coffee stain I saw you looking at as you came in. I don't know if you know, but there has always been a group within the Agency that was concerned that the Frogs left Earth out of concern for our planet's future. But we figured that was nothing more than paranoia."

"I had the same thoughts."

"But our fears were just confirmed by Dr. Laura Smith, your friend Jason Parker's girlfriend."

Reed wanted to inform him their friendship was entirely platonic, and that Parker seemed to be happily married, even though Laura did seem a bit flirtatious at times. But then, with the entire U.S. Intelligence apparatus at his disposal, POTUS might actually know more about Parker and Laura than Reed did. That much he remembered from his days with the previous Presidents.

"How is that, Sir?"

"Dr. Smith did a frame by frame examination of the videos taken by our Navy divers during the discovery of the Frog Ship in the De Soto Canyon cave, the alien ship we now call XFS."

XFS Dioscuri, Reed wanted to tell him but didn't.

"As I think you know, the coded history and recitation of future events given to us by the Frogs are highly encrypted by what we believe is some sort of quantum code. It may indeed take us a hundred years to crack it, just as the Frogs said. But we had a lucky break. Dr. Smith caught on a single video frame a bit of unencrypted Frog writing which, like the Rosetta stone, we hoped would give us a glimpse of the ending. And after our fastest supercomputers worked for months on that critical ending, they found what we believe is a surprise message."

Please don't tell me it's a cookbook, Reed thought, thinking back on an old Twilight Zone episode called "How to Serve Man."

"We don't have a great deal of confidence in anything in particular yet, but we believe the ending tells of a worldwide catastrophic event."

"Like what happened to our Martians?"

POTUS nodded his head. "In a word, perhaps. We'd been worrying about an asteroid impact, and NASA was going apeshit trying to run the threat analyses for the next hundred years and coming up empty. But after the Martian event, we realized we might have been looking in all the wrong places. We need to be focusing much further out, and there's really no way to do that. We don't have the technology."

"I must admit Sir, as I was getting sicker and sicker on the Mars return trip, I spent a lot of time thinking about what would happen if that event had hit Earth. And I didn't like what my mind was telling me."

"For good reason. It could prove to be an extinction event. And that is precisely why that carpet behind you is soiled. My pants may be too, but I'm too busy to check."

Reed had to smile at that image coming from the President of the United States.

"Knowing that news is a heavy responsibility, I'm sure," Reed said.

"Can I do anything to share the load?"

"I think you can, and that's why you're here. So let me tell you something you might not know. For years we've had think tanks like the Rand Corporation and other folks you've never heard of thinking and planning for potential extinction events. The assumption has always been we'd have some warning. But now we realize we might have no warning at all."

"As I understand it, that is true if we're talking a GRB."

"Right. Now we are. And guess what every one of the think tanks has concluded?"

"I don't—"

Interrupting Reed, POTUS continued. "Diaspora. They all say that. We must, and I emphasize *must*, colonize the moon and Mars, and even the moons of the outer planets."

"I'm not surprised."

"Tell me what you think is the fallacy in that?"

"For the moon and Mars, they have either no or minimal atmosphere to protect from cosmic radiation. Whoever colonizes those bodies would be worse off than if they'd stayed on earth unless they'd burrowed underground."

The President smiled.

"They told me you were a smart cookie," Whitney said. "And you are exactly right."

"And to find a moon or planet with a protective atmosphere," Reed continued, "we're talking much more extreme environmental conditions."

"Even than Mars, right?" the President asked.

"Much worse Sir."

"Your past job was to protect the President and their family, at least medically. Putting that hat on again, what would you recommend I do?"

"Don't go into space, Sir. Hunker down under ground or under water."

POTUS smiled again. "Bingo. Now, why do you think the Rand and other groups don't like that idea?"

"Got me, Sir. The benefits are kind of obvious."

"There's not enough money in it. Space exploration and transportation are unimaginably expensive and might benefit very few humans. And that is a mighty big 'might.' For the same money, we could provide shelter for a cross-section of humanity, both underground and underwater. Of those two options, underground or undersea, what do you think would be better?"

"Sir, if you don't mind me borrowing some ideas from Jason Parker and Peter Green, I'd say underwater."

"And why so?"

"If they are correct that the atmosphere could be irreparably damaged for decades if not hundreds or thousands of years, then exposure to the atmosphere could kill whatever survivors we might have. Being in an underwater habitat assures an autonomous environment. Underground, on land, any seismic movement could crack a hermetically sealed bunker like Mount Weather or Raven Rock."

"See, that's what I've been thinking. But I'm going to get a lot of resistance from Congress, lobbyists, and corporations who want money for expansion in space. They don't seem to get the point. Space exploration is great, and I agree we should do it, but our first priority should be on saving some remnants of the human race from a deep space disaster. Otherwise, we're going to spend trillions, and then end up losing half of the colonizers, or more, like we just did on Mars."

Reed thought about that for a second, then said, "I once heard Peter Green or Parker, I forget which, say something that stuck with me. In all likelihood, even unfriendly extraterrestrial aliens are afraid of cosmic explosions. Those explosions are no respecter of life or civilizations."

"Absolutely."

"But Sir, I'm still curious, why do you think I can help you?"

"When I mentioned saving a cross-section of humanity, I meant it, and not just altruistically."

Reed pulled his head back in surprise. *What did that mean?*

"We will need to plan for the long-term medical care of whatever remnants we deal with, and that includes our new Troll population. I hear you've already had to deal with the medical issues of those folks."

"True, we don't know much about their medical care. Trolls are not identically human. But the good news is that since we moved them out West, they seem to be staying pretty healthy."

"I'm glad you're keeping tabs on them. Genetically, how different are they?"

"Five Percent, based on some DNA samples I took from a sick Troll girl."

"How did that happen?"

"She was my first and so-far only sick Troll patient, and lacking any genetic information about her I surreptitiously took some samples of her DNA and sent them off for analysis by Emory University in Atlanta and the Max Planck Institute for Evolutionary Anthropology in Leipzig, Germany."

"And?"

"She had 95% match with the human genome."

"Well, that's good then. Right?"

"To put that into perspective, the difference between humans and chimpanzees is only 1.2 percent."

"You're losing me, Doctor. They can't be more different from us than chimpanzees."

"Looks can be deceiving. It very much depends on which genes are different."

"Speaking of, let me run a hypothetical past you."

"I love hypotheticals, Sir."

"I thought you would. Let's suppose there are ET species who were artificially bred to serve as slaves to other ET species."

"Like the Trolls were slaves for the Frogs?"

"But different. Let's say this other species had reproductive organs, but they couldn't produce babies."

"As in deliberately made sterile?"

"Maybe, to limit their numbers. Or perhaps it was an accident of hybridization, like mules being a sterile cross of horses and donkeys. But here's the hypothetical question. If that species had the know-how to do gene editing and produce fertile versions of themselves, how would they do it?"

"They could do something we're trying to do, turn normal tissue cells into functioning sex cells."

"I'll take your word for it. But that would take a lot of laboratory equipment, wouldn't it?"

"Some. It's not a simple process, that's why we can't do it yet."

"But if we provided the equipment, and they provided the know-how, would that be something worth doing?"

"That's a stimulating hypothetical, Sir. We would help save their species, while at the same time making a quantum leap in our understanding of both genetic engineering and ET species."

"So, you would see that as a win-win?"

"Sure would. The more we encounter non-humans, the more we need to understand them. I'd love to understand Troll genetics better so we can treat them if the need arose."

"Okay, you have definitely broadened my horizons, Emery. No wonder the other Presidents liked you. But just remember, this is all hypothetical, so please keep our conversation close to your chest."

"Aye, aye Sir. Will do."

By Presidential order, Dr. Reed was leading the completion of the DNA genomics investigation of the Trolls. According to some geneticists, the initial research had been sloppily done, with misleading results. The new survey was attempting to replicate and expand the earlier study. Because of the potentially alarming findings, the old results had been classified after the fact, and all further work would be done by government scientists at Walter Reed Army Medical Center, and remain classified.

On the surface, the government was trying to learn how to medically treat these people, newly minted U.S. citizens. The nine-year-old sick Troll girl had been a major scare for the few medical caregivers who knew who the Trolls really were.

But under that surface—and there is always something under the surface—they wanted to learn as much as they could about the genes the Frogs had contributed to the mainly human genome the Trolls contained.

At the same time, no one really wanted to think about how the Frogs had obtained those human genes.

CHAPTER 31. ETH ZURICH

Thursday night, late, Jason Parker received two genetics reports from Zurich. He had more or less forgotten about it, given all the other distractions of late. When he opened the attached PDF, he found the laboratory name, GeneList Technologies, Inc., about the only easy to read information in the report.

The first report was divided into three sections, corresponding to the three samples submitted. One, the most anticipated, was on the "Guacamole," the presumed alien sample removed from the compressed craft found in Antarctica. The other two were prepared blood samples, one from Dr. Reed, and one from Parker himself. Those two were control samples added to check for any irregularities in the genomics testing or reporting process. It was standard procedure.

The good news about the Guacamole sample was that, according to the report, it was genuinely alien. As Parker read down the list of findings, he saw that the extracted material was full of complex DNA, not merely primitive DNA from fungi, bacteria, or unicellular algae.

Thank goodness for that, Parker thought, rubbing his temples.

In the second report, that from the sick nine-year-old girl troll, the most surprising finding of the analyses was that the five percent unidentified genetic material from the Troll was also found in the so-called inheritable, germ portion of the presumed alien sample. In other words, whatever organism that sample was from, several chunks of its DNA had found their way into the Troll's DNA. Whether that was coincidence or purposeful was hard to tell.

In other words, there was a possibility that the Troll girl was a chimera, a hybrid between humans and the unknown organism.

There was one other genetic finding worth further exploration. One gene marker was shared among the alien material, the Troll, and Jason Parker. At first, Parker thought that was simply an expression of the genetic code unique to mammals. After all, the Trolls and Parker were mammals, so perhaps the alien was as well.

But that thought dissolved when Parker noticed that same genetic marker was absent from Reed's data.

What on Earth could I have in common with this unknown alien stuff and the Troll girl? Why would Reed not have it?

As he stared at the computer screen, puzzling over that genetic relationship, he kept having a nagging question.

What in the hell is that alien stuff?

Parker desperately needed to go to Switzerland to check on the Guacamole reconstruction effort.

Jason Parker's commercial flight arrived in Zurich in the early morning. His appointment with Professor Helmut Reuter was in the afternoon, so his first priority on arriving was to take a cab to his downtown hotel near ETH University and get some sleep.

After a few hours' nap, he was recovered enough from his jetlag to walk from the hotel to a park at the northern head of Lake Zurich, purchase a luncheon brat from a vendor's cart, then walk the very few blocks to the University.

While lunching on the edge of that lake created by glaciers during the last ice age, he wondered two things. One was why it was that in Europe it was considered normal for parents to give wine to their children, whereas in the States that was deemed to be verboten.

Secondly, he thought back to the last ice age, an event with a catastrophic effect in some early human's opinion, or perhaps a beneficial effect on Europe when viewed from a geological timescale. Likewise, would a gamma-ray burst possibly have a beneficial impact on Earth when viewed from a geological epoch perspective?

What strange thoughts encroach on your mind when sleep-deprived and thrust into a new environment. But Parker realized he had to clear his mind of such thoughts before meeting Professor Reuter. The professor had promised that what Parker would see, would be more bizarre than anything imaginable. Parker had seen a lot of strange things in his relatively short adult life, so his imagination was primed for anything.

Or almost anything.

After washing down his last bite of bratwurst with a little Pinot Noir, Parker found his way back to the University. Following directions emailed to him by Professor Reuter, he wound his way up several flights of stairs, then walked down old stone halls to find Room 402,

Reuter's office and laboratory. After knocking on the heavy wooden door, Parker heard a shuffling sound accented by tapping just before the door opened. The door swung inward silently, revealing a tall, slightly skinny and disheveled man with a full mane of bushy white hair and old-fashioned *pince-nez* glasses, leaning on an elaborately carved cane. He looked like a relic from a bygone era, but his technical skill was reputed to exceed the state of the art.

"Ah, the famous Dr. Parker. You are right on time. Please come in."

As Reuter led him into his office, he said, "In my day I used to be quite fleet on the football field. Soccer, as you Americans call it for some reason. But apparently, the constant abuse resulted in arthritis in my hip. As you see, I use a cane to get around. That's rather ironic. You say 'Use it or lose it,' but sometimes you lose it anyway."

Parker had not been wondering about the man's limp or his cane, or anything else really. He just wanted to know what all the mystery was about.

"Can I offer you some cognac?" The professor asked.

"No, thank you, I'm fine."

"So, I suppose you want to know why I called you here rather than simply sending you a report."

"Precisely," Parker said.

"You really have to see this to believe it."

"I can hardly wait," Parker admitted.

"Your patience will be rewarded, I assure you."

With some effort, Reuter led Parker to a bank of computer screens. When he moved a computer mouse a large screen brightened, revealing a greenish amorphous blob with irregular edges and an irregular shape that bore a slight resemblance to melted and refrozen pistachio ice cream.

"This is what you sent us, based on the three-dimensional scans you obtained, well, wherever you obtained it. Frankly, I can't imagine where you found this."

Reuter looked at Parker with a curious glance, but Parker knew not to give any clue as to where the scan came from.

"You didn't give us much to go on. We usually know if we're dealing with a person or an animal, but we had no clue what this was. And I assume you don't know either, or you wouldn't have hired us."

"I hope that was a wise choice on our part," Parker said, smiling at Reuter.

"Oh, you have no idea how wise it was," Reuter responded thoughtfully. "I've explained before how our modeling takes advantage of biological symmetry. Almost anything other than an amoeba has symmetry, so we started with that assumption. The left side of our bodies is essentially a mirror image of the right side of our bodies. That applies to our face, brain, lungs, limbs, breasts, kidneys, ovaries, and testicles. It's universal throughout our animal kingdom."

"Redundancy in biology is a good thing I suppose," Parker mused out loud.

"It's also pretty universal that animal structures are longer than wide, with a clearly defined front and back. What goes in one end must come out the back, in general. And so animals can see what they're eating, eyes tend to be arranged at the front end."

Parker was growing impatient. *When are we getting to the good stuff?*

"So now, you apply these rules to all the basic animal forms, real or imagined, in our animal inventory, or even the literature, and then digitally squash them with either a simulated steamroller, or a millennium-old ice deposit, and see which of the results match the best, statistically, with what you scanned."

"And you did this first with Otzi?" Parker asked.

"Indeed, but what I'll show you in a moment is from more modern corpses, unlucky Elizabethan hikers. I have a video of how the reconstruction occurred in their case."

On the computer screen popped up a scanned image of what was discovered after the alpine ice melted, finally revealing the two tortuously intertwined bodies.

"As you can see, we didn't have much to go on. We could only guess their sex by their clothing, which was fairly typical for that era."

"What were they?"

"Male and female. You'll see more as the reconstruction begins."

Parker watched intently as the computer unfolded and untwisted the crumpled bodies.

"Keep in mind, this process is not random. The forces applied to the digital bodies were the opposite of the forces that have been measured inside crevasses as they move down a mountain. Scientists have buried sensors inside crevasses all over Switzerland, and elsewhere, so those measured forces are being applied to each of these body parts."

"How do you know the same forces were in play?"

"We don't, but taking the average of many such measurements, we come up with our best estimate, which is all we need in this case. So watch this."

As if watching time run backward, the computer screen unraveled the estimated forces to reveal what was clearly a male and female hiker.

"Wow," Parker said.

"We don't know who they were, but they were young, and seemed to have survived their fall, at least for a bit. Although over time their bones were broken by the movement of the ice, those breaks appear to have been post-mortem. Which means they may have frozen to death rather than been killed in the fall. In fact, the best way to explain their extremely close proximity is that they may have been hugging each other for warmth until they froze to death."

Parker found that poignant detail disturbing.

Reuter noticed Parker's reaction and added, "The Alps are a dangerous place, Dr. Parker. And you're not the first person to be so affected. But I have a cure for that, the real reason you are here."

Parker looked at Reuter and smiled. Indeed, he was ready to move on.

"Considering what you and your team saw, it took a lot of computer processing time for a recognizable life form to emerge from the goo. It was made all the more difficult by the absence of bony structures. Its skeleton, such as it is, was mostly cartilaginous. Only the skull appeared to have been ossified."

"I assume you had other morphological forms which were unlikely based on what we know of biological structure."

"Indeed. If one of the computer's suggestions was a flying Tyrannosaurus Rex, we would rule that out as not being consistent with the amount of lift available on wings—as we know them."

"I get that, but that would also preclude the possibility of flying dragons."

Reuter laughed. "Yes, that would be very unlikely, but as you know, monsters do not have to be real to be interesting."

While the conversation about dragons was going on, the computer could be seen running through all the possibilities for the original biological structure. But all chit chat slowed to a standstill when the first image of a possible structure began to appear out of the probabilistic haze.

"So now you see something interesting, don't you?"

"It looks vaguely humanoid."

"Just wait. The solutions are finally beginning to converge, and I think you will soon be surprised."

Indeed, as the contours of the most probable life form began to fill out, Parker grabbed a chair to steady himself. "Are you serious?" he asked Reuter. The question was purely rhetorical since Reuter was not one to kid about his life's work.

"This is my question for you, Dr. Parker. Have you ever seen a mermaid before?"

Parker stammered, knowing full well that what he was gazing at was a fair approximation of what he had once seen in a Russian medical freezer.

But the words would not leave his mouth.

Chapter 32. Svalbard

Svalbard sits like a frozen half-way house between Norway and the North Pole. The icy island sits high above the Barents Sea, with mountains thrust up by the motion of the nearby oceanic rift between the North American and Eurasian Tectonic Plates.

While Jason Parker was traveling to Switzerland, Svalbard was hosting a rare and highly secretive meeting of political giants, aimed at healing economic rifts between the most powerful countries riding on those North American and Eurasian geological plates.

Through combined political earnestness and strategic deception, the President of the United States, Harmon Whitney, had arranged to meet his counterparts from Russia and China. The purpose of the meeting was ostensibly to discuss China's interest in the Arctic, an interest that lay geographically distant but strategically close to China's national interests as exemplified by the concept of the Polar Silk Road, an aggressive effort launched in partnership with Russia.

There was a covert purpose for the meeting that would no doubt come as a shock to the Eurasian Presidents. Dr. Emery Reed was one of the few people on Earth who would be there to witness their dismay. It was, after all, the Doctor's urging that the secret that had been so closely held by the U.S. President and his Security Council should by all rights be shared with the leaders of the Earth's most populous nations, even if they were frequently at odds politically. The message the President wished to share was a dire message affecting the entire planet.

As for the supposed intention for the meeting, POTUS could not have cared less. Countries squabble over land, something that can be occupied, and defended. But in spite of what alarmists had been shouting, the Arctic was nothing more than deep water with varying degrees of sea ice covering it, just as it had been for millennia. On occasion, those areas that were ice-free were navigable, and all nations had a right to navigate them. As for the Arctic oil, once fusion reactors made their way out of the black military world to enter civilian service, they would put a significant dent in the financial gains from deep sea drilling in one of the most environmentally hostile regions of the planet.

And if scientists and engineers could ever figure out what propelled the Frog Ships, world energy concerns might completely disappear. Or so it seemed.

The grunt work for yet another draft Arctic Treaty had been accomplished by tirelessly laboring staffs at home. But today, the POTUS had a field trip on the schedule. He wanted his colleagues to view the Doomsday vault above the Longyearbyen airport. He had a lesson planned for them.

The Svalbard Global Seed Vault was built into a hillside, with an entrance less than half a mile from the east end of the Longyearbyen runway. As the three Presidents arrived at the brightly decorated entrance to the mountain tunnel in separate explosion-proof vehicles, Norwegian Special Forces operators guarded the short column from fore, aft and flank positions. Top cover was provided by F-35 aircraft fully loaded for any contingency.

Once the Presidents were inside the vault, its massive inner and outer doors were closed, shielding the dignitaries from anything short of a direct thermonuclear strike.

After the customary tour led by the keepers of the frozen, ice-clad seed vault, the Presidents gathered again in the larger anteroom. No one else was in the room except for the Presidents and their translators, and Dr. Reed. There the American President's voice could be clearly heard, reverberating among the icy rock walls.

"And so it is here, in hidden icy places deep inside granite mountains that the vestiges of civilization's agriculture might one day reside. If we ever have to hit the reset button after a calamity brought to bear by ourselves, or the cosmos, this, and a few other sites like it, is where we must come. But what about us, human beings? Have we built a sanctuary for the human race?"

He looked back and forth between the other Presidents. "That was a rhetorical question. I already know the answer. It's no."

The other Presidents looked like they would rather be anywhere besides listening to President Whitney.

He continued. "The official reason we are here is to sign an agreement that places such seed repositories high among our mutual national interests. After all, an asteroid could hit the most fertile wheat fields of the central U.S., or Russia, or the rice fields of China and our very sustenance could be at risk. But I now ask you to consider a greater calamity, one that I will not speak of again after we go our separate ways."

The Russian and Chinese Presidents briefly looked at each other, apparently puzzled.

"While we busy ourselves with ways of deflecting an incoming asteroid, what about some other cosmic event that can destroy humankind with zero warning? The Earth is defenseless against a gamma-ray burst."

The other presidents smiled as if thinking the Americans were up to their melodrama once again. After all, the American political apparatus seemed to thrive on prophecies of impending doom.

"The U.S. lost communications with several Mars rovers at precisely the same moment, while scattered across distant locations on the Martian surface."

Sometimes presidents cannot afford to be completely candid. A half-truth would have to do for now.

"Our analysis of the last signals coming from those rovers indicates the same seemingly anomalous signals occurred just a millisecond before the total loss of contact. Those signals have now been interpreted as an overwhelming pulse of gamma radiation. Mars was hit by a gamma-ray burst or GRB."

"The good news for us is that Mars was at the time as far removed from the Earth as is physically possible. Earth and Mars were on opposite sides of the solar system. The bad news is that if some intergalactic, or even extragalactic gamma-ray source has its sights aimed at that particular point in space for a repeat performance, then Earth is moving ever closer into that target zone. Just as we were taken by surprise on Mars, we will be taken by surprise on Earth. And there is absolutely nothing we can do about it."

The look of disbelief on the other President's faces was palpable.

"I know you will no doubt huddle with your scientists and examine what the consequences of such a GRB would be on Earth. What you will find is a broad spectrum of possibilities, ranging from destruction of the ozone layer, increasing the exposure of all of us to harmful cosmic radiation, and a spike in skin cancer rates from ultraviolet radiation. If that happens, we would all be fortunate. In a worse case, the gamma-rays would force through our protective ozone layers and immediately kill all living things directly exposed to the GRB.

"In this worst case, our atmosphere could be largely stripped away, and what little oxygen would remain could be converted to toxic forms. Life as we know it would be gone forever."

The Russian President seemed comfortable enough with POTUS to mock him.

"Please, Whitney, do you really believe that rubbish?"

"Lest you think it an absurd possibility, we need to look no further than Mars itself. Mars' atmosphere used to be far more substantial than it currently is. And now we must entertain one possibility of why that has changed. This may not be the first GRB to hit our neighbor. What we are now viewing through our rover's eyes is a look at a potential future Earth."

Dr. Reed had never seen the Chinese President's eyes roll. Until now.

"So now this is the challenge we need to address. What can we do about it? If we believe science fiction forecasts of our future, we can say we'll send the eggs and sperm of the human population out into the cosmos."

He swept his hands out in a circle encompassing the frozen seeds of agriculture, mere yards away from them at that very moment.

"But to what end? And at what cost? And to what success? Space is a perilous place, and few potential landing sites would have the ozone levels providing us with the protection we currently have. And if we should find such a unique atmosphere, would it support human life? It's not very likely."

The U.S. President's oratory and gesticulation were greeted with a smug smile from the Chinese President, and an outright smirk from the Russian President.

Captain Emery Reed's official role in this revelation was nothing more than making sure his President's health did not suffer from the Arctic's bitter weather. But as Reed observed the lack of response, and seeming lack of interest from these geopolitical rivals, Russia and China, he thought back to the rows of dead Space Corp astronauts stacked like cordwood outside the opening to the Martian cave at Pavonis Mons. Perhaps if these world leaders had seen what he saw, men and women with their faces contorted by seizures and unimaginable pain, they would take POTUS a little more seriously.

But of course, that image forever frozen in Reed's mind could never be made public. Because of his position, a piece of Mars and its effect on him would have to remain locked deep within his brain, never to see the light of day.

The photo-op of the year came soon after the ominous warnings in the Svalbard Global Seed Vault. The Longyearbyen town hall was the venue for the historic signing, but before the ceremony, several vetted media outlets busied themselves with photographing the signs on bank doors prohibiting the carriage of guns into banks. Elsewhere in Longyearbyen, high powered rifles were required once one strayed a few blocks from the main city streets. The threat of polar bear attack was just that great.

Of course, during the "Three Leaders" visit, no firearms were allowed except for the state security forces scouring every square inch of land, both in the surrounding mountains and elsewhere, for any threat to those they guarded.

On-scene military commanders recognized the risk posed by having the highly specialized but inherently competitive SPECOP forces working together for the first time on such a high-profile protection mission. But in spite of many misgivings, the protection mission came off without a hitch. After the requisite photo-op, the world reveled in the fact that the world's greatest superpowers had agreed on anything, even something of as little import as seeds. Of course, the real challenge faced by all the planet's nations would likely remain deeply buried beneath the granite mountains of Svalbard.

Chapter 33. Return to Base

Parker's return flight from Zurich on Delta arrived at Dulles airport in Washington on Tuesday afternoon. It was peak season for the Cherry Blossoms around the Washington D.C. Tidal Basin, but he didn't have the energy or inclination to head downtown for sightseeing. Instead, he checked into the Dulles Marriott.

On Friday he was scheduled to pick up his Baby Jet at the Manassas Airport for a flight to Nevada to pay his first visit to the now relocated Trolls. For that flight, he needed to be well-rested.

After eating a thickly cut filet mignon at his favorite steak house a close walking distance from the Marriott, he lay on his bed to catch up on the news.

After the news, he was planning to call Sandy and see how she and the grown kids were doing.

He didn't wake up until late Thursday morning.

After an early departure Friday morning, Jason Parker's satellite phone rang while he was 40,000 feet above Fayetteville, Arkansas.

"You rang?"

He had assumed it was Laura Smith, but he was wrong. Both the number and the calling party was blocked, which it always was for his Intelligence contacts.

"Don't know who you were expecting, but this is Kelly Brightman."

"Kelly! What a surprise. Great to hear from you. You'll never guess where I am."

"Actually, I know exactly where you are."

"I should have known," Parker admitted.

"I also know you're headed to see our old friend Baltazar. I would tell you to say "hi" to him, except you're not really going to see him."

"I'm not? Why not?"

"I need you to do a one-eighty and return to D.C. just as fast as your little jet will fly."

"Are you serious? I'm on an ODNI mission."

"This is ODNI business," Kelly replied.

"Am I supposed to be impressed?"

"You better be."

"Did Laura put you up to this?"

"No, her boss did," Kelly responded. "And speak of the devil, she just walked in. I'm putting you on speakerphone."

"Hi, Jason," Laura spoke up. Not having heard the previous conversation, she asked, "Where are you?"

"Just about on top of Razorback Stadium in Fayetteville, Arkansas. Wooo Pig, suwee."

"What did you say?"

"Razorback Hog call."

"I didn't know you were a Razorback fan."

"There's a lot you don't know about me, Laura. You haven't known me long enough."

She laughed, ever so slightly.

"So Laura, is it true the Director's changed his mind and now wants me back in D.C, like right now?"

"It's true. Something's come up."

"Okay then, but you guys are buying my fuel."

"We always do Kemosabe," Brightman said. "What's your ETA?"

"I'll have to get back to you. I need to alert ATC and get rerouted, find a place to get fuel, and then flight plan… yet again."

"I need something now. Give me a rough estimate."

"Okay, a guesstimate is three and a half hours."

"That long? I thought jets were fast."

"They are, but mine's not the fastest, and flight planning and refueling are time-consuming. But I'll do my best on the schedule."

"You landing at Andrews?"

"That seems like the most convenient. They know me there."

"We'll have a car waiting for you. Don't shut her down, we'll have someone pull it into the hangar for you."

"No way, not my baby!"

"It's not yours, Jason," Laura reminded him. "We're just letting you fly it, for exactly this type of flexibility. So enjoy being chauffeured during rush hour," Brightman said. "We don't want to risk a traffic accident. We need you here ASAP."

"Geesh, Kelly, what's so damned important?"

"I'm out here."

Parker heard a click. "Laura, you still there?"

When his question returned only silence, he said, "Okay, I guess not."

Just as he had predicted, Parker landed at Andrews Air Force Base during the height of early rush hour on a Friday afternoon. The timing could not have been worse.

After deplaning, Parker gave the man walking up to taxi the jet a suspicious look.

"Don't bend my bird, please. I need it to get home."

"Not to worry Sir, I'm thoroughly checked out in these baby jets."

Sounds a bit like famous last words, Parker thought, but he had no choice but to trust the folks at Andrews. If they took care of Air Force One and Two, they could probably handle his personal jet.

Hearing the din of the nearby Beltway traffic, Parker understood the wisdom in having a driver who could quickly navigate the Outer Beltway from Andrews, heading west to the Potomac River, then north up 295. At least heading north on 295 they were driving against the traffic going west and south to the Maryland and Virginia bedroom communities.

A few minutes later they turned off the freeway at the exit to Joint Base Anacostia-Bolling, directly across the Potomac from Ronald Reagan Washington National Airport. Parker was not surprised to see they were the only car entering the base, compared to the constant line of cars exiting for the weekend getaway.

Having passed through the guard gates on MacDill Boulevard, the Air Force vehicle twisted and turned to the point where Parker felt lost. However, within a few minutes, they pulled up to the DIA compound where Parker was met by an Air Force sergeant for escort into the presumed meeting place with Kelly Brightman and Laura Smith. Other than those two, he had no idea who else he'd be meeting, or why. Maybe it would be with no one else. Perhaps he would just get a briefing.

Must be an important briefing, he thought.

The sergeant opened a door and beckoned Parker to enter, then took up a position outside. It was then that Parker noticed the man was armed. How he could have missed that, he didn't know. Too many distractions perhaps. Way too much mystery.

As soon as he stepped into the room, he heard a voice to his right. It was Brightman's.

"Better late than never, old friend."

Sitting at a table beside Brightman was Laura. No one else was in the room.

"Good to see you, Kelly and Laura. But what the hell's going on?"

"You better have a seat first."

Brightman motioned to a seat in front of the table, facing his two friends.

"It's that bad, eh?" Parker said as he walked over to the table.

"No. This is all good."

As Parker took his seat, Laura spoke. "Jason, we have another alien craft. It's in Sasebo, Japan."

"How did it get there?"

"We recovered it from deep water off of Taiwan. Then we towed it to Japan."

"Sounds like a huge operation. Why wasn't I told about this before? Did you know about it, Laura?"

"Yes. The recovery started two months ago."

Looking at Laura with a look of distrust, "And you didn't let me know?"

Brightman spoke up, "You've already been kidnapped by the Russians once, and if it happened again, we couldn't let you know anything about this. Until now."

"Why now?"

Brightman and Laura looked at each other, seemingly not believing what was about to be said.

Brightman did the speaking. "Because we now need you and Laura to interview the man who raised it from the depths."

Parker looked back and forth between the two.

"We didn't recover it?"

"We did, but we only found out about it because of the man you're about to meet."

"I'm really confused," Parker admitted.

"I'll cut to the chase. Jason, this man is a Buddhist monk from Thailand. But he hitched a ride on a Taiwanese fishing boat, and somehow raised an alien craft up from the deep. As luck would have it, it got fouled in the boat's fishing nets, and almost sank the whole damn boat."

Looking at Laura, Parker asked, "Is this a joke?"

"No, Jason. We're deadly serious."

Still looking only at Laura, Parker said, "And what do you and I have to do with this?"

"It seems he can do what we can do," she explained. "Communicate with the ship. He doesn't know how he does it, and you and I need to find out how."

"But he hasn't flown in it?"

"No. And he only activated it once."

"Doesn't leave us much to go on."

"Just talk to him," Brightman said. "He'll be accompanied by one of our agents who has a little experience with being a Buddhist monk. He ordained briefly."

Briefly ordained? I didn't know that was an option?

"With his personal knowledge and experience, our man was able to talk his way into several Taiwanese monasteries until we finally found this guy."

"Do I know the guy who found him?"

"I doubt it. Mark Fuller's his name."

Parker shook his head, signaling he didn't know Fuller.

"He's been hidden away as one of the better CIA analysts until we activated him for this mission."

"I'm surprised the CIA loaned you their guy?"

"We had CIA backup, but due to the military relevance, we were given the lead. Now, are you ready to meet the monk?"

Parker stared at Brightman, smiling but too distracted to immediately respond to Brightman's question.

Brightman looked at Parker, inquisitively. "What?"

"I'm very proud of you, Kelly. You've come a long way since our days diving in Mexico."

"Well, thanks."

Without breaking his stride, Brightman continued, "Now his Monk name is Phra Theratapati, but the agency just calls him the Ship Monk."

"The chipmunk? Why?"

"No, Jason. The Ship Monk. He was a Monk on a fishing boat. But he prefers to have us call him Thera since we don't seem to be able to pronounce his real name correctly."

Parker smiled, thinking about the Troll with the unpronounceable name, the one he dubbed Baltazar.

Looking at Laura, still smiling, he said, "Yeah Laura and I keep running into those difficult names."

"Okay then, let's get this over with," Parker said.

Parker was not looking forward to this interview. Could it really be that someone besides he, Laura, and Baltazar could control an alien ship? It was an unsettling thought.

CHAPTER 34. INTERVIEW

A tall, bald-headed black man walked in the door with a shorter, more Asian looking man. Immediately, Parker, Laura, and Kelly rose to greet the Thai Monk.

"Thera, good to see you again," Brightman said.

Thera smiled. "These must be my inquisitors, the spaceship experts."

"Such as we are," Laura replied.

"And this must be the famous Dr. Parker who is looking at me strangely. Maybe you were expecting me to be wearing orange robes?"

Thera was right; Parker had not been expecting a monk in jeans and a plaid shirt. He lifted his eyes in agreement.

"Buddha said there is a time and place for everything," the monk said.

"Buddha said that? I thought it was my mother."

"All mothers say that," Laura said.

"I agree," Thera said with a chuckle. "The Buddha probably heard that from his mother."

They all laughed.

"Monks are not to draw attention to themselves outside of our natural habitat," Thera noted. "Robes would attract attention in Washington."

"I suppose so," Parker said.

Brightman, pointing to Fuller, said, "Jason, this imposing-looking man is our analyst Mark Fuller. He was once ordained as a temporary Monk in, where was it, Mark?"

"Myanmar."

"That experience helped him locate our talented friend Thera here."

Fuller held out his hand to Parker, who shook it warmly.

"I suspect that was like finding a needle in a haystack," Parker said.

"My hunches paid off," Fuller said, smiling at Phra Theratapati. "He wasn't hiding as well as he thought he was."

Pointing to the rectangular faux-wood table with six chairs around it, Brightman invited his guests to sit. "I'm sure dinner is on our collective minds, so why don't we get started with our meeting."

Once the chairs were filled, Brightman began the important conversation.

"Thera, as you know, both Laura and Jason want to learn more about you, and how you came to be on a boat in Taiwan."

Parker nodded and said, "Thera, since I seem to be the one with the most catching up to do, I'd like to educate myself on how you became a monk in the first place. In Thailand, did I hear?"

"Yes, a monastery not far from Bangkok. I was the only surviving child of my family. My father had been an aerospace engineer, and my mother was a school teacher. She taught English and world history in what would be your equivalent of high school. We lived in Bangkok until I was about nine years old. Then the accident happened."

"May I ask about that?" Parker asked.

"It was about thirty years ago, and we were driving back from a beach vacation in Pattaya, southeast of Bangkok. We were almost home and driving on the newly opened Chon Buri Expressway. It's really a very long bridge, and close to Bangkok, you're driving maybe three stories above city buildings and streets. My parents were in the front seats of our Isuzu, and my sister and I were in the back. Suddenly a car on our right hit the wall, then bounced off and then hit us directly on our right side, throwing us up into the air and over the left side of the bridge. The impact from the side ripped off the back-right door where I was sitting and threw me free of the car. The car and my entire family fell three stories and landed on a gas station below us. As you can imagine, there was a terrible explosion. Multiple explosions actually. I, on the other hand, should have been killed instantly on impact, but I fell through the canopy of several palm trees, eventually landing on an awning and then a large pile of compost. When I landed, I saw the ball of fire from the explosions. I couldn't have been more than thirty meters away. I could feel the heat on my face."

"Oh my God, Thera, I'm so sorry," Laura said.

"Were you injured?" Parker asked.

"Certainly. I had two broken legs, a broken arm and ribs, and a punctured lung. I was in the hospital for three months, and during that time of being an orphan, a Buddhist monastery took me in, cared for me, and picked up where my schooling left off."

"No grandparents?" Laura asked.

"None living. And it's standard procedure for orphans in Thailand. They're taken in by the monasteries and educated. Some educations are better than others, but something is better than nothing. In Thailand, education is not mandatory, like it is here in the United States."

"So that experience led you to become an ordained Monk?" Parker asked.

"After a while. At first, I was too young to dedicate myself to the teachings of Buddha and the monastic way of life. But eventually I got used to meditating, and by the time I ordained, meditation brought me the peace that nothing else could."

Parker thought about that comment for a moment, then steered the conversation towards their immediate interest. "I hear that meditation is what brought you to join a Taiwanese fishing boat. How did that happen?"

"For me, meditation is a gateway to, well, I guess you would call it paranormal experiences."

"Really? What kind?" Laura asked.

"My father and I were really close. And when I'm in the deepest meditation state, I feel a connection to him."

"You said he was an engineer?" Parker asked.

"An aeronautical engineer."

Laura asked, "Did he have anything to do with your going to Taiwan and going on board a fishing boat?"

"Have you ever meditated?" Thera asked Laura.

"No, not really."

"That's what I thought, or you wouldn't have asked that question. Deep meditation frees your mind from the distraction of the world and lets you focus on nothingness. Sometimes out of that nothingness comes very clear thoughts. Most of it is internal in origin. That's how Mark decided he did not want to be a professor but wanted to join the U.S. government, as a civic duty. Isn't that right, Mark?"

"Don't worry, he isn't psychic," Mark said. "I told him that on the way over here. But he's right. During meditation, I could see clearly that I was not on the right path for my life."

"Okay, then, did you think of the fishing boat?" Laura continued.

"As I was saying, some meditative thoughts come from within. But other thoughts seem to come from outside. That's what I call the paranormal experience."

"How so?" Parker asked.

"I began seeing myself on a fishing boat, and at my command, that boat cast a net and pulled in a net full of fish. That cannot be an internal thought, so it must be external."

"Why not?" Laura asked.

"I would not willingly step foot on a boat any smaller than an ocean liner. I get seasick very easily."

"Some random thought, then. Why did you act on it?" Parker asked.

"I didn't at first. But the same image kept coming back to me, every time I meditated deeply enough. But then one night I had a dream where Siddhartha showed me the name of a particular fishing boat, the *Shy Chan*. Below it was the name Taipei. I woke up and wrote the name down, thinking the boat could not possibly really exist. After all, it was just a dream."

Laura said, "I have tried to read things in my dreams, but I never have been able to make out words."

"I could. And in the morning, I did a little research, and found out there really was a *Shy Chan* fishing boat, registered in Taipei. So, it truly was a sign."

Laura looked at Parker, Mark, and Kelly, shrugging her shoulders. She had to admit that was strange.

"I still didn't take action until the image in meditation and in other dreams kept coming back. Something or someone was sending me an inescapable message. But I couldn't afford even a one-way ticket to Taiwan. We monks are poor, with no real possessions. But one morning after another night of dreaming that dream with the same boat name, always the same, someone placed in my alms basket exactly enough money to buy a one-way ticket to Taipei, and enough train fare for me to get to the boatyard in Southern Taiwan where the boat was being prepared for its next fishing trip."

"Whoa, that was generous," Laura remarked.

"It was proof that my trip was meant to be."

"What did the boat Captain say when you told him your story?" Parker asked.

"Well, I didn't exactly tell him the whole story, just the part about Siddhartha appearing to me in a vision and telling me to go find a fishing boat."

"Did he? I mean, can a dead Buddha do that?"

Thera averted his eyes by looking down at the floor.

After a long pause, he said, "It's a difficult thing for nonbelievers to understand. And to be honest, I don't know. But the information came from somewhere. Perhaps it was cosmic consciousness. But I could tell the Captain was more impressed by Siddhartha than the cosmos."

"What did he say when you told him you get seasick easily?" Laura asked.

"He laughed and said no one gets seasick on his boat. But he lied."

"So, you did get sick," she noted.

"Most assuredly. But the day when we caught the thing, the sea was strangely calm. The Captain said we were becalmed, and fishing was not going to be good. I guess he was right since we didn't catch any fish."

"You had no idea what was coming up?" Parker asked.

"The fish finder indicated it was a big school of fish. We were all excited but also worried our net wouldn't set in time. The thing was accelerating upward."

"And when you finally saw it?"

"I couldn't understand what I was seeing. It must have been a trick of the eyes. But then when it started lifting the stern of the boat, we started to panic."

"And what had you been doing until that point?" Laura asked.

"I was meditating, of course. That's what I do."

"And what feelings or impressions did you have during that meditation?" she continued.

"That's hard to say. Meditation is not a feeling—more a knowing. And I knew I was doing the right thing. Until of course, I realized we were all about to die."

"And that is when it dropped back down into the water?" Parker asked.

"Yes, but we were still going to die if the deckhands hadn't been fast with the axes."

"I see," Parker said.

"I don't think you do. I was crushed to think that I had been so wrong, and it almost cost the entire crew's lives."

"You mentioned cosmic consciousness," Parker said. "Could you explain that to me? Do you think the cosmos wanted you to find that spaceship?"

"I cannot explain something for which no words apply. Westerners use the word *fate*, and *destiny*, or *predestination*. Can you explain *fate* to me, Mr. Parker?"

"That something is 'supposed to happen,' perhaps?"

"You see, that is an explanation that explains nothing. It is a rationalization."

"Well, you didn't give me much time to think about it," Parker replied.

"No, I believe you spoke the truth the first time. Now let me ask a question. Have you recovered the spaceship?"

Brightman broke in at this point. "We're not at liberty to say."

Laura spoke next. "Do you have any more questions, Jason?"

"One last question. When you were meditating, do you think you established some sort of mental connection with that ship?"

"Without a doubt. I felt like it wanted to be found."

Laura winced. "Are you serious?"

"I'm not kidding Dr. Smith. It wanted to be found, but I just didn't know what *it* was."

"So you sensed a connection with something," Parker said, "but you had no idea what."

Thera stretched his arms up and away from him. "That's why we call it Cosmic Consciousness, Dr. Parker."

Brightman spoke up again, "Thank you for your time, Thera. We appreciate your candor. You have any plans for the weekend?"

Looking at Fuller, Thera said, "Mark promised he'd take me to see the Smithsonian Air and Space Museum."

"That's always a winner. Enjoy yourself Thera, and if we have any more questions, we'll contact you on Monday."

"Can any of you recommend a good Chinese restaurant?" Fuller asked.

"Oddly enough," Parker answered cheerfully, "I was thinking about going to Chinatown this evening. Do you know the Wok and Roll on H Street?"

"I've been by it, but never stopped."

"What do you say we meet there about seven-thirty?" Parker said.

"OK. Is it near a subway stop?" Fuller asked.

"Gallery Place-Chinatown stop. Walk under the Chinatown Arch and Wok and Roll's less than a block away on your right."

"Sounds wonderful," Thera said. "This will be my first Chinese meal in America."

Thera sounded genuinely enthusiastic.

"Thera, I do have one more question before you leave," Laura interjected. "In Taiwan, you told Mark you had wanted to get back to Bangkok, but instead you came here with him. Why?"

"Well, let me put it this way," he said hesitantly. "You Americans made me an offer I could not refuse."

Laura smiled. "Thank you for coming in," Laura said, rising to shake his hand.

Just before he left, Thera gave the customary Thai *wai* with hands clasped together pointed upward, and a slight bow and smile, as a symbol of respect.

Parker clumsily tried to copy the gesture.

Thera smiled. "It takes practice, Dr. Parker."

Brightman's flag-level boss, a Ms. Foster in the Senior Executive Service, asked them in the privacy of her office, "So what do you think?"

"Did you catch it all?" Laura asked.

"Pretty much. Did it make any sense to you?"

Brightman's big boss was surprisingly young for a senior bureaucrat. Her body exuded energy, and her large brown eyes invited conversation. She was an excellent communicator tasked with communicating to her bosses something as intangible as superhuman capabilities.

"It sounds like typical Eastern mysticism to me," Laura said.

"Even some Russians have that sort of woo-woo thinking," Parker added, remembering his conversations with the smart but strange Russian parapsychologist Oleg Kiselev during their captivity near Irkutsk in Siberia. I've heard them call it the *noosphere* instead of cosmic consciousness."

"Woo-woo thinking?" Foster repeated, her right eyebrow raised questioningly.

"Pseudo-scientific, paranormal."

"And yet, Dr. Parker, you and Laura can control a spaceship with your mind. Is that not paranormal?"

"I don't see that as paranormal. The ship picks up our brainwaves, interprets what those brainwaves mean, and then it figures out how to act on it. That's science, not paranormality, in my humble opinion."

"Then why can't anyone else fly it?"

"That I don't know."

"Laura, what do you think?" the woman asked.

"I think this monk just might be able to fly our ship, or at least the new one. Clearly, it responds to him."

"Do you really think it beckoned him?"

"Well, let's say either it did, or something in the cosmic consciousness realm led him to it?"

"Like?"

"I wouldn't want to speculate Ma'am."

"Well, I would. I asked you a valid, and I might add an important question. So let me put it another way. Would you consider it possible for a disembodied spirit, oh like maybe this man's aerospace engineer father, to not only know about the spaceship but to communicate to his son about it during meditation?"

"I don't know how to answer that," Laura admitted.

"Well, just so you know," she said, "DARPA is asking these sorts of questions, just as the Russians are. You know why the CIA started their remote viewing research during the last century's cold war? They did it because the Russians did it first. And the noosphere? We know about that. And that raises a whole new level of potential intelligence gathering and potential weaponization."

"I suspected as much," Parker said with a wry grin.

"So, when I ask these questions, it's not frivolous. I want you two to think about what the monk said, and get back to me."

"Ma'am, with all due respect, I don't work for you," Laura said, risking insubordination.

Ms. Foster smiled. "Your boss said you do now, until we figure out what to do with this Thai monk. My gut feeling is this man is a prize we don't want to lose to the Chinese or Russians."

"But can he fly the spaceship?" Laura asked.

"Can I fly the ship?" Parker added.

"You'll find out soon enough," the bureaucrat stated decisively.

Parker exited the Chinatown Metro stop at 6:50 PM, preferring to be early rather than late. As he turned to face the multi-tiered colorful and ornate Friendship Archway on his right, he stopped to admire its beauty.

He also thought of the irony that when that colorful archway was dedicated in 1986, how different the world was then than now. Beijing was Washington D.C.'s "Sister City," and the Archway, designed by an

American architect who left his Taiwanese birthplace in his youth, celebrating the beauty and character of not only Washington's Chinatown but of China in general. But now, decades later, that friendship was being strained by Beijing's continuing provocations.

As Parker walked north on H Street, he passed the ubiquitous signs for shops and restaurants written in those incredibly complex and subtle Chinese characters. He deeply respected any native English speakers who developed fluency in Chinese.

He stopped in front of a white brick building, three and a half stories tall, with two dormer windows. According to the plaque at the entrance to the building, it was built in 1843. The building had once been a boarding house, but during the last century, the bottom floor had been converted to commercial space. That was where the Wok and Roll was located.

Parker turned into the restaurant and found Thera and Fuller waiting for him.

As Parker approached, Fuller said, "I think I'm going to love this place. The menu looks awesome."

"As you may have noticed, this is a historical building. It was a boarding house during the civil war, and supposedly a meeting place for those plotting the murder of Abraham Lincoln.

"Who's he?" Thera asked.

"A great American President who ended slavery in America. The house was owned by a Mary Surratt, who was later hanged for her part in the conspiracy."

"I would suppose that would be a suitable punishment."

To this day, some people contest her guilt, saying she was innocent. And for that reason, some say her ghost still haunts this building."

"Phi," Thera said.

"Excuse me?"

"Phi is the Thai word for ghost."

"I was just about to ask you if Thai's believe in ghosts."

"It is part of our culture. We have many ghosts. They are almost guaranteed when there has been a sudden and tragic death, like that of my family."

Mark spoke up. "It's like that throughout the Far East. It's a tenet of Buddhism and Taoism, prevalent in China, Vietnam, and Taiwan."

"That's interesting," Parker said. "So, if someone innocent was wrongly executed, like perhaps Mary Surratt, then you would not be surprised if she turned into a ghost?"

"Not at all. She would probably want to be avenged."

Parker laughed. "Well, that could take a very long time."

Thera surprised Parker when he said without expression, "Ghosts have all the time in the world."

"Are you serious?"

"Hardly ever."

Fuller laughed.

"So, tell me this, Thera. Do you think the force that led you to your surprise on the boat could have been the ghost of your father?"

"I did at the time."

"But you've changed your mind?"

"I'm not so sure now. I think it wasn't."

"Then what? If you don't mind my prying."

"Buddha said that our theories of reality are no more valuable than those which a chick has before it's broken through its shell."

"You have to die to know the truth?" Fuller asked.

"Not at all. The eggshell around each of us is the eggshell of preconceived notions. Once we break through that shell, we can truly understand."

"Did Buddha say that too?" Fuller asked.

"No. That was from Phra Theratapati."

"Isn't that you?" Parker asked, frowning in confusion.

"Yes."

"Then that's food for thought, as they say," Parker noted. "And speaking of food and eggs, I think I see my Egg Drop Soup and Tuna Sashimi headed this way."

"Excellent," Thera said, almost salivating.

After the dinner had finished without the ghost of Mary Surratt making an appearance, and after the men had gone their way, Parker was riding the Metro back to his Crystal City hotel. As lights flashed by and passengers jostled for seats, he was deep in thought about the before-dinner conversation.

Earlier in the day, Laura had been somewhat dismissive of Thera's "typical Eastern mysticism," as she put it. But even though Thera had not added any clarity about the source of his calling to the fishing boat, he did say something interesting. Buddha may have said the part about the eggshell around each of us, but Parker liked Thera's elaboration.

Perhaps Parker's communications with Frogs and his ability to fly Frog ships was the result of his first peek above the confines of his eggshell. Perhaps he was finally awakening.

CHAPTER 35. SASEBO

The U.S. Navy Base in Sasebo Japan had a secret. Inside that secret was sitting a crew of three men about as diverse in origin as pebbles washed up on the nearby Japanese beaches. One was Jason Parker, there to see if he could fly yet another alien spacecraft. Another was an ordained Buddhist monk from Thailand, also there to see if he could fly an alien spacecraft. The third was a test pilot's test pilot, an American man equally at home in the latest American Air Force and Navy Jets. He didn't have a need to fly an alien spaceship, but instead, he was there to take note of how the alien craft, whose official name was *XFS Taiwan,* would respond to Jason Parker and Phra Theratapati.

The test pilot's real name was Colonel William Morgan, but his call sign, the only name by which military pilots wish to be addressed, was *Sparky.* No one seemed to remember why that call sign had stuck with him, and he wasn't telling. Perhaps it had been due to a lightning strike, or a main-bus overvoltage, or nearly getting himself electrocuted. Whatever the origin, that name and the man behind it had become a part of Navy and Air Force legend. Everyone in the tactical aviation community seemed to know Sparky. That is precisely why he had been assigned to this flight, even though he admitted to Parker that he wasn't sure what his role was. But that was not unusual, he was one of the few men in the military who got paid to "wing it."

The first thing the select crew of engineers at the Naval Base had noted during the craft's inspection upon arriving from the long transit through the waters of the East China Sea, was that entry to the craft was relatively easy. Unlike the case with *XFS Dioscuri* and its Russian sister ship, it was just a matter of where you pushed on the smooth hull. This craft was about one-third smaller than the ship flown to Mars, and had a classic disk shape, at least classic for UFOs. In size and shape, it matched well the craft being recovered from the ice in Antarctica. The only difference was that this craft did not contain frozen biological material.

The one thing that made all three of the crew slightly nervous was the fact that no one knew yet if this craft would fly, or if it had the pleasing flight characteristics of *Dioscuri,* or if it really could lock onto

Parker's mind as well as did that more famous craft. Aside from its discoid shape, it had none of the external lights that seemed to be involved in the directional control of *Dioscuri*. In other words, no one knew anything about it other than it had been determined to be pressure-tight, and like the triangle, had no discernable propulsion engines, or any other machinery for that matter. The only thing the Navy investigators knew about it for sure was that it had been called from the deep by a Buddhist monk.

When a new aircraft prototype is being tested, after numerous tests of the engines, engine controls, and startup and shutdown procedures, there comes a carefully scripted series of system tests of the electronics, navigation systems, and emergency procedures before the prototype is taxied out of the hangar for its first taxi tests. None of that could happen with alien spacecraft since their propulsion and navigation systems were somehow incorporated into the craft's intelligent hull. The fact that it had no wheels meant there could be no taxi tests. Instead, Parker called it a hover test. If the craft could be awakened from its mechanical slumber, connected through brain waves with the craft's pilot, and then levitated just off the tarmac where it rested, then the hover test was considered a success.

Its first attempted hover test, and if that was successful, flight, was a risky adventure. But those few who knew about it in Washington thought it a risk worth taking. That was also the one thing the crew inside that craft also agreed upon.

It was 0050 hours in the moonless morning in a secret location without a name, not far from the Sasebo base. Navy engineers had already pressure and vacuum tested the craft for leaks, as best they could, but since they were facing the unknown, the three men inside were wearing EVA spacewalking astronaut suits. If they were inadvertently exposed to the vacuum of space, they would at least survive long enough to leave behind a record of their demise.

On the other side of the world, in New York, it was almost noontime, and mid-morning in Groom Lake where they were hopefully headed, on the other side of the world. Sparky had long been accustomed to being the only pilot in his test aircraft, but for this flight, he was tucked away in an observer's seat midway between and behind Parker and the fellow now irreverently nicknamed "The Ship Monk."

On their first arrival in Japan, Parker had entered the craft alone and established that the ship's initial response to him was similar to *Dioscuri.* Once activated by his thought processes, a view in front of the cockpit area became transparent. Presumably, all space-faring creatures enjoyed seeing where they're going.

"I'm ready when you are Jason," Sparky prodded. "Let's get this baby airborne."

"You ready?" Parker asked, turning to Thera.

"Can't wait any longer," he replied.

"Okay, let's do this." Then, addressing the ship, Parker said, "Up, up, and away!"

Nothing happened.

"Not to worry guys," he said, "this can be a slow process until we find the proper incantation."

"You're assuming this thing will fly," Sparky said. He sounded unimpressed.

"It does fly," Thera said.

Parker made another attempt. "Superman wants to fly."

There was no result.

"This could take forever," Sparky said. "Let a real pilot try it."

"Okay, your turn."

"Let's leave the Earth behind, you miserable bucket of bolts."

Nothing happened.

"Apparently, insulting it's not the trick either," Parker noted.

"Well, it always works for me."

"That plus a throttle," Parker reminded him. "Okay Thera, it's your chance."

Thera did not respond.

"Thera, you want to give it a try?"

"I already did. We're hovering."

Parker whipped his neck around to look at Sparky. "I didn't feel a thing."

Me neither, the test pilot mouthed.

Parker realized he had to take control. "Thera, I'm going to get us headed in the right direction."

"She's all yours," Thera said.

At which point the craft dropped a foot or so back to the ground, jarring their spines and reverberating through the ship with a resonant, metallic *bong* sound.

"Damn it," Parker shouted involuntarily.

Sparky held his words for a second, and then said, "Flight crew coordination folks."

"Okay, we're learning," Parker said. "Thera, whatever you did, do it again, but then hold it until I can mentally transmit the landing coordinates."

"I understand."

"Let's try it again."

"Okay, we're off the ground," Thera said.

"I don't feel anything, but I'll take your word for it. I'm visualizing Groom Lake now!"

Sparky was grinning at the ridiculousness of it all. But not for long.

G-forces pushed the men down in their seats and then caused them to strain against their harnesses as lateral acceleration increased.

Outside, only those with thermal and night vision lenses could see the craft leap up and then shoot at an ever-increasing angle out of sight. Within seconds they were climbing over the western border of southern Japan, across the Sea of Japan, crossing east of Hokkaido, and then out over the Pacific Ocean up to the Aleutian Islands, on a course for America.

"That wasn't so bad," Sparky said. "Jason, I thought you said we'd blackout. Our G-meter pegged at only five Gs."

"Yeah, this thing seems underpowered compared to *Dioscuri*."

"Well, you can't tell by looking at it. Our Inertial Nav says we're going faster than I ever have, looks to be about twelve thousand miles an hour. We could outrun a missile."

"Not if it's coming from in front," Parker reminded him.

"We should be crossing the coast near the Oregon-California border in about twenty minutes at this rate, and coming up on Groom Lake in twenty-five minutes."

"How high are we?" Thera asked.

"Don't have a great estimate on that, but roughly 100 miles," Sparky said.

"High as the Space Station?"

"No, we're way below it."

"How fast is the Space Station moving?"

"It's about five thousand miles an hour faster. But remember we have to slow down again, and it doesn't."

"How do we know we won't go higher and run into it?"

"Our launch window. The Space Station is on the other side of the world right now."

"Good," Thera said, seeming relieved.

For a man accustomed to receding deep into his own mind, meditating on nothing, or everything, yet leaving little mark on the physical world, Thera was exultant that he had just discovered that he, and he alone, had the mental ability and motive power to levitate an alien spaceship. In spite of what others had said, he had not believed, until now, that he had actually caused the ship to leave its resting spot in the deep sea and rise to the surface off Taiwan. He thought, with great guilt, that he had merely coerced the Captain of the *Shy Chan No. 5* into placing the fishing boat and crew in a dangerous spot at a dangerous time. He had really thought it was a coincidence that the boat arrived on station just as the alien craft was rising, with nearly disastrous consequences.

Coincidence is one thing, but causation is something altogether. If in fact, he had caused the rising, as he was now beginning to believe, his role in a potential disaster at sea would be undeniable. The only saving grace was that if all souls had been lost, there would have been no record that he was the cause. He would have been nothing more than an interesting side note in the accident investigation report which might have read, "There was also a Buddhist monk on board."

The alien craft crossed the northern California border more or less where expected as the G-forces of deceleration were becoming noticeable. After staring at his Inertial Navigation System they had brought on board, Sparky said in his usual calm voice, "We have a five-degree deviation in our course. You need to add in a five-degree correction to the right, Jason."

"How do you propose I do that?"

"Focus, Jason. Focus. Thera, can you help us out?"

"I don't think so," the Ship Monk said. "I don't know where we're going."

"Never mind then," Sparky said. "Jason, are you focusing?"

"As hard as I can. I have Groom Lake squarely in my mind."

"Well, it's not helping. At this rate, the INS is predicting we'll miss it by at least fifty miles."

"Where does that put us?"

"In the middle of the desert somewhere."

"Long as it's not in the middle of a mountain."

"It could. There are plenty out there."

Parker sighed. "Guys, I'm doing the best I can."

"We're not slowing down fast enough," Sparky said with some urgency. "I think we're going to overshoot our target."

"Fucking great," Jason blurted.

Speaking in a mock airline pilot tone, Sparky said "Well folks, those of you sitting on the right should be able to see Groom Lake as we go whizzing past it at supersonic speed. If you don't know, Groom Lake is reported to be the home of captured UFOs and space aliens. I suggest you tighten your seat belts because we'll be landing shortly."

Thera looked back at Sparky. "Where?"

"Damned if I know."

Thera then asked, "What's that big gash in the ground up ahead?"

"Uh, let me see," Sparky said. Even though the deceleration was making it difficult to move his limbs and his large helmeted head, he was able to look down and check out the INS.

"That just might be our landing site. I think it's the Grand Canyon."

"How exciting," Thera said. "I've been thinking I wanted to see the Grand Canyon."

"You've been thinking it recently?" Parker said with alarm in his voice.

"Yes. What else am I going to think about?"

By now, linear deceleration had slowed considerably, and the chasm of the mid-portion of the Grand Canyon was clearly visible dead ahead. In fact, the oblique view of the canyon filled their forward view and then shifted below them as the craft began a controlled descent.

"Jason get us out of here!" Sparky said. "There's nowhere to land except the river, and that has big rapids."

"I know, I'm trying. Thera for God's sake shut your brain down." Parker was not asking, he was demanding.

"How?"

"Meditate. On nothing."

Sparky also insisted, "That's what you do, so do it now!"

From the view out front, the crew could see they were now below the top of the canyon, sinking past rough and precipitous rock walls, with the churning waters of the Colorado River fast approaching.

Sparky saw he had no choice except to shut Thera down. Releasing his harness, he stood and slammed his gloved fist into the left side of Thera's helmet.

Thera's head impacted the left side of his helmet with enough force to stun him, but not knock him unconscious. No one had given a space helmet a left hook before, and so Sparky was unsure what the effect would be. It was a risky move. The impact would either distract Thera from thinking about the canyon, whose treacherous walls were becoming difficult not to think about, or break his attention on his effort to meditate on nothingness. But Sparky was used to making quick decisions, right or wrong. His instinct and quick reflexes had saved his life many times before.

In the same instant, Parker was able to regain control of the craft and blasted it vertically, well clear of the canyon walls and then above the spotty Arizona clouds before the craft headed at last towards Groom Lake over 200 miles to the West-Northwest.

As the ship was settling into the dry lake bed of Groom Lake, Thera broke his stunned silence.

"What happened? Did we crash?"

His question remained unanswered until they were firmly on the ground at Groom Lake.

"No, Thera," Parker answered, "we did not crash."

Sparky, satisfied that his instincts were once again proven right, decided that Thera's answer would be fully settled later.

And that it was, as that evening Thera sipped the first beer he had ever been allowed or wanted, to taste, while the three men watched the nightly news featuring tourist video of a UFO swooping into the Grand Canyon.

He didn't particularly like the taste of the beer, but Sparky told him it would calm his nerves, and that was something he needed.

As always, the newsmen, trying to be as dramatic as they could, ended the piece with the line, "Was it ours, or was it theirs?"

In truth, it was both.

Chapter 36. Samuel Putnam

Parker flew commercial back to Washington from Vegas. He was staying in Manassas, Virginia to be close to his government-owned, privately-operated jet parked at the Chantilly Air charter and maintenance facility. He had spent the morning talking to the jet repair facility about scheduling an annual inspection and other required maintenance on the jet when he received an email from someone he had not heard from in quite some time, the writer Samuel Putnam.

Parker and Putnam had been thrust together in the middle of some of the strangest imaginable happenings associated with the slowly evolving reveal of the marine alien species that Parker originally called Frogs. Putnam went dark shortly after informing the world about the aliens by publishing his now-famous piece in the *Fortean Times.* That article revealed the role of Jason Parker, Laura Smith, and the U.S. government in uncovering one of the greatest stories of all time. After that publication, Putnam stopped communicating with Parker so abruptly that Parker had feared for his friend's life.

But social media hits from time to time showed that Putnam was still alive, occasionally expressing his views on social injustice just like he used to do, and sometimes plugging his new book. He just wasn't interested in aliens anymore, at least not publicly. Ever since the Frogs' sudden departure, Putnam had been skeptical of their explanation that they had suddenly located their home planet far away in another arm of our galaxy. Being the cynical investigative journalist that he was, his internal antennas had been twitching. He feared that there was another reason, one of which we humans were not yet aware.

Putnam's email revealed that he immersed himself in something altogether different, a travelogue of sorts of the entire Mississippi River, a work commissioned by his local university.

The email showed the front cover of the book, and as Parker sat admiring it, he had an almost overwhelming desire to talk to his friend. If nothing else, he should congratulate him on the success of his new book. He dialed the phone number on the contact information on the email. Even that had changed.

"Jason, what a surprise to hear from you," the familiar and cheerful voice said on the phone.

"Well, now that I have your phone number, you might be hearing from me more often."

"Let me walk over to a quieter area. I'm at a publisher's convention in Anaheim, and it's kind of noisy here."

"Talking about your new book?"

"Oh yeah, the publisher is parading me around like a new prizefighter."

"I figured you were pissed off at me for some reason," Parker said.

"I'm sorry I didn't get back to you when you and Laura hit the news again. Trolls? I could hardly believe my ears. And you flying a Frog ship out of Russia? That must have been fucking amazing."

"I'm not claiming that. I was only a passenger while the ship was on autopilot. But still, I was surprised you didn't send me a Christmas card or something."

"If I'd known you cared, I might have. But frankly, shortly after my article was published in FT, I was visited by some strange people claiming to be from the Air Force, but who somehow didn't really have that Uniformed Services persona, if you know what I mean. They were fishing for more information than I was able to give or at least wanted to give. They might have been foreign agents for all I know."

"That would explain a lot."

"I'm rebranding myself, Jason. Investigative journalism can be stressful, and I don't need any more stress in my life. So now I'm a modern-day explorer of sorts, funded by public institutions. And you know the best part? I've had zero spooks visiting me since I started this kind of writing."

"But you still have deadlines, I assume."

"Well yeah, there's always that. Comes with the territory if you want to get paid."

"So what's your next project?"

"Actually, this morning I had breakfast with two Chinese publishers who love my Mississippi project. They were talking to me about the Yangtze River. The river's about the same length as the Mississippi but passes through far more interesting countryside."

"I didn't know that."

"I think that's the point. Not many Americans know about China and the Yangtze. And of course, not many Chinese know about the Mississippi. So, they've invited me to speak at the Hong Kong

International Literary Festival about my new book. I'm going to do a little research on the Yangtze before I go, just in case it comes up."

"When is the meeting?"

"Next week. They'll pay expenses."

"Next week?"

"Yes. You don't sound happy for me, Jason."

"It's just a little ironic. One minute you're saying there are no foreign agents in your life, and in the next, you say you're being courted by the Chinese."

"It's a river project, Jason. Not an alien project. Besides, the Mississippi work is already done. If they want to offer me a new project, I'm not in a financial position to refuse. That's the downside of academic life."

"I understand. The only advice I can offer you are things I've learned the hard way. First, there is no free lunch, or breakfast, for that matter. And second, not everyone who smiles at you is your friend. Or your country's friend."

"Jason, I'm not a schoolboy, so spare me the lectures."

"I just want you to be safe, Samuel. You worried me when you went dark on me.

"I had a lot going on."

"I'm glad to know that, but before you go, when are you scheduled to show up in Hong Kong?"

"The 14th."

"Which hotel?"

"The old Peninsula Hong Kong. Why do you ask?"

"Just curious. You flying out of LAX?"

"Yeah, I'm going to stick around until Tuesday. No reason to go back to Oklahoma for such a short time. I may visit Disney Land tomorrow. I've never been there. Have you?"

"Once as a kid."

"Oops, my publisher is headed this way. He doesn't look happy that I'm not schmoozing with his cohorts. You've got my new contact info, so stay in touch."

"I will. Best of luck to you, and your book."

"Thanks. And I will be careful, Jason, so don't fret."

After they hung up, Parker set a reminder in his phone. He had some research to do.

Parker found flights leaving LAX for Hong Kong, and knowing Putnam as well as he did, figured he'd be on the 10:20 PM Cathay Pacific Flight leaving LAX on the 12th, arriving in Hong Kong sixteen hours after departure, about 6 AM on the 14th, or 4 PM Central Standard Time on the 13th. Just to make sure of his guess, he called Samuel about the time he thought he would be boarding and wished him a good flight.

Parker had guessed correctly.

When the CIA hired Joshua Nilsson for his spectacular remote viewing talents, they had made several concessions. The first was that he could telework. After all, remote viewing required Joshua's mind to travel, not his body. Secondly, on days when his presence was needed at the office, he'd be transported from his condominium in the suburb of McLean, Virginia to Langley, Virginia, CIA headquarters. Transport to and from work would be by a nondescript government auto, with bulletproof glass.

The last concession was that when at work, his government-issued guide dog would remain at his side, except for periodic bathroom breaks for the dog. The job of performing dog escort seemed to always fall upon the shoulders of the most junior CIA intern, much to their chagrin.

What Nilsson did not know was that Harry Kincaide was the most influential person making introductions for him, and dictating the terms of his employment. Kincaide was nothing less than in awe of Nilsson's psychic capabilities. He had trained the best psychic spies in the U.S. government employ, and Nilsson's homegrown talents far exceeded the combined skills of the rest of Kincaide's special agents.

Nilsson had been brought in to work early this morning because there were several in the intelligence agency who were curious about what the Chinese had in mind for the journalist and writer, Samuel Putnam. For obvious reasons, the Chinese were very perturbed about what had happened to their submarine on the Blake Plateau. But for equally obvious reasons they had remained very quiet about the incident, at least according to Agency monitoring. The Chinese did not know that the US Government knew they could park their submarine at 3000 feet, and lockout divers at that depth. The U.S. did not have that diving capability, and the Chinese were in no hurry to reveal one of their best secrets.

Nilsson had studied everything he could find on Samuel Putnam, including the relationship between Putnam, Jason Parker and the undersea telepathic aliens, the so-called Frogs. After reviewing Putnam's article in the Fortean Times, Nilsson and everyone else at the CIA knew the Chinese understood the connection between Putnam and the aliens. Perhaps if the Chinese suspected the craft that flew past their sub at such an incredible speed was an alien craft, then the Chinese might be very interested in extracting information from Putnam.

Of course, that put Putnam at personal risk. But that risk could perhaps be mitigated by Nilsson's remote viewing. The CIA had suggested to those questioning the wisdom of Putnam's travels that they could provide top cover for the writer. Cleverly, they had not mentioned that the top cover was only psychic.

There were quite a few things about the CIA's prolonged but carefully hidden psychic spying program that the Agency was not ready to mention, even to Congress, or POTUS.

Nilsson was in a soundproof room, and other interested parties were seated behind a one-way glass partition. Nilsson didn't need that degree of isolation to do his job. It was primarily to make sure that involuntary exclamations from the listeners did not interrupt his thoughts.

Speaking out loud, Nilsson said, "I'm standing at an airport gate in Hong Kong, and the Cathay Pacific 757 just pulled up. I'll wait here until I see Putnam get off the plane."

One of the less well-indoctrinated supervisors turned to a colleague and asked softly, "No one can see Nilsson, right?"

The more knowledgeable person smiled, and then responded,

"No, they can't," she said nodding towards Nilsson sitting behind the glass, "because he's right here."

"Yeah. Of course."

"His mind's there, but his body is here," she explained.

The man nodded his head, looked embarrassed, and turned back towards the one-way window.

"I see him now," Nilsson said. "He's one of the first off the plane. He must have flown First Class."

Someone else muttered, "The Chinese are grooming him."

A minute later, Nilsson said, "He's being escorted by someone in a nice suit, down towards the baggage claim."

Several of the listeners looked at each other in surprise. They had not expected that degree of detail in Nilsson's viewing session.

"Now I'm in the main lobby of the Peninsula Hong Kong Hotel. From my vantage point, I'm sitting on an old but gorgeous fabric-covered bench. Lots of red in it. And you'll never guess who's sitting right next to me, a uniformed Chinese Officer of some sort. He's staring at the entrance, and … here comes Putnam now. A bellman is carrying his bags on a cart as Putnam checks in at the desk."

The non-informed CIA supervisor turned once again to the lady next to him. "That doesn't make sense. Not enough time has elapsed. He couldn't have gotten from the airport to the hotel already."

She looked around to see if anyone else was paying attention. They weren't.

"Remote Viewing is a funny thing. Time and distance are not the same as it is for us."

He looked at her with a look of dismay. She'd seen that look before.

"No one knows why. It's … strange."

He looked back towards the glass again and said only one thing. "Huh."

Many in the CIA thought Kincaide's Remote Viewing program was incredibly weird. But it produced actionable results, without risk of detection, and therefore was the best intelligence methodology in their spying arsenal, as long as you didn't have boots on the ground. If you did, ground truth added confidence in the RV'ing results. No one understood it, but it worked.

Finally, the questioning but highly intelligent supervisor asked his neighbor. "How far apart can time get displaced?"

"Don't know for sure, but typically it's no more than a few minutes, maybe half an hour at most."

The man just shook his head.

Nilsson looked over at the folks behind the window. "I can't keep this up all day, you know."

The senior member of the observing group signaled the end of the session by moving his finger across his throat. They had seen enough to know that Nilsson was having no problem targeting Putnam and that Putnam was receiving more than his share of attention from the Chinese, for a guest speaker talking about an American river.

The Mississippi River is interesting, but not that interesting.

Two days later, Parker received an email from Putnam. According to Putnam, the Chinese had loved his presentation, loved his book, and loved the idea of sending him to the highland source of the Yangtze—immediately. They had already booked both air and boat transportation down the river, arranged for several guides, and gave him a generous advance.

Everything was happening at a dizzying pace. And yes, he was thoroughly enjoying being a celebrity. Best of all, he would earn more for his writing than he could make in three years of teaching creative writing and journalism.

Parker's one-line response summed up exactly his concern.

"I'm glad for you, Samuel. But remember what Virgil once said: 'Beware Greeks bearing gifts.'"

CHAPTER 37. DISPATCH FROM LIJIANG

The high-altitude flight from the origin of the Yangtze River to the first significant town on the river, Lijiang, roughly 632 miles from their departure point, had gone far better than Samuel Putnam had imagined. Although Putnam would have preferred to be on the river in a kayak or small boat, the first part of the Yangtze, called by the Chinese the Jinsha River, was not navigable. But a slow-moving ultralight was able to fly as low as Putnam wanted so he could get the best photographs.

The real advantage of their mode of transportation came when they had to climb over the many dams used for hydroelectric power generation. At the very high altitude of the upper river, a climb was a slow and painful process, but it could be done as long as they carried oxygen with them. An altitude of 15,000 feet is not to be trifled with.

As they flew down the river, the river's altitude dropped until they were down to 12,000 feet about 200 miles from their departure point. They were then able to drop off their oxygen bottles. Their flight performance benefited greatly from the loss of weight. And frankly, Putnam thought the bombing practice, dropping the steel bottles from altitude, was a nice break in the routine of banking through changes in the valley direction, with nothing to really see except barren mountains reaching far above them, and an occasional sandy beach.

After the first few miles of rapid-fire photography, Putnam realized everything was looking pretty much the same. Rugged, while at the same time, bleak. The vegetation he expected to see did not take well to the high altitudes at the westernmost portion of the Jinsha River.

Due to the altitude, it was cold, even in the summer, but fortunately, their battery-powered garments kept the pilot and his writer passenger from freezing to death. They weren't comfortable, but at least functioning. After spending a bitterly cold night on a sandbar, Putnam was looking forward to the relative warmth of Lijiang, and its 7800-foot altitude. At least Lijiang offered the two men a warm meal and warm blankets.

When they arrived in their hotel, Putnam could barely stay awake through dinner. He was famished, but more than that, he was exhausted. He had greatly underestimated the amount of energy it took to fight the cold at high altitude, all while focusing on his primary mission, photography.

Of course, he was getting paid to write about what he saw, but he was too tired to put those words together until morning. With luck, the words he would send off to the Kansas City Star would form in his mind as he slept. That's how it happened, usually.

But in the morning, the proper words did not find him. Perhaps it was the altitude and fatigue. In fact, it was not until the evening of the next day, after they arrived in Panzhihua at an elevation of 3800 feet, that his first dispatch came together.

He was a day behind schedule posting, but the K.C. Star had been warned that he might get behind schedule. And true to the form of Samuel Putnam, his first Yangtze Dispatch was worth waiting for. His Chinese hosts were pleased.

> Our aerial voyage began at high altitude and horrendously cold, frost-biting temperatures. As our small, noisy eagle of an airplane descended towards lower altitudes, it seemed to attract only a passing glance from mountain sheep which somehow found footing on slivers of granite, appearing to risk death with each step, but somehow averting what would be for humans, tragedy. As we throttled back the engine and soared in the air currents being thrust up the steep canyon walls, occasionally a magnificent, solitary golden eagle joined us. We were a strange flight of eagles, but a flight nevertheless, at least for a while.
>
> It was at that point that I began to feel that China was starting to accept me and my machine, as a novelty if not an equal. Clearly an equal we were not, but, to the Eagles at least, we were not too scary.
>
> One of them came close enough for me to see him eyeing us as if deciding if we were fit company for his regal presence. As I took his photo, I felt honored that he remained in formation for as long as he did.

The next day was the last day of flying. Their destination was Yibin, about 264 miles to the east. A modern city of five million people, Yibin was the place where the Chinese considered the proper Yangtze River to begin to flow to Shanghai and the sea, an incredible 1800 miles away. The Chinese have named the eastern portion of the river "Chang Jiang," for Great River.

After landing at the large Yibin airport, Putnam parted ways with his pilot and was taken by a courtesy car to his accommodation for the night. In the morning, he would begin the rest of the journey by wooden boat. But first, he had to write another dispatch for the K.C. Star. They were anxiously waiting for the next installment, as were his Chinese sponsors.

> As our flight drew to a close, and as the ground below us grew more verdant in the temperate climate of lower altitudes, we caught the smell of the earth of China. It was the odor of well-fertilized soil, enriched by cyclic floods from the river Yangtze.
>
> The soil had formed over eons as the high mountains, now far to the west, had been slowly ground down by the relentless course of rains and rivers. The dirt from which the sustenance of the Chinese people grew, formed long before the rise of western civilization. It was a humbling thought.

The noise of the city morning came earlier than Putnam had wanted, but this was to be his first day on the River Yangtze, so he didn't really mind the early awakening. Still, his body was complaining from the days-long trip in turbulent air. Small aircraft get batted back and forth under conditions that commercial aircraft wouldn't even notice.

He had been advised that at about eight o'clock local time, he would be picked up at his hotel and taken to the boat waiting for him at the base of the Zhongba bridge. Getting up at 6 AM, he had time to settle into the hotel breakfast room and enjoy a meal of fried noodles, steamed buns stuffed with pork, a boiled egg, and orange juice. He also had time to reflect on how pleasantly he had been surprised by the Chinese people, and especially the Chinese pilot who he had gotten to know reasonably well after spending a cold night on a sandbar on the upper reaches of the Yangtze. If it weren't for his not surprisingly stilted English, Putnam would have thought he was spending the night with a fly-fishing guide back home in Oklahoma.

He looked up to see a graying Chinese man standing in the door of the restaurant, glancing about as if looking for someone. When his eyes locked on Putnam, the only American in the eating area, the man started walking his way. He was taller and better dressed than many of the other Chinese Putnam had met.

Cautiously, Putnam called his name before the man had a chance to speak. "Mister Wang?"

"And you must be the famous Samuel Putnam. So glad to meet you at last."

Mister Wang's accented English was so impeccable that Putnam guessed he had spent considerable time in the States.

As Putnam stood to meet the man, Wang took Putnam's hand and shook it vigorously.

"Your departure has been delayed a few hours due to an engine maintenance issue. You'll be on your way today but just a little late."

"Maintenance is good. I don't want to break down soon as we get started."

"Indeed. Actually, I thought that would give us time for our local government officials to talk to you about your trip so far. We want to find out if you've had enough support, and if there is anything we can add for your comfort on the rest of the trip."

"That's very hospitable of you. If we have time, I'd love to go for a walk."

"We'll drive you. The office is a few miles away, but we have a car waiting for you outside. While we chat, we'll have your belongings transferred to the boat so you won't be delayed further."

Putnam thought that was to be a mixed blessing. It would give whoever was interested, time to plunder through his notes and computer, but so far at least those notes were entirely benign. So he didn't see the harm.

The nondescript vehicle carried the two men southeast across the river using a suspension bridge, motoring deep into the bustling center of Yibin city. Although Yibin was considered to be a Western tourist destination due to being the official beginning of the Yangtze River, Putnam saw no sign of Westerners here. He sensed that he was an anomaly.

They stopped at a government building even more nondescript than the car which brought them. The sign on the building was in

Chinese hanzi script, with no English translation offered. It could have been a brothel for all he knew, although it would have been a very drab one.

No one was guarding the building, so this meeting promised to be every bit as uninteresting as Putnam had assumed. It was just a way to pass the time while waiting for the beginning of his 1800-mile voyage.

Wang led Putnam down a hall, making a right turn past two elevators, and then to the end of the hall. At the very end was a door with a frosted glass pane, again with writing that Putnam could not decipher. At this point, he was wishing he had better prepared for the trip by learning more about written Chinese. He could speak just enough Mandarin to get by, but the writing was a skill which he had labored to acquire, and finally forsook. His guides had promised him that skill would not be necessary.

Wang dropped Putnam in the middle of a comfortable looking room, stocked with aging furniture that would have been right at home in a 1950s government office. Another man came in the same door in which they had entered, and just as suddenly, Wang excused himself.

The unidentified man held out his hand in greeting. "Mr. Putnam, please forego any effort to bow. We understand that it is not an American custom, so we do not expect it. Frankly, to us, it's an indication of personal weakness for a Westerner to bow."

"And you are?"

"Mr. Wang didn't tell you? Shame on him. I am Liu Wei, and I'm the counterpart of your Public Affairs Officers. I'm here to make sure your visit to China is satisfactory and will continue to be. I trust it has so far. Right?"

"Yes, entirely."

"Good. Now perhaps you can settle a nagging question I've had ever since I heard your name. Are you by chance related to the Putnam's of the great publishing empire?"

Putnam laughed. "No, not that I know of. I don't know of any rich relatives."

"Well, maybe you should check. I hear that you Americans are so, shall I say, insecure about your ancestry, that millions of you are donating DNA samples."

"I think it's more out of curiosity, not insecurity. How about you?"

"No. For us, our personal identity is sacred. We would never make that public."

"Well, our DNA information is not at all public."

He smiled. "Maybe you should read the fine print. But that's not what I want to talk about. As I'm sure you know, we were very impressed with the fine job you did on the Mississippi River book. I'm sure your work on the Yangtze will be every bit as monumental."

"I'll do my best. But it's an odd thing, really. You never know how it will turn out until it's done."

"I understand. But you know what really interests me goes before the Mississippi River book. That was the time you spent with Jason Parker and Laura Smith."

Putnam laughed. "Oh, so you know about that."

"Of course. The whole world does. Your story in the Fortean Times was what broke the story wide open. Was it all true?"

"Every bit."

"Ended on a very precautionary note. You seemed concerned that the Frogs' departure was not necessarily good news."

Putnam smiled at that, but Liu was not smiling.

"That's what a writer does, you know. You have to pique the reader's interest so they'll be more likely to remember the story."

"I suppose so. But are you sure there wasn't some genuine concern in your words?"

Putnam paused, thinking of an appropriate answer.

"This seems far removed from the River Yangtze, but to answer your question, none of us know the future."

"If what you say is true, then the Frogs do. Is that not correct?"

"Well, that's what was reported to me by Jason Parker. And he was told that by a Frog. So, as far as I know, it's true. But remember we won't know what the next decades hold until those decades are long past."

"Apparently, yes. But I wonder if that is true. Our sources tell us that part of the alien code has been broken."

Putnam smiled once again, but this time it was a nervous smile, not a friendly smile.

"Then your sources are far better than mine. I know nothing more than what you read in the Times."

"Are you sure?"

"Absolutely."

"You see, this question is really about the Yangtze after all, the lifeblood of our country. The future of our world is, of course, the future of China."

"I don't think you need to be quite so draconian. I suspect our planet will do just fine, just like it always has since the beginning of human history."

"Hopefully, you're right. But consider this, if you know anything, who knows, we might be able to upgrade your boat. You know, something with more reliable engines, quieter, faster, less likely to leak. It could make the next part of your journey more predictable, shorter, and much more enjoyable."

"Since your government sponsored my trip, it surely would provide entirely adequate arrangements. Don't you agree?"

"Yes, of course. It is as you say. Just remember my offer."

"I will, but let me remind you, if there was some secret knowledge, I'm the last person they would tell. I'm an investigative journalist, so revealing hidden things is what I do for a living."

Chapter 38. Langley

When the CIA's secret weapon, the blind remote viewer Joshua Nilsson, revealed that the Chinese may have an ulterior motive for inviting Samuel Putnam to China, the Agency urged the NSA to put Putnam on a watch list during his stay in China.

Dutifully, the NSA had been intercepting Putnam's dispatches to the Kansas City Star, running their usual analysis on writing styles, and then passing both the dispatch and the NSA analysis on to the CIA. This was the best way, under the circumstances, of keeping a careful watch out for any Chinese transgressions that might put Putnam at risk, and more importantly, reveal Chinese intentions without risking discovery of CIA human intelligence sources. It was a way of tapping into Putnam's brain without literally tapping into his brain.

A CIA analyst was reading Samuel Putnam's latest dispatch from China, titled "Slow Boat Through China." Putnam's latest had been flagged as having a fifty-five percent chance of being written by someone other than Putnam, and a ninety percent chance that if Putnam had written it, his emotional or mental state had deteriorated compared to his first dispatch.

There was cause for concern.

> "Welcome to Luzhou," my guide said emphatically after our first day on the river Yangtze. We had a late start, engine troubles they said, but even with long hours of summer daylight, it was dark as we stopped at Luzhou, our first city down river.
>
> As I ate my modest dinner of noodles, fatigued from seven hours on the water, I came to see the river as something other than what it appeared to be.
>
> For all the days I've spent on the Mississippi River I'd come to see the river water as, well, water. But today something was different.
>
> Two of the most abundant atoms in the universe are hydrogen and oxygen. Oxygen allows us to breathe, powering the molecular engines in every human cell.

> The other element forms the basis of a hydrogen bomb, with the potential of vaporizing millions of those lives. But when those two elements mix and are sparked, they explode and water forms, the water which pervades and sustains life.
>
> In unimaginable quantities that water flows through the hearts of two of the greatest nations on Earth, the United States and China. It feeds, it sustains, and on its back, it transports the goods of agriculture and industry. And yet, if you once again apply energy, this time in the form of electricity, it forms what it was, hydrogen and oxygen. It is, in that sense, reincarnated in a potentially endless cycle of explosion, birth, and rebirth. All it takes is energy, and a will to create or destroy, or both.
>
> In a way, great nations are the same. Our separate pieces come together, are tempered by heat and fire, then through war are torn asunder, to once again combine, different yet the same.
>
> The great rivers like the Mississippi and the Yangtze are indeed mirrors of the nations through which they flow.

"What the hell?" Sharon Wizer muttered out loud, attracting the attention of the analyst in the next cubical.

"What's up, Sharon?"

"Oh, it's that American journalist in China. I think he's going off the deep end. Unfortunately, knowing the Chinese like I do, there could be repercussions."

The next morning in central China, Putnam rose from his bunk to relieve himself, and when he returned to his cabin, he found unknown Chinese carrying his belongings, including his computer, out of his cabin and placing them in a heap on the pier.

Putnam gestured anxiously and shouted, "What are you doing?" The men did not react to him but kept filing in to rid the boat of every last scrap of paper the author had brought with him.

As Putnam bounded up the gangplank, snatching up his laptop computer and standing protectively over the rest of the pile of his belongings, he shouted for his translator and guide. But no one responded.

After some shouts he could not understand from the boat captain who had just started the engine, the deckhands cast off lines, and the boat eased away from the pier.

Like a piece of detritus, Putnam had been cast off. The noise of the boat's departure had obscured the sound of a van pulling up behind Putnam. But he clearly heard the voice of a Chinese man offering to help. The man pulled a large rectangular plastic bin from the back of the van and started placing Putnam's things into the container.

Putnam, clutching his laptop, asked, "Do you speak English?"

"I do," he said.

"Are you robbing me?"

"No."

"What's going on?"

"I'm about to take you to see some people. I think you've met one of them. He's sponsoring your trip. Don't worry, this could be good news."

Along with Liu Wei, the Chinese Public Affairs official Putnam had met in Lijiang, there was another man who looked beefier than most Chinese and cultivated a menacing presence.

"Mr. Putnam, it is good to meet you, but I am tired. Because of you, I took an early morning flight from Beijing just to visit you. That was not what I had planned for the day, so if you don't mind, we'll skip the formalities."

"And you would be?"

"It doesn't matter. I was awakened by an outraged voice who told me to tell you that your email last night was drivel. It was not up to either your or our expected standards."

"It was honest. It was what I had on my mind."

"I'm sure your mind thinks about sex from time to time, but the Chinese government is not paying you to write about your sexual fantasies. And we certainly aren't interested in having you write about hydrogen bombs and reincarnating water."

Liu Wei broke in, "Your charter is to write about the Yangtze River and the history of China surrounding it, just as you wrote about the Mississippi. Nothing more, nothing less."

"How can I write anything without a boat?"

The dour bureaucrat spoke again. "There can be two outcomes for this conversation Mr. Putnam. One is that you get a better, faster boat as your friend Liu Wei here suggested, or we send you home."

"I have a contract."

The tall man favored him with a curled, pernicious smile.

"Good luck suing the Chinese government, Mr. Putnam. And besides," nodding toward his Public Affairs colleague, "this man is interested in the river as a cultural exchange. We invite American tourists to ride our boats."

"All the more reason to get me a better boat, one worthy of the writing."

"I really do not care what you say about our boats. I want to know about the message the Frogs left behind. Is it as dire as our sources imply?"

Putnam sat silently, contemplating his next words.

"I should have known this would follow me wherever I went."

The dour man sat motionless, staring straight at Putnam, expectantly.

Putnam continued, "I already told your friend here that once I filed that story with the *Fortean Times*, I walked away. It was done, and so was I."

"Forgive me for being skeptical Mr. Putnam, but how can anyone walk away from the biggest story of the twenty-first century? I don't believe you."

"Even though you Chinese seem to rummage through our government's most sensitive files at will, we commoners are not privy to top-secret matters. There's a reason for that, and I'm guessing this encounter here is one of those reasons. If people don't tell me things, then I can't tell you things."

"Let me put it this way," the increasingly baleful Chinaman sneered. "I understand your government may be wary of revealing national secrets. We are no different. But what I don't think you realize Mr. Putnam is that we may be talking about all humanity being affected by the Frogs' message, not just your country. The U.S. has a responsibility to share with all peoples the knowledge gained from extraterrestrial visitors."

"Noble intentions, I'm sure," Putnam said. "However, I think you assume too much. I would not assume that anyone knows the message. In fact, as I reported, it will take another ninety years before we understand the message."

"I'm not so sure."

"Let me say it clearly. Even if I did know something, which I don't, I would not prostitute myself, and my country. I do feel certain that our nation's morals are such that if there were a message for humanity, we would share it with the United Nations."

"That's funny, I thought the entire cylindrical gift from the Frogs was intended to be shared with the United Nations already. Didn't you say that?"

"Maybe it has."

"Ah Mr. Putnam, you are so naïve. I assure you that because of the naiveté of the American people, China will continue to exploit every means available to discover what is in our national, and world, interest. Your country would no doubt do the same."

Turning to the PAO by his side, the bureaucrat said, "Mr. Wei, this boat trip is over. I'll be escorting Mr. Putnam back to Hong Kong for his flight back to America. His mission failed. Please have someone pack his belongings."

Putnam was speechless.

CHAPTER 39. FALSE FLAG

Jason Parker's satellite phone rang while he was 38,000 feet above southern Illinois, about to cross into Missouri, headed for New Mexico. Once again, he assumed it was Laura Smith, and this time he was right.

"Jason, we need you to make a little detour to Pawhuska, Oklahoma."

"Not again."

"We need you to talk Samuel Putnam into writing an information piece for us. Preferably a book if he's a fast writer."

"I thought he was in China? He's back? The so-and-so didn't call me."

"Actually, he was kicked out of China," Laura said.

Parker laughed. "Yeah, I can see that. What kind of book is he supposed to write?"

"We'll tell you after you land and we have more secure comms. But we're guessing since the Chinese didn't pay up, he's probably hungry enough to take some Washington money."

"As you know, Laura, Samuel's pretty darned independent."

"We'll see about that," Laura retorted.

"Is it something I could write? I could use the money."

"I'm sure you could, Jason, but Putnam's gaining a national following. And we want someone independent of the government. Plus ... he's a better writer."

"Ouch, that hurt, but you're right. So, you want him to write the government's words, in his own words?"

"That's one way to put it."

"Do you know if he's in Pawhuska now?"

"Actually, he's in Bartlesville, but we've arranged to have him pick you up at the Bartlesville airport and drive you to Pawhuska."

"Well, at least Bartlesville won't be far out of my way."

"That's the spirit."

Just as arranged, Putnam met Parker at the Bartlesville, Oklahoma airport. The drive to Pawhuska on Highway 60 would only take thirty minutes or so.

Parker shook Putnam's hand and then pulled him in for a manly hug.

"Damn good to see you, my friend. It's been too long. I hope picking me up over here wasn't too much of an inconvenience."

"Not at all. I'm teaching at the local branch of Rogers State University, so I have to be here anyway. And since it's time for me to head home, you couldn't have planned it better."

"You're teaching now."

"Yes, journalism and creative writing, and my wife's an adjunct professor at the main campus in Claremore. She occasionally teaches since our daughter Cindy's gone away to school, and Susan gets bored hanging around Pawhuska."

"What's she teaching?"

"Well, she's half Osage, so she's teaching Native American History whenever she gets the chance."

"That's terrific."

"Strangely, they have a sophomore course on the Cherokee, but none on the Osage. Susan is trying to get that added to the curriculum since there's a hell of a lot more Osage than Cherokee around here."

"How'd you end up teaching here?"

"After my Fortean Times article, I had several good teaching offers come my way, but they were all about aliens if you can believe that. I want to teach writing, not aliens."

"Makes good sense to me," Parker said.

"And hell, what do I know about aliens? You and Laura had all the experience."

"Well, your Fortean Times article was spot on. You picked up on a lot, for someone who had never seen them."

"They're really gone now?"

"Yep."

"They ever phone home?"

"Not to me, anyway."

They both sat quietly for a moment as Putnam turned his jeep onto Highway 60, headed west towards Pawhuska.

"How are the wife and kids?" Putnam asked.

"They're okay, I guess. Our daughter-in-law is pregnant, so we're excited about that. But as for Sandy, well, after all these years she's pulled the plug."

"You're divorced?"

"We're separated."

"Oh, I am so sorry."

"It's my fault, really. I kept making promises I couldn't keep. I guess I felt like I had a higher calling than being a homebody. But I should have seen how she was suffering."

"So I guess divorce is coming."

"Most likely. But what do you say we change the subject? Did the Chinese beat you up or anything?"

"They got pretty thuggish, but nothing physical. They apparently didn't like where I was going with my writing."

Parker chuckled, remembering his first experience with a bona fide writer. Putnam looked over at him, no doubt wondering what was so funny.

"The first time I met a professional writer," Parker reminisced, "I was in graduate school, working with the Navy on a diving training program. The writer was a graduate student too. I had never met a real writer before, but she uttered one well-crafted sentence that absolutely blew me away. I'll never forget it."

"Do tell."

"We were on a boat decompressing between dives, and one of the guys brought a sea cucumber up from the bottom, and as he climbed on deck, he handed it to her saying, 'I got a pet for you.' Well, she placed that cucumber directly in front of me, and just off to her right side. And like you would any pet, she began stroking it. As she did, it tensed up. It was apparently not used to being stroked."

Putnam started smiling, imagining how this might end.

"I guess you could say it became turgid. That would be the proper medical term."

"Like a dick?"

"Exactly."

"As she kept stroking it, it finally became annoyed enough that it squirted a strong stream of water from one end, in her direction."

"You serious?"

"And that was when she calmly uttered those absolutely perfect words, *Isn't it amazing, the consistency of nature?"*

Putnam laughed heartily.

"I was at a complete loss of words," Parker admitted.

"You mind if I borrow that story for my writing class?"

"Sure, if you think you can get away with it. It's pretty bawdy."

"Hey, it's nature."

"What's your next writing project?" Parker asked.

"I'm not sure. Since my Yangtze River project failed, my schedule is free, except for teaching."

"I'm delighted to hear that, Samuel."

"How so?"

"I have a writing job for you."

"What kind of writing job?"

"A good one. It pays well."

"That's not the most important thing, you know. If my name is on it."

"I know Samuel. But I think you'll like this."

"What's it about?"

"Expanding your horizons."

"How far?"

"To the cosmos."

Putnam diverted his eyes from the road just enough to give Parker a questioning stare.

"Damn Jason, this isn't about the Frogs, is it?"

"No, it isn't. But let's go back to that time. You wondered if there was a reason why the Frogs left Earth in a hurry."

"Jason, I just went through this with the Chinese."

"But I want to move beyond that, to a speculative piece. Let's think about the consequences if you were right and some calamity was about to strike the Earth. Hypothetically speaking, what would we do?"

For the next few moments, only the sound of the tires on the road reached Parker's ears as Putnam was thinking.

"Hypothetically—such an interesting word. I teach my students that it's like Schrödinger's cat, you don't know if it's alive or dead until you open the box."

I've never heard that association before, Parker thought.

"Likewise, until you look into the speaker's mind, you don't know if the word "hypothetical" means *hypothetical,* or if it means *reality.* I know you won't tell me, so I'll have to take you at your word."

"You're stalling Samuel."

"Okay, so have NASA blast the damn asteroid, or if that doesn't work, leave the planet, I suppose."

Parker smiled. "Exactly right, that is the conventional wisdom. We, the government, fund NASA to do all that, but no one wants to contemplate how dangerous, and ineffective a mass evacuation would be."

"It worked for the Frogs."

"And in a million years it might work for us. But here's the point. We want you to do a piece on the realities of space evacuation, including the likelihood that Mars may be no better off than Earth when it comes to surviving threats from the cosmos."

"Maybe less, because there's no infrastructure there," Putnam said.

"Yes, and not that much of an atmosphere. But if we bypass Mars, where else could we go?"

"I see. And we're only talking about a very few people anyway," Putnam noted. "The odds of finding a suitable new Earth are astronomically small."

"And the evacuees' odds of survival while searching is also astronomically small," Parker said.

"That sounds like a downer of a book."

"But it doesn't have to be. The Earth is a much more resilient refuge than people think, especially compared to space."

"Well if you believe that, why don't you write that book?"

"Because I'm a guvvy, and the government cannot be seen pouring huge quantities of taxpayer money into space exploration while at the same time poo-pooing the population survival benefit of that investment."

Putnam frowned, apparently not liking what he was hearing.

"Yeah, that could get ugly on Capitol Hill."

"We do not want NASA defunded. It's our greatest outreach, especially since we now know other advanced civilizations exist, and our long-term survival may depend on us learning survival skills from them. But until then, we need to fund alternatives."

"What sort of alternatives?"

"Deep sea alternatives."

Putnam laughed. "Ha, you Navy guys are jealous of the aerospace budgets. I get it."

Parker shook his head. "Samuel, this is not a Navy idea or a Navy request. It comes from the top."

"The top?"

"The very top."

It took a few seconds before Putnam responded with a simple, "Oh. Well then, I'll need some help, some experts to interview."

"I can make that happen."

"And this will not be a quick turn around," Putnam warned.

"Understand."

"And also not cheap."

"Not a problem. But I'll need an outline before I can advance you anything above a hundred thou."

Putnam smiled. "Wow, deep pockets."

"That tells you how important this is."

"Will this be targeted as a mass market paperback?"

"No. Hardcover followed up by paperback and electrons."

"Publisher?"

"Your call."

"My call? That's not how it works, Jason."

Parker laughed. "Don't you worry, dollars speak volumes, pun not intended. Tell us who you want, and we'll get them on board."

Putnam paused, smiling. "Well, this is an interesting turn of events."

After a few minutes more of Putnam pointing out the very few landmarks to the east of Pawhuska, they pulled into town. Putnam wheeled the jeep into an angled parking spot within sight of what appeared to be the courthouse.

"Susan is hosting a reading group at our house this evening," he said. "Do you mind if we talk about this project at a restaurant?"

"You'll never catch me complaining about talking over dinner."

"Good. Then assuming you like down-home cooking, I know the perfect place to talk. Not too noisy."

They got out and approached a stand-alone, one-story building with a sign that read BUFFALO JOES.

"That sign's not hype, Jason. There really is a wild buffalo herd in the prairie north of here."

"Are they on the menu?"

"No. We're trying to grow the herd, not eat it."

Buffalo Joes was a modern-looking restaurant with the ambiance of most any barbeque or pancake restaurant. Simple, but it got the job done.

Sitting in a corner table by the front window was a middle-aged man with short, graying hair and the weathered look of an old salt. Putnam smiled the moment he saw him.

"Luke, fancy seeing you here this early," Putnam called out.

With a mouth full of snacks, the man could only wave his hand.

Putnam pointed to Parker and said, "This is good timing. Luke, this is none other than Jason Parker. Jason, this is Luke Warmwater. I believe you two have a lot in common. He's a former Marine recon diver and has a personal heads up on some of your experiences. I've been hoping to get you two together. Plus, keeping with the Navy theme, he calls himself *the Pirate*."

Warmwater scooted his chair back and stood up, offering his hand to Parker. Parker grabbed it eagerly. Who wouldn't talk to a Marine diver who called himself *the Pirate?*

"He's also a full-blooded Osage," Putnam added.

"What's not to like?" Parker said.

"Please, join me," Warmwater said gesturing to the empty seats at his table. I just placed my order."

"If you don't mind, we will," Putnam said.

As Parker pulled out a chair and sat down, he asked Luke, "So I assume you're one of the local Osage?"

"Sure am. My clan is the Cheezhu wash doggie. We're all over Osage County."

"How do you spell that?"

"It's T·z·u W·a·s·h·t·a·k·i. And before you ask, regarding my name, my parents did have a sense of humor."

Putnam and Parker smiled. "I see that," Parker said, "and I guess you do too. Why do you call yourself the Pirate?"

"It's because of me sailing vessel, the *Gahitha*. And before you ask, that's Osage for 'moves by the wind.' So what brings Jason Parker back to Pawhuska? There's not much going on here since the *Killers of the Flower Moon* movie came out."

"Yeah, I heard about that. Absolutely tragic story."

"You see why we don't trust white people all that much."

"Yes, I get that. But actually, I came to talk Samuel into writing a new book."

"What about?"

"The unrealistic expectations of space travel as a refuge from global calamity."

"That sounds like a good book title right there," said Warmwater. "Are you interested?"

Samuel gave him a sly look. "We'll see. We've just begun the conversation."

"Well, some chicken fried steak and Miller draft should expedite that."

Parker grinned at Warmwater and said, "Samuel tells me you were a Marine Recon Diver. I've worked with those folks, they're awesome. How did you decide to become a Marine Diver?"

Looking Parker straight in the eye, Luke said, "You don't *decide* to become a Marine diver. You *hope* to become a Marine diver. Many try, few succeed."

"*The Few, the Proud.* It's not just a saying, right?"

Luke smiled, apparently pleased that Parker remembered the old Marine Corps slogan.

"But actually, I became a diver through a strange occurrence. Before I tell you, I have to know, do you believe in ghosts, Mr. Parker?"

Parker laughed, a laugh which brought an immediate scowl on Luke's face.

"I'm not laughing at you, Luke. I'm laughing at the irony of your question. I discovered the E.T. Frogs, but I've never met one in the flesh, just their apparitions. I don't know what that apparition is exactly, but I've both seen and touched it, so whether you call it a ghost, or spirit, or whatever, I'd have to say yes. I believe in them."

"Okay then," Luke said, "When I was a youngster, one of my role models was a great uncle. He was an Army medic in World War II and as handsome an Osage as you'll ever see. He inspired me to apply to medical school, which I did. In my first year, during a rotation in pathology, I saw naked spirits in the morgue, mostly disturbingly young adults, male and female. They were talking to each other, seemingly surprised to see their bodies there. It was so disturbing to me that I quit medical school and became a Marine diver."

Parker sat stunned.

"And the rest is history, as they say," Luke added.

"Well, I've heard lots of reasons for leaving medical school," Parker finally said, "but that one takes the cake."

Putnam added, "The native peoples have always been more closely attuned to the spirit world than the rest of us."

"Luke, there seems to be a lot of paranormal stuff going on these days," Parker said, "and I must say the Frogs are about as paranormal as it comes. But I'm also curious about your 'head's up' on my experiences. But first, I'm hungry. You recommend the chicken fried steak?"

"Sure do. Your cardiologist needs the work."

Parker and Putnam both laughed.

"You only live once, Luke," Putnam said. "Let's enjoy what we have."

Whenever Parker heard that truism, he thought of Laura Smith's odd belief that we live multiple times.

She is a strange bird, he thought.

But then Parker remembered that the last time he was in Pawhuska, Putnam's wife, Susan, pointed out that numerous Native peoples also believed in reincarnation.

Luke waved the waitress over, "Triple that order, please. But make Samuel's a Heineken if I remember correctly."

Putnam nodded his affirmation and then smiled at Parker. "You're going to like this story even more."

Taking a swig of his beer, Luke started his tale. "I hear from Samuel that you've seen all sorts of crazy things, and done incredible things, so what I'm about to say may be no big deal to you. But I'm just your average Indian, so I thought you'd want to hear what the average Joe has experienced."

"Of course."

"Let me give you a little background first. When I was a kid about eight, we moved from Oklahoma to Kansas City, to a town called Shawnee Mission. The tribe owned mineral rights to the oil on our land in Osage County. When Phillip's Petroleum Company needed a good petroleum engineer, my Dad was sent to Bartlesville for company training, and then we moved to Kansas City where they have a refinery. So there we were, Osage Indians living in Shawnee country. It was a little weird for me."

"Was it a Shawnee reservation?"

"Oh no, no reservations there. This was all white man country. Anyway, we later moved to a suburb called Prairie Village. We lived there when I was about ten. It was nice because I didn't sense any prejudice against us, being Indians and all. We had enough money to look affluent, and that's all it took to fit in."

Parker was curious to know where this conversation was headed. Putnam smiled, perhaps anticipating what was coming.

"During the summer, my Mom would often send me on my bike to ride the mile or so to the shopping center of the Village to get small grocery items for her. One afternoon my older brother and I rode our bikes together down to the Village for something. Well, on this one day we were riding back at dusk. We were about halfway back home when we saw it."

"Saw what?"

"A big, triangular UFO, with large, colored lights around its edges. It was hovering, low down, and close, not far from what used to be Porter Elementary school."

A Triangle with lights, Parker thought, *like Dioscuri?* This was the first historical sighting he'd encountered.

"Oh, I see," was all Parker could manage.

Parker had to be careful. While the public knew about the Triangle recovered from the ocean floor, the lights had been PhotoShopped out of all the public images. The presence of those lights was top secret since they had something to do with controlling the craft, but how that worked was still a mystery. He would have to avoid any mention of lights.

Fortunately, the Russian and American Presidents had agreed during a rare moment of mutual interest to keep that fact hidden from the public. And if a photo leaked, they would both claim the pictures had been doctored somehow.

Luke continued speaking softly, discretely, but nevertheless conveying a sense of awe.

"I have burned into my memory the image of us stopping our bikes on the sidewalk, straddling them, and staring at that thing. It was motionless, didn't make a sound. But we could see it in sharp detail, the metallic look of the main body, and the round lights along the periphery, each in a bright primary color. They were red, blue, yellow, and maybe green also."

This was hitting awfully close to home. Parker had to work hard to hide his reaction to what he was hearing.

"And then it was gone. Neither of us had any memory of what happened. We didn't see it fly away. In fact, the next thing we remember was riding our bikes home as fast as we could. I ran into the kitchen and told Mom we'd seen a UFO, but my damn brother immediately denied it. "No, we didn't see anything," Warmwater said in a mocking tone.

"Mom did not respond. I have no idea what she was thinking. In fact, that event was never mentioned again until my parents were long gone. Much later, I asked my brother if he remembered lying about that UFO. He just laughed and admitted that he did remember."

"Has he ever told anyone?"

"No."

Good, Parker thought.

"And now he's passed away. That remained my secret until I told Samuel, and now you."

"Well, we now know they do exist."

"The ones with the lights?"

Parker hated lying, but he had no choice. "I don't know about that. But I guess anything's possible."

Nodding to Putnam, Parker followed up with, "but we do need to be discrete."

"No problem," Luke said. "I'm a Marine, so I know how to keep my mouth shut."

But after he swallowed a mouthful of tea, Luke continued, "But I'm curious, why must we be discrete?"

"Just because."

"Okay boss. I can take a hint."

Parker had not eaten chicken fried steak in years, so it was a treat. After he ordered apple pie for dessert, Warmwater could no longer contain himself.

"The old WaZhaZhe were not always Christian, you know. They believed in Wa-kon-da, which was our name for God. WaZhaZhe means 'little people," which is our way of being humble before God."

Parker nodded his head.

"Anyway, we believe what we see, which is that Wa-kon-da brings us cycles of birth and death."

He looked around to make sure no one was listening to the conversation.

"Ever since my magical moment with the UFO, I have known instinctively that a new cycle of life is beginning. And now that we know about the existence of other Triangles, and of undersea aliens, and now the Trolls, our tribal elders are in full agreement with me."

"That what? A new cycle is beginning?"

"Yes."

"I actually agree with that," Parker said.

"Good. But there's a downside."

Putnam was staring at Parker with anticipation. He apparently knew what was coming.

"Wa-kon-da knows that with the start of each new cycle, there's a lot of dying as the old cycle passes away."

Parker was not expecting that. In Western civilization, there are indeed cycles, but each one builds upon the last. The Osage apparently saw life as a zero-sum game. And that was not a pleasant thought.

"I don't know what to say."

"And it's not just the Osage. The Hopi have long spoken of nine signs of the end days. The last one is especially interesting since you seem to be focusing on space and the Cosmos." The timbre of his voice shifted slightly. *"You will hear of a dwelling-place in the heavens, above the earth, that shall fall with a great crash. It will appear as a blue star. Very soon after this, the ceremonies of my people will cease."*

"You have that memorized?" Parker asked.

"I think about it a lot. And supposedly an old Seneca prophet may have predicted the destruction of the ozone layer."

"Seriously?"

"That's one way to interpret it. And then, you have to consider the Frogs left Earth for a reason, didn't they?"

"Maybe they left because they could?" Parker said, keeping up pretenses, pretenses that he did not fully believe himself.

"That's not what our elders think."

Looking in Putnam's direction but speaking to Luke, Parker said, "So it's not just Samuel who is skeptical of the Frogs' motives."

"No. You may be one of the few who are not suspicious," Warmwater answered.

Parker noticed that a couple at the closest table was now looking their way.

Lowering his voice, Parker responded, "That's what a lot of smart folks in Washington think. They left because they could. Too damn much insanity here on Earth."

Luke smiled. "Didn't know they had smart folks in D.C."

Parker laughed at the abruptness and clarity of the comment. "I can see why you might think that. But I also think maybe you WaZhaZhe hold a grudge for a long time."

"For good reason," Luke reaffirmed.

As Luke's tale was wrapping up, the server brought their meals, and the conversation dropped off considerably as they ate.

Pointing a fork at Luke, Parker said, "Getting back to the reason I'm here, I'd be interested in your opinion, Luke."

"Let me get this straight. You want Samuel to write about how the world could come to an end. Some cosmic calamity may strike the Earth, and we have the choice of heading out into space or hunkering down on Earth. Did I get that right?"

"You did," Parker said.

"Well, quoting that famous astronaut, Rocket Man, space is cold as hell and no place to raise your kids. But if we go the other way, like deep underwater, then count me in. I'm your man."

"You would rather stay here?"

"Not like we really have a choice. We don't have thousands of spaceships like the Frogs had."

"What do you think, Samuel?" Parker asked.

"I'm undecided. I'll let you know after I research it."

"If Laura or I can help, just let me know," Parker offered.

"Oh, so Laura's in on this?"

"She is."

Luke's eyes got big, and a smile crossed his face. "Hey Jason, isn't Laura the hottie who had a crush on you?"

"Whoever gave you such an idea?"

Luke cut his eyes over to Putnam. "I'll never tell."

"Well, she is an interesting young lady with what has to be the most interesting job in the government. But tell me, Luke, how did you end up being a man of the sea? The ocean's a long way from Oklahoma."

"Nothing like changing the subject," Luke said with a smile. "But since you asked, I do love my birthplace, but after a while, you want to experience something other than heat, cold and tornadoes. And like you said, the ocean's a long way from Oklahoma."

Luke leaned forward in his seat and with a gleam in his eyes said, "After being a Marine, saltwater gets in your blood. I just come back here to visit family. And ol' Samuel here."

As the waitress cleared off the plates and made the customary offer of deserts, an offer not taken, Parker laid down his napkin and said, "Gents, that was a great meal and great company. I hate to eat and run, but Samuel I'm wondering if you can take me back to the airport. I need to be in New Mexico by morning."

"You flying out of this little airfield at night?" Luke asked.

"No, Bartlesville."

"What's the rush?" Putnam asked.

"Or I can get a cab."

"Don't you think of it. I promised your assistant I'd take good care of you."

"Well, thanks. I have an appointment with a Troll, and I don't want to be late."

"A Troll, you say," Warmwater smiled and shook his head gently. "I never thought I'd live long enough to hear that."

"Wish I could go along," Putnam added.

"Samuel, you start writing that book, and I'll make introductions."

"I am thinking about it."

Luke smiled. "I just hope you folks treat the Trolls better than you treated us Indians."

"We're trying our best, Luke," Parker said. "That's one reason I'm going."

A short time later, Putnam was driving his white jeep back up the road towards the Bartlesville Airport. It was a dark night, and the moon had not yet risen, allowing the two to clearly see the Milky Way.

"It's beautiful up there tonight," Parker said.

"But as Luke reminded us, cold as hell," Putnam said.

"I'm sorry I didn't get to see Susan this time. Please give her my best."

"I sure will. But I'm happy you got to meet the Pirate. What do you think about him?"

"Seems like a Renaissance man. I've met a lot of people, but never one quite like him. That was good luck running into him."

"Sometimes, things are just meant to be."

"Like you writing that book?" Parker prodded.

Putnam did not answer. Both men were silent as the Jeep's lights lit up the curves in the road as they drove east. As shrubby trees and occasional glowing eyes passed by on the side of the road, Parker was thinking back to the time he was called *Ta'veren* by the Trolls in Mexico. Having later researched the fictional term, he realized that as the writer Robert Jordan described it, *Ta'veren* cause things to happen to correct the Wheel of Time. *But if I am Ta'veren in any way, it's because I seem to meet unusual people who cause things to happen. They have the superpowers, not me. And this Osage boat Captain named Luke Warmwater might be one of those.*

"Remember that night in the Prairie?" Putnam asked, also reminiscing.

"The story about the Black Triangle that wasn't a UFO, but one of ours? I'll never forget it."

"There's a lot going on up there in space that we simply cannot understand. We humans are not capable."

Parker looked at him and broke out into a big smile. "I'm glad you're coming around to my way of thinking. We're not the brightest bulbs in the cosmic neighborhood."

"But I still think that if the really bright ones moved out of the stellar neighborhood," Putnam added, "maybe we should consider following suit."

"But where Samuel? That's the question."

"I know," Putnam said. "I'll have to think about it."

"How about writing while you're thinking about it."

"Okay, I give up. I will, but I can't promise you how it will end. Or when."

None of us can, Parker thought.

"Good," Parker said. "I'll get the paperwork started."

Parker felt satisfied as they pulled up to the Bartlesville airport general aviation ramp. After he had thanked Putnam for the ride and wished him good luck, he checked out his baby jet all the while smiling and thinking, *I'm having way too much fun.*

Chapter 40. Lechuguilla

For most of the night, Parker's flight had inexplicably been on a traffic hold issued by Albuquerque Air Traffic Control. Early in the morning, he was finally released for takeoff on his short one-hour flight. His repeated queries as to the cause of the delay had always been answered by a curt, "We don't know. Do you wish to cancel your clearance request?"

No, he certainly did not, now more than ever.

By the time he began his descent, dawn had just begun to tint the eastern edge of the Guadalupe Escarpment as he was vectored over the sparse lights of Whites City, then turned to the northeast to join the final approach course for runway 03 at the Cavern City Airport. As his jet's main wheels squeaked onto the striped asphalt runway, it was light enough for him to see the tarmac was crowded with planes of various sorts. Alarmingly, some of them had FBI markings.

As he entered the Fixed Base Operator's building, a building that normally sat begging for attention, he found a dozen or so men and women, all looking severe, staring at him and his government I.D. badge. From a distance, they probably couldn't figure out who he was, but the badge looked official enough for them to relax their gaze and return to their separate conversations.

After a brief restroom break where he saw rows of photos from the World War II days of the former Carlsbad Army Airfield, he was escorted by a sergeant into an olive drab green sedan with Army markings which soon turned south on the National Parks Highway headed back towards White's City.

"What on earth is going on here, Sergeant?"

"All I know is there's been an accident. You'll get briefed when you check-in."

"Why the FBI presence?"

"Like I said, you'll get briefed when you arrive."

The two men remained silent for the rest of the trip. Before long the sedan turned to the right to the road leading up to the secured entrance to the Lechuguilla Cave.

Dr. Emery Reed's and the CDC's health concerns for the Trolls had resulted in all of the Trolls being moved from the sultry and mold-prone climate of the Florida Panhandle to a more hospitable and roomier part of the much drier Lechuguilla Cave, not far from Carlsbad Caverns in New Mexico. Initially, the Mexican and Siberian Trolls had settled in different portions of the cave system, but gradually the two populations were mixing. Sexual opportunity and boredom had a way of causing that.

President Whitney had another purpose for relocating the Trolls. He had promised Reed that he expected to quell any taxpayer concerns by taking the Trolls off the dole and giving them real jobs. Conveniently, the jobs he had in mind were jobs replacing well paid civil servants, National Park Service personnel, with contract labor, Troll contract labor. After all, looking after the New Mexico cave systems, Lechuguilla Cave and Carlsbad, was in the Trolls' best-interest. And best of all, they were cheap. Their salary, once suitably taxed, was placed in a trust fund.

Whitney's plan may not have been terribly original, but it was convenient.

In that delicate underground ecosystem where the Trolls were placed, admission of visitors was carefully controlled. In fact, in the part of the cave where the Trolls were located, a cadre of Marines and militant Trolls kept guard. Of course, the Marines had guns, and the Trolls did not. But then, as a Mexican troll had once proved in the jungle of Quintana Roo, their weapons were their hands. A single male troll had simultaneously disarmed and tossed about two young Marine guards in the Yucatan jungle.

But the Marines working the Lechuguilla site did not know of that jungle history, an embarrassment no Marine wished to retell. The local platoon had merely been warned not to fraternize with the Trolls, and to let them do their thing, whatever that was. But based on the extensive federal presence, something must have gone wrong.

Jason Parker had not previously visited Truman Baltazar, or Argxtre as he insisted on being called, in their new environment. He had expected a much less clamorous meeting.

On their arrival, Parker was met by a Marine Lieutenant who ushered Parker into the backroom of the secure reception center.

"There's been an accident. One of the non-troll visiting scientists was crushed by a falling stalactite. Maybe you know him. His name is McKetchen, Oscar McKetchen."

"Never heard that name before. Were any Trolls hurt?"

"No."

"Why is the FBI here?"

"It looks like it was an unfortunate accident, but the FBI is investigating anyway, just in case."

"Are there any other visitors here now?"

"No."

"So the FBI is investigating the Trolls?"

"A formality only. Are you here to see anyone in particular?"

"Yes, the troll we call Truman Baltazar."

"Oh, the Head Troll. Let me check and see if he's available for a visit."

Well, Parker thought, *I sure as hell hope he is after I've come this far.*

The man called on his personal radio, "Thomas here. Is Baltazar free to visit Dr. Jason Parker? He came in from," turning to Parker, he asked, "Where are you from?"

"D.C."

"He flew in from Washington," the Captain said.

After listening for a moment on his earbud, the Lieutenant turned away from his radio and said, "Give them thirty minutes. They're finishing up an interview."

"They who?"

"The FBI."

"Okay, do you have a waiting room?"

"Turn right past the male head and past the candy machine, and the waiting room is through the first door on the right."

"Okay, that's where I'll be."

"Copy that."

The small windowless room had a well-worn leatherette sofa and eight uncomfortable-looking chairs. Without sitting, Parker pulled his phone from his pocket and placed a call to Laura Smith. She picked up immediately.

"Laura, who the hell is Oscar McKetchen?"

"Oh god Jason, I didn't have time to warn you. McKetchen is a visiting graduate student from Harvard. He's studying the differences between the two troll populations."

"You mean, he was. Now he's dead."

"Yes, that's what I meant. We got the word yesterday while you were in Pawhuska."

"Well, that's quite a surprise. There's a significant FBI presence. Are the Trolls suspected?"

"I don't know how the investigation's going, but I think it was just a tragic accident."

"I'm meeting with Baltazar in a little bit. Is this likely to come up?"

"I doubt it. It was just an accident. Caves can be dangerous."

Truman Baltazar had emerged as a leader of the Trolls when they lived in Quintana Roo. He and his hybrid people had "skin lights," UV projecting sites that enabled them to see from both UV light reflected from cave walls, and from the UV-excited fluorescence of the cave minerals around them.

The fact that their skin was an ever-present light source meant that in their normally dark habitat they usually wore as little clothing as they could. But now that humans had installed lighting in the current cave system, to benefit the fully human visitors, the Trolls had taken a liking to rugged western clothing. They looked more like cowboys and cowgirls than Trolls. Except for the boots. They preferred sneakers—surer footing in the caves.

When Parker and Kelly Brightman first met Argxtre in a Mexican cave, he looked like Tarzan in a loincloth. Now he would fit into any crowd, as long as the lights didn't go out and he didn't start disrobing.

A Marine Corporal entered the room with Baltazar.

"Dr. Parker, as you requested. You can chat with him all you wish, but everything in here gets recorded. If you need privacy, I suggest you step outside."

"Thank you, Corporal."

Baltazar wore dark sunglasses when outside the cave to protect his eyes. A Navy ophthalmologist was concerned about the possibility of cataracts in the Trolls, and Baltazar took that concern seriously. Besides, he thought he looked cool in sunglasses.

Their greeting conversation was telepathic.

Jason, it's good to see you, but your timing is not so good.

Baltazar did not reach out his hand to Parker. That was not their custom.

Parker responded telepathically.

You're right, Truman.

Speaking out loud out in exasperation, "Come on, Jason, is my name really that hard to pronounce?"

"I can't help it that we can't pronounce your names." I can call you Mr. A, or Truman. Which do you prefer?"

"I prefer we talk outside, in private."

"Can we talk in the cave? I haven't seen it."

"No. It's sealed until the investigators leave."

"So, what the hell happened here?"

"I don't understand how profanity helps you people talk. It adds nothing to the conversation."

"It makes us feel better," Parker answered.

"What happened is a big rock fell on Oscar's head."

"Did your people like Oscar?"

"You sound like the FBI. Did you come all this way to repeat their questions?"

"No. I actually have something more important."

"I know."

"Look, Truman, do me a favor and pretend you don't know what I'm going to say."

"Okay, sometimes I don't."

"I need to talk to you about what your people are likely to do if the world were to come to an end, from something like a gamma-ray burst."

"See, I know about that already," Baltazar said, smiling.

"Then that will save me some time," Parker said. "Have you thought about what you would do to save your people?"

"For anything other than an asteroid landing on top of us, we're good."

"How can you say that?"

"Mother Earth protects us. I know your concern, but she can shield us from even a gamma-ray burst."

"What about the aftermath? What if the Earth's oxygen levels plummet because of the effects of the gamma-rays?"

"That would be tragic for you humans, I'm sure. But what you haven't figured out yet, is that our creators, those you call the Frogs for some reason, could only exist in a low oxygen environment. As you now know, we are genetically engineered from a species that can only tolerate a small amount of oxygen. Earth's atmosphere is highly toxic to it. What you apparently haven't figured out yet is that we are what you call facultative anaerobes. Given enough time, we can switch to a biochemical pathway that operates just fine in low levels of oxygen."

Parker's forehead wrinkled as he thought. "You mean fermentation?"

"Since you're a science guy, it's more precisely micro-aerobic metabolism. Just like the Frogs, we prefer a little oxygen. But given enough time, we can convert over to an oxygen-absent environment. Time is the key."

"What kind of time?"

"Our children can switch over very quickly—the younger, the better. But we adults require a few weeks of supplemental oxygen. Perhaps you have noticed our request for a lot of oxygen concentrators."

"Dr. Smith said that was for low oxygen portions of the cave."

Baltazar smiled. "They have a dual purpose."

"What about food? Livestock requires oxygen."

"Okay, we'll call it a triple purpose for the oxygen concentrators. But when we're not in the mood for a steak, the cave is a great place to grow and harvest anaerobic bacteria."

"Not at all appetizing," Parker said, frowning.

"Your sensitivity may be the death of you yet, my friend."

"How do you know all this stuff? You said in Mexico that your minds could read whatever you wish? But how?"

"Have you ever read something in your dreams?"

"Once or twice."

"Once or twice is all it takes to prove you can do it. You don't need a physical book in front of you."

Parker smiled. "Interesting. Once I read a letter that had not even been written yet. Once the actual letter arrived, I knew I had not imagined it."

"You do know, but you're just unwilling to believe. If you want to know the answer to your question, believe what you know."

"Can you access anything that has been written?"

"We're a lot better at it than you are Jason Parker. And like you, we can also access things that have not yet been written. But again, this is routine for us. Not so for you."

"Then do you know we are considering undersea habitats?"

"Of course you are. You don't have much choice. With the oxygen largely depleted from the atmosphere, that low oxygen will eventually seep into whatever underground refuge you have. And unlike us, your biology does not adapt to low oxygen levels."

"Some people tolerate hypoxia very well," Parker said.

"But not as low as it can get."

"Did you read that somewhere?"

"No, it is not written. When that happens, the writing will stop."

"Hell's bells, Truman, you're just full of cheerful news."

"We believe in being prepared. But I predict you will not be prepared. Soon there will be no one left except us Trolls and cockroaches. And of course, we'll eat the roaches."

"Do you know that for a fact?"

"Yes, roaches are not that bad, and full of protein."

"I mean, do you know we will be unprepared?"

"No, I don't know for sure. I guess it is up to you, Jason Parker. After all, you are Ta'veren. Make things happen."

Parker laughed. There was that word again.

"I was just thinking about that word yesterday."

"Here's a secret for you Jason, writers like Robert Jordan who described Ta'veren, know a lot more than people give them credit for. You would be wise to take them a little more seriously."

"Whatever you say, Truman."

"Dammit, I really hate that name."

"I thought you didn't cuss."

"For you, I make an exception," Baltazar said.

"Speaking of seriously, what can you tell me about how Oscar McKetchen died?"

Baltazar grew suddenly quiet, frowning.

"We are being brutally honest here, my friend," Parker continued, trying to encourage the Troll to be more forthcoming.

"He was careless. Fortunately, we did not eat him. That would have been hard to explain to the FBI."

Parker laughed involuntarily. "Yes, I guess it would."

"I sense you want to do me a favor," Baltazar said, pivoting the conversation.

"Of course. What do you need?"

"First, tell Washington we want no more scientists studying us. We are not experimental animals. If they have a question, all they have to do is ask. We probably understand how science works better than your scientists do. And second, send them our thanks for moving us to this habitat. It is far roomier and healthier than the Marianna Caverns. Plus, we like having our Siberian cousins right next door."

"So, I take it you are happy with the move," Parker asked in conclusion.

"Yes, entirely. We could stay here forever. In fact, I think we will."

Chapter 41. SSGN Austin

The submarine USS *Austin*, SSGN-879, slipped silently through the South China Sea. Its course cut through an area 470 miles east of Ho Chi Minh City, formerly Saigon, Vietnam, 170 miles west of the nearest island in the Philippines, and 645 miles southeast of Hainan, the closest Chinese Island. The vessel had just reached its primary target, slowing to a stop 700 feet below the surface, and 100 feet below a circular dome resting on the edge of a subsea precipice.

Within a few minutes of the sub coming to a hover, Navy SEALs dropped out of the submarine and using their silent running propulsors headed towards a surprise rendezvous with the opaque dome of unknown content and purpose, recently installed by the Chinese Navy. Due diligence required the U.S. Navy to take a closer look at what the Chinese were doing.

It was only a reconnaissance mission, nothing more. The SEAL team was composed of six divers, each with twin propulsors attached to their legs, and a guidance, stabilization and communication system held on a tactical board in front of them. One of the divers was to hide a disguised listening device below the dome while another diver kept watch over his buddy. The others were to encircle the dome in buddy pairs looking for some telltale indications of its purpose. The plan was for the four pairs to approach the dome from the four ordinal directions, and then move counterclockwise in a circular search pattern.

It was the SEALs' favorite time of day, early morning, time of maximum darkness on a moonless and calm night. No Chinese naval vessels were operating near that location at that time, in what is otherwise a busy international shipping channel.

While one SEAL had his attention turned towards the smooth surface of the dome, the second of the buddy pair was acting as his overwatch, standing behind and offset in distance from the dome. His job was to make sure his buddy encountered no surprises. Unfortunately, there was no overwatch for the overwatch.

E-5 Neal Phillips, or Flips as he was called by his team members, was twenty feet outboard from the diver he was watching through his night-vision diving mask. While keeping a light-amplified eye on his buddy, he was also attuned to the haptic threat detector which would give a vibrating warning around his chest pointing out a potential threat. The position on his body indicated the direction of the threat, and the intensity of the vibration revealed the closeness of that threat.

The brains of the sensor screened out biologics, focusing only on anything that would indicate the operation of a life support system. Electrical signals, breath sounds, gas flowing through tubes, solenoid clicks, sonar reflection off a hard object, all would indicate a non-natural entity in the SEALs presence, thus posing a potential threat.

The sensing system was highly tuned to the low-frequency acoustic locator beacon of each of the SEAL divers, so locating a team member in the black and cold deep water of the South China Sea would be easy.

With no threats nearby, Flips watched his buddy, willing that he be successful in finding some entrance or other indication of the dome's purpose. Being a SEAL, his current prayer life was centered mostly on a desire for mission success, and an always silent prayer that if his time came, he would die honorably.

Flips' prayer for success was suddenly and forcibly interrupted by multiple things wrapping around his body, pulling on his arms, legs, neck, and facemask. His immediate thought was of a giant octopus since his sensors had not alerted him. As he felt his facemask slipping from his head, and not being able to move his arms to secure it, or to reach his alarm signaler, he was only able to utter a muffled shout.

Flips instinctively held his breath as his face was fully exposed to the cold water. Breath-holding for a minute or more was something he had been trained to do, in a pool. But under attack, and restrained as he was, he could not take a deep breath due to the boa constrictor-like grasp of the tentacles. Within seconds, not minutes, his partially empty lungs began sending low oxygen blood to this brain. As he felt the wooziness from suffocation take over his being, he realized that his death was upon him, and it was not the honorable death he had always imagined. Heroic SEALs do not drown.

They just don't.

Kelly Brightman, the DIA Alien Analyst involved in the Buddhist Monk incident and the XFS Taiwan, phoned Jason Parker as he was planning his flight back to Washington.

"How are things out West?"

"Warm and dry, as always."

"What do you think about Baltazar and his friends?"

"I think they're more like humans than we fully appreciate. But for the rest of the story, I think we should wait for the FBI report."

"Fair enough. Are you ready to travel?"

"Why do I think I'm not coming back to Washington?"

"Because you're not. We need you at WARCOM ASAP."

What the hell could be going on now? Parker wondered.

"Okay, I can be wheels up in thirty minutes," Parker said.

After the short flight to San Diego, Parker picked up a rental car and drove over the high and curving San Diego-Coronado bridge to Coronado, on the ocean side of San Diego Bay. His assignment was to talk to COMNAVSPECWARCOM, a Rear Admiral, Commander of Naval Special Warfare Command. Upon Parker's arrival at SPECWARCOM Headquarters, he still had no idea what the meeting was about.

Parker was escorted into a secure and relatively small briefing room. Within minutes of his arrival, the Senior Enlisted called out "Attention on Deck," marking the arrival of Admiral Langston.

"Gentlemen, my time is short, so I'll give the initial brief, and the rest of you can answer Dr. Parker's questions. I remind you, I need some clear guidance by 1800 today, so that gives you four hours."

Parker and the Admiral had previously met at a SPECWAR conference, so the Admiral dispensed with formalities at this point. "Jason, we have an ongoing submarine op in the South China Sea, and yesterday we almost lost one of our SEALs on a reconnaissance op. It was not a UBA malfunction. It was this."

At that moment a dark and indistinct photo appeared on a large screen. In it, the unconscious body of E-5 Neal Phillips could be seen limp but held tightly by four appendages that at first looked like octopus tentacles, but within a moment of mental processing, it was not at all an octopus. At the same time, what appeared to be two sets of red eyes, one near the diver's neck, and one close to his waist, arose out of the blackness.

"What is this?" Parker asked.

"Okay gentlemen, I have other things to do, but I will be most interested in the discussion that follows." Remember, three hours and fifty-five minutes. The clock is ticking."

As all in attendance stood as the Admiral left the room, he commanded, “As you were. Now get to work.”

Having received no answer, Parker repeated his query. “What is this?”

“We don’t know, but whatever it is, it attacked our SEAL, somehow immobilized him, and ripped his full facemask off. His buddy, who was maybe twenty feet away broke light discipline to take this photograph. As he approached our diver, the creatures dropped our SEAL and fled. This next and last photo shows an astonishing thing. It looks like two small humanoids, with no breathing apparatus on their back. If you look at both photos carefully after they had been enhanced, you can see that what they’re showing are, from the front no hoses or mouthpiece, and from the back, no gas bottles. And most interesting, the analysis software had concluded that we’re looking at two smallish humanoids.”

“This is astonishing,” Parker said. “What happened to the SEAL?”

“By all rights, he should be dead,” came a familiar voice. It was Captain Emery Reed.

Parker broke into a smile when he saw his old friend and *Dioscuri* crewmate. It was good to have a friend in the room.

Without breaking his stride, Reed continued. “But perhaps the cold saved him. Since he was on the rebreather you designed, his buddy was able to turn on the high-frequency oscillation to get some oxygen into his water-logged lungs during the transport back to the sub. If it weren’t for that, he would have died.”

“He’s on the sub now?”

“He’s being transported back to a hospital in Taiwan as we speak. The sub had to transit to Philippine waters before surfacing for a helo extraction. He’s in guarded condition, but we think he’ll pull through. Or I should say, we hope he pulls through.”

Parker nodded his head.

The senior SEAL Captain, Richard Bloom, came straight to the point.

“Parker, we need to know if this was the work of your Frogs?”

Parker pulled his head back in surprise. “Frogs? No, they’re gone. All of them.”

“How do you know?”

“They told me.”

“Oh great,” a SEAL Lieutenant moaned.

“And besides, they look nothing like that.”

"How do you know?"

"I call them Frogs because, well, they look like frogs."

"But what you've seen is a mental image. They weren't physically there. Right?"

"No, and for very good reason."

"I know. If they were, they would die."

"Exactly."

"Then what else could it be?"

"I'll tell you in a minute."

Parker asked to review the images from the dive video.

"Let me think about this a moment."

"We don't have long Jason," Bloom reminded him.

Parker paced in front of the large screen, looking at it, then pacing some more, looking down at the floor, then back to the screen. He turned abruptly, scanning the dozen or so faces gathered in the room.

"I think the Chinese have snookered us. I think we are not willing to accept the reality of what we see in these photos. What I see tells me that while we've had our backs turned, the Chinese have made huge advances in genetic engineering. Unlike us, they are not constrained by human research ethics committees. They can do as they please with human embryos."

"But why? What would they do with embryos?"

"Create gills."

There was a stir in the room, but oddly the two most senior people were smiling, Reed and Captain Bloom.

Reed said, "Jason, somehow we thought you might go there. And I told Captain Bloom and the Admiral that you'd be the best to suggest a way forward."

Captain Bloom, still in the back of the room, spoke up. "Emery, the way forward is for us to capture one of the sonsabitches and find out what they're made of."

"But there's one big problem," Reed said. "Our best guess is that if the Chinese have succeeded in implanting gills in people, and I use the term people loosely, the last thing they would want is those creatures to be captured. I imagine they are psychologically programmed to self-destruct."

"Oh, that's all you're concerned about," Parker said. "I have a solution for that. They can't self-destruct if they're not conscious."

"And how do you plan to knock them out?"

Parker smiled, "Easy day. They'll do it to themselves."

CHAPTER 42. ENCOUNTER

Rear Admiral Langston passed Parker's plan up the chain, with CNO getting concurrence from the Chiefs of Staff, who forwarded it to POTUS for final approval. Within a matter of hours, operational orders were transmitted to the Skipper of the *Austin*.

The mission concept was identical to the previous exploratory mission, but now, anticipating contact with Chinese-bred life-forms, the rules of engagement had changed. Lethal force was approved if needed for self-defense, but killing was not the point of the mission. Capturing and exploitation were.

At zero hours local time, six SEALs exited the submarine once again at 700 feet, using their dual leg thrusters to propel them up to the 600-foot depth while closing in on the dome. This time the targeting sensors had been reprogrammed to shut off the biologics filter so anything fishy, or even a hybrid humanoid, would be detected. This time there would be no surprises.

This time, the N-W TeK null-wave transmitters and receivers outfitted on all SSGNs were turned on, with miniature transmitter-receivers attached to each SEAL. That meant the underwater action could be followed both onboard the sub, and even back in WARCOM Command Center in San Diego. Null-wave technology represented the world's most secure, and most classified, communication system using a portion of electromagnetic waves that is undetectable without a sensor based on specially-tuned SQUIDs, Superconducting Quantum Interference Devices. That technology had revolutionized secure submarine to submarine, and diver to submarine communication.

Approximately one hundred yards from the dome, the detection and targeting sensors began vibrating. The targets were so numerous that the vibrations became uninterpretable, and the divers had to switch on their less stealthy optical displays. What they saw was exactly what they wanted to see—twelve or more biologics headed on an intercepting path.

"Time to take them down," the team leader ordered.

The divers kicked over and headed rapidly down the forty-five-degree slope of the mound on which the dome rested. By the time the SEALs reached the one-thousand-foot depth, the following humanoids had thinned out in numbers, also as anticipated. Now, the match was more even, and the SEALs were looking forward to meeting the leading targets who, unlike the SEALs, were riding on scooters. Putting their leg thrusters on full power, the SEALs turned and attacked. The two opposing forces closed the remaining distance in seconds. The SEAL's only intention was to knock the humanoids from their mounts, just like in a jousting match. Once that had been accomplished, they would taunt the humanoids into swimming by switching their own propulsor units off and dropping even deeper.

Upon first contact, all of the targets were easily dislodged. Three of the targets, who now looked almost identical to muscular preadolescent children, regained their mounts and retreated back towards the dome.

"Let the runners go. Keep ahead of the swimmers," was the verbal order heard by all the dive team members, as well as Austin's control center.

Back in San Diego, Admiral Langston and a handful of his most trusted staff were breathlessly watching the night vision displays and audio from the SEAL team members.

Even swimming at top speed, the "Deux ex Machina," or D.E.M. rebreather designed by Parker and adopted by the Navy for deep missions, easily kept up with the breathing needs of the divers. The targets, seeing the men swimming, and confident in their own ability, swam ever closer to the SEALS. The fastest swimming of the hybrids suddenly stopped motionless in the water, unconscious. His fellow attackers, seeing their leader helpless, turned and swam away as hard as they could. Unfortunately for them, within seconds they also were overtaken by unconsciousness.

"Take the closest swimmer, and doc, get him sedated. He'll come around soon."

"Doc" was the SEAL with the most medical training.

The entire SEAL squad surrounded the closest unconscious target, bound it, and injected a sedative to keep it asleep. Knowing their captive might still revive in spite of the narcotic, it was attached to a harness and tether. The SEAL squad then began towing it towards the submarine which had settled to the deeper depth to receive the SEAL team and their bounty.

"He's just a freaking kid," one of the divers said.

"This kid would kill you in a heartbeat," the team leader reminded them all. "Make sure he's secured."

Explosive Ordnance Disposal divers met the team at a safe distance from the submarine and conducted a scan for explosives implanted within the hybrid. Minutes later the scan on the limp child was completed, and the capture of a Chinese gill-bearing mutant was accomplished.

The close-up view of the unconscious kid before he was loaded into the submarine caused celebration back in San Diego.

The Admiral turned to his staff and said, "Folks, we now have in our possession the Western world's first Merman. A *Hooyah* is in order!"

Captain Emery Reed had been recalled to the White House to brief POTUS on what the SEAL team had accomplished. Harmon Whitney knew Reed was plain-spoken, and unlike the Chiefs of Staff, was not beholden to military jargon, a fact the President appreciated.

It was 0600 hours, and the capture of the Chinese had happened mere hours before. Whitney had left his desk for a more intimate setting with his confidant. They were seated just feet apart on a sofa with more historical significance than either of the men knew.

"Mr. President, I heard you were a competitive swimmer in high school and college."

"Yes, I was a sprinter. I was best up to 200 meters, but anything beyond that, well, I sucked at it. Why do you ask?"

"Then you understand that the faster you swim, the more oxygen you're consuming."

"Oh yeah, I learned that the hard way. I was out of breath a lot in my day."

"And the more carbon dioxide you're producing. When you 'take a breather,' you're blowing off carbon dioxide and taking on board more oxygen."

"Never thought of it that way, but I suppose so."

"Too much CO_2 in your bloodstream makes you breathless, but if you have too little oxygen, you don't know it. You just pass out."

Whitney laughed. "I hear too much alcohol has the same effect." He rolled his eyes up toward the ceiling for effect. "Of course, I wouldn't know from experience."

"Our divers carry as much oxygen as they need in their oxygen bottles, but gills are not like that at all. They have to extract oxygen from the water. Water doesn't contain much oxygen under the best of circumstances, and when you go deep, there's even less. Plus, oxygen availability varies with season and other events. Jason Parker told me his first clue that something strange was happening in the Gulf of Mexico was when there was a large fish kill due to low oxygen water in the De Soto Canyon being forced up by a Frog ship diving into the canyon."

Whitney looked at Reed with his head askew. "Really, I'd never heard that story. And I thought I'd been briefed on all the Frog stuff."

"You might want to have a sit-down with Parker one of these days. But anyway, with gills, there has to be a careful balance between oxygen demand and availability."

"Okay, I get that."

"Also, the smaller you are, the less oxygen you need to pull out of the water."

"Is that why the hybrids are children?"

"Maybe. It could also be that these hybrids are fairly young since the technology to make them has not been around all that long. They're still growing up."

"So they could outgrow their gills?"

"Possibly, unless the kids have been genetically modified to always remain small. Inactivating growth hormone would do that nicely, I suppose."

"Geesh, the Chinese can do that?"

"With genetic manipulation, you can do anything you want. Of course, you'll have millions of dead embryos before you find one genetic combination that works. So ethically, we'll never do that. But the Chinese ... well, let's just say they have many millions of embryos to experiment on."

"Damn. So how did the SEALS capture that hybrid without hurting it?"

"That was the easy part. They bumped him off his scooter and made him swim. The SEALs let him think he was closing in, but the kid didn't realize his gills were not supplying the oxygen he needed for a race. His mind said, swim faster, but his gills were failing him, and he had no idea. Finally, when the oxygen in his blood got too low, it was lights out."

"Could he have died?"

"Only if his heart reacted badly. It was a risk, but we thought a small one under the circumstances."

"But wouldn't it wake up once it quit swimming?"

"Sure would. And that's why it was sedated."

"Is that safe? It sounds risky for the kid."

"It is risky since we know even less about their physiology and metabolism than we do the Trolls. But again, he, or it, has value dead or alive."

"How do you know all that? Aren't you and Parker just guessing?"

Reed laughed. "Actually sir, I learned it from a frog."

"An ET?"

Reed chuckled. "Not that kind of frog Sir, a real frog, like you find in ponds. One of them took a liking to my swimming pool in Florida. I tried to fish him out with a net before I poured chlorine in the pool, but he didn't want to be caught. Every time I got the net close to him, he'd take off again to another part of the pool. After chasing him for several minutes, he stopped swimming and just settled to the bottom. At that point, scooping him up was no problem. I laid him on the grass, but he didn't recover. He died."

"Died? Why?"

"I think it was timing. I was so shocked to see the frog quit swimming that I was too slow getting it out of the water. With later frogs, if I were quicker, they'd recover fully."

"Maybe you need to make your pool less inviting."

"I'm trying, Mr. President."

"You know what I've told you before about saying, Mr. President. 'Sir' will do just fine."

"Roger that, Sir."

"But regarding your frog chase, I didn't think frogs have gills? Only tadpoles do, right?"

"That's right. But the adult frog skin is permeable to oxygen and carbon dioxide. It's like a gill in that respect. As long as they're sitting on the bottom, or moving slowly, they get plenty of oxygen. But if you make them race, they will run until they go unconscious. Like us, they're not very good at detecting hypoxia before it's lights out."

"Interesting. So these kids are just like frogs. I get it. But they really do have gills?"

"They sure do, internal gills. Apparently, it's easier to turn lungs into gills than it is to turn skin into a gas-permeable organ."

"Wow," said Whitney, staring at Reed. "The only thing I can say is, *wow.* The Chinese went to all that trouble to make some sort of mermaid, and those creatures can be defeated simply by making them race. So much for their dream of creating super soldiers."

"Well, I'm guessing they now see the error in their ways."

"I'm just glad the sub was able to make it to a hospital ship where that little guy could be taken care of."

"From what I hear, he's one pissed-off little merman."

"I am too. Pissed off, that is."

"Oh?"

"The Chinese must not have understood a word I said in Svalbard. Here they are wasting their energy creating weak monsters, protecting themselves from a non-existent threat, us, and we have a global threat from the cosmos that could strike at any moment."

"Well, the Chinese will never admit they make mer-kids, unless we parade this one around."

"Let's not. They may have assumed he simply drowned. We'll hold that card close to our chest for the time being, until I break this thing wide open by going to the U.N. This self-destructive nonsense has got to end."

Reed was taken aback by that. Would he really reveal the Mars base?

"What do you think about that, Emery?"

"Sir, I'm the last person who should be advising you on that."

"Well hell, everyone on my staff has their own personal agenda. But you, you were on Mars, and you almost died there. I think that gives you a better-informed opinion than anyone else in DC."

"Honestly, I think it's a risky move, but I agree it needs to be done."

President Whitney sat silently for a moment with his gaze resting on the carpet. Then he looked Reed straight in the eye and said quietly, "Yes, it is risky if I do it, but potentially apocalyptic if I don't." They watched each other for a heartbeat, then Whitney stood and asked, "Have I ever shown you my chaos wheels?"

"No Sir."

He beckoned Reed over to his desk. "They're a hand-me-down from my predecessor. It's all math and physics, these wheels. You see, you take both hands and spin them, and then you watch what happens."

To illustrate, he spun both wheels clockwise. They weren't really wheels, but each had a central hub riding on a low friction pin, and from each hub extended three spokes. Instead of a wheel rim connecting the spokes, each spoke had a bulbous end. The spokes were only connected to the hub.

"Nothing interesting is happening when I first spin them but watch as the wheels begin to slow down."

Reed moved closer to the desk to better watch the demonstration.

"For me, these wheels are symbolic. One wheel is me, and the other can be whatever I'm thinking about. And right now, it's the U.N."

As friction began to slow the spinning wheels, their motion started becoming less smooth, and then it became erratic. Eventually, the two wheels began bouncing to and fro in opposite directions. And then they stopped.

"Why did they do that?" Reed asked.

Pointing to the enlargements at the ends of the spokes, Whitney said, "These produce invisible forces. When they get close, they repel each other. Eventually, they end up pushing each other around, erratically and unpredictably."

Invisible forces? Reed said to himself.

Speaking slowly, being careful of his words around the President, Reed said, "So these would be magnets?"

Whitney seemed to be enjoying his often-repeated game. "Yes, in this case, they are. But in the real world, there are all sorts of invisible forces at work. And we can't predict what they are, or when and where they're working."

"Chaos. I can see that," Reed said, beginning to understand where the President was headed.

"The motion of these wheels as they're slowing down is never the same. And that's what troubles me about going to the U.N. I have no idea how it will end. People are too damned unpredictable."

"It's too bad we don't have a crystal ball," Reed joked.

"Actually, did you know President Reagan's wife consulted an astrologer before he made any decisions?"

"No, I didn't. That's a little bizarre, don't you think?"

Whitney raised his eyebrows. "I'm surprised you didn't hear about it during your last White House stint. I'm sure these sorts of decisions weigh heavily on every President."

"I suppose they do, Sir," Reed said.

John Clarke

After pausing for effect, Whitney said, "You don't happen to know any good astrologers, do you?"

CHAPTER 43. U.N. SECURITY COUNCIL

President Whitney wielded the gavel in the U.N. Security Council Chamber at the United Nations headquarters in New York. He sat at the head position of the almost circular conference table which had been designed to comfortably fit the five permanent members of the Security Council and ten other members taking their place on the Council on a rotating schedule. Two circular rows of seats were reserved for ambassadorial support staff, and on three of the four sides of the Council Chamber were additional seats for a few onlookers. Among them were Jason Parker, Laura Smith, and Emery Reed. They had no speaking or supportive role, but due to their deep personal support for the President's soon to be revealed agenda, they were present as witnesses.

The atmosphere in the large chamber was one of hushed uncertainty. The agenda for the meeting had not been published, and all media had been cleared from the room. Seated on President Whitney's right was the U.N. Secretary General from Switzerland, and on his left, the Under-Secretary-General from Bolivia. The U.S. Ambassador was seated behind and to the President's left. Both Secretaries General were just as much in the dark as the rest of the delegates.

On the wall behind the President was a digital display showing the fifteen by twenty-seven-foot symbolic mural by Norwegian painter Per Krohg. Before taking his seat, President Whitney had surveyed the image which showed a phoenix rising from a dark and chaotic landscape, harkening back to the horrors of World War II, into a light-filled world of peace and progress. As Whitney had returned to his seat at the head of the table, a strange and fleeting thought crossed his always perceptive mind. The mural was upside down.

Whitney was the only President to preside over the U.S. when the world was going the other way, plummeting in a literal instant from peace into oblivion. For Whitney, the irony of the juxtaposition of the optimistic Krohg mural and his own secret fear was almost overwhelming.

At the cue of the meeting gongs, the noise in the room abated. After a nod to the Secretary-General, Whitney spoke.

"Thank you very much. The eleven thousandth eight hundred and fifty-fourth meeting of the Security Council is called to order."

He struck the gavel to formally start the meeting.

"I am honored to be here today to chair this meeting of the United Nations Security Council. I will open with a statement in my capacity as the President of the United States of America. It is also a great honor to be at this U.N. Security Council briefing to discuss a matter of urgent importance. It is nothing less than the survival of all humanity."

Parker noted that that seemed to get everyone's attention, except for the skeptical few who put little credence in anything the U.S. had to say.

"For decades now scientists and politicians have been arguing over the influence of man on the world's climate. Yet at the same time, proposals have been made for man to geo-engineer the climate on Mars. If the one issue is debatable, how are we to believe we can radically alter the atmosphere of another planet? There are vast differences between the Martian and Earth atmospheres. And certainly, our track record for improving our own planetary atmosphere has not been stellar. It is neither an easy nor certain endeavor."

He got that right, Parker thought.

"Instead, it seems an easier task to engineer animals to be sustainable on Mars, to feed a growing human population on Mars, at least until we achieve the wide-scale production of manufactured, palatable protein. Taking the long view, perhaps in some distant future humans themselves can be re-engineered to breathe the Martian atmosphere."

The sound of titters and coughs filled the room.

"Of course, those creations would no longer be human. They would be something else. But can we edit the genes of humans to change them into a new species, with capabilities far beyond our own? Indeed, we can, and we know the Chinese are doing exactly that."

Whitney stared at the Chinese Minister who sat with no expression to betray his thoughts.

"But we are not here to discuss the ethics of bioengineering. Instead, I am here to warn you of imminent danger, a danger that makes our national competitiveness and hostility seem banal in comparison. I am not talking about nuclear war or killer aliens or killer asteroids. No, I'm talking about something much worse."

The esteemed group started muttering to those within their delegations.

"Before I describe that threat, I need to reveal that the U.S. had a secret military base on Mars for the last ten years."

Audible gasps and murmurs filled the great room as ministers throughout the chamber turned their heads to speak to their deputies located behind them.

"But rest assured its purpose was not military. It posed no threat to any nation on Earth."

He let his eyes sweep the room, to let each Minister and assistant know they were included in Whitney's promise. Being an astute speaker, his eyes fleetingly acknowledged anyone responding with a nod.

"It was a base where we could safely conduct animal genetic research adapting rodents to the Martian atmosphere. It was done on Mars because of the risk of an accidental release of genetically modified animals on Earth. That is a risk no nation should take."

Whitney again looked around those seated before him. He knew full well that some nations, China, in particular, had little concern for the release of modified organisms, a fact confirmed by the sullen look on the Chinese Minister's face.

As Whitney was speaking, the digital mural behind him turned into a white display screen.

"But perhaps you've noticed I've been using the past tense for this Martian base located at an ancient volcano called Pavonis Mons."

The screen behind him showed a satellite view of the volcano and a formerly classified close-up of the Space Corp base. Whitney twisted his body to his right to point to the close-up.

"The base has been destroyed by the very threat I've come to talk to you about. And that threat came from no enemy of the U.S., or even of the Earth. It came from an uncaring Cosmos. It was a gamma-ray burst."

The normally quiet and stately chamber erupted in a cacophony of words spoken in all the languages of the members. The combined intonation suggested disbelief.

"Our scientists can give your scientists a much deeper understanding of the incident, but know this, it came from a distant source hidden within our galaxy, and even at the cosmic distances involved, was powerful enough to devastate any human or animal caught in its beam. Worst of all, traveling at the speed of light, it was undetectable until it hit."

Laura quietly whispered to Parker, "I think the crowd is a bit stunned."

Whitney continued. "The source seems to be a powerful gamma-ray burster beamed in the direction of Mars. Mars was on the opposite side of the sun from Earth at that time.

A computer animation of the inner solar system with the varying positions of the planets played on the large screen.

"But think about this: As the Earth moves around the sun, and as the sun moves around the galaxy, our scientists predict we will soon be in the line of fire for the next burst. It is merely a matter of time, and of luck, or lack thereof."

The animation changed and zoomed in on the Earth being hit by a cosmic blast.

"If a GRB similar to what struck Mars were to strike Earth, the results will be even more catastrophic than it was on Mars. Millions of lives will be lost instantly."

There was increased stirring in the great hall.

"But it gets worse."

Whitney paused as the delegates looked around at each other, perhaps looking for affirmation they had really heard that.

"Part of our atmosphere may be blown away. We know that because sensors left behind on Mars show that it now has even less oxygen than it did before the strike. Those in the beam's direct path will surely be killed if exposed, but even those taking shelter will die from the inevitable change to the atmosphere where much of our planet's remaining oxygen will be converted into a toxic gas. Sooner or later, civilization as we know it will end."

The stirring ceased, replaced by shocked silence.

"But what's to be done? Diaspora is the age-old word used to describe the spreading of humanity from land to land on Earth, and now from planet to planet in the cosmos. Now, let me ask a rhetorical question. How many of you are willing and able to send a group of your finest and strongest humans out into space in the hopes of someday seeding a new planet? Not many of you have that technology, or the budgets to support it.

"But even if you do, do you think safe harbor would be found? A GRB impacting a spaceship would surely destroy it and all life on board. And what habitable planet would you seek out? Mars? Once you see what happened to Mars, you will not feel secure in that assumption."

The screen then displayed a table of the gaseous constituents of the Martian atmosphere measured before and after the GRB.

"As you see, along with the loss of oxygen, much of the existing carbon dioxide atmosphere has been depleted, making Mars even colder. Those seeking shelter there would die a cold and lonely death.

"So, what to do? I have already spoken directly to the presidents of Russia and China about creating an international effort to save humanity similar to the seed vaults of Svalbard. We, as a body, have agreed to find a safe place for plant seeds in case of a catastrophic loss of our local agriculture. Yet what good are seeds if there is no one alive to plant them?

"To my knowledge that concern has so far fallen on the deaf ears of Russia and China. That is why I have chosen this forum to break the news about the potential for a future calamity. And in comparison to space, the planet Earth may be our only refuge. Not a refuge on land, but a sanctuary underwater, protected from gamma-rays, autonomous, isolated from the surface and the poisonous atmosphere which could result from a GRB. The sea might be the only sanctuary available to all nations on Earth.

"Not for every person, unfortunately, but at least a sampling of populations from every nation. What is essential is water that is shallow enough to not overtax our subsea engineering, but deep enough to provide protection from cosmic events and to encourage autonomy and independence from shore."

The French delegation was leaning into each other, whispering.

"Where are we talking about? Here is a survey of what we consider suitable subsea locations, located in relatively shallow underwater plains."

A chart of the globe was projected on the display, slowly rotating with colored lines connecting geographical names with the respective location on the globe.

"In our initial survey, we see potential sites in the Bay of Campeche, waters off the Yucatan Peninsula, Texas, Florida, Brazil, Argentina, East China Sea, Yellow Sea, Gulf of Thailand, Java Sea, Timor Sea, Hong Kong, tip of South Africa, Hudson Bay, North Sea, the English Channel, Celtic Sea, Bass Strait of Tasmania, and the Great Australian Bight."

Whitney remained quiet as the display highlighted each of the listed areas as the globe turned.

"Ideally, these locations could eventually host an assortment of multicultural and multinational undersea bases. The U.S. is willing to share our technology for deep subsea habitation, in exchange for rights to establish our own colonies around the globe. At the same time, we invite each of you to establish your own bases on our plateaus on the Gulf of Mexico, and the east coast of Florida and Georgia."

The display zoomed into the sites mentioned in the southern U.S. "What I have just revealed should make our national and ideological rivalries seem petty in comparison. Fighting over boundaries and tariffs matter not one bit if the Earth's population is gone. So, in closing, I implore you all not to let long-standing rivalries interfere with a united effort of all nations to protect at least a portion of humanity, a portion that may eventually seed a new Earth. Thank you."

There was uncharacteristic applause from those nations who viewed President Whitney's briefing as a magnanimous offering to the world. Characteristically, the Chinese minister and his staff were glowering, smarting from some of the words they had just heard.

"I now resume my function as President of the Security Council, and give the floor to the President of France."

As he finished, Whitney struck the gavel, formally yielding the floor.

France was a nation historically comfortable with deep sea ventures. Their president, Alexandre Delauze, asked only one simple question in French that was translated as he spoke. "Thank you, Mr. President. Dear Colleagues, Secretary-General, I will be brief. What about asteroid impacts? Aren't they much more likely?"

Whitney responded, "Your question is well-founded, Mr. President. That is what we thought as well until the Mars incident occurred, and we discovered the nature of the GRB source. But to answer your question, as the U.S. envisions it, these bases would provide a diaspora unlike any other. If an asteroid takes out the South China Sea, the survival of the Chinese people would be ensured elsewhere on the Earth. After all, the Security Council is chartered to maintain the security of all the peoples of the Earth, and not just those outside of the impact zone of an asteroid. Exactly the same principle applies to a GRB. The only difference is, with an asteroid we might have advance warning. With a GRB, we would not. There will be no time for arguments, committees, and all the other things nations do during a crisis. The work has to begin now, not ten years from now. We have just received our only warning."

Whitney added, "Thank you, Mr. Delauze, for your response. I now give the floor to the Minister for Foreign Affairs of China."

An angry frown had creased the Chinese Minister's forehead for the past several minutes, and just before he spoke, his mouth started twitching. He slowly dragged his stout body into a half-standing position, leaning on both arms with knuckles flat on the table in front of him.

"Mr. President, let me be clear," he spoke forcefully through a reddened face, "we will never share our South China Sea territory with the Americans or any other nation. That is all I have to say."

As he lowered himself again to his seat, he turned to give a half-smile to his deputy.

President Whitney was quick to respond. "Minister Wu, the world is well aware of your view on territorial limits and your country's opinion of the validity of international law. But what the world may not be aware of is that the only product of the Chinese people to survive a cosmic catastrophe might just be this."

At that moment, an underwater photo appeared on the screen of the aquatic child created by the Chinese and now sequestered by the Americans.

The minister's mouth gaped open.

"This is an aquatic species that can no longer exist on land but uses gills to survive underwater. It is a product of internationally-banned human experimentation by the Chinese who created what is, in effect, a new species. It is an alien, created for military purposes."

There was near bedlam in the room.

Over the noise, Whitney raised his voice. "As you see, it and its brethren are mere preadolescent children. What you cannot see are the child's gills since they are internal. But like a fish, he has no lungs and cannot survive in air."

"How dare you!" Minister Wu retorted, slamming his fist on the table in front of him. "This is cheap Hollywood trickery. Such a thing does not exist."

Denials were fully expected. "We can arrange a face to face meeting," Whitney responded, "if any of you wish to decide for yourself. The child is quite happy to remain with us indefinitely. He does not wish to be returned to China."

"This is nonsense!" Mr. Wu and his delegation abruptly stood up and stalked out of the room.

Whitney had expected chaos, but instead, the noise subsided, and he was met with stunned silence except for the sharp echoes of the shoes of the Chinese delegation as they left.

Whitney cleared his throat. "As we say in America, seeing is believing. I can assure you this young creature is very real. We can provide whatever proof you need, but the DNA proof is by far the most telling. My reason for mentioning this is that, ironically, if what our scientists have forecasted indeed happens, this may well be the only remnant of the human race to survive. What we propose is that others of us, with normal human DNA, join this creature underwater for the long-term survival of the human race."

After several more moments of subdued mumbling in the chamber, the UK Ambassador asked to speak.

Whitney nodded. "I now give the floor to the Prime Minister of the United Kingdom."

"Thank you, Mr. President, and thank you for convening this debate. I'm sure what you claim about genetically modified children is easily verifiable, so I would like to follow up on your remarkable revelation about your Mars base. Are we to believe that your genetically modified rodents breathed the carbon dioxide atmosphere of Mars?"

"Thank you, Mr. Prime Minister. The answer is no. We grew plants that converted the highly toxic carbon dioxide into oxygen for the animals while simultaneously providing food for the animals. In turn, the rodents made high-quality protein for the astronauts."

The reactions within the audience were very much culturally determined. Some country's ministers winced at the thought of eating rodents, while some found it unremarkable.

"But the plants cannot make as much oxygen as normal rodents require. The animals have therefore been bioengineered to take advantage of genes which provide tolerance to low oxygen concentrations. Those genes are found in some mammals and numerous invertebrates."

"Even people?" the UK Minister asked.

"Yes. The *Epas1* gene found in Tibetans living at high altitude. But I'm afraid if you want any more detail, you'll have to talk to my Chief Project Scientist, Dr. Jason Parker, or my Chief Medical Advisor, Dr. Emery Reed."

Jason Parker and Emery Reed looked at each other in shock, and simultaneously said, "Did he just say that?"

Laura Smith, sitting next to Jason, whispered, "I didn't see that coming."

CHAPTER 44. DEEP BASE ONE

Deep Base One had been secured to the bedrock lying below hundreds of feet of marine sediment on the east coast of the Blake Plateau. For that reason, the base was affectionately termed the *Plateau Chateau.*

For the previous two months, NASA engineers had been monitoring the tectonic stability of the site at the Stetson Mesa roughly a hundred miles east of Jacksonville. They had also been observing the pressure integrity of the large undersea donut-shaped structure which would soon house its first cadre of military and NASA aquanauts. The pressure inside the base had remained constant at the sea level pressure of air, or one atmosphere, even though the water pressure surrounding it at two-thousand feet was sixty atmospheres. Only when all measurements of inside pressure, and stress and strain measurements on the structure were utterly stable, could the manning of the station begin.

Deep Base One, often shortened to DB1, was designed to eventually become completely independent of shore resupply missions. It was planned as the first of ten deep-sea refuges being quietly assembled. Once the engineers and experimental divers had worked out all the bugs on DB1, the DB system would become an ever-growing refuge for a select group of Americans dedicated to assuring the longevity of the human race in the face of a threat that might never come. On the other hand, that threat could arrive at any moment, so as far as black budgets went, this one was on the top of the nation's secret priority list.

Once the first team of experimental aquanauts was transferred through the pressure lock, they would be very slowly compressed to the ambient pressure of just over 1100 pounds per square inch. Slow compression occurs from the controlled electrolysis of desalinated seawater which produces both hydrogen and oxygen. The lightest of all gases, hydrogen is critical to maintaining a breathable density of gas at the dome's eventual depth, and to also suppressing the signs of the high-pressure nervous syndrome. Although it was still very much debated, the scientific consensus seemed to be that the very slow addition of hydrogen gas would be the best way to prevent the sometimes-bizarre manifestations of hydrogen toxicity that had previously resulted in psychotic delusions and mania at depth.

For two weeks, Parker and Laura had interviewed the first candidate aquanauts at the Naval Station Mayport near Jacksonville. Before Parker's interviews had begun, those candidates had already passed security clearances and rigorous medical and psychiatric exams at Naval Hospital Jacksonville.

Shortly before his inaugural passenger-carrying flight to DB1, waiting for the first engineering crew to complete their training and indoctrination, Jason Parker wandered into a room looking out upon runway 5-23 and the flight line at Mayport Air Base. Every once in a while, the walls would vibrate from the sound of high-powered aircraft departing. From that same runway, Parker would soon coax *Dioscuri* into taking off and flying to DB1 with the first operational test crew.

The room with a view of the flight line was painted in Navy gray with virtually no color-relief save some white trimmed photos. One of those photos was of the *XFS Dioscuri* sitting on Phobos, the photo taken by Emery Reed. It was the first time he had seen it. Sure enough, standing there in the open hatch were three people in spacesuits and helmets. You couldn't tell who the people were inside the suits, but he knew.

As he examined the photo, Parker thought of the Dr. Seuss book, "Oh, the Places You'll Go." When his parents read that book to him as a kid, neither they nor he had any idea just where he would go in his lifetime. In that photo taken on the diminutive moon of Mars, three of the four crewmembers assumed they were about to head home. But that was not to be, at least not right away. In the interim, their world view would be shaken to its core.

Although Dr. Seuss and his parents were convinced that he, like all kids, would travel to exotic places and do exciting things, no one could have guessed the future. His family, his teachers, his wife and children, his friends at work, no one, would have thought he would end up flying a rescue team to Phobos, and then on to Mars, and return with a load of secret Martian astronauts. And who would have dreamed he'd do all this is an alien spaceship, a ship equally at home in the deep sea and outer space?

No wonder Sandy is fed up, he thought. *When she married me, there was no inkling of what was to come. I had not yet met Laura, could not even imagine there really were ET aliens, had not encountered covert and corrupt government agents, had not been shot down, or along with Laura been captured and betrayed by a friend, or shot through the chest and saved by Frogs, or prevented a war with the Frogs. Laura and I had not been kidnapped by Russians or escaped from Siberia in a Russian-salvaged spaceship. There was no sign I'd be disappearing for unknown periods, facing unknown risks.*

Hell, if the roles were switched, I would have long ago told Sandy to take a hike.

Without fanfare, Jason Parker delivered the first twenty aquanaut engineers to DB1 using *Dioscuri.* Among them were NASA's Don Baxter and DIA's Kelly Brightman, who was a spook by occupation but an electrical engineer by training. Supposedly, Brightman was taking a leave of absence from his job just because he could not turn down the opportunity to make the longest deep saturation dive in history. Since Parker was a friend and diving buddy, Brightman was selected as a member of the team the moment he expressed interest.

After delivering the engineers, Parker returned to Mayport the same day awaiting the engineers' report that the ingress recycling system was working at peak efficiency.

Each time the ship "locked in," a mixture of helium and oxygen had to be used for flushing the seawater from the transfer lock. That gas was generated and stored as a byproduct of the power station's fusion reactor and the electrolysis of desalinated seawater.

For that process to be sustainable, no gas could be lost, and the addition of helium to Deep Base would contribute to the slow compression of the atmosphere inside the base.

Fortunately, all was working as planned. The next and final transfer would bring the total number of aquanauts to 150, approximately half of the full complement.

As far as Parker was concerned, the key crew members were an eclectic bunch. Emery Reed had recovered from his irradiation incident and seemed none the worse for wear. He was eager to join another saturation dive as the Senior Medical Officer. Samuel Putnam was on board, tasked with finishing his book. The divers J.R. and Tom were there for any deep diving operations that might be required, as was the Marine diver and self-proclaimed pirate, Luke Warmwater. When it comes to deep sea diving, you never know when you'll need a pirate.

The most hardened crew member was Clarice Williams. Recently retired from the Space Corp, she was ready to move on to more down-to-Earth adventure. She never wanted to go to Space again, and no one could blame her.

The most eclectic crew member was Lieutenant Larissa Slocum, a female nuclear physicist, five foot five inches tall, tightly tucked auburn hair, and a face full of seriousness and intellect. That's what you would expect for an Engineering Duty Officer and Navy diver who happened to have a Ph.D. from MIT.

The reason Dr. Slocum was on the team was that her doctoral dissertation was on the inertial confinement fusion reactor system or ICF used at the National Ignition Facility of Lawrence Livermore Laboratory. Her stated goal was to not only be a rock star saturation diver but to also pick the brain of Don Baxter, the inventor of the compact Tokamak. The Tokamaks were being used wherever small reactors were needed, such as Deep Base, and she wanted to learn all she could about them.

As Parker was settling into the pilot's position in the alien cockpit of *Dioscuri*, Laura peered around the corner.

"Got room for one more?"

"Wow, you bet we do. Get your butt up here. I might need your magic words this time."

"How did it go last time? Weren't you alone?"

"Yeah, and I adopted the Monk's approach—no incantation required. Merely some deep thoughts."

"You sure I won't disturb your deep thoughts?"

In truth, Laura always disturbed Parker's deep thoughts, but he had a solution in mind that might work.

"Not if we observe sterile cockpit discipline."

"Which means ..."

"No talking during critical phases of flight."

"Believe it or not, Jason, I can actually do that."

Parker just smiled. He was thinking, *We'll see,* but some things are best left unsaid.

"Are we in a critical phase yet?"

"In a minute," Parker replied.

"I heard President Whitney insisted Emery Reed replace the preselected senior medical officer on board."

"Yep, he's supposed to be strapped down in his seat back there as we speak. And I do feel much better about him coming along. He's the most experienced flight and undersea medicine doc we have."

"Great. So when I can't talk to you, I can talk to him?"

"Knock yourself out. But you do know this is a very short flight. You'll have plenty of time to chat when we lock-in."

"Okay. I'm excited. Let's go."

I can tell, Parker thought.

A radio transmission from the aft cabin signaled that all the passengers were settled in.

Parker radioed to the back passengers, "Folks, we are first in line for takeoff. Please make sure all loose items are secured. We will be airborne shortly."

Parker looked over at Laura. "You ready to go?"

"Sure you don't need my help?"

"I'll let you know," Parker said.

"You're having fun, aren't you?" she asked.

"I can neither confirm nor deny that."

"Why don't you try cloaking this baby?" Laura asked.

Parker smirked. "Already tried that. Nothing happened. Now silence, if you please."

Seeing how the Monk levitated the craft with little fanfare, Parker silently cleared the front screen and hovered a few feet off the ground, waiting for a green light from the tower at the Mayport Naval Air Station. That meant that the airspace east of Jacksonville had been cleared for the few minutes it would take for *Dioscuri* to remain airborne. When the light came, *Dioscuri* immediately accelerated at two Gs headed due east for the Blake Plateau.

The total distance traveled was ninety-eight miles; the airborne distance eighty miles. Once the ocean bottom dropped to one-thousand feet deep, *Dioscuri* entered the water, supercavitating the last eighteen miles to the site of DB1, the Plateau Chateau.

Ten minutes after departure, *Dioscuri* pulled into the DB1 hangar.

DB1 was arranged as a series of concentric toroids, looking not unlike several donuts, each one placed inside the hole of the next larger one. The fusion reactor for DB1 was located in the most central hole, supplying power to the entire base. That central area was also where essential engineering functions occurred such as desalination, and electrolysis.

In case of a problem with the fusion reactor, the hangar for *Dioscuri* was attached to the outer edge of the furthest ring. When it comes to nuclear processes, distance makes safety, and luckily, water is an excellent radiation shield.

From above, the arrangement of rings looked much like the Pentagon, except the toroids were smoothly circular, not pentagonal.

Like the Pentagon, spokes were connecting each ring, but unlike the Pentagon, each ring had emergency doors that isolated each ring, and each of five segments within each ring. A sudden flooding event would no doubt claim lives, but it would not destroy the entire base.

As far as Don Baxter's creations went, it was the most beautiful, and potentially the most important. It was without a doubt the most expensive, but serving as a prototype for saving a segment of humanity from cosmic disaster, the money was well invested.

The beginning of slow compression was one of those rare moments when then there was little for Parker to do, except getting better acquainted with the Deep Base residents. If any medical problems or emotional derangements were to appear, this would be the time to find out. Pressure-wise, they were not far from the surface pressure, so return to the surface and its one-atmosphere pressure would not be difficult.

Every underwater habitat built to date had a viewing area so the occupants could see the fish and other creatures outside. Don Baxter had made sure this creation, designed for long-term habitation, had a viewing area conspicuously rising above the hangar. Those interested could watch the arrival and departure of transport vehicles and observe the ever-changing parade of fish just outside the habitat. At two-thousand feet there was no natural light, so floodlights illuminated the sea bottom.

Or, if the viewers so chose, the lights could be turned off. After allowing for human eyes to adjust to the darkness, the viewers could witness the occasional sparkle of fish using luminescent biological lures to attract their prey. For that reason, the viewing room was a popular and sometimes crowded venue for eating lunches.

During one such lunch period, Parker spotted Larissa Slocum looking pensively out the viewing window. Slocum's long auburn hair tumbled down her back and shoulders, standing in sharp contrast to the light blue background of the requisite DB1 working uniform, coveralls. Each coverall featured a patch with a design of dark blue wavy lines and a bright red downward facing arrow. It was only a slightly altered version of the original Man in the Sea, Sea Lab emblem of the last century.

Beside Slocum sat Samuel Putnam.

"Do you mind if I join you?" Parker asked.

Slocum looked up at him smiling. "You're welcome any time, Dr. Parker."

"Oh no, that will never do. Call me Jason."

"Where's your lunch?" Putnam asked.

"I'll eat later. Am I interrupting anything, Samuel?"

"I was just asking her how she came to join the Navy. Did you know she used to work at the National Ignition Facility?"

"I did. Larissa, did Samuel warn you that he's a writer? You're liable to wind up in his new book."

Slocum laughed. "Yes, he warned me."

"Fair enough then," Parker said, taking a seat.

"To answer your question, Samuel," said Slocum, "when I started working in the field, we were making great progress in creating a fusion power source. But we weren't there yet. That was the entire purpose of the National Ignition Facility."

"Who was funding the research?"

"Mostly the Department of Energy, but a lot of money came from the Department of Defense."

"Classified programs, I assume."

"Yes, very."

"So, what happened?"

"All of a sudden, the DoD money dried up."

"Why?"

"No one said at first, but it was about the time twelve years ago or so when the Navy discovered the deep Gulf of Mexico cave in the De Soto Canyon, just south of Pensacola, Florida."

"Really?"

"And from what I hear, that's where your alien ship, *Dioscuri,* was discovered."

"That's completely true. It was," Parker said.

"And this is where things get speculative," Slocum continued. "About that time, NASA announced a breakthrough in their own fusion research program aimed at a fusion-driven spacecraft and demonstrated a completely functioning, compact fusion reactor. It's not ready for flight yet, but that's what I want to work on with Don Baxter."

"That's pretty far afield from diving," Putnam noted.

"I suspect that my time here in Deep Base is going to be the pinnacle of my diving career. I can't wait to dive outside once we reach two-thousand feet, but what could possibly follow that? After this, I can't bear the thought of wasting my remaining career doing admin work. It'll be time to move on to space travel. I want to go to Mars, either with or without a fusion-driven ship."

"You seem to be a little suspicious of NASA's discovery," Putnam said.

"Oh, I think they discovered something alright, but my suspicion is it's alien technology recovered from the De Soto Canyon cave."

"Why?"

"I'm from that field. There is no way the work done up to the time of NASA's announcement could have resulted in a working, compact fusion reactor."

"*No way* is a dangerous claim to make," Putnam said.

"I repeat, there is no way," she said more firmly.

Putnam looked at Parker. "Do you know anything about that, Jason?"

"No, but that's not surprising. After Laura and I were kidnapped by the Russians, a lot may have happened that we don't know about."

Putnam picked up where he'd left off. "Okay, well Larissa, I guess you never got around to telling me why you joined the Navy."

"That's simple. When I was working at NIF, the Ignition Facility, we were still striving to make more energy than we were consuming. That was the Holy Grail, even in a facility as large as ours. In our funding and milestone estimates, our best guess was that it would take fifty years or more before we could produce a compact fusion reactor. So that timeline would keep me happily engaged for my entire career. And then, out of the blue, that timeline was destroyed by Dr. Baxter's revelation of the compact fusion reactor."

"But that was a wonderful thing, don't you think?"

"Oh, I fully agree. But I had to completely revamp my career plans. There was no longer a *raison d'être* for my research."

"I see."

"But happily, by being a Navy engineering duty officer, I found out about the opportunity to work with Dr. Baxter and the fusion reactor powering our Deep Base. And if the rumors are correct, there's also one on Mars and Phobos."

"Speaking of Phobos, have you met Clarice Williams yet?"

"Yes, I have. We're buds now. She's the one who told me about the Phobos Base."

"She's a fortunate lady. If the fusion reactor had been damaged by the shuttle debris, she would have quickly frozen to death."

"Believe me, she knows that. Anyway, if my suspicion is correct, by working with Don Baxter, I'll have a once in a lifetime chance to work with alien technology. And because he's a NASA engineer, I know he's thinking about the next step toward flight-worthy fusion reactors. That would be super-cool."

"*Dioscuri*'s very cool alien technology too," Parker said, more defensively than he meant. "And at this point, no one knows how it works. Maybe you could be thinking about that?"

"True, but here's the thing. My tools are in thermonuclear engineering. I'm not a cosmologist or astrophysicist. I've had no training in cosmic matters like dark energy and matter. So, I don't have the background."

"But you have a smart brain. After having had one ride in *Dioscuri* already, all I ask is that you think about it, outside of the proverbial box. If you manage to understand one compact fusion reactor, perhaps you can understand another alien technology."

She looked at him, squinting her eyes. "Did you just say that?"

Damn, did I just say that? Act dumb, Parker. That shouldn't be hard for you.

"Say what?"

"Alien technology," she answered. "You just confirmed the reactors are alien technology."

Parker sighed. In his effort to inspire Larissa, he had just made a stupid mistake. But rather than comment further, he simply said, "I'm sure you'll learn a great deal from Dr. Baxter. He built them, and he's no alien."

Slocum gave Parker a knowing smile. "Yep, that's why I'm here, to learn from Don Baxter."

Chapter 45. Breaking Pots

Parker and Laura were returning to Parker's office when Tom Thomas, one of the two most experienced saturation divers in the Navy, came out of one of the DB1 spokes just ahead of them.

Parker stopped him. "Tom, I've been meaning to ask how you and J.R. are faring with the hydrogen addition? Is J.R. doing Okay?"

"So far, so good. No repetitions of the DeSoto Canyon narcosis."

"Good," Parker said. "We're doing things right then."

Laura smiled at Tom. "Seems like you and J.R. are partners in crime. Do you hang together during your off time?"

"I guess I'm sort of like a big brother to J.R. I try to get him to keep his pecker in his pants, but it's tough. The chicks adore him."

"That's a high calling, Tom," Laura remarked, grinning.

"Actually Jason, I have a question for you if you have a sec?" Tom asked.

"We're just headed to my office. What's up?"

"Did all that scanning of the guacamole down in Antarctica turn up anything interesting?"

Parker unconsciously looked at Laura. She did not react, so he wasn't sure if she'd been briefed or not.

"Do you know about the guacamole?" Parker asked her.

"Please continue," she said noncommittally.

"To answer your question, Tom, yes and no. DNA analysis didn't match anything we know about, but the computer reconstruction was even more puzzling. The damn thing looked like a merman."

"You mean a mermaid?"

"Yes."

"You've got to be kidding me. Right?" Tom noted with a questioning look on his face.

"Like I said, it's puzzling."

"J.R. and I froze our asses off," Tom said, "so I hope some good came from it."

"I'm sure more is to come," Parker said.

"Thanks, Doc. Please keep us advised. It's good to see you, Laura," Tom said, turning to continue towards the chow hall.

Laura looked at Parker and asked, "You mean merman, like what we saw in Siberia?"

Parker looked at her with a wry grin, "Kind of."

"Well, that's an interesting coincidence. When were you going to tell me?" she asked, sounding peeved.

"I'll brief you in my office. I assumed you knew."

"You know what they say about *assume*," she reminded him.

The meeting with Laura was intended to be only administrative. However, it quickly morphed into a discussion of the computer reconstruction in Zurich of the biological goop in the Antarctic ship, the so-called *guacamole*.

Laura's reaction to what Parker was telling her was far different from her usual repartee. She mostly sat there, with some *hmms* thrown in, with an occasional, *Really?*

In the end, Parker asked, "So what do you think, Laura?"

She didn't answer immediately. But when she did, she had an outstanding thought.

"There's no ground truth here. The only thing we have to compare to the computer modeling results are fanciful drawings."

"In my opinion, what we saw in the freezer in Russia was a pretty close match."

Laura shook her head. "But they didn't pull it out of the freezer. It was folded up in there, so we didn't get to properly examine it."

"All true," Jason admitted. "But neither you nor I had any doubt what it was."

"I'll give you that, Jason."

"And I have no doubt what this is," Parker concluded, shaking his head in emphasis.

"That's rather ironic, don't you think, Jason?" Laura said. "You're the most objective scientist I know, and I hear no objectivity here."

Parker laughed. "I see your point. But a lot has happened to us lately that defies any attempt at objectivity."

"But so far we have nothing I can brief up my chain. The IC community would laugh me out of Washington."

After Parker's and Laura's dueling logic had expended itself, Laura returned to her berth, and Parker swung by the viewing area to see who was there. Tonight, his Osage Marine friend, Luke Warmwater, was sitting by himself.

Although Warmwater had been out of the Marines for a decade or so, he still looked like one, except for his haircut which was more long-haired Osage and less high and tight. He was square-jawed, easy spoken, and easy smiling.

Parker stood back quietly, remembering his Mayport interview with Warmwater.

As Warmwater entered the interview room with Laura and Parker, Warmwater said, "I told you I would if I could, Jason. So here I am."

The two men shook hands, while Parker gave him an up and down look-over, smiling.

"Laura, I want you to meet one of the most interesting people you'll ever meet."

"Oh please," Warmwater protested.

"See Laura? He's my new best friend."

"Is Jason serious?" Laura asked. "Your name really is Luke Warmwater?"

"It is. My parents had a sense of humor."

Just then the photo of *Dioscuri* on Phobos caught Warmwater's eye.

"Holy cow! That's it, Jason," he said excitedly. "That's what I saw. Except those bulbous things are lights. They were lit up in different colors. That's exactly how I saw it—just that close. Amazing!"

"Really? That's a lot closer than most UFO sightings back then."

"I never thought I'd see it again," he said almost breathlessly.

Laura was looking at Parker with a puzzled look on her face.

Parker explained, "Luke and his brother saw one of these when he was a kid."

"Yeah," Luke said. "It changed my life."

Warmwater kept staring at it, and Parker was not willing to interrupt his reverie.

"Hey, wait a minute, you turkey," Warmwater said as he turned away from the photo and towards Parker. "You told me you didn't know if there were lights on the Triangle? You knew all along there were."

"What do you mean? I don't see any lights," Parker said, smiling.

Parker had that uncomfortable yet in some ways humorous feeling you get when you know you've been caught in a harmless lie.

Warmwater poked his finger at the bulbous lens-like projections arranged along the edge of the craft. "These things. They're not lit up in this photo, but they glow brightly when it's hovering. Right?"

Laura looked alarmed. That bit of information was a secret that was to only be revealed once the applicant had been selected for the final aquanaut team. Until then, the lights were top secret.

"Laura, we have a problem," Parker said. "Either we have to select Luke for the Deep Base team, or we have to shoot him. What's it going to be?"

"I think I see what's going on here. So, Luke, it seems you have some special knowledge about this craft. How did you acquire it?"

"I was a kid. My brother and I saw it." Looking back at the photo, he said, "We were at least as close as this, and it was hovering only a hundred feet up or so, with all its lights lit up."

"Were you in a field somewhere?"

"Oh hell no. We were in a suburb of Kansas City."

"What did it do?" she asked.

"It just hovered. Then it disappeared."

"Really?"

"The next thing I remember is us riding our bikes home as fast as we could."

"Did you have missing time?"

"You mean like being abducted? I don't know. My Mom was not particularly worried when we got home so we couldn't have been gone long. She wasn't out looking for us."

"You told her what you'd seen?" Laura asked.

"I did, but my brother denied it."

"Did he? As a parent that must have been a little strange, two siblings with wildly different views of what had happened. One seeing something bizarre, and one claiming to have seen nothing. Did you later confront your brother about his lie?"

"I sure did. He thought it was funny that I called him on it."

"He admitted it?"

"Immediately. He knew damned well what we had seen, and what he had done."

"I know you're back there, Jason," Warmwater said without turning his head. "Don't you know you can't sneak up on me?"

"Why is that Luke? Because you're Osage?"

"No, because I'm Marine Recon. Is something on your mind?"

Parker came closer and found a seat a couple of feet away from Warmwater.

"I was just thinking about our interview in Mayport where you were telling Laura about your Kansas UFO sighting. And now, thanks to an extraordinary sequence of events you've flown in one of them."

"That's ironic, Jason. I too was thinking about that and trying to figure out if that sighting had any deeper meaning. That sighting was both miraculous and brief but came at a formative age for me. In a way, it was like the spirits of those dead young adults in the hospital morgue that disrupted my entire career path."

"And you wonder why it happened to you?"

"Wonder why it happened period. Why would this craft, which is obviously very real, appear literally out of the blue for a few seconds, and then disappear again? And those young adults in the morgue, what was up with that?"

"What do you think?" Parker asked.

Warmwater smiled, peering out into water outside the habitat. Without looking at Parker, he said, "I think nature is fucking with us. Every once in a while, it gives us a glimpse of reality, just to keep us humble, to let us know that we're living in a delusion. What we think is real is only a tiny fragment of what is truly real."

"That makes sense to me," Parker said.

"Take women, for example. Same basic biology, just different equipment, yet sometimes worlds apart from us. You know why?"

"No clue."

"Because we can't see beyond the veil separating us from them. We can't get inside their head because they see things we cannot."

"You're divorced now, aren't you?"

"Oh yeah. Recon life is hard on spouses."

"Why is that?" Parker asked, already knowing the answer.

"One spouse is running around the world doing fun but dangerous stuff, and the other is stuck at home. The homebodies get rootbound."

"What do you mean?"

"You put a beautiful plant in a pot, give it light, food and water, and it will flourish, but only for a while. But even though it gets everything it needs, sooner or later the roots will keep growing and strangle themselves in the pot. The plant becomes root-bound. It can no longer flourish. There's only one cure for that."

"What's that?" Parker asked.

"You break the pot because you can't pull the plant out with the pot intact, and then you put it in a larger pot. That's what I call divorce, breaking pots."

"That's an interesting viewpoint."

"A gardener can do everything in their power to keep their flower flourishing, but underground where you can't see, the flower is strangling. It's not the gardener's fault or the flower's fault. It's just nature."

I can relate to that, Parker thought.

"So, there are worse things than divorce," Warmwater concluded.

"Good to know," Parker said.

"How about your marriage, Jason? With all the running around you do, are you and your wife doing okay?"

"We're not to the breaking pots stage yet, so I guess we're okay."

"Then I wish you the best of luck. A road warrior's lifestyle is tough on the spouses."

Chapter 46. Seeing Things

When the inside pressure was equivalent to 1,480 feet seawater, still approaching its final pressure of two-thousand feet, Luke Warmwater was sitting alone in the viewing area, day-dreaming while munching on a ham and cheese sandwich. In his thoughts, he was allowing himself to be absorbed into a primal part of the Osage cosmology where spirits from the sky bestowed life upon the peoples of the Middle Waters, the Osage and other Native Americans. At that very moment, he felt that he was an integral part of the Lower Waters, a region he had only skimmed back in his days as a Marine recon diver. But now he was fully immersed in it.

While chewing on his sandwich, he was watching a deep-water fish close up to the viewing port. It was a type he had not seen before. He looked down to his electronic fish identification display, figuring it might be a *Coryphaenoides* or Rattail fish. The common name Rattail pretty well described the shape of the gray, deep water fish.

As he looked up from his device, he caught a glimpse of something moving at the fringes of the lighted water. As he focused on that twilight area, he saw nothing. Perhaps it had been a shark, or maybe it had actually been nothing but his imagination. Whatever it was, the Rattail in the center of the viewport seemed unperturbed. It seemed more interested in the light inside the Deep Base, and perhaps in the man sitting there watching its every move.

Then, in a flash, the fish disappeared. The sudden disappearance startled Warmwater, who then pressed his face to the viewport looking for any sign of the fish.

A second later a green humanoid shape appeared close to the viewport, well-lit by both the internal and external lights. Its face seemed human in form, and sticking out of its mouth was the longest tongue Warmwater had ever seen. The tongue quivered and thrashed in a very untongue-like way. Warmwater then realized it was the long tail of the Ratfish, just as the creature slurped it down. The creature then smiled in an almost human way.

You should try them, Warmwater heard in his head. *A bit mushy but very nutritious.*

And then it was gone.

It didn't take Warmwater long to find Parker as he was delivering a lecture on deep diving physiology. He had given that instruction before they left Mayport, but since they were approaching the maximum depth of the dive, a repeat lecture was in order.

"And I remind you, once we reach the bottom depth," Parker said, "those of you who have received the training on the UBA, and who wish, may venture outside. You will, of course, be securely tethered for your safety. Any questions?"

A young red-headed male, part of the genetics research crew, was there as a technician, not a diver, so he had been consistently taunting the experienced divers.

"Just an opinion, really. The idea of a tethered diver sounds to me a lot like bait on a line. Has any diver ever been eaten while out there?"

Parker laughed. "Not to my knowledge. But there's always a first time, so you're not required to go outside unless you're part of the maintenance crew."

From the looks on the assembled faces, the laughter he heard was in some part nervous laughter.

Addressing the group again, Parker said, "Okay, you know where to find me. I'll be headed out for an excursion as soon as we're within reach of the bottom depth and I'll let you know how it is. It should be a piece of cake, although very cold cake. So, until next time, you're dismissed."

That was the third and final lecture Parker had delivered that day, so Parker was glad to see his friend Luke Warmwater waiting to see him.

"So why did you select a wise guy for this mission?" Warmwater asked.

"You noticed? Well, aside from being a jokester, he is one of the potential breeders. We don't want the redhead gene lost from any potential survivors, you know, just in case."

Warmwater looked at him with a funny look. "Are you serious, Jason?"

Parker laughed. "Of course not. He's one of our most experienced genetics techs. He's so good he claims he could make mermaid babies."

"It's funny you should say that because I just saw something peculiar. Can we step into your office? I'd like to talk in private."

"Okay, but every living thing down here is peculiar," Parker said.

On deep dives, there is rarely any privacy, but Parker had successfully argued that for long-term habitation's sake, individual bunks, showers, toilets, and a few offices had to be free of monitoring. Anything else would cause paranoia to sweep DB1, and that was a risk no one was willing to take.

Once they were in Parker's combined office/bunk area, with the door locked, Warmwater said, "I'll tell you something about peculiar. This was like mermaid peculiar."

Parker laughed.

"It's not funny, man," Warmwater said. "I watched it eat a rattail fish, sucking the whole thing down like a noodle. And it spoke to me in my head."

"Really? What did it say?"

"It said I should try them. And that they're delicious."

Parker stared at Warmwater for a moment, then smiled. "Okay, I'm sorry I joked about the ginger kid. Now, what really happened?"

"No, for real."

"Oh. Well, we do have hydrogen in the gas mix now, and that has certainly caused hallucinations in the past. Not usually at this low percentage, but everyone is different."

"I thought we were avoiding that by such a slow compression rate."

"Very true," Parker answered. "So I'm not convinced that's the explanation. For instance, you once told me about seeing ghosts in a morgue. Any chance that's what it could be?"

Warmwater thought about that for a moment. "Well—I'm not sure which is worse, a ghost mermaid or a real mermaid."

Parker smiled. "Just between us boys, that's funny."

That seemed to take the edge off. Warmwater smiled for the first time since his sighting. "Too bad we don't have video monitoring. I'd love to have proof."

"We are fairly Spartan down here, so we lack a lot of things. But I tell you what, if you want to announce this, we can see if anyone else sees one."

Warmwater shook his head. "This will remain our little secret. I'm not blabbing."

"When I go out there," Parker said, "I'll keep my eyes open."

"You better. We're not on our home turf anymore," Warmwater reminded him.

When Parker was alone in his room, he thought about the coincidence of mermaid sightings. Mermaids were make-believe, but Helmut Reuter showed what his life-form reconstructing computer did with the crushed alien guacamole. And there was the creature killed by excessive oxygen and stored in the Russian medical freezer. And now there was Warmwater's experience.

This was clearly more than coincidence.

At 0230 hours, Parker awoke from a scary dream. He didn't remember what it was about, except that it was bizarre. It might be the effect of the hydrogen or the fact that they were at 1,500 feet of water pressure, with the pressure getting closer every day to that at two-thousand feet of seawater.

Being awake anyway, and not feeling drowsy enough to immediately fall asleep again, Parker wandered into the engineering monitoring center. The midwatch was usually sedate since nothing of note was scheduled for the middle of the night. But the five people there seemed agitated and glued to a monitoring screen. A red alarm light was flashing.

"What's going on here, folks?" Parker asked. "Anything I should be concerned about?"

Lieutenant Larissa Slocum was the night shift duty engineer. "Good timing, Jason. We were doing our usual camera scanning of the piping system coming from the fusion reactor and stopped when we saw a spider crab crawling on the piping. We were guessing it liked the warmth from it. But as we zoomed in, it disappeared. At first, we thought it had fallen off the pipe, but when we replayed the recording, we saw it got sucked up into a tiny crack where the weld should be joining the pipe and a junction. Apparently, the weld cracked, and the pressure difference forced the crab through the crack. We immediately got an overpressure alarm."

"That sounds serious."

"Our safety valve is dumping some of that pressure, but we have to fix it before we lose our reactor cooling fluid. In the system I'm used to, it just shuts down. But in a small magnetic Tokamak reactor like this one, it's a cause for concern. There's less metal mass to draw away the heat in case of a disruption to coolant flow."

"What's the differential pressure?"

"About 445 psi."

"Can we use our ROV to reweld it?" Parker asked.

At that moment, Don Baxter, the DB1 designer walked back into the engineering office. "Already tried that. It can't reach the crack to make the weld."

"But it has to be welded," Parker said, looking at Tom, "or we'll have to abort the mission."

"I know. That means J.R. and I have to do it."

"But we've never done a 500-foot downward excursion before," Parker reminded Tom.

"There's always a first time, Doc," Tom said, grinning at Parker.

Dr. Emery Reed walked in. "I don't like what I just heard. Downward excursion? That wasn't part of the plan."

Samuel Putnam showed up right behind Dr. Reed.

Parker was surprised to see Putnam. "You're losing some good snooze time, Samuel."

"Dr. Reed woke me," he said. "I can't chronicle the events down here if I'm sleeping. What's going on?"

"Our divers will have to do what our ROV can't do."

"Is that unusual?" Putnam asked.

"Not at all," Parker said, speaking from experience.

CHAPTER 47. OUTSIDE

The crowd gathering in the engineers' ops center grew noticeably louder when J.R. Jackson showed up. Tom Thomas had buzzed him awake, with a call to report.

"Did I hear diving? Hooyah! Where's my coffee?"

"We have a welding job outside," Tom said. "You need to weld a crack the ROV cathodes can't reach. But I have to warn you, there's suction on that crack. We already watched a crab getting crushed and sucked inside the pipe. So please keep a respectful distance. We can't turn the flow off since it's part of the reactor cooling system."

"Not even for a few minutes?" the diver asked.

"Not even."

"Well that's a little scary," J.R. said. "But I can handle it."

Two hours later, as a morning glow began to color the Eastern sky, J.R. was on the bottom at two thousand feet. Down there it could have been noon time, but no light penetrated from the surface. The water above DB1 was perpetually black. However, the bottom was well lit by floodlights where J.R. was standing.

"How are you feeling J.R.?" Parker asked.

"Like I'm going to need some good loving after this."

The topside crew laughed, but Tom, who knew J.R. the best, came on the line.

"They're waiting for you J.R., but first, you have a job to do."

Dr. Reed interrupted. "Any High-Pressure Nervous symptoms, J.R.?" He would have been surprised if there weren't. By his calculation, the hydrogen content was not yet high enough to entirely suppress the effects of a 500-foot plunge at that depth.

"I'm a little shaky," J.R. said. "Didn't you boost my H2 gas?"

"A little, but we didn't want you hallucinating on us, so we're being cautious."

"Too bad, I think I could have used a bit more of that magic gas. But hey, I'm good to go."

Reed nodded his head to Baxter, who was going to direct J.R. to the worksite.

"Okay, J.R.," Baxter said, "the pipe inlet is about sixty feet straight ahead. Let me know when you have a visual."

"Roger that."

The visibility was excellent; J.R.'s boots stirred up a little sediment with each step, but it was carried away in a slight current. He'd only walked about thirty feet when he called *contact.*

"Alright, J.R. Now follow that pipe to your right. It's heading up and over the outside toroid, but the flange you're looking for is at the juncture of the upward heading pipe. Again, approach that juncture with extreme caution."

A minute later, J.R. called out, "Okay, I'm at the pipe juncture, but your robot is blocking my access. Will you please release the clamp from the pipe?"

"Copy that. Stand back because it may fall a few inches. Don't want to trap any body parts."

"Roger that. I want to keep all my body parts."

After a pause of several seconds, nothing was happening.

"Uh, any time would be good," J.R. said.

"We hit the release," Baxter said. "It should be free."

"Well news flash, it isn't. Can't you see that?"

"Yeah, we sure do. Trying it again… and again."

Tom asked, "Any better ideas, Don?"

"Hmmm. We didn't expect this."

Someone else came on the comms. "Hit it with a hammer."

J.R. laughed. "That may work on a car starter, but I'm fresh out of hammers. You see any down here?"

"No, but I see rocks," Parker said. "How about smacking it with a rock?"

J.R. turned around and walked towards an object visible about eight yards behind him.

As he was reaching down to grab it, he stopped. "Oh fuck, that's no rock. It's a stonefish."

"At two-thousand feet?" Parker asked. Seems way too deep and dark for them."

"Or something a lot like it," J.R. said. "I'm not touching it. But it's a brazen son of a bitch. It didn't move the slightest bit."

"Cos it's not afraid of you," Parker said.

"I'm not afraid of much, but whatever it is, I'm afraid of it."

Now J.R. was looking around and finally saw a suitably sized stone he could wield. He was out of the field of view of the Sub Base cameras, but the lights and camera on his helmet showed what he was after.

Once he got there, he stopped. "Before I pick this sucker up, I want to make sure we all agree it's just a rock."

Parker looked around the room, and everyone's head nodded.

"Yep, we're all in concurrence. It's just a rock. Not paper, not scissors, not a poisonous fish."

J.R. laughed, then bent over and picked it up. A few moments later he was back to the stuck ROV clamp. "Any spot better to whack it than another?"

"Use your best judgment," Baxter said.

J.R. whacked the clamp hard, disintegrating the partially softened rock. The ROV piping clamp sprang open, allowing him to lift the apparatus and move it to the side. With utmost care, J.R. pulled from the large pockets on his dry suit a curved patching plate that had been quickly milled out of stainless steel. Using a pad eye already welded to the outer surface of the plate, J.R. was able to safely place the patching plate over the torn piping. He then plugged his own electrodes into the high amperage auxiliary source on the ROV and after lowering his welding visor, started welding the patching plate to the reactor intake pipe.

Welding stainless steel is not easy, and doing it well underwater is an order of magnitude more difficult than on land. But the finished welded bead was almost a work of art.

"Well that should last a thousand years," J.R. said.

"Great job, J.R.," Baxter said. The pressure is dropping back down where it needs to be. We're getting good suction now."

Dr. Reed had been silent during the repair operation, but now he was taking over.

"Dr. Reed here. J.R. now we need to work on getting you back. First, we're going to bump up your oxygen partial pressure from 1.3 atmospheres to 1.6 atmospheres. Let us know if you start getting any oxygen toxicity symptoms. And remember, if you do have an oxygen seizure, you'll be fine in the helmet, and the rig will immediately drop the rig oxygen partial pressure back to 1.3 atmospheres."

"Roger that. Let's do it."

"O2 is coming up," Reed announced. "Make your way back to the hangar so we can get you into the pressure chamber to start decompression."

"Are we doing an upward excursion?" J.R. asked. "I'm anxious to get back."

"We'll let you know soonest."

"Copy that," J.R. said.

A moment later, J.R. paused, not moving.

"What are you doing, J.R.?" Tom asked. "Peeing in your drysuit?"

"Holy shit! Did you see that?" J.R. shouted.

"See what J.R.?"

"Is the hydrogen still high Doc?"

"Sure is. I can't lower it until we start decompression."

"Well, I think I just had a hallucinogen."

"A what?" Reed asked.

"What did you see J.R.?" Parker asked. He understood what J.R. meant, and had been concerned this might happen. There was a little too much human experimentation going on during this dive.

"For just a second," J.R. said breathlessly. "Looked like a fuckin mermaid with long blond hair, but ugly as hell."

"What was it doing?"

"It looked straight in my helmet. Like he was checking me out. Then boom, it was gone. I guess it didn't like what it saw."

The first thing Tom thought to say was, "How do you know it was a he?"

"Duh, no tits," J.R. answered.

Reed turned to Parker, "It didn't show up on the helmet camera. Could it be the hydrogen? Didn't you say J.R. hallucinated on the 2500-foot dive?"

"But not like this," Parker said.

Returning his attention to the mike, Parker asked, "How are you feeling J.R.?"

"I'm great. Just glad that mermaid didn't decide to take a bite. Had wicked looking teeth."

"What about the oxygen?" Reed asked Parker off-mike.

"One point six is not that much. NOAA uses it, but not at two-thousand feet. Frankly, Emery, I'd recommend getting him out of the water as soon as possible with an upward excursion in the chamber."

"I wasn't planning on it," Reed said, "but I've changed my mind. Let me wang out a new decompression profile with a hundred-foot excursion."

"Hey Jason," J.R. said, "Remember when I saw something in the De Soto Canyon? I still have a sample of its hair."

"You do?"

"Somewhere. I'll have to look for it when I get back," J.R. said. "But this looked just like it."

"This is becoming a regular thing for you," Parker noted.

What Parker didn't say is that when making deep experimental dives with hydrogen, divers seeing strange things may or may not be seeing what they think they are. Hydrogen narcosis can be deceiving.

"Doc Reed, you don't think I'm fucked up, do you?" J.R. asked.

Fortunately, J.R. could not see Captain Reed shrug his shoulders.

"I'm sure you'll be fine once you get back inside."

"That would be nice fellas. Bring me home."

What the hell is going on? Parker wondered. *Luke Warmwater just saw something similar. And his sighting occurred at a much lower dose of hydrogen. But this time it should have shown up on the helmet camera, but oddly, it didn't. Must have been interference.*

Strange.

CHAPTER 48. SICK BAY

Dr. Reed and his corpsman assistant had just finished up sick call for the morning when Parker came into Reed's office. "How's Rhonda holding up to the pressure?" Parker asked, watching her as she exited the room.

Under normal circumstances that would lead to an entirely different conversation, but in truth, all he wanted to know was if the combined effects of pressure and exotic gases were impacting the performance of the medical personnel on board.

"She's a trooper."

"Good."

"So how are you holding up Jason?"

"I'm doing fine. But I need to know what you have in your pharmacy for psychiatric disorders."

Reed's eyebrows raised. "For you or someone else?"

"Just a general question. No one in particular."

"Based on the Duke University experience with dives in the two-thousand-foot range I've stocked up on chlorpromazine and diazepam. And then there's the ever-popular lithium. But, if you're worried about J.R., he checked out perfectly normal."

"Then we have a problem."

"Why do you say that?" Reed asked.

"Luke Warmwater claims he saw something similar while sitting in the observation room. And he was not in the water, also not at full depth, and he was breathing the same oxygen and hydrogen we are."

"What do you want me to say? We don't know what's happening. We're making new science down here."

"New science? You might be right Emery. I'll have to think about it."

"But you've piqued my curiosity," Reed said. "Do you mind if I talk to Warmwater?"

"If he'll talk to you about it. But he might not."

As Parker turned to leave Reed's office, he was met at the door by Laura Smith.

"Knock knock," Laura said. "Emery, can we come in? We need to talk."

"Always welcome, Laura."

"Kelly and Clarice are with me too," Laura said, as they stepped in close behind her.

Laura looked at Parker with a straight face. "I figured I'd find you here. If you don't mind Emery, I'm going to lock the door."

"Oh, it's one of those meetings. What did I do wrong this time?"

"Nothing," she said, her face remaining expressionless. "We have something to share with you two."

"Is this about J.R.?" Parker asked.

"Yes and no."

"Please pull up whatever chair you find," Reed said.

Clarice said, "I'll stand."

By habit, Reed reached for a pen as if preparing to copy a patient history.

"Please put the pen down, Emery. No note-taking." Laura's tone was firm.

He raised his eyebrows at her and set the pen down on the pad.

After nervously clearing her throat, Laura said, "This habitat is a ruse. The world just might end tomorrow, like President Whitney claims. That's the white version of why we're here. But the black world reason is that what J.R. saw is real. He's not imagining things."

"Real what?" Parker asked.

"That we don't know. But let me start from the beginning. There is a reason why both ODNI and DIA established the positions Kelly and I are in. And there's a reason why we were the only candidates seriously considered."

"That doesn't surprise me in the least," Parker said with one eyebrow raised.

"But I think this will. When the Frogs left with their spacecraft, the number of biological targets detected near both NURA habitats in the Gulf of Mexico dropped off dramatically. So, the intelligence community assumed they'd all left. And those remaining targets were thought to be non-alien biologics. Big sharks, small whales, something at the edge of our identification abilities."

Parker had been making the same assumption.

"The aliens had never been detected far from deep water canyons, like the DeSoto Canyon, the Mariana Trench, or the Puerto Rico Trench. That's why before you came along Jason, the Intel community called them the Canyoneers. However, after a while we started seeing targets appearing at the edges of the Florida continental shelf, heading south."

Parker cocked his head. That revelation was a surprise.

"And as soon as planning started on Deep Base, we started getting contacts on the Blake Plateau."

"No way," Parker said, shaking his head.

Laura continued without skipping a beat. "Those contacts increased once the Deep Base structure was on the bottom and increased, even more, when the engineering checkout team arrived. It's almost like they knew what we'd be doing before we even knew it."

"Frogs?" Reed asked, smirking.

"Again, we don't know what the contacts are," Laura continued, "or why they do what they do, but both military and civilian intelligence wanted Kelly and me to figure out what was going on."

"Why? Are they perceived as a threat?" Parker asked.

"We don't know. They don't act hostile, but then we're also not provoking them. We're just watching them."

"And they match what J.R. saw?" Parker said, pointing in the general direction of the viewing alcove.

"Pretty much. I don't know why his camera didn't record them, but based on what J.R. described, I'd say yes."

"Luke Warmwater saw one too," Parker said. "It even spoke to him telepathically."

"Where?"

"In the viewing port. Luke was eating a sandwich, and the damned thing ate a rattail fish, whole, right in front of him."

"Holy cow!" Clarice exclaimed, wide-eyed.

Laura turned towards Brightman and looked at him with raised eyebrows.

"So, where do we go from here?" Parker asked. "What's the plan?"

"You're the plan, Jason. So pay attention."

"Me?"

"Afraid so. I'll let Clarice fill you in on the big picture."

"Thanks, Laura." Clarice cleared her throat. "The things I saw manhandling my husband on Phobos were very real, and their ship too. Dr. Reed, you probably thought I'd lost my marbles, but I didn't. Although we still think what killed our astronauts on Mars was a GRB, we strongly suspect it was not a GRB that cooked our cargo ship en route to Phobos. It was more likely a free-electron laser, not gamma-rays."

"How'd you come to that conclusion?" Parker asked.

"Our cargo ship inspection probe didn't survive long, but its last transmission was an image of the cargo ship being charred, an effect we don't think we'd get with gamma-rays. And based on the visit of the Beetle ship to Phobos, they're a likely suspect."

Parker looked puzzled. "Not to change the subject, but Laura, you said Deep Base was a ruse."

"It is," Laura said. "Sort of. There is an ulterior motive to Deep Base One. It's true that it's a proof of concept for a refuge from GRBs. If it works, and we survive, then there will hopefully be many more. We have no idea if the international community is taking Whitney's warning seriously, but at least he's done the right thing by warning them."

Parker interrupted. "Laura, please?"

"Hold your horses, Jason, I'm getting there."

Parker sighed. Patience was not his strong suit.

"Deep Base can also be a hideout from unfriendly aliens. Any weapon they want to use other than a nuclear bomb would be made ineffective by two-thousand feet of seawater. But now we're talking about a long-term underwater presence by humans. And for that, the Chinese had the right idea about genetic body modification."

"Really?" Reed said.

"Of course, what the Chinese did was morally reprehensible, but in a post-apocalyptic world with a damaged atmosphere, gills would have survival value. But Jason, as you pointed out, the weakness in the Chinese approach is that they did not succeed in designing-in hypoxia tolerance. We know there are genes for that in high altitude living Tibetans. And Emery, as you may know, those same genes were successfully amplified in the Martian rodents. But the human genome is far more resistant to that degree of tampering."

"Laura, where's the ruse?" Parker asked again.

As interesting as all this is, Parker was thinking, *what about DB1 and us?*

"Almost there Jason," she said, casting him her own impatient look.

"Do you remember how you and the Frogs had telepathic communication?"

"And the Trolls," Parker replied. "Don't forget them."

"Right. Well, Joshua Nilsson has not had the clear communication you did Jason, but he has developed a compelling sense that these mermaids, or whatever they are, want to help us achieve that genetic modification."

Reed and Parker burst out laughing together, but Laura's stern look calmed them down.

Reed said, "So that's not a joke?"

"Actually, the joke is on you, Jason," Laura said with a devilish smile. "You were the one who taught us that human gills could not work unless we developed a genetic ability to tolerate low oxygen levels. You showed us how the Chinese effort had failed, and we took advantage of that. But we do know for a fact that these real mermaids, or whatever you want to call them, the ones we're seeing here, do have hypoxia tolerance. For long term survival, we need to build in that same hypoxia tolerance. If we do suffer a GRB, the survivors will likely need that capability because our atmosphere's oxygen level will probably be lower than it is now."

"But even if there is never a GRB, sooner or later we will meet an enemy that has an aquatic swimming and attack capability far in excess of our Navy SEALs. Once the hypoxia tolerance bit is solved, humans with gills will be a viable military threat. And that is the real reason we are here."

"What?" Parker exclaimed, shocked.

"GRBs and Diaspora is just a cover story for the real interest in using these creatures, whatever they are, to help us build a military capability we don't currently have."

There was a long pause in Reed's small office as both he and Parker thought about what Laura had just revealed.

Finally, Parker spoke. "Why am I not surprised? It's a perfect cover story."

"It is. We just have to make sure Samuel Putnam does not get wind of this. Knowing your backgrounds, I know you two understand."

"Putnam's my friend," Parker said. "We hired him to write the story of underwater versus space refuges, but we now have to hide the real story?"

"I can assure you there will be a time and a place for a reveal. But who knows what the bigger story will even be? Let's just say we're hedging our bets. This place cost a bazillion dollars, and if the world doesn't end, then we need to tell Congress what the taxpayers got for their money. Interspecies research and development sounds like a smart idea, and a bargain. And if the world does end, well that money will not only keep some of us alive but help the survivors survive long enough to repopulate the Earth. Now, what's so bad about that?"

"But you know, these new creatures you're talking about won't be human, Parker said. "Not entirely."

"We know," she said calmly. "Neither are Trolls. We're getting used to that."

"I don't see why the joke is on me. None of this is funny."

Parker's friend Brightman smiled. "When we reach two-thousand feet, we need you to lockout and meet these creatures face to face."

Laura quickly added, "We need clear communication with whatever is out there, to make sure they're willing to hold up their end of the bargain."

"Wait. Bargain?" Parker exclaimed. "We've already negotiated with them? How?"

Laura got a great deal of pleasure, knowing things Parker did not.

"You can thank Joshua Nilsson for that. He's got ways."

"And what was the bargain?" Parker asked.

"We supply the materials, and they supply the know-how."

Parker was looking around the small office, smiling. "Now I know you're kidding me."

But no one else was smiling.

Parker's former work colleague and diving buddy, Brightman, said, "Afraid not Jason. This is coming from the top."

"Whitney?"

"None other. POTUS."

Parker was shaking his head. "This is un-fucking-believable."

Laura continued. "Nilsson's conviction is so credible that our Deep Base has a wet genetics laboratory."

"I know that," Parker said. "But Baxter designed it all wrong. It looks like it would flood very easily."

"Don was instructed to design it that way," she said. "You see, the wet lab is not for us. It's for them."

Chapter 49. Making Gills

Parker and Doctor Reed were trying to make sense of what they had just been told. Kelly Brightman was also joining them in Reed's office. Brightman knew the overall plan that Laura had revealed, but being an electrical engineer, he didn't understand the feasibility of genetically engineering an aquatic species with gills. Obviously, the Chinese did, and the three men in that room were playing catchup.

"Emery, there are two parts to this task," Parker said. "The first part is interfering with normal lung creation."

"Organogenesis." Reed was clicking and unclicking his ballpoint pen, an old habit when he was thinking.

"Yes. And the second is hypoxia tolerance. Of those two, changing the development of lungs to create gills is far more complicated. There are scores of genes and growth factors involved, but apparently, the Chinese succeeded in that effort. That would be Nobel prize-winning work. If it wasn't illegal."

"But how on Earth did they manage that?" Reed asked.

"We taught them, as always," Parker said. "You start with a Chinese national with a B.S. degree from China. They come to the U.S. to get a Ph.D. from someplace prestigious like Yale or Harvard, do a postdoc at a U.S. medical school and a research hospital, then get a faculty position at a good U.S. school on the West Coast with a healthy Chinese population so Chinese contacts would not attract attention. Once they've risen through the academic ranks to become a full professor in the genetics department of that University, specializing in organogenesis of lungs, and have become a leader in your field, their native country invites them back. A Chinese University such as Shanghai Jiao Tong University would do nicely. It has a good medical school, and a large University affiliation with an outreach to all sorts of academic and engineering fields."

"Yes," Reed admitted. "This does happen, far more than we would like."

Parker continued. "And then another prestigious university with a large population of Chinese postdocs trains up another Chinese national in the methods of using CRISPR to cut out defective genes. Of course, the temptation would be to use that skill to edit genes in human embryos, which then grow into gene-edited babies."

Reed nodded towards Brightman. "That also has happened in China, but it's considered unethical in the western world."

"So, the U.S. trained postdoc goes back to China," Parker said, "to do exactly what is outlawed here. Now armed with the information about which genes to snip out and which to replace with gill-developing genes and growth factors, you have all the information you need to make gills by creating a chimera, a hybrid cross with genes from another species."

"Sounds like our academic and medical knowledge would in effect be weaponized by foreign entities," Brightman said.

"Absolutely," Parker said.

Reed looked puzzled. "But what troubles me is that the Chinese didn't recognize the need for hypoxia tolerance. That's what you and our SEALs discovered. We're talking maybe a single gene, EPAS1, and its variant coming from the Denisovans, a gene which is prevalent in high altitude Tibetans. Because of that variant gene, Tibetans don't get mountain sickness."

Parker said, "Laura was right. On Mars, we were able to use gene editing to greatly amplify the EPAS1 gene in our Martian rodents, but underwater there may be far more complications than we know about. Perhaps the genetic changes required for the generation of gills interferes with EPAS1."

Brightman cocked his head. "In plain English please."

"Right now," Parker explained, "we don't have the know-how to make it all work."

Remembering the "hypothetical" conversation Reed had with President Whitney in the Oval Office, Reed smiled, realizing there was nothing hypothetical about it, at all. We humans don't have the knowledge to make it all work, but we know who does.

"So now I get it," Reed said. "The aliens have that worked out, both internal gills and hypoxia tolerance. So, I think that is the compelling reason why we are in effect subcontracting our gene-editing effort to the aliens."

"Nice," Brightman said. "We supply the lab equipment, and they supply the know-how. That said, I do see a strategic military advantage if our merfolk are hypoxia-tolerant. But there are ethical concerns," Brightman said. "Based on what little we can piece together about the

Frogs, their entire culture seems to have been based on their bioengineering of creatures which did their bidding. They created their own slaves. Isn't that right?"

Parker and Reed were silent for a moment, thinking.

"I suppose you could argue that," Parker finally admitted.

"Then we better be damned sure we're not helping merfolk do the same thing. Maybe that's the reason they're so willing to help us?"

Reed was not willing to be that cynical, based on what POTUS had suggested, hypothetically.

"Maybe they just want to have kids," Reed offered. "I'm not sure they can reproduce without genetic assistance."

"Maybe we should ask them," Parker said.

"That should make for interesting dinner conversation with them," Reed said. "Hey, can you guys make babies?"

Chapter 50. Trapped

Parker retired to his room and found a message waiting for him on his computer. It said *Call Home*.

Worried that something might be wrong, he wasted no time calling.

"Hi love, how are you doing?"

"I've had better days."

"Oh, are the kids okay?"

"Yeah, they're great. Nancy's pregnancy is progressing well."

"I'm sure both she and Danny are excited. When is she due?"

"Mid-September. And it's a girl."

Parker would have expected Sandy to be gleeful about the birth of her first grandchild, but she did not sound happy.

"Is there a problem with the baby?"

"No, she's fine."

"Then why so glum?" he asked.

"I'm filing for divorce."

"OK, Sandy, we don't joke around like that. Really, what's bugging you?"

"No joke. I can't take the worry anymore, Jason. After you came back from Guam and the Frogship, after you'd been shot through the chest, you promised me you wouldn't do that to me ever again. But you lied. I was worried sick when you and Laura were kidnapped, and no one would tell where you were. You were in Russia for God's sake. I might have never seen you again. But that wasn't enough drama for you. Next, you somehow fly a spaceship out into space, and you're not even an astronaut. Now you're sitting two-thousand feet underwater using experimental diving protocols. When you leave the house each morning, Jason, I never know if you'll be back."

Parker was stunned. "Sandy, I don't believe this. You want to throw away twenty-five years of marriage?"

"Don't you realize that fifteen of those years were terrifying for me? I'm seeing a cardiologist for heart palpitations. He asked me what's going on. I told him it's you. According to the Doctor, you're killing me, Jason. I'd rather be divorced than dead."

"Well damn, Sandy, if you're insistent, can't we at least do a trial separation?"

"That's rich, Jason. For all practical purposes, we are separated, and have been for most of fifteen years, ever since the Frogs showed up."

"Is it Laura you're worried about?"

"Oh, hell no. She's a sweet girl, a little wacky, but she's not the problem, Jason. It's you. You just can't help yourself."

"You couldn't wait to have this conversation until I got back? I'm locked in here for a while yet."

"Maybe that's a good thing, Jason."

"It's shitty, what it is."

"I'm sorry," she said. And then the call ended.

Parker sat mindlessly staring at the communicator until there was a knock on his door.

"Come in," he said with no enthusiasm.

It was Laura.

"Just checking on you," she said. "You have a big day in the morning. Anything I can do to help?"

Every time Parker would question whether there was anything to Laura's imagined connection with him, past life or otherwise, she would do something that made rejection of that notion more difficult. This was one of those times.

"No thanks, I'm good."

"You sure? You don't sound very convincing."

"Well, there's nothing you can do about it. I just got off the line with Sandy. She filed for divorce."

Laura gasped.

"Oh my God, Jason. I can't believe it."

"Me neither. Our marriage was perfect for me, but when I look at it from her perspective, the last fifteen years have been hell. I get that. While you and I knew what was happening, while we were living in the moment, she was left wondering if she'd ever see me again."

"Is she mad at me?" Laura asked.

"You? Not at all. It has nothing to do with you. She sees you as a sweet kid. It's all me."

"Well, it's pretty damn inconsiderate to spring that on you when you're trapped down here."

“That’s what I thought too, but you know what? It happens. Troops deploy to combat zones and find out overseas that they’ve been dumped. It happens more than it should. But I guess I thought it would never happen to me.”

“But twenty-five years? Wow.”

“So, no, Laura, there’s nothing you can do.”

“I’m so sorry, Jason.”

“Actually, coming by so I could talk about it, helped. Your timing was uncanny.”

“I knew, Jason. I could feel that something was up.”

“You’re a very surprising woman, Laura.”

She smiled and nodded her head. “I know.”

CHAPTER 51. CONTACT

Jason Parker set his foot on the Blake Plateau for the first time at 0700 the next morning. The silt stirred up by his footsteps was soon swept away by the gentle current that scoured the bottom, the very deepest segment of the Gulf Stream. He'd been signaled to suit up when DAWSS-1 detected biologicals quickly rising up the steep slope of the escarpment. There were multiple targets, and once they crested the escarpment and entered the plateau, they hugged the bottom, traveling at a phenomenal rate for a biological, approaching 100 meters a second. At that rate, it would take them 49 minutes to transit the 183 miles from the escarpment to Deep Base. Parker was waiting for them.

As J.R. and Tom had reported, the combination of Parker's D.E.M. diving rig, onboard heater, and whole-body tube suit kept him almost as comfortable as making a scuba dive in the Caribbean.

The heads-up display in his diving helmet showed him critical information like depth, water temperature, and compass heading. The onboard guidance system would also show him a bearing to a detected target, but as he headed slowly away from the habitat, no target was showing.

But the more powerful sensors on the habitat had detected something, and Laura was at the comms giving Parker guidance.

Deep Base One was tied into a series of Deep-Water Sensing Stations—the DAWSS, as it was called—extending east across the plateau and onto the edge of the Blake Escarpment. The first sensing station, DAWSS 1, was at a depth of 4,000 feet, at the edge of the escarpment, and located about twenty-five miles south of the Blake spur and thirty-five miles southeast of where Parker and *Dioscuri* encountered the Chinese submarine. The station looked out over the Blake Abyssal Plain which bottomed out at 16,000 feet.

DAWSS-2 was closer to DB1 and sat on the bottom of the plateau at a depth of 2,500 feet. On an easterly heading from DAWSS-2, the plateau sloped downward and eastward toward the escarpment.

"The group has stopped about a quarter-mile out," Laura said over the comms, "and now a single target is approaching at a much slower speed, steady at two meters a second."

"That's a brisk walking speed," Parker said. "I can't wait to see this thing."

Only a handful of the habitat's occupants were aware of what was going on. This first interspecies meeting was not being advertised since the intelligence agencies' expectations could be seriously in error.

"Are you nervous, Jason?" Laura asked.

"Oh hell yeah."

"I suggest you don't make any sudden movements," Laura said, her voiced tinged with anxiety.

"I'm picking it up on my helmet sensor now," Parker said. "But has it stopped?"

"It has. Maybe it's checking you out."

"This is creepy as hell since I can't see it."

"Uh Jason, if it makes a dash for you, I want you to scamper back here pronto."

"Scamper? You can't scamper underwater. I doubt I would have time to make it."

He had walked into a more dimly lit portion of the habitat's surroundings, thinking that bright lights might scare away the creatures. But then again that thinking could have been a mistake. Now he was farther from safety.

"Well, try anyway," Laura urged.

"Maybe you should have armed me after all," Parker said.

"Hush, it's moving again, slowly."

There was now silence over the comms and in the diving control room. Just the sound of Parker's breath inside his mask and his pulse whooshing in his ears.

Parker's heads-up display began pulsing yellow, indicating an approaching target. And then, out of the dimness, a dark shape began to emerge. From that distance, it looked vaguely humanoid.

And then it stopped again.

It's good to meet you, at last, Parker heard in his head.

"I can't really see you," Parker said.

No need to shout Jason. Just think.

"No, I need to speak. My friends are listening. Can you come closer?"

A little. The bright lights hurt my eyes.

"Are you here to talk?"

"Yes, and do not worry. I don't plan to eat you."

The creature approached a little closer so Parker could see more details. What he saw surprised him. It looked eerily similar to the creature that had been digitally generated from the squashed guacamole in the crushed disc in Antarctica. Professor Reuter's computer had been spot-on.

"What are you?"

We are what we are and what we have always been. We are Human.

"Funny, you don't look human."

Parker thought it ironic that this creature and the King Frog he'd come to know also claimed he and his people were Human. In this dim lighting, it looked greenish-black, rough, maybe scaly skin. Nothing seemed human except the presence of arms, neck, and head.

"Do you have a name?"

Wqfuye.

"Sorry I asked," Parker said, smirking. "Are you one of the Frogs, the builders of the Frogships?"

The Masters didn't like being called Frogs. And no, we are Guardians. We were created to protect the Frogs and their spacecraft. We did the manual labor underwater, while the Trolls did the manual work on the land. The Trolls can tolerant high oxygen concentrations, but both the Masters and we cannot.

"Good, you don't look like a Frog."

Of course, science fiction is replete with shape-shifting ETs, so as far as Parker was concerned, the verdict on what he was talking to, was not yet settled.

"Can you fly the Frogships?" Parker asked.

Yes. In the Masters' mind, that is manual labor. They spend their time doing more cerebral things.

"Like what?"

Searching the galaxy for our home, deciding when they should leave, and enlisting the help of Ta'veren like you.

Oh good grief, Parker thought. *Not you too.*

The merman's smile was not as cute as a Frog's, but it was a human smile all the same.

Hearing Parker's announcement, Laura laughed with a combination of surprise and relief. Reed, Baxter and the rest of the Intel crew were standing with their mouths agape, or whatever expression of shock best suited them.

Do I know you? Parker thought.

No.

Why didn't you leave with the rest of your kind, in your ships? Parker asked.

Because Earth's waters suit us.

"Why have you come to our base?" This time Parker remembered to speak.

I have been invited, by someone you call Nilsson. I make new creatures, but my laboratory left on one of our Frogships. So, you have built a laboratory for me.

Parker was not sure if he should confirm that or not, so he kept silent. But he could not hide his thoughts from the creature.

When do I start work? The creature asked.

"Who came with you?" Parker asked.

My helpers.

"What will you do for us?" Parker asked out loud.

Make gills. That is something you will need sooner than you think.

Remembering the discussion he had previously with Reed and Brightman, Parker asked, are you able to reproduce yourselves?"

"No. The Masters made sure of that. But we know how to fix that once we work in your laboratory. When can we see it?"

"Uh, Dive Control," Parker called out. "I think they want to come aboard."

"How many?" Laura asked.

Twelve, the Guardian thought.

"Make that an even dozen," Parker said.

"Oh crap," Laura said.

CHAPTER 52. WET LAB

Deep Base One quickly became the most exciting scientific laboratory in the world. Although the *Guardians,* as they were being called, were prevented by their physiology from mixing with the aquanauts outside of the water, both they and the aquanauts enjoyed telepathic contact.

There was a symbiotic relationship in this pairing of species. Although divers like J.R., Don, Parker and Kelly Brightman often ventured forth to spearfish for food, the Guardians were much better at bringing home the groceries, so to speak. The cooperative relationship was cemented by the U.S government-provided workspace within Deep Base, and the aquanauts who generously provided genetic material and laboratory equipment necessary for the Guardians to do their work. Dr. Reed was responsible for the collection of much of that genetic material.

Aside from Parker and Laura, Space Corp Technical Sergeant Retired Clarice Williams had the easiest time relating to the aquatic, mermaid-like creatures who thought of themselves as *Humans.* She had seen far more frightening creatures. Compared to the beetles which fondled her dead husband, the Guardians were warm and cuddly.

It was bittersweet parting when the dry portion of DB1 began its decompression to return the aquanauts to the surface. Their mission was completed earlier than planned because of the need to check all welds with human occupants outside of the facility. Don Baxter had checked and rechecked the patch put on by J.R., and it had not been leaking. But still, it was critically important to inspect every other weld on the complex.

Ironically, during the inspection process, the Guardians continued their work in the Wet Lab which remained flooded at the two-thousand-foot depth. With the secret blessings of the U.S. government, they had unfettered access to the laboratory, and seemed to enjoy the opportunity to do human hybrid production, and more importantly, to start producing fertile versions of themselves.

As the dry portion of DB1 was decompressing, Samuel Putnam spent countless hours quietly watching through the thick but transparent pressure boundary the Guardians working in the Wet Lab. He understood their need for self-reproduction. Without the right gene-editing equipment, their species would eventually die out. However, harboring a suspicion which seemed to be the hallmark of investigative reporting, Putnam wondered why our government was supporting this alien species in making human-alien hybrids.

Of course, a select group of government scientists was monitoring the work and learning a great deal about the process of making new forms of humanity. The scientific advances were unequaled anywhere, except perhaps in China. But then, in the spirit of competition, the Department of Defense was convinced that our hybrids would be better than their hybrids. After all, the Chinese did not have access to aliens from outer space, so far as anybody knew.

Having finally gathered enough material for his commissioned book, once the DB1 crew surfaced, Samuel Putnam returned to Oklahoma to edit his work. As he had once alluded to Parker back in Pawhuska, the book ending would not be precisely what the government desired. But he had to be true to his muse.

Shortly after Don Baxter surfaced from the first Deep Base mission, NASA assigned him another equally important task: To return to Mars to bring home the bodies of the dead astronauts, and to see if the Mars Base on Pavonis Mons could be restarted. If anyone could start up the fusion reactor, it would be Baxter since he designed it and the rest of the base.

With a persuasive letter of support from both Jason Parker and Laura Smith, recently promoted Lieutenant Commander Larissa Slocum was added to the crew list at the last minute as an assistant to Donald Baxter in starting and hopefully maintaining the Pavonis Mons fusion reactor.

While President Whitney had initially chosen to abandon Mars Base because of the belief that it had been attacked by some unknown enemy, the further analysis had concluded that the so-called attack had been of natural origin. With the talk of Diaspora to save some of humanity in case of future natural disasters, it only made sense to attempt a restart of Mars Base.

As for potential pilots for the Mars mission, Jason Parker was busy with Deep Base 1 and was using *Dioscuri* to support that mission. The Trolls who had flown *Dioscuri* had not yet been tested on the *XFS Taiwan.* And lately, they seemed more interested in shoring up the comfort and security of their new home in New Mexico. They were simply not interested in leaving the Earth.

The only person with a known ability and desire to fly the alien disc called *Taiwan* was the Buddhist Monk Phra Theratapati. To watch over Theratapati, the Space Corp assigned the test pilot, and Thera's onetime flight companion, Colonel William "Sparky" Morgan. The two men had finally made their peace after Thera realized that Morgan had knocked him unconscious to save the *Taiwan*, and all their lives, from the turbulent waters of the Colorado River.

The third member of the flight crew was Joshua Nilsson, the CIA's blind remote viewer. Although the Agency had complained bitterly about sending their most prized asset off into space, Laura's boss, the Director of National Intelligence, explained to his subordinates in straightforward terms that the new Mars Mission required a remote viewer. The risks were simply too high to not have a backup since Jason Parker was spending his time two-thousand feet beneath the sea.

Once the new flight crew had been determined, Jason Parker gave Thera, Sparky, and Nilsson a detailed briefing on the previous flight in *Dioscuri.* The hard part for Sparky was the idea of trusting the ship to make and fly its own flight plan. As a test pilot, he had been trained to not believe the machine. However, his flight from Sasebo in the *Taiwan* with both Thera and Parker had somewhat set his mind at ease.

What concerned Sparky most about the upcoming flight was *Dioscuri*'s previous close shave with the Moon and the uncertainties of flying past the Sun to Mars. After the Janus Silver mission, Earth had caught up with Mars and then passed it in its orbit around the sun. Now, once again, the two planets were on opposites sides of the solar system.

Aside from *Taiwan*'s flight crew, there was also a large complement of NASA and military men and women who had volunteered to either bring home our nation's dead, or if it worked out, to establish a new and larger colony on Mars. Newly promoted Commander Chris Meyers was resuming command, and two of the surviving Space Corp personnel from the last Mars duty rotation were returning as well.

A crescent moon sat low on the Eastern horizon, so *Taiwan*'s vertical launch into the clear night was not as nerve-wracking as had been *Dioscuri*'s. There was no close-up view of the moon as the ship made its initial course corrections. To Sparky that was both a relief and a disappointment.

Chapter 53. Ta'veren

Three months of rest, recreation and mechanical inspection occurred over the Christmas season. After that, the DB1 crew reassembled at Mayport.

The crew for this mission had been expanded to include the full complement of 325 men and women. Of the inaugural team, other than Parker and Laura, only the Navy divers J.R. and Tom, the former Marine Luke Warmwater, DIA analyst Kelly Brightman and Dr. Emery Reed returned for the full deployment.

The younger crew members were selected for their open-mindedness, intelligence, diving experience, absence of psychological abnormalities, and their reproductive potential, just in case. As expected, J.R. was giddy thinking of the possibilities.

Laura was Parker's copilot again for this flight carrying the full operational crew for Deep Base. His only conversation with her was to say, "If I can't get this heavy baby to hover, I may need your help."

"I'm here for you, Jason."

When it came time to hover, Parker did not need Laura's help after all. *Dioscuri* took off and flew in both air and water just as it had before.

As they pulled into the DB1 hangar, Laura looked over at Parker and said, "We make a pretty good flight crew, don't you think?"

"Don't jinx us, Laura. Remember, this thing is listening."

"I'm not worried. Besides, it likes me better than it does you."

Parker knew better than to argue that point. Quite possibly, she was right.

After the excitement of the new crew members finding their cabins, and the requisite tour and safety lectures, Parker and Laura found themselves alone in the viewing room. During the last mission, this small alcove had become their only respite from the continuous onslaught of questions and complaints. The current mission was starting out no differently.

There was a distinctive sign hanging above the alcove which proclaimed in large letters, *No Bitching Allowed*. Amazingly, the sign worked. The Viewing Alcove was usually quiet.

Laura was the first one to speak. "How do you think the new folks reacted to hearing about the alien workers?"

Parker shrugged. "These people are selected for their open-mindedness, and as a result, I think they took it in stride. They know we're on a special mission, and I think they're just glad to be a part of making history."

"That we are, Jason. Who would have thought we'd be doing this?"

"You know, I was thinking about just how far you've come, Laura. When we first met, you were this bright graduate student, but also kind of a weirdo. You were the first person I knew who actually believed in aliens and UFOs. And look at us now. We have aliens working for us, and we're flying former UFOs across the solar system at relativistic speeds."

"And we've walked on both Mars and one of its moons," she added.

"And you've walked on the ocean bottom two thousand feet down using a powered rebreather you invented. Look at all we've accomplished in the course of a scant fifteen to twenty years. It takes your breath away to think about it."

Laura reached over and affectionately put her hand on Parker's knee.

"I've been thinking about Thera," Laura said. "I think he disproved my pet theory."

Parker turned his gaze away from the window and looked into Laura's eyes.

"Which theory is that?"

"The one where I thought you and I were soul mates from a previous life together as Frogs."

"Well, if you're going to disprove a theory," Parker said, "that's a great one to start with. But Buddhists like Thera believe in reincarnation. I would have thought he would simply reinforce your feelings."

"I get the feeling he communicates with the *Taiwan* simply by meditating," Laura said, "putting his mind in a different place than his body. And now that you've started emulating his technique, you have more consistent results getting *Dioscuri* ready for flight. It all seems to be based on mental concentration."

"That certainly makes more sense than some supposed affinity leftover from a previous life."

"But then," she said, "a lot more people can concentrate than can fly these alien craft."

"That makes sense too," Parker said.

He really had no idea where she was going with this conversation.

"Knowing you, Jason, you probably aren't going to like what I'm going to say next."

Parker shifted his gaze from the window again, ducking his head in a questioning manner.

"The Trolls call you Ta'veren, and I think I remember the Frogs might have too."

Parker laughed. "But I know you know that is a fictitious name. It's all fantasy."

"I know, but if the shoe fits."

"What are you saying?"

"Ta'veren are at the center of the wheel of time. They make things happen."

"I'm sorry, Laura, but that's really a silly idea. Even as a graduate student, you didn't talk like that."

"Don't be so dismissive, Jason. Think about what has happened. The Frogs chose you. They claimed that we were once Frogs, and that's something we can never confirm, but the fact remains, they chose you. They appeared to you and talked to you until you finally believed in them. And because of that, we were able to prevent a war between the Frogs and our government, a potential war that few in the government even know about. I'm not even sure President Whitney knows about it."

"I would hope he does," Parker said.

"And we were able to get an International Treaty signed giving the Frogs safe passage off the planet. I mean, think about it. That was the world's first absolutely clear and unequivocal proof that ETs have been in our deep oceans for thousands of years."

"I will grant you that," Parker said, nodding his head.

"And of course, if it weren't for you, we wouldn't have the Trolls. We've invited a whole new species into the citizen's club, thanks to you."

"I'm hoping that doesn't backfire," Parker said, "but so far I'm really enjoying having Baltazar around. As cavemen go, he's pretty damn interesting."

"The world doesn't know about the war we prevented," she continued, "but they do know that we have alien spacecraft that we're flying across the solar system. You were the first one to figure out how to fly the damn things. And thanks to that discovery, we now have a growing number of compact fusion reactors. Reverse engineered alien technology."

"You know what's funny about that? Larissa Slocum's not read into a lot of stuff, but she figured that out on her own."

"I'm going to miss her, but she should enjoy her trip to Mars. And speaking of Mars, we wouldn't have been able to rescue the Phobos and Martian Space Corp folks without you and the *Dioscuri*. So, like I was saying, you're the center of it all, Jason. You really are Ta'veren, and somehow the Frogs knew that."

"Well don't forget, Laura, they can see a little way into the future. Which makes both Samuel and me wonder if there really was a reason why they left so suddenly."

"You're worried about a gamma-ray burst?" she asked.

"Sure. That's why the Frogs left their planet in the first place. So, I imagine they're a bit skittish about them. I suspect GRBs and Supernovas are what all ETs are afraid of. The Cosmos doesn't give a shit about living things."

"Well, then again, think about your role in that. We're sitting right now in a deep-sea refuge. That's the public reason we're here, of course. And you know the other reason why we're here. Without our trip to Phobos and Mars, we wouldn't have that warning about a cosmic catastrophe, and we wouldn't have aliens helping us keep up with the Chinese. So, no matter what happens, the world is better off because of you. That's the definition of Ta'veren."

"You know Laura, I didn't ask for this pep talk."

"I know. But you know what I just thought of, at this very moment?"

Parker smiled, gently shaking his head. "I have no idea."

"You know what male lions do when they take over a pride of lionesses?"

Parker laughed. "There's probably a lot of sex involved."

"First order of business is to kill all the previous male's cubs. It's all about preserving the new male's genes, over those of the vanquished."

"That's pretty brutal."

"It's instinct. So, what did the Frogs accomplish by choosing you?"

"Well, for one thing, we kept them from being killed by an underwater nuclear war."

"But what are we doing right now, at this very moment?"

"Uh, surviving. What are you thinking?"

"In our hybrid children, we're enriching our gene pool with the genes of their hybrids. So, in effect, we're passing on Frog genes."

"Well, I guess, sort of. But why are you so interested in their fate?"

"Jason, it's my job. We need that sort of biological diversity and capability."

"Why?"

"Think about it. I work for the ONI. The Chinese are making a new aquatic species, as you well know. We have to compete just to maintain the status quo. It was no different when the Russians started a psychic spying program based on remote viewing. We had to respond and did so quite spectacularly. After all, you are one of those remote viewers."

"As is Joshua Nilsson. And the NSA's Hans Richter, I might add," said Parker.

"Exactly. Using the aliens is a win-win proposition. They help us survive, we help them survive. And although you claim ignorance, who else do you think would have thought to do that? You're the only person on Earth who has a good enough relationship with these mind-reading aquatic species to trust them to subcontract the gene-editing for us."

"Obviously, someone in D.C. did, since you told me to go meet these guys on their own turf, two-thousand feet down."

"Yes, but you planted the seed."

Parker thought about that for a minute. "I guess I did, didn't I," Parker admitted.

"So, like the Trolls and Frogs say, you are Ta'veren," she said, smiling.

"Oh please, Laura, cut out the crap," Parker said, also smiling.

One of the new additions to the DB1 crew was a female Navy Lieutenant Ph.D. psychologist trained in Navy diving. Her unique assignment on this mission was to dive with the female contributors of genetic material, biological mothers if you will, when they first met their laboratory-raised offspring in the child's natural habitat, seawater. The scientific question being posed was whether or not it was possible for a psychological bond to form between mother and child when the child is a hybrid.

That was a first-of-a-kind research study because nature decreed that the product of a union between different species is not viable. It will never survive. No matter how aggressively a confused dog might try to mate with a cat, a cat-dog hybrid could never result. However, through the tricks of laboratory genetics, that natural barrier had been repeatedly violated. What was not sure was whether the natural loving bond between parent and child would survive the genetic differences. If it did not, the long-term survival of the hybrid child might be in jeopardy.

During the human crew's three-month absence from DB1, an embryo containing the DNA of Laura Smith combined in a test tube with the DNA of a Guardian geneticist had rapidly grown to the size of a human newborn. It spent its days maturing in the nursery portion of the Wet Lab, touched only by the alien caretakers. That is, until the day when Laura and the research psychologist donned their diving gear and entered the wet nursery.

Laura was anxious, just as most new mothers are when asked to hold their firstborn. The fact that Laura had not carried this strange-looking child in her womb was of little concern to her. In fact, it seemed like a great convenience. Of more interest was whether she would know how to hold the child without hurting it.

As the Mermaid nursery attendant handed her offspring to her, Laura heard a voice in her head.

Do not worry. She is small but not delicate. The water supports her body.

The baby lay on Laura's arms, sleeping, gently breathing seawater into and out of her gilled lungs. Her facial expressions changed as if she was dreaming, twitching her mouth, then cracking a quick smile. Then she opened her eyes, stared at Laura's face for a moment, and started making squeaky crying noises. They were loud noises, even underwater.

Again, Laura heard a voice in her head, seemingly directed to her by the nursing attendant. *Hold her close.*

Instinctively Laura pulled the baby to her chest and gently embraced her. The crying stopped, and with a gentle swaying motion, Laura managed to lull the baby back to sleep.

As the baby lay in her arms, Laura experienced the sharp-edged conflict between tenderness and fear. The tenderness was from loving the creature that was part her and part water creature, and the fear was of forever losing the child to the water world. As much as Laura, an oceanographer, loved the water, she could never be a part of it.

Yet, there was a bitter-sweet irony that she had contributed to the world a creature who really could be a part of the ocean. Laura realized while holding that sleeping new creation, that perhaps that contribution was her most noble destiny.

The Navy psychologist noted that Laura Smith, new mother to a hybrid creature, sat smiling a satisfied smile, moving in a soothing motion calming to both child and mother.

The Lieutenant wrote in her scientific log, "Bonding between mother and child has begun."

CHAPTER 54. HELLFIRE

It was a miserably wet and cold November morning in Washington, D.C. when at 1 AM every secure phone in the White House and Pentagon rang at virtually the same instant. There had been a devastating radiation event of some sort in the south Pacific.

When POTUS took the call from the Secretary of Defense, he was told it might be an Electromagnetic Pulse from a nuclear weapon detonated high above the ocean. Every satellite gamma-ray detector on that side of the Earth was either out of commission or if far enough away, signaling a large gamma pulse commensurate with an aerial nuclear detonation.

As a result, the U.S. Military was on Defense Readiness Condition 1, meaning nuclear war was believed imminent.

Within twenty minutes, various wartime scenarios were being evaluated in the Presidential Emergency Operations Center. Knowing that both China and North Korea had boasted of the potential use of an EMP weapon against the United States, that was the first possibility to be examined.

The outer atmosphere above Tahiti seemed to be the epicenter of the blast, but militarily that made no sense at all. Tahiti was nowhere near the expected path of a ballistic missile fired from China, North Korea, or Russia.

Could it have been a practice EMP attack originating from any of those nations? That would undoubtedly be a reckless and self-destructive move, one that would more than likely result in a nuclear exchange of the highest order. World War III would be at hand.

Since no missiles had been detected either during boost phase or midcourse glide phase, it was quickly becoming a concern that the bomb had been satellite launched. Some satellites of uncertain purpose had been over the South Pacific at the time of the blast.

The known trajectory of one of them, a Chinese satellite, would have taken it over Washington D.C. and New York an hour or so later. It suddenly became possible that a planned EMP attack had been foiled by something as simple as a timing error. A blast planned for the East coast of the United States might have detonated prematurely.

Quite possibly, though, a backup attack satellite was already homing in on the U.S.

The call was made to send the Designated Survivor to his safe place, and to start wakening senior members of Congress and the military, and shuttling them to the Ravens Rock Complex in Pennsylvania.

The U.S. President was on the phone with the President of China when a video from the International Space Station came in from the NASA feed to the EOC. A huge burnt-orange cloud was covering the entire southern Pacific, extending all the way up to Hawaii and down to New Zealand. This was no ordinary nuclear explosion.

Coincidentally, General Morrison, the man who had briefed the SecDef on the Mars attack was in the Operations Center. He heard the President of China vehemently deny they had anything to do with the event, followed by a similar denial from Russia and the Supreme Leader of North Korea. Seeing the colossal cloud covering the South Pacific, he scribbled something on a note and handed it to SecDef.

SecDef studied the note for a moment and then spoke up as President Whitney was ending his communication.

"Mr. President, there is an alternative explanation for what happened."

Whitney stared at him for a moment, expressionless. Slowly he said, "Okay if you're going to tell me that we're not at war, I'd be quite happy to hear it."

SecDef paused for a moment, knowing his next words could be of historical significance. "Remember the gamma-ray burst incident on Mars?"

"Of course," Whitney said, his voice showing signs of stress.

"Based on the NASA feed, General Morrison and I are thinking this is a gamma-ray burst."

"Well, that's just great. So, you're saying we're not at war, but we're doomed anyway."

"Something like that, Mr. President."

Feeling a shudder deep inside Lechuguilla Cave, the Troll leader Argxtre woke just in time to hear four-million-year-old stalactites falling from the ceiling of the cave in non-housing areas. While the other Trolls remained asleep, he wandered the cave to inspect the damage caused by what he assumed was an earthquake. Using his skin lights to illuminate the calcite containing walls of the cave, he found relatively minor damage in the inhabited deeper portions of the cavern. As he climbed closer to the cave opening, the number of new rockfalls increased.

The civilian guard at the entrance to the cave was asleep when Argxtre grabbed a flashlight from those stored nearby. Apparently, the vibration and noise that had disturbed the Troll were not enough to rouse the man from his slumber.

Walking outside the cave entrance, Argxtre shone the bright light on the desert surroundings. Seeing nothing, he turned back to the cave. Whatever had happened, was not visible from the outside.

As he passed the still sleeping guard, his sensitive ears picked up the click-clack of many chitinous feet moving quickly towards him. He spun his body and the flashlight just in time to light up the carapace of a beetle as large as a small pony as it ran at breakneck speed into the cave.

Jason Parker got the call from Sea Base's Communication Center as he was in the middle of a dream about the Mermaid-type creatures, the so-called Guardians. He listened to the caller without saying a word, and then ended the call. Next, he called Laura.

"Sorry to wake you, Laura, but something happened."

"That's okay. I couldn't sleep. What's up?"

"A GRB just hit the South Pacific. Not knowing what it was, POTUS almost started World War Three."

"Oh my God, Jason."

Chapter 55. XFS Taiwan

The arrival of the *XFS Taiwan* back at Pavonis Mons after several days of cross solar system flight was smooth but inconsequential, which made Thera and the rest of the crew deliriously happy. Trusting a former Buddhist Monk to fly a spaceship was almost more than the *Taiwan*'s passengers could bear. But as they say, all's well that ends well.

Unfortunately, the scene greeting them on their arrival was not what was expected. Nothing was as it had been. The carefully stacked corpses were now strewn about, their spacesuits ripped open and the freeze-dried contents ravaged. Even the cages containing the radiation-killed Nutria were demolished, with no sign of the rodents remaining. It was as if everything organic had been devoured.

When Commander Meyers inspected the thick doors at the entrance to the base, they had deep claw marks in them, as did the hard basalt walls surrounding the opening. Once the doors were opened, however, everything inside was intact. The doors had been attacked but not breached.

The volunteer personnel leaving the *Taiwan* filed into the relative safety of the cave having cast a troubled eye on the claw marks as they passed by them. To them, a trip to Mars was suddenly far less appealing than they had anticipated.

Once Don Baxter and Larissa Slocum had the fusion reactor running, and power had been restored, the stored gas bottles were opened, flooding the habitable space in the cave with air. After air quality was checked, space suits were removed, and the base personnel gathered within the comms center as Commander Meyers activated it to send a status report back to Houston.

Anticipating a lengthy time delay for a response from Houston due to the vast distance between Earth and Mars, Meyers began a review for the newcomers of the Base's safety procedures.

As Meyers was nearing the end of his detailed briefing, he looked over at Baxter and pointed to his watch. Oddly, there had been no response back from Houston at the expected time.

After multiple tries, Meyers pulled the flight crew, Baxter, Slocum, and communication technicians aside to discuss troubleshooting ideas.

"No matter how bizarre your thoughts may be," Meyers said, "I want to hear them. Our instrumentation says the signal is going out with plenty of power."

The full bird Colonel William Morgan, or Sparky, offered, "Could be a stupid question, but are we positive the transmitting and receiving antennas are pointing to Earth?"

"Everything should be lined up according to our indications here," Meyers said.

"Maybe we should send someone outside to check them," Colonel Morgan said. "After all, we seem to have suffered some damage out there."

Very mindful of the external damage, Meyers hesitated.

"I'm not running the show here," Sparky insisted, "but I'll go. It will be the first useful thing I've done so far."

Although uninvited to the troubleshooting discussion, Joshua Nilsson had been listening from an inconspicuous position at the door to the comms center.

"That won't be necessary," Nilsson said softly, and then repeated more loudly until he got everyone's attention. "It won't be necessary to check the antennas. They're not there."

"The antennas?" Meyers asked.

"No, it's Houston. They're missing. Everyone."

There was total silence in the room.

Everyone on the mission had been briefed on the concept of Diaspora and had, in fact, realized that they could, in theory, be the last vestiges of humanity cast-off to another planet to ensure the survival of the human race. It would be a noble gesture.

But that was just an idea, an improbable idea at best. Ideas are always more heroic-sounding than is reality.

Commander Meyers was well-versed on the history and capabilities of each of his crew, and that included the CIA Remote Viewer Joshua Nilsson. The only reason Meyers assumed responsibility for a blind person on Mars was because Nilsson's mind-sight was much more of an asset than anyone's eyesight. But still, he questioned the psychic.

"Where are they, you ask?" Nilsson repeated. "I don't know. That's why I said they're missing. They could be in hiding."

"From what?"

"I'm not sure. Something happened on a big scale."

"How big?" Meyers asked.

"I don't know."

Later that day as Commander Meyers assembled the Mars Base staff, Larissa Slocum squeezed her way to the front. Meyers stood before them with a flat expression impossible for Slocum to read.

"I have some good news and some bad news. The good news is that last night the Deep Space Network station came online just long enough to tell us what's been happening back on Earth. The bad news is that the Southern Pacific was hit by a strong gamma-ray burst about the time we were arriving at Pavonis Base. The effects of that blast knocked out of commission both the 70-meter Goldstone antenna and the one in Canberra, Australia. The Madrid antenna had been taken down for maintenance before the GRB, and getting it up and operational took a minor miracle. But the Spanish crew kept at it until they could send us the news."

Meyers' words echoed throughout the volcanic cave, making them seem even more surreal to Larissa.

"To make matters worse, the GRB produced an incredible amount of nitrogen dioxide smog that has spread throughout the planet, wreaking havoc on those with a weakened respiratory system. Sunlight has been greatly weakened by the smog, and brutal winter conditions now exist in the northern hemisphere. With electrical grids knocked out of commission, people can't keep warm and are dying in large numbers. If you have family in the States, and I suspect all of you do, then this would be a good time for your thoughts and prayers. Frankly, from here, there is nothing we can do to help."

Oh my God, is there nothing we can do? Slocum wondered.

"However, as physicians say, tincture of time may be the ultimate cure. If the environment does not reach the tipping point, the atmosphere may eventually recover. But at this point, it's too early to tell. If it goes over the tipping point, there may be no reason for us to return to our former home. Certainly, for the foreseeable future, we should call Mars our home. Our standing orders are to remain in place, for the good of the country. Everything that can be done at home is being done. We have nothing here that can help our countrymen at this point."

Slocum could no longer resist the temptation to break in.

"Sir, are we likely to get additional updates from Madrid?"

"Well, apparently it's time for questions now. Unfortunately, Larissa, that may have been our only communication. Things are deteriorating in Spain, just like everywhere else."

Don Baxter, the senior civilian on Mars Base, and usually the most stoic, was visibly shaken, as were the rest of those gathered in that part of the cave.

Baxter spoke. "Sir, you mentioned good news. I'm not sure we've heard any good news."

"The only good news is that we now know what's going on, and we got out just in time. We owe it to those who had the wisdom to send us back to Mars, to make a go of it here as best we can."

A Lieutenant Research Physiologist who volunteered for a second deployment to Mars spoke next.

"Sir, being part of the last crew, I know we did a lot of genetic work with rodents. Apparently, none of them survived, so do we have a continuing genetics research mission, now that we're back?"

"Thank you, Dodson, for your willingness to come back. Your experience will be vital to our resumption of operations. But to answer your question, the short answer is no. That work is being continued by an underwater base and laboratory off the coast of Florida. It's called Deep Base 1. If you're interested, our Engineering Duty Officer, Larissa Slocum, can fill you in on details of that operation, as can our Chief Engineer, Don Baxter. They both recently left that base to come on this mission."

"Can we go back for a visit the next time Mars is close to Earth?" Lieutenant Dodson asked.

"We'll cross that bridge when we get to it. We have about a year to think about it. In the meantime, we should assume we are the only surviving remnants of the human race. In other words, be mentally, physically, and emotionally prepared for the worse. And I might add, take excellent care of our Buddhist Monk here. Thera's our pilot, and our only way home."

One of the enlisted corpsmen raised his hand. "Sir, there's one thing I've been thinking about a lot lately. Since we may be the only human survivors, can we have a relaxation of the military non-fraternization policy?"

One of the enlisted members shouted out, "Horn Dog."

Meyers smiled. "That policy has always been needed to maintain good order and discipline between the officers and enlisted. But in the current circumstances, let me use a Latin medical term. *Ad libitum.* With you being a corpsman, you know what that means."

Looking around the room, Meyers saw no more hands raised.

"Are there any saved rounds?"

"Just one, Sir. What do we do about the creatures that were trying to get in here?"

"Assume you're in a combat zone. Be ever vigilant, and get some practice at the shooting range. Chief Petty Officer Lawson is our Small Arms Marksmanship Instructor, as well as the Crew Served Weapons Instructor. If you want training on the 20 mm Gatling gun perched overhead, he can give that as well. Whatever your weapon of choice, make sure your qualifications are current. Treat this just like any other deployment to hostile territory."

"Sounds like fun," someone said with a hint of sarcasm.

"With no more questions, carry-on smartly Shipmates."

"Attention on deck!" someone yelled from the back of the group.

"As you were," Meyers responded.

As you were, Larissa Slocum thought as she headed back to the engineering spaces. *We will never be as we were, ever again.*

Chapter 56. Aftermath

Barometers around the world began inexorably inching downward, eventually pegging off scale. The "stormy" weather they forecast was an understatement. A large portion of the atmosphere facing the GRB impact was lost, causing massive decreases in atmospheric pressure. The unimpacted atmosphere on the side opposite to the impact tried frantically to equalize pressure, producing horrendous winds as air flowed from high pressure to low.

Ultimately, the Earth's normal atmospheric pressure dropped far below that of the strongest hurricane, causing both hurricane-force winds and a killing decrease in the availability of oxygen.

The GRB caused the Chinese to abandon their underwater habitat and leave their remaining Water Children to their own devices. Beijing was distracted, dealing with two million GRB-induced fatalities from hypoxia in high altitude cities like Xining, not far from where Samuel Putnam began his high-altitude flight down the origin of the Yangtze River.

Those losses were minor compared to the eighteen million lost due to hypoxia in Mexico, fourteen percent of the population of the entire country. The most significant loss of life was in Mexico City, the capital.

The highest percentage human cost in South America was in Columbia, where 22% of the population, over ten million lives, were lost.

The loss of 150,000 people in Santa Fe, New Mexico was a massive crisis for the U.S. Unfortunately, body recovery had to be abandoned after the risk to first-responders proved too high as they repeatedly ran low on bottled oxygen during the search and recovery effort. Due to the risk of contagion spread by body decomposition, the CDC placed the entire city and its surroundings under quarantine. The National Guard was called upon to set up a perimeter around the town to deter looters who did little more than add a Karmic increase in the body count.

Sadly, there were numerous other small cities in the Western United States where the dead lay where they fell. There was too few recovery personnel with portable oxygen units to remove them. Nature was allowed to take its course.

To many religious people steeped in the prophecy of the end days, the appearance of corpses strewn asunder seemed to be the scene expected during the *rapture*. The Godly were gone, seemingly in keeping with Biblical scripture.

> "For the Lord Himself will descend from heaven with a shout, with the voice of an archangel, and with the trumpet of God. And the dead in Christ will rise first. Then we who are alive and remain shall be caught up together with them in the clouds to meet the Lord in the air." *1 Thessalonians 4:16-17.*

The ghastly scenes made grist for Sunday sermons, as long as you didn't look too closely at the facts. The facts were that quite a few ungodly folks died along with the saints. Hypoxia is no respecter of persons.

In keeping with what Argxtre had told Jason Parker, the Trolls in Lechuguilla Cave were fine. Even though the land near Carlsbad, New Mexico was at four thousand feet or so before the loss of planetary atmosphere, and was now at a post-event 12,000-foot equivalent altitude, the Troll population was well-adapted to that environment. Daily, their metabolism was shifting over to become ever more tolerant of the hypoxia that was putting all human life at risk.

When U.S. Marshals came to confiscate the oxygen-concentrators the Trolls had amassed before the GRB, the Trolls put up some resistance. Before too much blood was shed, Argxtre relented. The oxygen concentrators were needed more desperately in over a hundred other U.S. cities in Colorado, Nevada, Arizona, and New Mexico.

Things became very interesting, however, when during the search for hidden oxygenators, one of the Marshals found a guarded tunnel.

Turning to Argxtre, the Marshal asked, "What's this?"

"This is a sacred area. It is our burial ground."

"And it's guarded, why?"

"Like I said, it's sacred to us. You humans are not allowed."

Mindful of the FBI's lingering suspicions about the death of the Harvard graduate student Oscar McKetchen, the Marshal pressed Argxtre further.

"Actually, the State Department requires us to notify them of any deaths of your people on or off government property."

Like the other Trolls, Argxtre had enough awareness of the near future to realize that further deception would not end well for them.

The Marshal narrowed his eyes and tightened his lips. "Just because we can't read your minds, it doesn't mean we're stupid. What are you hiding?"

"It's not us."

"What then, a human?"

"No."

Growing impatient, the Marshal yelled, "What the hell is it, then?"

Slumping his shoulders in resignation, Argxtre waved the guard aside and beckoned to the Marshal, "Follow me. I will show you."

Out of habit, the Marshal radioed for backup before following the Troll deeper into the twisted confines of the sacred portion of the cave. His radio returned nothing but static.

Keeping a wary eye on both Argxtre and the closing-in ceiling and walls of the tunnel, the Marshal rested his right hand on his holstered pistol as they trekked 100 feet or so on the sandy cave floor.

As the tunnel closed in narrower and narrower, the Marshal noticed a pungent smell that irritated his nostrils. It was not the usual smell of death that he was accustomed to. It was different.

At a solid wall marking the end of the tunnel, Argxtre stopped at an area covered in a light dusting of sand. Protruding from that sand were what seemed to be dismembered appendages of something large and hard.

The Marshal's mouth gaped open in shock. "What am I looking at?"

"Bug. Big bug."

"A cave bug?"

"No. A space bug. We buried the rest of them in their ship, outside."

With widened eyes, the Marshal stared at the insect's limbs. "How big are we talking?"

"Big."

"You killed it?"

"It put up a good fight," Argxtre said.

The Marshal took a deep breath in. "Holy shit."

The chaos that ensued in Mexico after the human destruction of their capital was threatening to tear the country apart. At the request of the surviving Mexican Vice President who had been engaged in trade talks in Washington at the time of the Event, President Whitney sent the U.S. Army to restore order and prevent the large-scale encroachment of China and Russia into Mexico. From SecDef and Whitney's perspective, the talk of "humanitarian assistance" by those Communist countries was a poorly disguised attempt to gain a foothold on the U.S. Southern border.

Once joint U.S. and Mexican Army units were in place to stabilize Mexico, the Mexican Vice President, the only survivor of his government, returned to Cancun, an oxygen-safe sea-level city, to establish a new government.

Nuclear ballistic missile submarines of the U.S. Navy maintained a hair-trigger status, just in case one nation or another tried to take advantage of the precarious worldwide situation. Hypersonic land-based missile batteries were also on alert status, as were satellite-based weapons. The Earth had suffered enough without some aggressor losing their mind and making matters worse.

Reminiscent of manufacturers switching product lines in World War II to aid the war effort, medical supply manufacturers were pressed into service to turn out vast numbers of oxygen concentrators to meet the need of people having respiratory difficulty as the result of the low sea level oxygen concentration. Those concentrators made available weeks after the event were most useful to those with acquired infections such as pneumonia. Those with respiratory weakness due to the nitrogen dioxide smog occurring immediately post-event had died quickly. As usually happens, the youngest and the oldest populations were the most vulnerable.

Upon the reports of both General Jim Morrison and the Director of National Intelligence, President Whitney summarily fired his Science Adviser, Commander Patricia Werner. He filled her vacated position with the synesthete Cosmologist, Dr. Peter Green. Of all of President Whitney's potential replacement Science Advisers, Green was the only one who had given both a warning and an explanation for the gamma-ray burst that had wrecked so much havoc on the world.

For Green, Werner's firing was sweet revenge that could only be bested if there was a special place in hell for those of her ilk. Lacking eternal damnation, being replaced by the one person she had publicly humiliated during Morrison's meeting at Area 51, was a suitable judgment. It was cosmic justice.

Within a few days of the GRB event, Peter Green had been summoned to the President's hiding place. He and his staff were considering a move back into the White House, but first Whitney wanted a better understanding of both the Event and the likely sequelae. To gain that understanding, POTUS was tapping into the mind of his new Science Adviser, Peter Green.

"Peter, after your early warnings, I was briefed on what might happen after a GRB. None of it was good news, but at least I expected the nitrogen dioxide smog and the damage to the ozone layer. And I know you warned your friend Jason Parker and the ODNI's gal, Dr. Laura Smith, about the potential loss of atmosphere. So, can you explain that to me?"

"Sure. It's how we think Mars lost its atmosphere. Both the solar wind and a gamma-ray burst ejects not only high energy radiation but also high energy cosmic particles. It had always been questioned whether so-called cosmic ray neutrons, and electrons, accompany a GRB, but my best guess is this time they did. But even without that, there's something called electromagnetic radiation pressure. Due to wave-particle duality, high energy light has momentum, and can transfer that momentum to air molecules."

"I did not know that," Whitney said.

"When high energy radiation and cosmic rays hit air molecules, it's like a pool stick breaking racked billiard balls. After a collision with an energetic ray, the molecules go every which way, which means they can actually escape the atmosphere. It's believed that the Martian atmosphere used to be much thicker than it is now. But over eons of time, the solar wind blew those molecules out into space."

Whitney frowned. "But the Earth is even closer to the Sun, isn't it?"

"It is. The only reason Earth does not look like Mars right now is that we have a strong magnetic field which normally protects us. Mars does not. We believe Mars used to, billions of years ago, which meant life could have once flourished, but once the planet's liquid iron core solidified, the dynamo producing the magnetic field stopped. Mars now has no magnetic field to protect it. We still do, and hopefully always will."

"Then what happened to our atmosphere after the GRB?" Whitney asked.

"In this case, its protection was not perfect. The magnetic shield was breached in places by the onslaught of the powerful radiation pressure. For about two centuries now, our planet's magnetic field has been weakening. Over the past few decades, the strength of the magnetosphere has been weakening by 5% per decade. And on top of that, we have something called a South Atlantic Anomaly. The magnetic field is particularly weak there."

"How large is that anomaly?"

"It reaches all the way across South America and across the Atlantic to the West Coast of Africa. It's huge. So now, if you combine a GRB with a weakening magnetic field across the planet, and with an especially weak field across South America and the South Atlantic, then you have a lot of radiation energy getting through the magnetosphere to knock nitrogen and oxygen molecules out into space."

"Yikes. Is that lost air gone forever?"

"We don't know. Hopefully, our gravitational field will eventually pull some of it back."

"I guess plants can make more oxygen," Whitney said.

"That's what we need, but that will take a very long time. And at the rate we're deforesting the planet, it won't happen until we humans are gone."

"Do you have any good news, Peter?"

"The good news is that most of us are still alive, for now."

Whitney raised his eyebrows. "That is true, Peter. Thank God for little favors."

Whitney leaned back in his chair, seemingly studying his new Science Advisor.

"Is there something else, Mr. President?"

"First of all, Peter, at this level, we use first names. Call me Harmon, and I'll call you Peter. Got that?"

"Yes sir."

Whitney laughed. "I'm sure it will take a while for you to get used to, but while you're acclimating, I have something else for you to chew on. Does the name Clarice Williams ring a bell?"

"She's one of the aquanauts on Deep Base One, isn't she?"

"She is. Do you know about her Space Corp experience?"

"I've heard rumors she might have gone space crazy after her husband was killed on Mars."

"I'm surprised you've heard that much," the President said. "But actually, he died on Phobos. But she's not crazy. She was right."

"About what Sir?"

"We still have to get you fully read in, but I can tell you this. She witnessed some ETs on Phobos, and those same ETs were apparently blown out of the sky by our GRB. They crashed, and their remains have now been discovered. I want you to book a flight to Carlsbad, New Mexico ASAP. I need a direct link to what's going on. I need to know if this ET matter is over, or just beginning. Your clearance will catch up with you on the flight over."

As Green left the room, Whitney thought, *I think Green might be the next Jason Parker.* He's y*oung, energetic, a free thinker, expanded awareness, not beholden to anyone.*

I need to get Harry Kincaide to train Green up on remote viewing.

Speaking on the intercom to his assistant, Whitney said, "Martha, get Harry Kincaide on secure comms."

Chapter 57. Plateau Chateau

Hearing the news about the GRB and the growing devastation on the surface, Jason Parker had to get away to the only place of solitude available to him.

Parker donned his multilayered thermal suits and diving gear, including his D.E.M. rebreather, and stepped out into the cold, inky blackness of the Blake Plateau. He moved deliberately, finning slowly to clear the outer edge of the hangar, then finning vigorously over the seafloor, getting some distance between him and the bright lights of DB1.

Where Parker stopped was only dimly lit, just enough for him to see his surroundings without turning on his helmet lights. He once again stood on the seabed, looking away from the base and waiting for his eyes to adapt to the darkness in front of him. As he did, he began to discern his faint shadow spread out before him.

When his eyes had become sufficiently dark adapted, he saw there were two shadows, one dimmer than his own. It was close behind him. Instinctively he turned around, and when he did, he saw silhouetted against the lights the outline of a Guardian.

Is that you? Parker thought. He didn't even try to pronounce the Guardian's unpronounceable name.

It is.

The Guardian moved beside and slightly in front of Parker so they could make eye contact without either of them facing the glare of the seabed lights.

Did you know? Parker continued to ask telepathically.

We did. It is written.

Where?

On the scrolls you were given.

Well, that didn't do us any good, now did it?

You did exactly what was needed. There is nothing more you could do.

So, what happens now?

Wait. Your atmosphere is severely damaged, but parts of it will heal.

Like what?

The smog will dissolve into acid rain and begin clearing the skies, allowing the sun to warm the Earth again.

What else?

A quarter of the nitrogen is gone.

A quarter?

Yes. Blown out into space.

Parker did a quick estimation. Eighteen thousand feet is half an atmosphere, and the 8000-foot cabin altitude in airliners is seventy-five percent of an atmosphere. So that must mean the atmospheric pressure now remaining was roughly eight thousand feet.

Holy cow!

I do not understand, was the thought coming from the alien.

That means healthy people living at sea level should have plenty enough oxygen to live. But folks in Denver may be in trouble. And anyone with respiratory disease may be dead or dying.

It could be worse. Earth was lucky, the Guardian relayed.

How long will the atmosphere take to heal?

That depends. The ozone layer is depleted, and it will take a while for that ozone to replenish itself. So in the meanwhile, ultraviolet radiation will be an extreme danger. The depleted nitrogen is more problematic. We know of no way to make more nitrogen. The nitrogen you had was blown off into space, but Earth's gravity may eventually bring it back. Until that happens, hypoxia will remain a problem for your people.

Well, you're just full of cheerful news, Parker noted.

And yet full-scale nuclear war for military reasons was always an option for you Sapiens. That would be much worse.

Sapiens? What is that? Parker asked.

You call yourselves Homo sapiens sapiens. We just call you Sapiens. But the most important thing you can do now is what you are doing. Sapiens need to be prepared for the possibility that the oxygen level you are used to will no longer be available. Those with genetic changes will do much better in the long run.

Like our Tibetans?

Yes, some of you Sapiens already have that mutation.

I wish you luck in creating those changes, Parker said in all sincerity.

The best way to protect yourselves from ultraviolet and other radiation is by remaining underwater. That's why we are making hybrids between Sapiens and Aquaticants.

Aquaticants?

"Us."

So, the best we can do, Parker said mentally, *based upon the future that you already know, is to make versions of us air breathers, with a hypoxia gene, and to give others of us gills like you. Aquaticants did you say?*

Since it confused you when the Masters called all of their creations Human, I have decided to give us another name. Call us Aquaticants.

And with a flick of his tail, the Aquaticant disappeared into the darkness.

Parker wasn't ready for him to leave, and as an afterthought, he called out in his mind, *Do you have an easy name? One I can pronounce?*

Call me David.

Everything had changed. Parker had no choice except to believe what David the Aquaticant told him. After all, all creatures sired by the Frogs used telepathic communication amongst themselves, and thus lying or exaggeration was not even a concept they understood. Their thoughts were fully transparent.

After returning to Deep Base and locking in through the hangar, Parker assembled the DB1 leadership to let them know what he had decided.

With the changing of the guard on the second Deep Base mission, those leaders were primarily Laura Smith, Dr. Captain Emery Reed, Kelly Brightman, J.R. and Tom, and the former Marine Diver Luke Warmwater from the Tzu Washtaki Clan.

First, he described the meeting he had outside with the Aquaticant who allowed the linguistically-challenged Sapiens to call him "David."

"As I thought about what David was saying, I realized our team on Mars, including Larissa Slocum and Don Baxter, have no idea what's going on down here. I assume they have no communication since a GRB would destroy the satellite and control network.

"Laura, you and I were one of the forces behind the return to Mars Base. Therefore, I feel a heavy responsibility to check on them and relay the news. They might be planning a return to Earth anytime, not knowing that the entire atmosphere has changed."

"How do you plan to do that?" Warmwater asked.

"If I were to take off now, the internal pressure of *Dioscuri* would be at two-thousand feet, and I'd have no way to exit the craft on Mars. But we have no reason to remain at this pressure except for access to the Aquaticants and the hybrid nursery. If we wanted to separate from them, pressure wise, we could split the complex, and start decompressing the part not attached."

"But Jason," Laura said, "I have a child in the nursery, so I'm not sure I want to leave her."

"Everyone here should make a choice. Stay at two-thousand, or approach the surface pressure. Regardless, we're still protected from topside events by two-thousand feet of water. If we're at surface pressure like a submarine, it just means we can exit directly to the surface once locked into the transfer vessel."

"Which would be what?" Tom asked.

"*Dioscuri* would be my number one choice, as long as it's down here," Parker said. "Plus, on the way back from Mars, we can stop and check out the conditions on the surface before returning here. However, David the Aquaticant did not seem at all optimistic about a quick recovery of the atmosphere."

"But once you leave for Mars, we'll have no way to get out," Brightman noted.

"That's true. You'll have to wait for our return."

"What could possibly go wrong with that plan," J.R. said wryly.

"But mind you," Parker said, "we might be bringing some Martian crew back with us. That's another reason we need to split the complex and bring part of it up to surface pressure so we can lock back in on our return."

"But we need to remember, once you decide to either stay at two-thousand feet or decompress to the surface, you're committed. We can fly to Mars faster than we can compress and decompress right here. So for those with mutant children, you need to decide where your affection lies."

"There's affection," Laura said, "and then there's a duty. I think my duty will be to maintain some adult leadership down here. And considering my job assignment, it makes sense for me to stay with the aliens or Aquaticants, or whatever they call themselves now."

"Remember, they call themselves *humans*, but made up a different name so we wouldn't get confused. I think they see us as being rather simple-minded."

"That's a fair assessment," Brightman offered.

Dioscuri always had an assortment of space suits in storage, with oxygen and carbon dioxide absorbent supplies just in case the ship went to high altitude. Certainly, going to Mars was as high altitude as you can get. However, the stores of suits and expendables limited the number that could travel with Parker.

After Parker's plan was announced to the assembled DB1 crew, only five wanted to accompany him to Mars, namely Tom, Kelly Brightman, Luke Warmwater, and two Special Forces operators, one female and one male. Those two, Theresa and Paul, had quickly bonded, and Theresa wanted to have one last hurrah before her pregnancy slowed her down too much. Those two were also the only DB1 crew authorized to handle blue-green laser weapons. Those weapons were equally effective underwater and on land. Of course, their primary use underwater was in incapacitating food fish. On land, well, who knew where they might be useful.

The DB1 complex was split, with the hangar and two-thirds of the base sealed and beginning slow decompression, and the remainder of the base staying at the pressure of the seafloor. Those at the bottom pressure could enter the genetics laboratory or the nursery, or enter the water surrounding Deep Base. But they could not enter the rest of the base due to the difference in pressure.

To decompress the habitat required a carefully coordinated operation of double-sealed "lockout" cylinders. Habitat gas would be sealed off by a bottom hatch, and then a top hatched would open, flooding the volume and sending the entrapped gas up to the surface. Once the top hatch was sealed, water would then be pumped out of the space, and fresh gas would enter from the habitat. In essence, the system was a vacuum pump, sucking the internal pressure closer and closer to surface pressure.

During the weeks of decompression required for the low-pressure side to approach the Earth's surface pressure, Parker made sure his combat crew was ready for any eventuality. Emery Reed also had to recompute the decompression profile since surface pressure had supposedly changed. What had previously been one atmosphere was now just three-quarters of an atmosphere, according to David the Aquaticant. When reaching mean sea level pressure, it would now be as if they were "flying after diving," which meant the risk of getting decompression sickness would be higher than usual.

The solution was to slow decompression even more.

Parker also practiced remote viewing since that was how he would steer *Dioscuri* to Mars. What he saw on Earth did not make him happy. The closest city, Jacksonville, looked dark and cold, at midday, in Florida. Snow appeared to be on the ground. A city customarily inundated with traffic was silent. Nothing seemed to be moving.

He then viewed his home in Panama City in the Florida Panhandle, on the Gulf Coast. There was no snow, but also no signs of life, just like Jacksonville. His home was intact, but there was no sign of his wife, Sandy. Her car was gone. If he had the extreme remote viewing skills of Joshua Nilsson, he would be able to locate her, but he didn't. There was nothing he could do except assume, for his sanity, that she and the children were alright. They had settled on plans of action for all eventualities during his absence, except for nuclear war. Unfortunately, the GRB event was very close to such a catastrophic event.

Mars, on the other hand, appeared as it always did. Cold and clear.

It was finally time to leave DB1. Parker had no choice except to fly without Laura, his experienced copilot. The others on board were merely passengers, with none of them having flown in a spaceship, much less an alien spaceship.

There was also another first for Parker. He had never flown from deep water out into space, and he also was lacking his support network that he'd depended on to come up with the ideal launch window. All he could do was use data downloaded before the GRB, and pray that the estimate of the space station and satellite location was accurate enough for launch. There had been no database updates since the GRB.

The potential passengers had already been briefed on that complication, which probably had a lot to do with the small number of people volunteering to ride with Parker to Mars. Those who did want to go were risk-takers, like Parker. He just hoped he wouldn't be responsible for killing them all.

Parker's old diving buddy, the cave diver Kelly Brightman who helped him discover the Trolls, volunteered to ride shotgun. With help from what he had learned from Thera the Monk, Parker gently coaxed *Dioscuri* into obedience. The ship backed out of the hangar and then bounded vertically towards the surface far above. The light coming from the now cleared cockpit windows went from the deepest black imaginable to a rapidly growing haze as they approached the surface two thousand feet above. Soft gray flooded around them as they entered the clouded atmosphere, but within seconds they broke out into almost blinding sunlight, a sight they had not seen for months.

Parker had purposefully launched at a time when his software said the moon should not be an obstacle, but for reasons of its own, *Dioscuri* headed towards the moon. This time, however, they passed by the moon at a safe distance, and then made the sharp left turn to once again head outside of the ecliptic.

You wouldn't think trained military personnel would giggle like kids, but with the continually changing G-forces, someone in the back was squealing. The others were just slightly more restrained.

Once the ship's velocity stabilized at its cruising speed, and all on board became weightless, there was a constant stream of men, and the one woman, floating forward to be dazzled by the view of the Sun and its solar system.

Two days after its departure, *Dioscuri* began its deceleration phase. Only the most adventuresome astronauts made their way forward against the relentless negative Gs to see the approach of Mars.

The enchanting trip was nearing completion all too soon for everyone except the one space-sick Special Forces Operator. He endured non-stop ribbing from his female counterpart, so as they neared the Martian atmosphere, he was relieved to soon be on solid ground again.

Parker was not so pleased. The Martian atmosphere near Pavonis Mons looked disturbed and cloudy. As they approached the equatorial region of Mars near the extinct volcano, he could clearly define the edge of the sand storm. Unfortunately, their target seemed to be in the middle of the worst part of the storm. Keeping his mental focus while landing on a target he could not see, even close up, would be yet another challenge for Jason Parker. As a result, he had asked Luke Warmwater to join him in the cockpit. For some reason, it seemed to

Parker that Luke's ability to see what the rest could not see, like ghosts, might have some benefit here. He knew that was an irrational thought, but it couldn't hurt to have his company and his sharp Recon eyes.

As the ship began its entry through the atmosphere, and then final vertical descent through the storm, Warmwater looked over at Parker with a worried look on his face and said, "How are you landing this?"

"I'm not," Parker said.

"Oh. Shit."

"*Dioscuri* has landed. Welcome to Mars," Parker announced to his passengers.

Warmwater panted, "I've done scary shit, man, but that was wild. My hands are shaking."

"Put them to good use then. It's time to get suited up," Parker said.

Chapter 58. Return to Mars

Safe inside the cave complex, Parker reached out to shake Commander Chris Meyers' hand.

"I had a hunch you might need more firepower," Parker said, "so I brought some warriors. Some are youngsters full of piss and vinegar, and some are old farts still handy with a weapon. So how are things here?" Parker asked.

"A lot better than back home, from what I hear," Meyers said.

It was a great homecoming as Parker and his DB1 crew met the Mars Base crew. Warmwater, Brightman and the two Special Forces operators broke off for a tour of the underground base, while Parker met with Larissa Slocum, Donald Baxter, and Joshua Nilsson. Thera, the Buddhist Monk, joined them.

"Well, Larissa, are you enjoying keeping the fusion reactor running?"

"I could not be happier!" she exclaimed. "This is what I was born for."

"I knew Don would treat you well. And I'm sure he's glad to have the company."

"As much as I appreciated being on Deep Base, Jason, I did miss the sunlight," Larissa said.

Baxter patted Larissa on the back. "My job would be three times harder if I didn't have this over-achiever helping out. Thank you, Jason, for getting her on the crew list."

"Always glad to put in a good word. Now Thera, how's the universe's only Buddhist spaceship driver liking it here?"

"I'm just glad I didn't kill everyone getting them here. And I might add, landing in a sand storm like you did would have been out of my league."

"Don't underestimate yourself, Thera. The Frogs made a damn good spacecraft, but I've often relied on what you taught me about focusing. I don't need any magic incantations anymore."

"Focusing is good. Meditation is better. And I've had plenty of time to meditate since I've been here."

"As far as monasteries go," Parker noted, "this one's the most unique."

"That's true. I'm in no hurry to leave."

Meyers smiled. "And we don't intend to let you go anytime soon, Thera. You're our ticket out of here."

Turning toward Nilsson, Parker asked, "How's the best remote viewer in the world doing?"

"Maybe *in the solar system* would be more accurate," Nilsson wryly suggested.

"Right you are."

"Are you up to speed on the situation on Earth?" Nilsson asked.

"I only know what a Mermaid told me."

Nilsson scrunched up his face. "A what?"

"One of the Frog's aquatic progeny. Anyway, what do you know?"

"It's like a nuclear winter. It's dark and cold. The old and sick are dying all over the planet, especially at higher altitudes."

"You have any good news?" Parker asked.

"Yes. I check in on Baltazar and his Troll clan at least once a day. They're doing just fine."

"Nilsson's the best source of information I have," Commander Meyers said proudly.

"I hate to ask," Parker added. "But any chance you know where my wife is?"

"Sandy?"

"Yes. I tried remote viewing her, but she's not at home," Parker said, "and I don't have your personnel locating skills."

"That's why amateurs like you should leave it to the pro, me."

"Is she OK?"

"She's more than OK. Being the good Doctor Parker's wife, she was flown to a secure facility in Savannah, Georgia. She's just fine, and being well taken care of."

Parker let out a sigh. "That's great to know. What about the others here?"

"You win some, you lose some. Considering this was a GRB, we are lucky anyone survived. If anyone else in your crew is curious, send them my way," Nilsson volunteered. "I'll do what I can."

"You're the best Joshua."

Nilsson laughed again. "Actually, that's a little bit true," he said.

The sandstorm was beginning to let up enough for the Mars Base crew to start hauling in the supplies that had been stowed aboard *Dioscuri*.

Climbing up the ladder was not particularly easy, but getting down off the ladder while carrying a load was the hardest part of the trip.

With cargo unloaded, and after breaking bread together with the rest of the Mars Base crew, Parker took his crew members aside. "Now that you're here do any of you want to stay?"

Warmwater answered first, without hesitation. "I think my people would be proud if they knew a member of the Tzu Washtaki clan of the Osage Tribe was the first Native American on Mars. I think I have to stay."

Parker smiled at Warmwater and patted him on the back. "Somehow, that does not surprise me at all."

"And besides, I'm still a pretty damn good shot," Warmwater added. "They just might need the services of a Recon Marine one of these days."

"Once a Marine, always a Marine," Parker responded. "I'll let Meyers know."

Looking around his small group, Parker asked, "Anyone else?"

Rina, the newly pregnant Spec Ops soldier, looked up at her boyfriend and said, "We've been thinking how awesome it would be to give birth to the first true Martian. So, we'd like to stay too."

"I don't know if you'll be first or not, but that sounds like an awesome goal to me. In fact, I think that's the whole idea behind Diaspora."

"Kelly, are you going back with me, or staying?" Parker asked, looking squarely at his old diving buddy and co-discoverer of the Trolls.

"I'm giving it some thought," Brightman answered. "I'll let you know before you shove off."

Later, Parker spoke to Meyers when Meyers had a free moment. "We have three folks wanting to stay. Do you have a problem with that?"

"I only have a problem if you're trying to get rid of them."

"Believe me, I'm not. They're part of my A-team. But I really think they'll be a military asset for you."

"That I could use," Meyers said.

"There's only one thing," Parker added. "One of them is pregnant."

"I don't see that being a problem. We have good medical care here, and we can certainly feed another mouth or two. And unless some of my crew is keeping secrets from me, this will be our first pregnancy. If she goes full term, she'll make history."

"Now, while we're at it, Commander, is there someone you're trying to get rid of?"

Meyers thought about that for a moment before answering. "Honestly, no. Everyone seems content here, especially since Earth is having problems. Their collective Type A personalities cause me problems sometimes, but I can manage it. Everyone is pulling their fair share, and more. But I must admit, I wish Clarice Williams had come with you."

"She's done with space, Chris. After what she experienced on Phobos, she never wants to leave home again, no matter how badly it's screwed up."

"I understand. I just miss her experience. Speaking of experience, how's Laura Smith doing?"

"She's two thousand feet down, doing her Alien Intelligence work, trying to understand our latest alien discovery. And on top of that, she is nurturing one of the world's first human-Mermaid hybrids. Those babies have gills, and they are fast-growing. She simply doesn't have time for any more space adventures."

"Roger that," the Commander said.

Looking back at their nuclear fusion expert, Parker asked, "How about Larissa?"

Meyers smiled. "I thank God for Larissa every day. You did us a great service getting her on board."

From the way the Commander was smiling, Parker wondered if there was anything romantic going on between those two.

Parker also wondered if that was the way he smiled when he talked about Laura.

The Navy's core values are Honor, Courage, and Commitment. It was that last value, *Commitment,* that swayed Brightman's decision to return to Earth to resume his functions at the DIA.

Commander Meyers pointed out that darkness was fast approaching, and maybe Parker and Brightman should bed down for the night, and head back to Earth in the morning. They would have to sleep in bunk beds, but at least those beds were comfortable.

"I've got the top bunk," Parker said, knowing the hulking Brightman would prefer the bottom bunk anyway.

As they lay in their bunks, nestling their heads in their pillows, trying to fall asleep, Brightman called out to Parker. "I can't believe I'm on Mars, Jason. This is freaking amazing."

"That it is, my friend."

"Do we have to go straight back?" Brightman asked. "I'd love to see more of Mars."

"Actually, I'm going to try a little sightseeing tomorrow. There are some things out there we just have to see. No telling when we'll be back."

"As long as you don't kill us in the process, Jason. No low-level buzzing, please."

"Ah, shucks, Kelly, you're no fun at all."

"Goodnight, Jason."

"Sleep tight," Parker said drowsily.

As he closed his eyes in repose, Parker reminisced how nice it was when he was the only human wearing the Frog's world history vial around his neck.

I wonder what it says? He thought. *Wonder if it says Jason Parker flew to Mars, twice. That is so awesome. I can't believe I'm here.*

Of course, I'll be long dead before we can decode the entire message. Laura's convinced of that. We just lucked out with the little snippet of apocalypse code we could translate. The rest is really complicated.

I feel like they wanted us to find the spaceships. Hell, the Taiwan jumped up and said, "Here I am."

I think the Frogs deserve more credit than they're getting. The Frogs couldn't protect us from the GRB, but they left us gifts. This ship, the Taiwan ship, the Russian ship.

Guess we should tell the Russians the secret to making their bird fly. Yeah—maybe someday.

Bet they're really pissed.

Parker laughed softly, amused by the trick the former President had pulled on the Russians.

Kidnap Laura and me? We'll get you for that, you Russkies.

And those crazy-smart merfolk genetic engineers? They may be the greatest gift of all.

Why have the Frogs been so nice to us?

Thank God we didn't nuke them.

CHAPTER 59. TOURING

The next morning, having said farewell to their friends, Parker and Brightman were ready to depart in the now dusty *Dioscuri.* Seated in the cockpit, Parker turned toward his longtime friend and said,

"Like I said last night, I'm going to try something different, a little sightseeing. Are you ready?"

"Ready as I'll ever be."

After sitting there for a moment, Parker said, "Have patience. This may not work."

Then after another few seconds, the craft levitated off the Martian ground beneath them and started moving slowly at first around the volcano called Pavonis Mons.

Unlike its usual departure path, it stayed relatively low, only slowly gaining altitude as it headed almost due west of their position.

Before them in the distance lay the highest volcano in the solar system, Olympus Mons. As Parker set his attention on that mountain, the ship accelerated, pinning the two men in their seats. In a few minutes, the acceleration had decreased, and they were effortlessly cruising in a wide circular pattern, just below the top of that hugely high mountain, three times the height of Mount Everest.

Dioscuri was now exquisitely sensitive to Parker's thoughts. Having flown a complete circle around Olympus, Volcano of the Gods, the craft headed back east, toward the three volcanic mounds arranged linearly in their view. Playfully now, becoming confident in his mental control of the craft, Parker said, "You say you want to do some buzzing?"

"No. I said no!"

"Okay, here we go," Parker laughed, ignoring his friend's objection.

Parker swung around to approach the triple mountains from the south. From the G-forces in the turn, he could tell they were traveling thousands of miles an hour now.

The first mountain in front of them was Arsia Mons, and then past that, Pavonis Mons, the site of the Mars Base.

As they sped over the military base, Parker said, "If I were in a plane, I'd wag my wings. But as you see, we don't have wings. I guess a sonic boom will have to do."

With Pavonis Base now behind them, Ascraeus Mons lay before them, the last giant pimple rising above the rusty looking Martian plains in front of them.

Once they had blasted over that mountain, Parker steered the ship into a tight right turn, pulling Gs, heading southeast toward a region strangely ripped by gigantically wide gullies.

"Holy mackerel," Brightman exclaimed. "What the hell is that?"

"NASA calls them Chasma, but if you ask me, they're huge erosion channels. It's kind of hard to believe there wasn't once a lot of water on Mars."

"This is incredible. I'm just amazed."

For a man who was usually reserved, if not taciturn, that comment from Brightman showed just how excited he really was.

After racing to the east along the tortured equatorial region of Mars, Parker had a mind to head home. Before he solidified that thought, knowing there was power in his thoughts, he turned to his cave diver friend. "Have you seen enough?"

"I could do this forever, but yeah, let's go home."

And with that, *Dioscuri* pulled away from the red planet, zipping past the miniature moon Phobos on the way out into deep space.

Parker thought about briefing Brightman on the horrors on Phobos experienced by Clarice Williams but thought better of it. Williams wanted that memory to die just as her husband had. There was no need to keep a nightmare alive.

The sun was dead ahead, and somewhere on the other side of it, hidden by the Sun's glare, lay Earth. That beautiful planet had been bruised and battered by a cosmic assault, and life on the surface would be forever changed. But in spite of it all, it seemed the human toll of death and destruction would be absorbed, and life would go on, just as it always has.

"Kelly, do you want to take us home?"

"I'm game. How do I do that?"

"Just think about home. *Dioscuri* will do the rest."

CHAPTER 60. EPILOGUE

It was summertime, and Jason and Laura Parker were sitting on the sand at Grayton Beach State Park on the Florida Gulf Coast. They were the only people remaining on the beach after dark. Their oldest daughter, five-year-old Cybil, frolicked in the luminescent waves as they broke upon the sand. Behind her, the Milky Way galaxy slanted across the Southern sky, and just below it, the once offending Sagittarius Constellation was rising.

Jason and Laura had brought their daughter to the park after hearing that the zooplankton was inshore and the conditions were right for the luminescent waters to appear. Jason had seen that light display once as a young man and looked forward to introducing both Laura and Cybil to the spectacle.

The couple sat in beach chairs facing the sparkling waters while keeping an eye on the five-year-old. They were reminiscing about the adventures behind them and imagining the adventures ahead of them. They were discussing the Mars Colony that was thriving with no more interference from monster bugs. The more Parker thought about that fact, the more he wondered if perhaps the GRB was like a cosmic version of a killing frost.

Their discussion abruptly ended when Cybil squealed with excitement, "Nice fishy."

That got their attention.

Cybil was moving far too quickly in the water, faster than a five-year-old can run, yelling "Wheee!"

Both parents sprang into action, rushing into the surf and snatching Cybil out of the water while the child kicked her feet in protest. She did not want to get off whatever it was she had been riding.

As Jason held little Cybil up high, checking her over best he could in the light cast by the glowing water, a dark figure rose, blue light dripping off its head and arms.

Before the couple had time to react, the figure turned towards Laura. Strained words came from its mouth, "Momma, do you love me?"

There, in the magical light, appeared a Mermaid the size of a ten-year-old girl, balancing on her tail to stand as tall as she was able, which was no more than four and a half feet. There was something about her voice, and her telepathically exuded love, that Laura instantly recognized.

As the creature held out its arms as if asking for an embrace, Laura started moving towards it. Parker reached out to hold Laura back, but she twisted out of his hands and moved deeper into the water. To the dismay of both Jason and Cybil, Laura and the Mermaid wrapped their arms around each other.

Then, as the waves broke, casting glittering azure light on their faces, the two kissed like parents and children do. After a moment of closeness, the Mermaid dove back into the oncoming waves, leaving a pulsing streak where her tail stirred the water into light.

The three humans stood motionless, mesmerized by what they had just seen. Finally, Cybil spoke in her sweet voice over the hiss of the waves.

"Mommy, why did that fishy call you Momma?"

After a long pause, Laura turned to her daughter with tears in her eyes.

"That's not a fish, Cybil. That's a Mermaid, and she's my daughter, and your sister."

Cybil's father, Jason Parker, told her, "But that's our secret, Cybil. We can never tell anyone about this."

"Why not, Daddy?" she asked.

"Because everyone knows Mermaids only exist in fairytales."

About the Author

John Clarke is an adventure-loving scientist, inventor, author, diver, aviator, amateur musician and world traveler who challenges preconceived notions about mankind and the universe. He holds a PhD in Physiology, and was a diving scientist with the U.S. Navy for forty years, conducting research specializing in the adaptations of people and animals to the deep-sea. His Navy research began at the Naval Medical Research Institute, Bethesda, MD and continued at the Navy Experimental Diving Unit (NEDU) in Panama City, Florida where he served as Scientific Director for 27 years. He is a Fellow of Undersea and Hyperbaric Medicine. After traveling to the Arctic and Antarctic for research and teaching, he served on the Diving Control Board for the National Science Foundation's U.S. Antarctic Diving Program. After retiring from the Navy, he returned to service for the Office of the Secretary of Defense (OSD), coinventing the FDA-approved Wilcox Patriot SAVR ventilator under Presidential orders as an assistant to the COVID-19 Task Force. Prior to his OSD service, he

John Clarke

was a Scientist Emeritus for the Naval Sea Systems Command. He continues to write both science fiction and non-fiction.

His websites are: jasonparkertrilogy.com and johnclarkeonline.com. He can be contacted at john@johnclarkeonline.com.

John and his wife Peggy live in Panama City Beach, Florida, USA.

Made in the USA
Middletown, DE
10 August 2020

·9R00225